Goblin

Goblin

Ever Dundas

**FREIGHT
BOOKS**

First published 2017
Freight Books
49–53 Virginia Street
Glasgow, G1 1TS
www.freightbooks.co.uk

ISBN 978-1-911332-29-9
eISBN 978-1-911332-30-5

Typeset by Freight in Plantin
Printed and bound by TJ International Ltd. Padstow

The publisher acknowledges investment from
Creative Scotland toward the publication of this book

For Rachel and all Goblins

In memory of the pets

'A story has no beginning or end.'
Graham Greene

'Blessed are the forgetful.'
Nietzsche

Chapter 1

Edinburgh, 17 June 2011

Bones, doll parts, a shrew head, a camera. The film, it said, is in remarkably good condition. The developed photographs are particularly valuable. Many of them record events in London during World War II. Most importantly, there is a photograph depicting the aftermath of the pet massacre, an event which remains largely undocumented. Some of the photographs, it said, could assist in identifying the photographer. There are several of what are assumed to be family members. Because of the angle from which most of the photographs are taken, it has been suggested the photographer was a child. Although, it said, there is much debate about this. It was decided the photographs of family members should be published in the hope someone will recognise them. It is hoped, it said, someone will come forward. It is said. It is thought. It is hoped. Someone will come forward. Time has collapsed and space has collapsed and they have emerged from the darkness below, Goblin and Devil and Monsta. It is hoped, it said, someone will claim these bones.

Edinburgh, 23 June 2011

Ben spits book at me. Rip, chew, spit.

'It's good to have ye back, old lady.'

'It's good to be back,' I say, watching people come and go in the library.

Rip, chew, spit.

'I'm glad yer feeling better.'

'I am,' I say, but the past is creeping in. A past I thought I held well. It was there, with all its beauty and canker, and

1

I held it well until those images were spread out before me, before millions; the first time I see the photographs and they're shared with the nation. But they weren't all there. They hadn't published them all. I knew that.

It was Ben who had shown me the article. It was Ben who had said 'Bones and dolls and shrew heads, that means witchcraft.'

And it's Ben who spits book at me.

'Stop it,' I say, eyeing the pile of spat-out book on the floor, hoping no one else will notice.

Rip, chew, spit.

'You can't eat every copy of *Ulysses*.'

'I'm not eating it,' he says. 'I'm chewing on it. I'm sucking the ink off.'

'It will poison you,' I say. 'That book will poison you.'

'What kinda person,' he says, squinting up at me, 'buries a shrew head, bits of doll and old cameras with pictures of dead animals?'

'What kind of person doesn't?'

Ben looks at me like I'm old and senile, like I'm the crazy one who chews on books. The newspapers had picked up on one of the developed photographs; a mound of dead animals, mainly cats and dogs. Experts on the Home Front were wheeled out, animal rights activists were asked their opinion. How could people kill their own pets?

'What kind of person wouldn't bury the past, Ben? Who lives in the past?'

Ben shakes the paper at me.

'Bones and dolls and shrew heads,' he says, 'that means witchcraft.'

He lays the paper on my desk and picks up *Ulysses*. He opens it up where he left off, over a hundred pages already missing. Rip – he tears out half a page; chew – I can see him counting as he masticates; spit – another sodden ball added to the pile.

'I know you need this space, but you can't eat the books.'

Rip, chew, spit.

'Ben.'

'Okay,' he says, 'fine.'

Rip, chew—

'Ben.'

Spit.

'I've got to finish what I started. What kinda person just chews part of a book?'

'Clean up after yourself at least.'

I let him be, wallowing in paper and spittle. He's hidden by a pillar, his chew-pile down by the side of my desk. When staff come to speak with me he puts on an innocent smile and pretends to read the desecrated book.

I tear the pet massacre article out of the paper and fold it up. Stuffing it in my pocket I forget it all, lost in the simple pleasure of putting together a list of books for an author's research.

I've been Reader in Residence at the library for years. It gets me by, and I write reviews for two national newspapers which brings in a bit extra. I have my own desk in a corner where I sit enjoying the smell of the books and the low hum of voices at the check-out desk.

I watch Ben, wondering how to get him to stop.

'What's a reader in residence?'

I turn, startled. A young man is sitting at the other side of my desk.

'Sorry,' I say, 'What was that?'

'Ms G Bradfield – Reader in Residence,' he says, reading the nameplate on my desk. 'What is that exactly?'

'People tell me their interests,' I say, 'they tell me the kind of things they like to read and I draw up a list of books for them. I also help writers and students who are doing research.'

'That's a job?'

'Can I help you with anything?' I say.

'I like blue books.'

'The blues? Music?'

'No, books that are blue.'

'Sad books?'

'Jesus, I can't believe you get paid for this. How old are you anyway? Shouldn't you be retired?'

'There's no need to be rude. I'm trying to help.'

'Then why don't you tell me where I can find all the books with blue covers?'

I stare at him for a moment.

'Well?'

'The library doesn't have a record of all the books that are blue but if you leave your details I can draw up a starter list for you.'

Ben leans over my desk.

'So, what about that witchcraft, eh? Do ye think they found the witch? Do ye think they'd admit it? I bet they're dead anyhow.'

'Ben, I'm with a customer.'

'It doesn't matter,' the blue book man says, 'you're no use to me.'

'Wait, I can—'

I watch the man walk off.

'Ben, you can't interrupt me when I'm with someone.'

'He wis a right time-wasting bastard, old lady. You know it.'

'That's not the point.'

'I bet the witch is dead,' he says, tearing out another page from *Ulysses*.

'Why would you say that? Why would you say they're dead?'

'It was bloody years ago, wasn't it? How old would they be? A hundred and fifty I'd reckon they'd be.'

'Eighty-one. They'd be eighty-one.'

I glance at him, and he's squinting at me.

'Eighty-one, eh?'

'The Second World War wasn't that long ago, Ben.'

'It feels it. It sure feels it.'

'Can you feel time?'

'I feel it in ma bones.'

London, March 1941

Ma?

So you're back? I thought you'd died. I told everyone you'd likely died and they all said what a shame it was.

She looked away and her head swayed from side to side as she said shame, shame, shame in a sing-song voice.

And here you are. Goblin-runt born blue. Nothing can kill you.

She looked Goblin in the eye.

You're like a cockroach.

Edinburgh, 4 July 2011

People die. In the library. Some people, they come and they die. We're told not to let anyone sleep horizontally.

'I don't see why,' I said, 'I'm sure you can be dead in any position.'

'It doesn't look good,' they said, 'people lying around and snoring with their feet on the seats. If they're vertical and not snoring, it's fine, let them be. Otherwise, you must wake them. If someone's dead,' they said, 'you need to be careful, you need to be subtle. Don't upset the customers.'

In this market economy they're called customers. In this time of cutbacks and closures. If the library closed, where would I go? I've worked here for years. Where would people like Ben go? Ben comes and he stays, hours and hours. He began by reading his way through the fiction section A-Z, and we'd discuss the books together in the evening. Then he got distracted, eating all the James Joyce – rip, chew, spit.

'Ben,' I say. 'Ben. The Tories are doing a good enough job without you helping them.'

'It's just James Joyce,' he says.

'It costs money. It costs the library. Why don't you pay for it?' But I pay for it. For every book he eats.

'Why don't you go back to reading?' I say. 'You can't just stop at J.'

'Aye, I will, old lady. I always finish what I've started. So I have to finish this.'

I leave him in his corner, chewing and spitting. When I finish my shift, Ben and his dog Sam walk me home.

'You got a place to stay tonight?'

'Aye, I wis begging this morning and got enough to pay for the hostel.'

'You don't need to spend it on a hostel. You can stay with me. You know that.'

'I dinnae want to take advantage.'

'Don't be daft.'

'I'm fine, old lady. Ye dinnae need to worry about me.'

Sam jumps up on a low garden wall and runs across it before sitting down and snuffling at some ivy.

'At least bring Devil back to mine for a bit. Mahler always likes to see him.'

'Devil?'

'Sam. I mean Sam.'

'He's well behaved. Sam's no devil.'

'I know, I didn't mean that. Devil was a dog I used to know.'

London, August 1939

Bulbous silver slugs glittered in the sky; a stunning sky, shot through with a hazy pink as twilight fell. Pure white clouds were erupting on the horizon, a shifting billowing mass bringing a cool breeze. Goblin climbed to the top of the wall, scraping and bruising her already scarred, bare legs. She watched as the breeze buffeted the silver slugs.

'The Martians have come!'

Goblin cantered on the wall, arms reaching up. Devil ran back and forth below, barking. Goblin sat on the wall, watching the sunset, the balloons swaying and glinting. Mackenzie turned up and pushed Devil up by the arse, his front paws scrabbling, Goblin hooking her arm round his neck, pulling. He sat by her side, panting, licking her ear. Mac climbed up after Devil, the three of them sitting, watching the lazy Martian invasion.

'Where's Stevie?'

Mac shrugged. 'His ma said he couldn't come out.'

'Why's that?'

'Dunno.'

Goblin pointed to the barrage balloons and said, 'The Martians have come.'

'They're to stop the Martians.'

'I suppose,' said Goblin. 'But they look like rocket ships.'

'Fat rocket ships.'

They sat in silence for a while, staring at the rocket ships, Goblin gently ruffling Devil's fur.

'Do you think there will be a war?' said Goblin.

'Mum says for certain after the Russians made that pact with Germany.'

'What's a pact anyway?'

'I dunno,' said Mac. He chewed on his lip and said, 'Think it just means they're on the same side.'

The sun had set and darkness crept in, catching them by surprise. It was like the tide, seemingly so far off, suddenly sweeping over them. The barrage balloons no longer seemed futuristic or comical, but simply ominous black masses weighing heavily across London. They clambered down, ineptly assisting Devil, who half-fell, landing across Mac. He writhed, yelling the Martians had got him and they ran after Devil in the darkness.

'Get the Martian!'

Edinburgh, 5 July 2011

Sitting at the top of Granny's Green Steps, Ben and I eat our lunch and watch the tourists down in the Grassmarket. Sam rests his head on Ben's knee, snoring.

'What's the book?' says Ben, peering into my bag.

'*War of the Worlds*,' I say, as he pulls it out. 'Haven't read it since I was a kid. Have you?'

'Seen the film.'

Ben holds it up to his nose before flicking through. He stops when he sees my bookmark.

'Who's this?'

'Mad, my mum. My new mum.'

'New?'

'She adopted me.'

I take the photo from him and smooth my hand across it as if to feel mum's skin.

'She usually had it perfectly pinned up,' I say, looking at the way her hair is tumbling over her shoulders, 'but not here. Look how carefree it is.'

She hadn't washed it for days. You can tell from the photo, if you look carefully, you can tell it has lost its sparkle. I remember it sparkling red in the sun. There's a curl of hair matted against her forehead. The rest is messy, framing her face. You can see the wrinkles forming around her lips, beautiful perfect lines. She's wearing lipstick, some of it straying into one of the lines. I can smell her. The warm smell of jasmine and earth, the smell of sweat and the grease that dulled her hair.

'I told you I was in the circus after the war, didn't I? My mum and dad ran it together. I helped out a bit. Mum was an aerialist.'

'Yer mum wis hot,' says Ben.

I laugh and nudge him.

'You're right.'

Her skin was paper thin, transparent. The freckles on her cheeks were sunken, dulled by the dirt and dust of a day's work. They used to dance. They used to dance across her skin and she glowed. Iridescent. She was glamour, and I loved her with an ache that made my dirty little heart know it wasn't all black and rotten through.

'My new dad, James, he found me in the Underground. Underground is where the lizard people live.'

'Yer an odd one, old lady.'

'I was, and that's why I belonged with them. They took me in.'

'The lizard people?'

'Mad and James, my new mum and dad. They rescued me.'

'From what?'

I don't respond. I put the photo in the book and close it.

'Rescued ye how?'

Ben takes the book from me and I say, 'Don't. I'm reading it.'

'I don't eat books anymore.'

'No?'

'No. I smell them.'

'You do what?'

'Smell them.'

'What do they smell of?'

'Doughnuts, vanilla, old pants.'

'Don't they smell of ink?'

'Not always. Some of the really old ones smell of rotten teabags.'

'What's your favourite book smell?'

'*A History of Scottish Canals*. It smells of chocolate, vanilla, and a hint of whisky.'

'Sounds good enough to eat.'

'But I don't do that anymore, eh? I smell them and I can tell ye the exact date a book wis bought by the library.'

'That's very specific.'

'I'm a very specific person.'

He pulls a book from his rucksack and thrusts it at me, moving it gently beneath my nose.

'I'm the bloody book connoisseur of Edinburgh,' he says, 'and that, old lady, is the shit.'

I can't smell much of anything other than a generic book smell.

'Better be getting back to work,' I say, looking at my watch.

'I'll chum ye before I go check on Mahler.'

We walk through the Grassmarket, weaving our way through the tourists.

'What's that all about, eh?' says Ben, gesturing at a woman walking towards us. 'What's she doing all dressed up like that? It's not the feckin festival yet and it isnae Halloween. Hey, love! It isnae Halloween.'

She stares at me. Not Ben, but me. She stares with her grey-green-blue eyes. The Lizard Queen. She glitters and glimmers and shimmers. She's dressed in black and has bright red hair pinned up at each side of her head. Her skin is porcelain white, studded with jewels and painted with patterns of cobalt blue struck through with green and wisps of red. Her lips are red.

'Bright red with the blood of insects,' I say.

'Eh?' says Ben. 'What wis that?'

'She's the Lizard Queen, but she's dead. She's in London, dead and gone.'

She passes us by.

'It's me,' I say to her, following her. I take hold of her arm. 'It's me,' I say as she turns to me. 'I'm the one who ventured into the depths of the lizard realm with her Monsta and her prayers. It's me. I knew your husband, the Lizard King.'

'Excuse me?' she says, pulling her arm free.

'You're dead,' I say. 'You were torn apart.'

She frowns and says, 'I'm sorry, but I don't know you.'

She walks away and I stand there, watching her go.

'Hey, old lady, what wis that all about, eh?'

'She's the Lizard Queen,' I say.

'What's this lizard thing all of a sudden?'

'The past creeping in.'

I see Monsta crawling round Ben's neck, the shrew head peering from behind his ear, the worm arm slithering across his cheek. I reach out to stroke Monsta's head but Monsta isn't there. I stroke Ben's cheek.

'Ye alright, old lady?'

'Ben,' I say, my hand hovering next to his cheek. 'Have you ever seen someone die? Someone you love?'

He eyes me for a moment and I fall into darkness, like Alice down the rabbit hole. When I wake, Ben is leaning over me, waving a book in my face.

'Old lady, ye alright? Ye had me worried.'

I try to focus on his face, but the book waving makes me dizzy.

'Ben,' I say. 'I don't want to smell your book.'

He drops the book by his side.

'I wis fanning ye. That's what they do in the movies when people faint. They slap people too, but I didnae want to do that.'

'I'm glad.'

'Alright, everybody,' Ben says to the people gathered around us. 'Show's over.'

'Is she okay?'

'She will be. I'm looking after her, now give us some space.'

They drift away. Sam slobbers on my face, licking me better.

'I'm well looked after,' I say, trying to get up.

'Aye, take it easy now.'

Ben helps me sit up and I watch the drifting crowd, some people still staring at me as they walk off.

'What am I doing on the ground?'

'Ye fainted like a girl.'

'Mac?'

'Mac what?'

I shake my head.

'Ye said Mac.'

'Did I?'

'Right, old lady, I'm taking ye home. I'll get us a taxi. Mahler will be glad to see ye anyway.'

'I've got to go to work.'

'Not in this state. I'll call in sick for ye.'

When we get back to the flat Mahler barks and paws at us, asking for his lunch. Ben feeds him as I lie on the couch.

'Here,' he says, coming back through, 'drink some water.

Yev had too much sun, old lady.'

'I'm fine, Ben.'

'Ye are now that I'm looking after ye.'

He sits at the table and rifles through the morning papers.

'There's more about this pet massacre business,' he says.

'I know.'

'It says how people were scared, how it wis mercy killings before the bombs.'

Mahler comes through, licking his lips. He jumps onto the couch and lays his head on my lap. I stroke his ear.

'But I dinnae buy it. I'd never kill my Sam, no matter what. I reckon it wis Nazis.'

'Nazis?'

'Aye, Nazis killed the pets wi' their propaganda. Stirring up fear.'

'Yeah,' I say, 'probably Nazis.'

London, Summer 1939

'Mac, you're Frankenstein's monsta,' said Goblin. 'I'll be the Martians, and Stevie's the Nazis.'

'I wanna be the Martians,' said Stevie.

Goblin, Mac and Stevie had come to the abandoned worksite after school. Their den had rubble piled up on all sides to keep enemies out, with a fire pit in the middle. Stevie sat poking at the bits of charred wood from yesterday's fire.

'Chew it, Stevie,' said Goblin. 'You're the Nazis. The den is London and the Nazis are invading, but the Martians and Frankenstein's monsta eat them and then they fight at the end and Frankenstein's monsta wins.'

'Who's Devil?' said Mac.

'Devil is the humans. Frankenstein protects Devil, then Devil fights Frankenstein and burns him in a windmill.'

'That's stupid,' said Stevie.

'The Martians are coming!'

Mac scrambled up the den walls and out of sight. Goblin stared at Stevie, who sighed and clambered out after Mac. Goblin gave Stevie a few seconds then she went next, Devil barking at her heels. She had rope dangling from her waist in a clumsy attempt to look like the invaders in *The War of the World*s. Skipping across the worksite rubble and machinery, imagining her legs to be spidery and nimble, she chased after Stevie, the lumbering Nazi. The ropes whipped around her. Devil barked furiously, convinced this was all for him, and snapped his jaw shut on one of the ropes. Goblin jerked backwards, her feet pulled out from under her. For a second she really was a Martian, floating. She felt she could float to the stars.

Goblin heard the swish of the ropes as she hit the ground. She lay, breath gone, staring at the clouds, catching the glint of a barrage balloon. Devil stood on her chest, licking her face as she struggled to breathe, unable to move. There was only silence. Devil stood alert, and bounded off. Goblin took an intake of breath, feeling an ache move through her body. She turned her head to the side and saw Devil disappear into a gaping hole.

'Jesus,' said Mac, staring down at Goblin.

'Mac,' said Goblin, 'I didn't even know that hole was there. You can't see it from above.'

Devil came racing back out of the hole, snapping at a rat's tail.

'Goblin, you need to just—'

'Shit, Mackenzie. That felt like flying.'

'Well you're not flying now.'

'Ah, I'm alright.'

'Goblin.'

Mackenzie reached to stop her, but Goblin stood up, feeling a warmth weave its way down her arm.

'I'm fine. What's the fuss?'

Goblin looked down and saw blood dripping from her arm.

'Jesus. Martians sure can bleed.'

Mackenzie doubled over. He looked as if he was going to be sick, but laughed.

'You're the craziest girl I've ever met.'

'I'm not a girl. I'm a goblin.'

Goblin stared at the sliver of metal that had gone through her arm.

'Those damn Nazis laid a trap. Let's get 'em!'

'You need a doctor.'

'Martians don't need doctors.'

'Goblins do.'

'Ayaiyaaaaai!'

Goblin ran across the worksite, heading straight for Stevie, blood spattering everywhere. She landed on him, pummelling him.

'You dirty milky, eh? Nazi traps can't kill Martians.'

He sank his finger into the wound, and she was gone.

★

'You sure faint like a girl,' was the first thing Mackenzie said when she woke up. He ruffled her hair like she was a kid and he was an adult.

'You'd faint like a girl too if a Nazi shoved his finger in your arm.'

'Where am I?'

'At mine, stupid. Your ma and da aren't back yet. Mum's looking after you.'

Goblin looked at her bandaged arm.

'I don't remember. Was I out the whole time?'

'You came round, but you were woozy, mumbling nonsense. The doc patched you up – you don't remember?'

Goblin shook her head and sat up in the bed before falling back again, wincing.

'Shit. It hurts.'

'Dunno how. Mum's been pouring whisky down your throat.'

'Ma's gonna kill me – how much was the doc?'

'Free,' said Mac. 'It was doc Wilson – he owed your da a favour.'

Goblin closed her eyes for a moment and said, 'I remember – da and I fixed his wireless. Hey,' she said, opening her eyes, 'where's Stevie?'

'Thinks you have a down on him.'

'Why would I? I was pummelling him. I would have done the same.'

'Yeah, I said that.'

'Get him here. We'll read *The Time Machine* again.'

'Nah, I've got to go. Mum said I can't wear you out.'

'I'm good. You're not wearing me out.'

'You look like shit, Goblin. You look like a ghost. You're all bled out.'

'Tomorrow then, eh?'

'Always. It's boring without you.'

Edinburgh, 6 July 2011

Mahler wakes me at five a.m., pawing at me, licking the ocean on my arm, snuffling at a faded ship. Bored of the taste of my tattooed skin he barks and runs off to his food bowl, skittering across the kitchen floor. I get up, follow him through, and scoop his food out. I pour myself a glass of whisky and shuffle my way to the sitting room. Seeing someone asleep on the couch, I jump, spilling whisky over my hand before realising it's Ben. I sit next to him, licking the whisky from my fingers. I shake him awake.

'Aye, alright, alright. I'm awake already.'

'You half frightened me to death,' I say. 'I don't remember you staying the night.'

'It wis to look after ye, remember?' he says, sitting up. 'After yer fainting fit. Issat whisky? Jesus, woman.'

He grabs the glass from me.

'Hey, watch it! What kind of guest are you?'

'The kind who makes ye a proper breakfast. Get yersel dressed and I'll rustle up a healthy fry up.'

'A healthy fry up?'

'Aye, well, healthier than whisky. Nae wonder yer all skin an bone.'

I go to the bedroom and pull on some clothes as I sip whisky from the bottle under my bed. I hear Ben rummaging through the kitchen and cursing. He knocks on the door.

'Ye decent?'

I hide the bottle.

'Yes.'

'Yer worse than I thought,' he says, putting his head round the door. 'Not a scrap in the cupboards or the fridge. Where's yer money?'

'Money?'

'Aye, yer money. I'm no gonna rob ye, ye old skeleton. I'm gonna get yer messages in.'

'I don't need any messages.'

'When all yev got in the kitchen is whisky, seeds, ketchup and some mouldy bread, ye need messages.'

Ben roots around in his pockets and counts out some coins.

'I've a few quid from yesterday, so I can put that towards whatever ye have. We'll both be sitting down to a proper breakfast.'

'My purse is in my bag,' I say. 'Take whatever you want.'

'Dinnae think I'll gyp ye. I'll get a receipt and ye can see exactly what I bought.'

'I trust you, Ben. It's fine.'

'Right. Sit tight, I willnae be long.'

'I need to take Mahler for a walk.'

'He can come shopping with me.'

'I walk him every morning before work.'

'Yer not doing anything until yer so stuffed full ye cannae do anything anyway.'

'I'm not an invalid,' I say, but he just whistles for Sam and

Mahler, who come running.

When he leaves I get the whisky out again and sit in the living room, enjoying the morning sun, feeling the warmth of the drink spreading through my belly. I go through to the kitchen and pick up the seed jar before heading down to the street. I sit on the front step, throwing seeds across the pavement for the pigeons. People passing by give me dirty looks, but I ignore them and listen to the happy noises the pigeons make.

Gio says, 'La Pazza dei Piccioni.'

I look up, startled, but it isn't him. He isn't there. Just a stranger, a man, staring down at me.

'Stupid woman,' he says.

'What was that?'

'They're rats,' he says, 'rats with wings.'

'I like rats,' I say.

'They spread disease. They should be exterminated.'

'Humans spread disease,' I say, narrowing my eyes. 'Should we exterminate them?'

'Old witch,' he says, kicking at the pigeons, causing them to scatter.

'Sonofabitch!' I yell. 'Get off my street.'

He sneers at me and walks off.

'Rats have better manners,' I say to the one pigeon left pecking at the seeds. I go back upstairs and slump on the couch, drinking more whisky. I doze off in the sun, waking to the sound of the door. I put the whisky bottle behind the couch and join Ben and the dogs in the kitchen. I peer into all the shopping bags, wrinkling my nose up.

'I'm not eating any animals,' I say.

'That's for me,' he says, snatching the sausages out of my hand as I go to put them in the bin. 'I bought them with my own money and I got ye some veggie sausages. God knows what they put in those, mind.'

'Fine,' I say, helping him unpack the rest of the shopping.

'Here's yer receipt,' he says, pulling it out of his pocket, a couple of pages of his secret chewing stash falling on the floor.

'So ye can see I spent yer money on necessities. I bought some cakes but that's cos we need to fatten ye up.'

'You better not be eating my books,' I say.

'What? Where'd that come from? That's appreciation for ye, getting yer messages in and ye jus go on about yer books.'

'I'm sorry, Ben,' I say. 'I appreciate you getting my messages.'

He looks at me, uncertain.

'Alright. Good.'

'We've been friends a few years, Ben. I know you're looking out for me.'

'Give it a rest about the books, then.'

'I will. I'm sorry.'

I nudge the book scraps under the table.

'They found the witch, ye know,' he says, waving the morning paper at me.

'Which witch?'

'Which witch? Which witch? Which witch?' he chants.

I roll my eyes and finish unpacking.

'Turns out it's not a witch.'

'What's not a witch?'

'The witch. The witch isn't a witch.'

'No?'

'It's a goblin.'

'A goblin?'

'Wasn't a witch at all, but I was nearly right. A nasty little goblin. It's in the paper.'

He spreads the paper on the counter and hunches over it.

'"Mr Brian Mackenzie came forward to say he knows who buried the assortment of objects. She's the child in one of the photographs and he knows her only as Goblin." That's what it says right there. And goblins can live for years, until at least a hundred and fifty.'

'Is there a photo?'

'Of the goblin? Yeah, look. There's all the dead pets behind her.'

'Not the goblin. Is there a photo of Brian?'

'Just the goblin. Here, ye can sit and read about it while I make breakfast. Fried eggs, sausages, toast and beans coming up!'

I sit at the table and stare at the name, Mr Brian Mackenzie. As I run my finger across Mac's name, Monsta's tentacle-arm slithers over my hand. Spectre-Monsta sits on the table, swaying gently, those deep black eyes glinting.

London, 1941

Underground is where the lizard people live, and I go in search. I don't want to stay with the people scrunched up with misery, squeezed in with their blankets and their stench. I hop on the train with Monsta, and we go in search.

I stay on for miles and miles and hours and hours, wheeeeee, we're on an adventure, Monsta! Lizard seekers. We must flick out our tongues and smell them, taste them, the lizard people in the darkness in the depths.

We pick our way through the recumbent bodies, little hillocks, obstacles to our search. I huff, the bodies snore, or yell out, oi kid fuck off, and I pretend I'm a Martian, floating, nimble, no Devils to bite my ropes, no Devils at all, just me and Monsta.

Monsta sees me stop and sway, uncertain. Monsta's head shakes gently, the worm arm floating to me. I've not to sink. There are no Devils, but there are Monstas, and the lizard people await. Gently gently Monsta climbs, encircling my neck with worm tentacles, gently gently, casting a spell of forgetfulness, forgetting the loss above, revelling in London below.

We're adventurers! Ayaiyaiaiai! Shoosh kid shut up fuck off Jesus! And I say my lizard prayers as we seek seek sneak, our lizard who art in heaven hallowed be thy name deliver me from light above to the darkness below and let us partake of your kingdom.

We sneak sneak creep through tunnels for miles and miles,

rumblings above, tremors. Listening, swaying, the bombs are plopping and we can't hear the boom, just plops like rain. Hallowed be thy name, hallowed be thy name, let us partake of your kingdom O lizards, seek seek creep. I could hear Mackenzie protesting, I could hear him say, 'Don't forget the Morlocks, Goblin. Don't forget. They'll eat you alive, crunch!' But Mac wasn't here and anyway I knew there were no Morlocks, the Morlocks are the future and this is the present. And in the present we walked, for hours in the darkness, through tunnels and caves, we rest in caves and we sleep, we drift and we sleep, dreaming the dream of the lizards with glinting eyes made of emeralds.

Edinburgh, 7 July 2011

The past is creeping up and I'm sick, spending days in bed. Ben is looking after me and he says, 'Why didn't ye tell me yer not the witch? Why didn't ye tell me yer the goblin?'

'What does it matter?'

'It matters,' he says. 'At least now I know what the "G" stands for.'

'You never asked. You always call me old lady.'

'Aye, well, it would be good to know if yer best mate is a goblin. I shouldnae have to ask.'

I get up to take Mahler for a walk but Ben won't let me.

'Yer sick, old lady. Yer feverish. The doc said ye need some rest.'

'I don't remember a doctor.'

'Ye need to get back to bed. I'm looking after Mahler. Ye dinnae need to worry about a thing.'

Ben looks after me and Ailsa from next door brings me soup. Monsta is always by my side.

'You're not real,' I say to spectre-Monsta. 'You were buried.'

But Monsta only sways in defiance, wrapping tentacles round my arm.

'You're not real,' I say. 'You were in the papers. Your remains are in London.'

The phone rings and I hear Ben talking in the hall. He knocks on my door and brings me the phone.

'There's a detective for ye.'

'I told you they'd find me.'

He offers me the phone and I shake my head.

'He wants to talk to ye about the things they found.'

I fold my arms and turn away.

'She cannae talk jus now, Detective. She isnae well.'

He goes silent, listening. I watch him.

'Just hang up,' I say.

I can hear the murmur of the detective's voice. Ben's brow is furrowed.

'I think ye should talk to 'im,' he says to me, still listening to the detective.

'Give me that! What did he say to you? What did he say? Let me speak to him.'

Ben hands me the phone.

'Detective,' I say. 'What did you say to him?'

'We need you in London,' he says. 'We need you down here.'

'You need me?'

'We need to discuss what we found.'

'I won't come, Detective. I can't go back there.'

'You don't have a choice.'

'I have a choice.'

'We can issue a court order.'

'There's no need. I won't come. I won't say a word. There's no need. Leave the past in the past.'

I put down the handset and give the phone back to Ben.

'I knew they'd find me. I won't take any more calls,' I say. 'Bring me that album,' I say, pointing at the shelf. 'Bring it to me.'

He hands me the album and I open it, looking at the photos.

'I was in the circus,' I say. 'Mad and James, they were my new mum and dad and we all worked in the circus. We were happy.'

'I think ye should go see the Detective,' says Ben. 'When yer better.'

'I was a clown. Did I tell you that?'

'I can believe it,' he says.

'And I looked after the animals.'

'Think on it,' he says, standing up to leave. 'Ye can think on it.'

'I loved looking after the animals.'

I drop off to sleep and wake up with the album clasped to my chest. Amelia is standing over me, offering me soup, and she says, 'I was executed in 1896.'

No, not you, it's not you who brings me soup. It's Ailsa. And you, dear Ailsa, you weren't executed at all.

I can control this. There is no sinking or falling.

'Ailsa, I don't need soup. I need a drink.'

'You need nourishment.'

Drink gives me nourishment.

Ailsa leaves, and clink clink clink go the treasures under my bed. I pour myself a glass and I'm in control. Until Ben comes and takes them all away.

'It's cold turkey for ye, old lady. Eat yer soup.'

And I eat my soup.

'Why didn't ye tell me yer not the witch? That yer the goblin? I thought we were friends.'

'It's nobody's business,' I say, 'whether I'm a witch or a goblin.'

I come out of my fever and I know that I need to be in control. The past will not sweep over me. I walk into it, with Monsta and Devil and a fortune in my pockets, a severed hand at my belly. A camera in my hand.

Goblin, I can tell you now, was never haunted by the past. She held the past in the palm of her hand. She travelled, she bathed in circus lights, she wove stories around history, brought to life the ghosts of Venice, treading the streets with the tourists. Goblin, I can tell you, was a storyteller. Goblin controlled time.

I'm a storyteller. I control the past. I greet it as it comes in fragments, in ink, in the ether. I shall greet it and we shall dance in the darkness, scuttling and climbing and speeding through tunnels with the lizards down below.

Everyone's gone, and it's me and Monsta, back in London. I'm too far ahead, and mixed up, back and forward. The memories just come and I let them. I must bring order, a little order, move away from the bombs and back to glorious thirty-nine, thirty-eight, thirty-seven.

They merge. Those years before the war. The long summers, the running wild, playing cowboys and Indians, Martians and humans. I don't remember when we first found the worksite, or when David first told me his dreams of the sea, or when I became friends with the Crazy Pigeon Woman of Amen Court. They merge, and I jump forward and back. I must bring order.

'What ye doing, old lady?'

'I'm writing,' I say. 'I'm in control.'

This is the past, this is my story of the war, of London; the realm above, the realm in-between, the realm down below.

Chapter 2

Disappearing into another world, ushered in by the guardian in the long white robes and still I felt I was sneak sneak sneaking. I followed Mac's family, dipping my fingers in the water, touching my fingers to my body. I couldn't see clearly what they were doing, so I copied clumsily, my fingers bouncing off my chest to a random rhythm of my own. Mackenzie smiled at me, shaking his head, so I stopped, feeling like an idiot. I watched as people knelt in the aisle, stood, and filed into the pews. I followed close behind Mac and did the same, my eyes flicking round the church, but no one was looking, no one noticed if I did anything wrong. I stumbled after Mac, sitting with him and his family.

The service was confusing and I was faint from the smoking incense and the mesmeric chanting – the Lord be with you and with you Holy Holy Holy forgive us our trespasses as we forgive those who trespass against us the body of Christ the blood of Christ in the name of the Father Son and Holy Ghost go in peace thanks be to God Amen. I swayed and hummed and tumbled out into the world, Mackenzie by my side.

'Jesus, that was boring, eh Goblin? Let's go kill Martians.'

'Aiyaiyai!' I answered, 'Holy Holy Holy, the blood of Christ!'

We sprinted off to the worksite, picking Devil up on the way. I anointed him, spraying water across his body.

'Amen!' I said, and he chased after us.

I never spoke to Mackenzie about how I felt about this other world but I turned up at his door every Sunday and off I went with him and his family, disappearing into worship. I loved the stories, turning them over in my head, weaving my own. I floated on the smell of incense, felt safe in the soft light.

I drove my brother mad as I turned our bedroom into a shrine. David would come home to find me surrounded by saints and Jesus and Mary, incense choking up the room, bible in my hand.

'David,' I'd say, 'David, you won't believe this story—'

'Jesus, Goblin, leave it.'

And he'd flop onto his bed, lean up on his elbow and put on a record. He'd listen to our grandad's old records: Liszt, Schubert, Berlioz. Grandad had died in The Great War, but gran had sat with David, listening to the records, telling him stories about grandad. I barely remember her; she died when I was four. Ma hated grandad's music so she let David keep the old gramophone in our room.

He'd lie on his bed, smoking his cigarette, pictures of Marlene Dietrich peeling off the wall behind him. He was the coolest thing there was. There was something about him. I knew one day he would conquer the world. Jack Alexander, Simon Mayhew and their gang didn't think so, though. They were a couple of years older than David and lived two streets down. David used to play with them, years before, but not now.

'Why'd they pick on you?'

David was lying back, staring at the ceiling, his left arm behind his head. He took a draw on his cigarette, exhaled, 'It's just the way they are.'

'But why you? You're the best.'

He laughed.

'What? You are.'

'They don't seem to know that.'

'They're idiot bastards.'

David sat up, crossed his legs and leaned against the wall, Marlene partly obscured by his shoulder.

'At least I have you on my side, G.'

'Always.'

He traced his hand through the smoke, swaying to the music.

'The other day, when we passed them, why'd they say you were "one of them"?'

'What?'

'One of them. Why'd they say that?'

'Because they're idiot bastards.'

'What did they mean, though?'

He took another draw on his cigarette and looked at me, eyes narrowed.

'I'm not one of them,' he said. 'They just call me that because I read.'

'Because you're smart?'

'Uh-huh.'

'Then they're right. You are smart, you are one of them.'

'That's not what— Jesus, Goblin. Just leave it, okay? Go back to your bible.'

'But you *are* smart. They're just jealous.'

David smiled and stubbed out his cigarette. He picked up a book and said, 'Just leave it, okay? I don't want to talk about idiot bastards.'

'What're you reading?'

'*Treasure Island.*'

'What's it about?'

'Treasure. On an island.'

'Ha!' I said, throwing my old bear at him. He ducked and it hit Marlene.

'It's about pirates,' he said, throwing the bear back at me. I caught it and hooked my arm round its neck, holding it close.

'When I save enough money,' he said, 'I'll sail around the world. I'll meet a girl and we'll make our home by the sea – a place where the sea is everything, where it changes people.'

'So you get fins and gills and become a sea monster.'

David laughed. 'Not quite what I meant, G. But maybe... why not? A place where anything is possible.'

'You should join the Navy.'

'I can't, G.'

'Why not?'

'Don't think I'd take orders well. And I don't want to kill anyone.'

'Be a pirate then.'

'I think pirates kill people too.'

'You don't have to kill people – you could get someone to do it for you.'

'That's just the same.'

'You'll just have to go alone then.'

David shook his head.

'No, G – it'd be me and you.'

I smiled.

'I'd kill people for you, then.'

'Would you now?'

'If I had to.'

'Best not, G.'

I flopped onto my stomach and opened the bible where I'd left off.

'People get killed all the time in the bible, but sometimes they pray for help and God makes everything okay, but only sometimes.'

'That right?'

'You could pray for help, you know.'

'With what? Going to the sea?'

'Getting Mayhew and Alexander off your back.'

'What good would praying do?'

'Maybe God would smite them or something.'

'Smite them how?'

'Lightning or floods or locusts.'

'You want storms and locusts in London?'

'Not all of London, stupid – just on them. You need to be specific so God doesn't mess up.'

David smiled, 'That right?'

'Mm-hmm.'

'Goblin!'

It was da, shouting from the bottom of the stairs.

'Coming!' I shouted as I tossed my bible aside.

I ran down the stairs, almost banging right into da.

'A wireless?'

He nodded and I followed him into the back garden. He was good at fixing things; a wireless, bikes, cars, pretty much anything, so the neighbours always went to him. They'd pay what they could, or give him some veg from their veg patch, or bake us a pie. Da had me helping out since as far back as I could remember. When I was really young he'd get me to hand him what he needed, teaching me the names of each tool, and I'd watch as he took things apart and put them together again. Soon I was helping out properly and he'd give me a few pennies, or extra pie at dinnertime. He didn't speak much as we worked, but I'd rattle off stories and he didn't seem to mind. Sometimes he'd grunt in response or say, 'That so?' There was only a couple of times when some old gramophone was giving him grief that he told me to be quiet so he could concentrate.

'Whose is it?' I asked as he opened up the wireless.

'Mrs West's.'

I sat cross-legged on the grass and lay out the tools. We'd sometimes work in people's houses, but da couldn't tolerate interference, so he started wheelbarrowing things over to ours. Ma went mad when we worked in the sitting room, so we worked in the garden, da saying one day me and him would build a workshed.

Da grunted.

'What is it?'

'Just a loose wire.'

'That all?'

He nodded.

'You sure, da?'

He gave me a foul look and I said, 'I was just hoping—'

'I know,' he said.

I watched him as he secured the wire and I said, 'You read the bible, da?'

He shook his head, so I rattled off some bible stories, speaking fast as I knew that wireless would be fixed in no time, but he was slow about it and when he finished he sat for a moment, his hand on the wireless, looking over at Devil who was chasing flies.

'…and she turned round and turned to salt!'

'That so?' he said.

'Mh-hmm. And he just left the salt-woman there. I would have scooped her up and kept her for soup.'

Dad laughed and I blushed.

'What's so funny?'

He shook his head and stood up.

'C'mon,' he said, 'help me wheel this back.'

He lifted the wireless into the barrow and I pushed it up the garden path.

*

I went to church every week with Mac, but I sometimes went on my own too – even to confession, but not to confess, only to talk about the bible stories. I was so excited about it that the priest would get all swept up and forget about my sins. But then it was ruined.

After confession I went to light a candle and pray. I asked God a question but he didn't reply so I went to ask the priest who was talking with an old man by the door. I stood next to them, shifting from one foot to another as they continued talking, the priest eyeing me now and then. The old man finally left and the priest wasn't even polite, he just frowned at me and said, 'What is it?'

'Can Devil come?'

'What?'

'Can Devil come and drink some blood of Christ too?'

There was silence. And I waited, patient.

'There are no devils here, child.'

'Not a demon-devil,' I said. 'A dog-devil. I want to bring my dog to eat some Christ too.'

Silence again, and I waited.

'Animals don't have souls,' he said.

He turned away from me. I stood, staring at his back,

watching the swaying robes, taking in the beautiful interior, the warmth and the smells. I took it all in, realising it was over. I walked up to that priest and I spat at his feet.

I never returned but sometimes I'd stand outside and breathe in the smells. That was before. That was before Kensal Green and before the Pigeon Woman of Amen Court who said to me, Goblin-child, you worship wherever you please. You make your own church.

*

The Crazy Pigeon Woman of Amen Court walked by our school every morning. If she walked by when we were on break we'd be at the fence, spitting and shouting. She'd shuffle along, talking to herself, spit sliding down her back. Soon, we got bored. We got bored after no reaction every morning. We would just mumble obscenities, shout lazily in her direction. There came a time we didn't notice her at all and spat and shouted at each other instead.

She would always have a troop of pigeons following her along the street. Some of the kids spat on the pigeons too, until I pummelled them. I spun tales about her magic abilities, that she collected our spit and used it in potions. She could kill you, I said. She has your essence. She only has to say the word and you'd drop down dead. The little kids peed their pants, the others told me to fuck off, you're as crazy as she is. I didn't pummel them. I pretended like I was the Pigeon Woman of Amen Court, all calm and aloof.

Soon I was the only one left at the fence and I'd watch her and her pigeon troop. One morning I saw her hair move, like it was alive, like it could move on its own. Then I saw the heads.

'Excuse me,' I said. 'Excuse me.'

As polite as can be, but she walked right by, muttering, scattering seeds. I jumped the fence and walked by her side, glancing up at her, staring at the little pigeon heads poking out from her mess of hair. It really was a bird's nest; matted here and there, with bits of twig sticking out.

'Are they babies?' I said. 'Baby pigeons in your hair?'

She muttered and I leaned in to hear but caught nothing. She grabbed my hand and I was ready to pummel her but I couldn't, not with pigeons in her hair. She dropped seeds in my hand, or tried to. It was all scrunched up in a fist and the seeds just bounced off, scattering for her troop.

'You can feed them,' she said. 'Don't you want to?'

She bent a little and I opened my hand, catching the seeds, and I fed the pigeons in her hair.

'We call you Pigeon,' I said, trying to be polite, not telling her what we really called her.

'I know what you call me,' she said.

She wasn't stupid, that crazy pigeon woman.

'Come inside,' she said, 'and have a cup of tea.'

We'd reached her house. I'd left school without really knowing it, and I stared back down the road, and at her troop, and at her house, and in I went.

Animals everywhere, staring fake.

'Taxidermy,' she said.

I didn't know what that meant and screwed up my face.

'I find them,' she said, 'and I preserve them. I take out their guts and make them like this.'

'Like an Egyptian mummy,' I said. 'Kind of.'

She just grunted. I ran my finger along one of the shelves, wanting to touch the mummified animals, but I was all unnerved by their glassy eyes. Pigeons walked amongst them, pecking at seeds. Seeds and pigeon shit were everywhere. The smell was strong; a welcoming musty animal smell.

'Why?' I said.

'Dead things can't die,' she said.

I nodded, as if I understood.

'Sit,' she said, and I sat. She shuffled off, a small troop following her even in the house. She brought me some tea and a biscuit. I inspected it for pigeon shit and shoved it in my mouth.

'You got more biscuits?'

'You hungry? You can stay for dinner.'

I shrugged, sipping my tea. A pigeon scrambled up my leg, its claws digging into me. I let it be and it stood on my knee, eating seeds from my hand. It settled on my leg, falling asleep, looking up at me suspiciously anytime I moved an inch. I drank my tea and stared at Pigeon. I squinted at her, trying to see the pigeons in her hair.

'They're sleeping,' she said, seeing me look at her head. 'All asleep in their nest. I can feel them, their little warm bodies. He likes you,' she said, gesturing at the sleeping pigeon on my knee.

I stroked his head. He cooed at me. I looked up at Pigeon, not sure if he was happy or annoyed with me. She smiled and nodded.

'He likes you,' she said.

'What's that?' I said, pointing to a mummified creature next to my chair. I leaned over and stroked its head the way I'd stroked the pigeon, almost expecting the mummy-creature to coo at me too.

'A shrew,' she said.

I kept stroking it, willing it to coo.

I didn't know what to say to Pigeon, so I just sat, stroking the shrew and staring round the room. There were framed photos everywhere, of what looked like Pigeon and her family. They were in-between all the mummy creatures, but I didn't pay much attention to them, except to notice they were the only things not covered in pigeon shit.

'Do you like stories?'

'Uh-huh.'

'I'll tell you stories. I'll tell you all about London,' she said. 'Of the realm below and the realm above.'

She paused, arching her eyebrow.

'Did you know,' she said, 'lizard people live in the realm below?'

I shook my head.

'They hide away in the myriad of tunnels and caves in the depths of London. It's their kingdom, where the Lizard Queen and Lizard King rule. They eat the big black insects that live there too. They're as big as my hand.'

Pigeon raised her hand, spreading her fingers.

'And the lizard people eat them – crunch! Do you know what would happen if they didn't?'

'No.'

'The insects would multiply and take over the realm below and the realm above.'

'Like in the bible,' I said, 'in Revelation – "And there came out of the smoke locusts upon the earth and unto them was given power, as the scorpions of the earth have power... And they had a king over them, which is the angel of the bottomless pit."'

'That's right. You understand, don't you?' said Pigeon, smiling and nodding. 'London would be ruled by these insects, but we have the lizard people. They come to the realm above, in the form of humans. But I recognise them, I know them. You can tell by their eyes. They keep their lizard eyes, and they glint emerald, all shades of blue, sometimes red. They come from below and they feed off the rays of the sun. The lizard people,' she said, 'are demigods. Part-god, part-divine.'

'Holy, Holy, Holy.'

'Shall I tell you of the realm above?'

'Uh-huh.'

'Have you heard,' she said, 'of the Queen of Hearts? It is said,' she said, leaning over and raising her eyebrows, 'that Queen Isabella walks these streets carrying the heart of her husband. But it's not true. The heart is pinned to her dress like a brooch. It still beats, dripping blood, staining Isabella's dress, leaving a trail on the ground. I've seen her,' she said. 'She haunts these streets.'

*

'I've seen her,' I said. 'She haunts these streets. Huge pins stab through her husband's heart and pierce right into her own heart. She wears it like a brooch, but its alive, still beating, dripping blood.'

Mackenzie and Stevie stared up at me, their mouths hanging open. They fell about laughing.

'I've seen her, I have! She haunts these streets, collecting blood for her husband's heart, to keep it fed.'

'Yeah, Goblin, uh-huh, I bet you've seen her.'

'You better watch out,' I said.

We poked the fire with sticks, biting into our apples, the juice dribbling down our chins. I imagined biting into a heart. Eating human flesh.

'I'll tell you another,' I said. 'You know Amen Court? There's a dog that prowls Amen Court, a black dog, as big as a horse, with dripping jaws. This dog wants revenge, he wants human flesh. But he didn't used to be a dog. He was a man called Scholler and he was a prisoner in Newgate, where the inmates were starved. They were so hungry that they turned on Scholler and ate him alive!'

Mackenzie and Stevie were spitting out apple and rolling on the ground. Mac grabbed Stevie and barked at him, biting his leg. Devil joined in but got confused when Mac tried to bite his hind legs. He whined and sat down, licking his paws.

'Lay off Devil, Mac. He doesn't know what you're doing.'

'Jesus, he's a dumb dog. Hey, Devil, eh? No hard feelings.'

Devil laid his head on Mac's knee and we poked the fire with our sticks, watching the flames in silence.

'Any more stories, Goblin?'

'There's a spectre that haunts Newgate Prison,' I said. 'Her name is Amelia and she was a prisoner in Newgate too, just like Scholler. Do you know why she was locked away?'

'She killed a man!'

'She ate Scholler!'

'Much worse,' I said. 'Much worse. She ran an orphanage. She was paid by the local Parish to take in homeless kids. They thought she was looking after them so they paid her money to house them and clothe them and feed them, but she wasn't doing that at all, she wasn't. She took the money but she killed them. Killed all those kids and kept the money for herself. Some of the younger ones she put in a sack and drowned in the river. She got found out and put in jail and was executed and now she haunts the streets looking for children to kill.'

Stevie looked nervous, but Mac pretended it didn't bother him at all. 'She wouldn't kill us,' he said, poking at the fire with a stick, 'we'd stab her with hot sticks.'

'You can't stab a ghost,' said Stevie.

'Can so,' said Mac.

'Can't.'

'You can if they take corporeal form,' I said.

'What's a corprill form?' said Stevie.

'Flesh,' I said, leaning over and pinching Stevie's arm.

'Hey!' he said, waving his stick at me.

I backed off.

'But you'd need a magic spell to make them flesh again.'

'Told you,' said Stevie.

'I was still right, though,' said Mac.

'So was I.'

'Was not.'

'Was.'

We were at the worksite everyday. Mackenzie and Stevie and me, we were like wild things. We tore through the streets with Devil, cutting down anyone in our path, scattering the Button kids, and landing in our den. The three of us played cowboys and Indians and I told stories as darkness came. We'd collect wood and make a fire in the centre of the den. Mackenzie would go scrumping before we met and him and Stevie would sit there, stuffing their faces with apples. I'd watch the juice glisten on their fingers. The light from the fire glittered in their eyes, casting shadows across their thin faces. I'd read them *The Island of Doctor Moreau*, a chapter each night, and the next day we'd run round the worksite pretending to be Beast Folk chasing Prendick. Sometimes I'd tell Pigeon's stories of London, but not the lizards. They were secret. I only told stories of the realm above. I didn't tell Mac and Stevie about Pigeon. I never told them where I got my stories from. Some nights we'd all hunch over *The Phantom*, a gift from my aunt in the U.S., who would cut the strip from the newspapers, paste them together and send them to David. Pigeon had given me *Alice's Adventures in Wonderland* and I'd read bits out, but Stevie thought it was nonsense. Sometimes I read our favourite bits of *The Time Machine* or *The War of the Worlds*. None of us would miss our worksite meetings for anything and that summer stretched out forever.

*

After school I'd usually run home, pick up Devil and meet Mac and Stevie at the worksite, but Mac had to go visit some sick aunt and I wasn't in the mood for just being with Stevie and didn't feel like seeing Pigeon. So I went home, took Devil for a walk, and headed back again to read and listen to David's records. When I got in, ma was in the kitchen holding a bloodied rag. She plunged it into the tub and scrubbed at it, frowning, a cigarette dangling from her mouth.

'You okay, ma? You hurt?'

She didn't look up, she just said, 'What're you doing home again?'

'Felt like it.'

She didn't respond.

'You hurt yourself, ma?'

She looked up at me.

'No,' she said. 'I didn't hurt myself.'

She stared right at me, still scrubbing. Her eyes were too much, so I looked away.

'Just going upstairs,' I said, heading for the door.

'Wait,' she said. 'Sit down, Goblin.'

I turned back to her and she nodded to the kitchen table. I sat down and Devil jumped up on my lap.

'What is it?' I said, thinking over all the things I'd done

the past few days, but I couldn't think of anything that might have made her angry. Devil circled on my lap three times and flopped down, his back legs hanging over my thigh, his front legs and head dangling over the other side. I scrunched my hand into his fur, kneading at his back.

She dropped the rag into the tub, poured herself a drink and sat opposite. She lit another cigarette and stared at me. I looked down at Devil and stroked his head.

'How old are you now?'

'Eight,' I said.

She nodded.

'I didn't want you, you know.'

'I know.'

'But you came and there I was stuck at home looking after a screaming goblin-runt. Nothing made you happy.'

I felt my stomach go all tight and I just kept stroking Devil, trying to concentrate on how his fur felt.

'Ma,' I said. 'I've got a book I need to read for school.'

'You'll sit right there until we're done,' she said.

I looked up at her and she took a draw on her cigarette. She exhaled, the smoke engulfing me.

'Women get the curse,' she said.

I stopped stroking Devil when I heard her say 'curse', thinking I was going to get something more interesting than the usual. I managed to look her in the eye as I waited for more and she finally said, 'You'll get it too when you grow up.'

She smiled slightly, looking satisfied, and stared at me as she smoked. I couldn't wait any longer so I said, 'What curse?'

'Women bleed. Every month. Their bellies ache and they bleed from between their legs. It hurts.'

'I'll get it too?'

'You will.'

'What if I'm not cursed?'

'You will be. All women are. You'll suffer like the rest of us.'

'When will I get it?'

'When you're a woman.'

'When's that?'

'I don't know. Anytime. It could afflict you anytime.'

'Anytime?'

'That's right.'

'When were you cursed?'

'Thirteen,' she said. She must have seen my relieved expression as I thought how far away thirteen was and she added, 'You might get it sooner.'

She finished her drink and poured herself another glass.

'Why are we cursed?'

'So we can have babies.'

'The blood means we can have babies?'

'That's right, but I didn't want you. You came anyway and I was stuck here day after day with only you.'

'How long does the bleeding last?'

'A week. More or less.'

'Don't you die if you bleed for a week?'

She laughed and shook her head.

'But I almost died having you. Giving birth to a goblin almost killed me but you killed the midwife instead because you were so—'

'I know, mum. I know the story.'

'So ugly,' she said.

I waited for more but a few minutes passed and she said nothing. She smoked her cigarette and stared out the kitchen window. I lifted Devil off my lap and said, 'I'm going upstairs.'

She didn't respond, just looked out the window.

I went upstairs and sneaked into ma and da's room, walking carefully, trying not to make a noise. The room was all ma – the smell of perfume and powder. I sat down at her dresser and looked at my face in her mirror, two more angles of me reflected either side. I scrunched up my nose. I bared my teeth. I leaned closer, pursing my lips like old Mrs West's cat-arse mouth, then I puffed up my cheeks and laughed then went all serious again as I leaned forward and stared at my face right up close, looking at my brown-green eyes. I stared all wide then fluttered my lashes and did kissing noises. I went serious again and leaned in even closer, inspecting; cheeks speckled with freckles, big pink lips all dry. I stared at my small forehead but found nothing there either. I couldn't see the goblin in me. I wasn't ugly, I was sure of it, because I looked like ma and she was beautiful. I wasn't beautiful, though. My face was dirty, my lips dry and cracked, my short self-cut blonde hair was greasy and sticking out at all angles. I looked like a dirty boy version of ma, but I wasn't blue, I wasn't goblin.

*

'Maybe,' I said. 'Maybe she can see under my skin and into my insides. I'm ugly inside and she can see it. Like sin.'

David just stared at me, his mouth open slightly, then he said, 'Fuckin 'ell, G,' and got up off his bed and sat next to me on mine. 'I knew all this bible stuff would be bad for you.'

'She must be able to see inside because I looked in her mirror, looked really close and all I saw was that I look just like her but more like a boy and dirty. But I know I'm not ugly. I'm not,' I said, looking up at him. 'Am I?'

He looked down at me and said, 'Of course you're not.'

He shifted his arse on the bed until he was right next to me and he put his arm round my shoulder and squeezed so hard it hurt, but I didn't mind.

'Ma said blood makes babies come alive,' I said.

'What?'

'She said women are cursed and every month they bleed. And the blood makes babies. But wouldn't there be more babies if it was every month?'

David laughed.

'I don't know much about the bleeding, G, but that's not how babies are made. Think she's just trying to scare you.'

'I was scared at first, but I thought about it and I don't mind blood and I don't care if it hurts.'

'Well, that's good.'

'But what about the babies?'

David sighed.

'You're too young, G.'

'Too young for what?'

'To know about where babies come from.'

'Why?'

'Because it's adult stuff.'

'Why?'

'Jesus, G. Give it a rest. I'll tell you when you're older, okay?'

'I'll be older tomorrow.'

David laughed.

'Just leave it be, alright? What's the rush to grow up?'

'I don't want to grow up. Adults are stupid.'

'There you go, then.'

We sat for a bit and I leaned into him, resting my head on his chest. I listened to his heartbeat and said, 'Why does ma hate me?'

'Jesus, G. What is with you today?'

'I was born blue and killed that woman. Is that why?'

'You didn't kill the midwife, G. She was old, she just had a heart attack and it was hours after you were born. It's not like ma says.'

'Really?'

'Really.'

'You remember?'

'I remember.'

'I wasn't born blue?'

'You were, but it was because the umbilical cord was tangled round your neck.'

'What's a umbila cord?'

'Um-bil-ical. It's something that keeps you attached to ma. When you're born, they cut it. But you were all tangled up in it. You almost died. But it doesn't mean anything.'

'Why does she hate me then?'

'I don't know, G. It has nothing to do with you. It's just the way it is.'

'How do you know it's not me?'

'I just know.'

I fiddled with my blanket and said, 'I think da likes me.'

'He does.'

'I like fixing things with him.'

'He likes it too.'

'But he doesn't really talk to me.'

'That's just the way he is. Look, G, forget about them. We have each other. And you've got Devil and Mac and Stevie, that's all you need.'

'And Pigeon,' I said, without meaning to.

'You befriended a pigeon now?'

'Yeah,' I said, blushing, not wanting to give my secret away.

'Of course you have,' he said, ruffling my hair. 'Just don't let ma and da's bollocks get you down. It's not worth it. Okay?'

*

Pigeon took me and Devil on long walks. For the first time I saw different parts of London. She took me on the Underground, hopping on and off, searching for lizard people. And, best of all, she took me to the circus.

We were on one of our Underground trips and as the train pulled into the station we could see a row of clowns on the platform. They stood so still, all creepy like statues but with coloured-in faces and silly clothes and hair and hats. They stared out at nothing as Pigeon grabbed my hand, pulling me up to get off the train. Devil was the first on the platform, sniffing at them, tail wagging as they came to life, one of them throwing balls in the air and the others scrambling to catch them. Devil lay flat on his belly and growled at the mess of them that wasn't a mess at all but clever as can be as they each caught a ball perfectly, freezing in position. Devil barked, Pigeon clapped, I gawped. I watched as a clown jerked to life again, perfectly-clumsily cart-wheeling to where we stood and offering us a fanned bunch of leaflets for the circus.

I stared into his huge painted face and plucked one of the leaflets from his hand, holding it like it might go poof! up in flames. He blew a raspberry at me and back-flipped over to the other clowns.

Another train was arriving and they were statues again, not moving an inch. Pigeon ushered me on to the stairs and we went up into the glare of London above.

'Can we go?'

She looked stern, then winked and grinned, a wonderful grin of brown teeth, gaping holes, and cracked lips.

'Of course we can,' she said.

I clutched the leaflet so hard it was crushed when I came to stick it on my wall next to Jesus and Mary and the saints.

*

We followed the buzzing crowd and the first thing I saw was the great tent, swooping up into the sky, the light of the gloaming making it pop – bright colours, bright lights. The pigeons in Pigeon's hair were alert and chirping and she was swarmed with kids thinking she was one of the acts. She was kind and patient and let them feed the birds. I disappeared into the crowd, wandering from one ride to another, clutching at my pennies, deciding which one to spend them on. I finally chose and climbed into the seat and wheeeeeeee! I spun round and round and it felt like flying, really like flying. I was a Martian, a plane, an eagle swooping in for the kill. I came off, dizzy and happy. I looked for Pigeon but saw a painted man and followed him through the crowd.

'Oi, Mister,' I said. 'Oi, Mister, how come you're painted all over? How come the paint doesn't just come off?'

His eyes were a pale blue so light they were almost white. He knelt down in front of me, the ships and anchors and sea rippling and shifting as he moved. He leant his elbow on his knee and I was face to face with a mermaid with faded red hair.

'It's magic paint, boy.'

'I'm not a boy,' I said, 'I'm a goblin.'

'You don't look like a goblin.'

'Well, I am. I'd like to be painted like you, 'cept I'd have a Jesus.'

'Right here, little goblin.'

He turned and showed me Jesus on his back.

'Just like that,' I said. 'Yeah, just like that.'

'You come for the show?'

I nodded vigorously.

'You got your ticket?'

'Pigeon has it.'

'Pigeon?'

'Yeah, she has it. I'll need to find her.'

'Pigeons and goblins. You belong here, boy.'

He stood and yelled across the crowd, 'Roll up! Roll up! The circus is about to begin!'

I bobbed through the streams of people, searching for Pigeon. I found her amongst a gabble of kids and we clasped hands, keeping close as we were swept along with the crowd, swept into the magical realm of a glittering aerialist, purple sequins catching the light as she flew through the air. The platform statue-clowns bumbled and tumbled into the ring and I said, Pigeon, there they are! We've seen those clowns. There they are! And some old man behind me hissed ssssh! through his squint teeth and some woman said keep quiet, will you? But I always talked and talked and I forgot to keep quiet and they weren't even listening to much of anything anyway, it was all to look at so what did it matter if I said, Pigeon, that elephant, that big as a house elephant looks stupid in that tiny hat on its huge house-head. The clowns clambered and fell on its back, knocking each other like skittles. The elephant sprayed them all sodden with water and they drip drip dripped and I jumped up and laughed and cheered. Down in front! said that stupid old man but I was down anyway by then, glued to my seat mouth hanging open as a lady on a horse, balanced on one arm, went round and round the ring. Then me and Pigeon laughed and clapped like mad as the dogs all jumped through hoops and last of all out came the painted man holding a sword above his head and I squeezed Pigeon's hand and said, I know him. I know that man! He has Jesus! Holy, Holy, Holy, I said as he walked around the ring, all great strides and flexing muscles before gripping the sword with both hands, his head back. There was a gasp from the crowd as he lowered it into his mouth and I said nothing but held Pigeon's hand tight, waiting for the blood and the death and the panic. He swallowed it whole. There were cheers and claps and stamping of feet. Out it came, slowly, slowly, and cheers erupted into a roar as he swept it through the air. I stamped and yelled with the rest of them. All the performers came running in, swarming around him, dancing and cart-wheeling round the ring, the aerialist lady dangling from the trapeze. Everyone stood, clapping and whistling. The performers turned to us and bowed and bowed again and again. Flowers were thrown into the ring as the performers filed out, a swish of the curtain, they were gone.

On the journey back all I could do was talk about the acts but I was tired and half-asleep, leaning on Pigeon, her arm around me. I tried to keep my eyes open, looking up at her, telling her how I wanted to be a clown, be painted and do acrobatics, but my head would droop and I'd drift. I remember hearing her say, 'I know you, you're mad as a bag of cats, so don't you go trying any swallowing of swords.' I drifted, floating on glitter and lights.

I didn't tell Mac and Stevie I'd been to the circus. I didn't want them to be jealous, I didn't want them to know about Pigeon. Instead, I made up stories about a painted man who ate swords for dinner, a troop of jesters with painted faces who entertained Queen Isabella, and a flying glittering spirit who cast mischievous spells far and wide across the city of London.

*

'What you doing, boy?'

'I'm not a boy,' I said. 'I'm a goblin.'

'You don't look like a goblin.'

'Well, I am.'

'What do you want?'

'Looking for Pigeon.'

'What?'

'The old lady. I'm looking for the old lady.'

The neighbour leaned over, looking down at me, his eyes narrowing.

'What do you want with her?'

'Nuthin.'

I whistled to Devil and scuffed my way up the path. The neighbour called after me.

'She's gone, boy. She's sick. Her family took her away.'

I looked down at Devil. He barked at me, but all I could hear was the drone of the insects. I swayed, mesmerised by the bees tumbling amongst the weeds.

'Boy?'

'Huh?'

'You alright?'

'Where'd they take her?'

'I don't know.'

I walked off. I felt dizzy and sat on the curb.

'So what?' I said to Devil.

I scuffed my feet on the ground.

'So what? She was a stupid crazy pigeon woman anyway.'

It wasn't until weeks later I thought about the pigeons. I went back, broke in through a window and there they were, all over the house, dead like the mummified things, but rotting and stinking. I'd let her birds die.

I cleaned up the best I could, got them all together and buried them in the garden. I remembered from somewhere that people buried things with pennies, so I put pennies on the pigeons and said a lizard prayer.

'Forgive me lizards, for I have sinned. Forgive me my trespasses better than I forgive those who trespass me.'

I stuck a bit of wood in the ground and wrote, 'Here lie Pigeon's pigeons. May they rest with the lizards below.'

★

When Mackenzie was laid up with flu I kicked around with Stevie but I was bored pretty quickly. After pummelling him a dozen times and beating him at every race, I lost interest. I liked Stevie, but it didn't work just the two of us and Devil. We needed Mac. He brought out the best in us.

Stevie and I were just sitting on a wall, kicking our feet, and I was all wound up, like I could just shoot off into the sky like a rocket. I kicked the wall and looked at Stevie, thinking maybe I could pummel him again, but got bored the moment I thought of it.

'When, Stevie? When d'ya reckon Mac'll be better?'

He didn't respond, just shook his head. He was staring over at some kids playing Buttons. He had this faraway look in his eyes. It hadn't occurred to me that Stevie could be just as sick of me as I was of him.

We kicked the wall some more, then he was gone. Just a vague 'I'm just gonna—' and he was running down the street to the Button kids.

I didn't know what to do, so I got down and circled them, looking all aloof and too mature for it, but then I muscled in.

'You kids can't throw for shit.'

I got beaten by this little runt of a kid, a kid even runtier than me, with shit-hot aim. Stevie, he seemed to be enjoying himself, even won a few buttons. I just huffed and scuffed my feet and thought about pummelling the runtier-than-me kid but couldn't really be bothered in the end. Instead, I just ruffled his hair like David did with me, but he didn't even pay me attention.

'Kid, you can't throw for shit,' I said, drawling it out like some cowboy in the movies, but no one was listening and Devil was all laid out in the street in the sun snoring like some old man.

'When d'ya reckon Mac'll be better, eh?'

No one was listening and I'd had enough of these runtier-than-me kids. I left Stevie to it, winning his buttons, finally good at something. I heard later that he got really into it and cut off all the buttons on his parent's clothes, even his dad's Sunday best. He got a hiding for that, so he stopped playing Buttons and came back to our den like nothing had happened, bringing some scrumped apples like a peace offering and trying to tell a story about how he got captured by Martians.

Devil and I, we just wandered down the street, leaving them to their buttons. I thought maybe I could find David and we could go see a film, but he wasn't home. He worked fixing cameras at weekends so I took Devil along to see if David was there, but he was busy. He pressed some money into my hand and said get lost, Goblin, I'm working, and he winked at me and I left.

'Just you and me, eh kid?' I said to Devil with my cowboy drawl.

David had given me enough for the cinema, so I thought I'd go to the matinee but it was just some romance so we went to the Underground instead.

'Let's go on an adventure, Devil. Let's explore and find treasures.'

We often skipped the tickets, never got caught. I could ride for hours on the Underground, hopping on and off, sitting in the station watching all the people.

We caught a train to Kensal Green. Pigeon had told me all about the cemetery, so off we got and off we went, exploring.

As we walked through the grand entranceway, under the arch, there was a change in the air and I felt a bit sick with the heavy smell of flowers.

'This is the in-between realm.'

I walked on, pretending like I was monarch of this in-between realm, returning after years of exile to claim my throne. Devil bound down the path, chasing shadows and squirrels.

'Devil, you're ruining it. How can I be a snooty king when you're showing me up?'

I followed Devil and we were lost among the gravestones, turning down one path, then another and another. I kept to the shade, the trees providing shelter from the late afternoon sun. I looked out across the gravestones with their ivy armour and wild flowers erupting between them, insects shimmering in the sunlight.

Devil leapt across the path ahead of me, chasing a squirrel, the squirrel's arching jumps besting Devil's sloppy leaps. It spiralled up a tree, leaving Devil below, barking, whining.

'Ssshh! You'll wake the dead.'

Devil lost interest in the squirrel and worried a bumble bee tumbling drunkenly on the path. I pulled him away and we walked further into the cemetery. We came to a big path that led to a pillared building. Devil cantered ahead of me and I walked towards it, feeling my skin tingle. We ran up the stairs and between the pillars, reaching the door. I pulled on it, but it was locked. We explored the outside of the building, running down a pillared corridor. I weaved my way in and out of the columns, chasing Devil who easily out-ran me. He suddenly stopped, snuffling and scratching at something. I caught up to him, ready to save him from a sting, but it wasn't a bee, it was a foot.

'You found treasure,' I said.

I lifted it. Devil pawed at me, before catching the sound of a leaf scuffling down the path in the breeze. He jumped on it, looking up at me with pride. I smiled at him and cradled the foot in the palm of my hand. It looked like a crow's foot. The leg bone had been stripped clean. The foot arched neatly, each toe ending in sharp, glinting talons. I decided it was a magic thing that would protect me and give me powers. I clutched it in my hand and wandered after Devil. We left the pillared building and headed to the cemetery boundary. I pushed Devil on to the wall and climbed up after him. The canal lay below, the sunset injecting it with orange and reds.

'The water runs red, Devil-dog. It's red with the blood of the enemies of this in-between realm.'

Devil jumped down and threw himself into the water. I stayed on the wall; I didn't know how to swim. I watched Devil as he followed the ducks who snapped at him and launched themselves into the air, leaving him behind in seconds. Darkness fell, turning the water black.

'It's the time of water snakes, Devil-dog. We must go, or they'll pull us down to drown in the darkness.'

I coaxed him out and we went back into the cemetery, Devil dripping water along the paths.

We slept there that night and many other nights. I kept a treasure box in one of the mausoleums, a box full of old coins, dried up worms, the crow foot, David's teeth, a teddy bear, pigeon wings, an old broken doll I found in the street, and little things I had sneaked from ma; old jewellery, needles and thread, discarded make-up, a half-empty cigarette pack. We returned again and again, but never told Mac or Stevie. This was our world. We were the Goblin and Devil of Kensal Green.

*

After the first night we spent in Kensal Green, Groo was waiting for us in my bedroom. Groo was around one year old and belonged to Mr Fenwick, my neighbour. Mr Fenwick was from Scotland. He'd fought in The Great War and had stayed in London when he returned from the front. That's all us neighbours knew about him, as he was a right curmudgeon and would mostly grunt at you if you asked him anything about his life. Mr Fenwick hadn't given Groo a name, just called her The Cat. He said he got her to catch mice and rats, but she was useless. I named her. I called her Groo, short for 'groomer', short for 'terror groomer' because she terrorised Devil. She loved him, but at first I wasn't quite sure and neither was Devil. She'd come round a lot, sneaking in a window, or brushing past you at the door so quickly and silently you weren't even sure it was her or a mischievous breeze tickling your skin. 'That's sure no breeze,' I'd say to Devil as we went into our room and found her on the bed, waiting. Devil would join her, tired from a day of adventure and they'd curl up together. I'd try to find some space to lie down and read my book, my limbs tangled up amongst paws and tails. I'd read, listening to their huffy snores and I'd drift off to the rhythm. Waking up in the middle of the night, I'd find David had put a blanket on me and Devil was sat at the end of the bed, his ears pinned back, his eyes wide with worry as Groo groomed him. If he moved an inch, she'd hiss and lash out and he'd settle back down with a whine.

'You leave my Devil alone, you old bully,' I'd say to her, scooping her up. She meowed, but was rag doll limp as I carried her down the stairs and put her in the garden.

'He's as clean as any dog should be, you terror-beast. You leave him alone.'

She'd yawn and stretch, wandering off into the darkness. But it would repeat – night after night Devil was terror-groomed. I was about to call a stop to it, build the barricades, mark Devil's territory, but after the first night we'd spent in Kensal Green Devil must have enjoyed the peace and decided he'd had enough. Groo was up to her usual terror grooming but this time Devil stood up, pawed her, pushed her over, barked and wandered off. She lay there, startled, before meowing and slinking over to me. I was shaking with laughter before I realised she was standing on my pillow, chewing on my hair.

'You're a strange one, old Groo,' I said to her. 'You really are.' I fell asleep as she chewed on my hair and licked my head.

*

The next day I went to visit Mac. His mum let me in this time. He was still sick, but a bit better. I told him about Devil giving Groo what for and how she terror-groomed me instead.

'I woke up with my hair in weird clumps from where she'd been licking and chewing, but there was no sign of her. She must have gone back to Mr Fenwick's for her breakfast.'

'She's a strange one, just like you,' he said, then had a coughing fit. His mum came in and shooed me out.

'But I've only been here a minute, Mrs Mac.'

'That's right, and you're already making him worse. Come back next week, I'm sure he'll be better by then. Now, get.'

I was pretty down in the dumps at the thought of another whole week without Mac. I went home and listened to some of David's records and just stared at the ceiling. Devil pawed at me and barked, so I took him for a walk but my heart wasn't in it and I went back home after he'd done his business. I was lying on the sitting room floor reading my book when da came back from work. He sat in the chair next to me and lit his cigarette.

'Goblin,' he said. 'Come 'ere. I'll tell you a story.'

He usually didn't talk much, so I just looked at him, not moving an inch.

'Come here,' he said, patting his knee.

I walked over to him and just stood there. I could smell the sweat and dirt of a day's work. He picked me up by the waist and put me on his knee. He didn't usually touch me, so I just looked at him, confused. He held up his hand, spreading his fingers.

'A man lost his finger at the factory today,' he said.

I looked at him, wide-eyed.

'How?'

'He was stupid. He used one of the machines wrong.'

'He used it wrong?'

He nodded.

'And, chop! Off came his finger.'

He held one of his fingers down with his thumb, pretending it was missing. I sat up, stiff, staring at him. Ma came in, glanced at us, and went over to the mirror.

'And that finger fell to the floor and it kept moving.'

'What are you doing?' said ma, checking her make-up.

'Telling a story,' he said, not taking his eyes off me. 'It moved along the ground like this, like a caterpillar, and it kept on going, crawling right across the factory floor.'

'No! No, it didn't. Fingers can't crawl on their own.'

'Of course they can,' he said, 'and we could have fixed it back on, but it crawled too far and was eaten up, *snap!* by the big jaws of a rat. Just like this!'

His huge hand snapped shut on mine and I yelped and fell on the floor. I rolled and laughed, and said 'No, no! You're telling tales.'

Ma put on another layer of lipstick and smiled into the mirror.

'Don't fill her head with more nonsense,' she said.

'It's just a story,' said da.

'She's too stupid to realise. She probably thinks it's the truth.'

'I know it's just a story,' I said.

'Get out from under our feet, runt. And go wash yourself, you stink like a sewer.'

'Go on,' da said, 'do what your ma says.'

I stood up and said, 'Thanks for the story.'

He nodded. Ma sat on da's lap and they kissed. She ran her hand through his hair. They laughed and I left, closing the door on them.

Edinburgh, 12 July 2011

I'm at my desk in the sitting room while Ben sits on the couch, Mahler's head on his lap, Sam squeezed in next to Mahler.

'That Detective called again last night.'

'I don't want to talk to him.'

'Yel need to eventually, eh?'

'I'm not ready.'

'For what?'

'I don't want to talk about it.'

'What're ye writing?'

'About when I was a kid in London.'

'I thought ye didnae want to think about all that.'

'It's too late now, isn't it?'

'But ye just said—'

'It wasn't all bad. I had a family of animals. And I got a new mum and dad.'

'What happened to yer old mum and dad?'

'Da went to fight the Nazis and never came back. Ma left too, eventually. But when the war started she had to go work in a factory and she'd come home, her hands blackened, stinking of sweat. When she paid any attention to me I was "dirty rotten Goblin-runt". She called me Goblin-runt from the day I was born and it stuck.'

'Join the club,' said Ben. 'My parents were right cunts too.'

'I had a good brother, though. I loved David and he loved me. He called me Goblin, not "runt" like ma called me, apart from once when he was in a mood, but I knew he felt bad about it. We shared a room since as far back as I remember, and he was good to me. Ma loved David. He mustn't have been born blue.'

London, 16 March 1939

I was nine years old on 16th March 1939 and David gave me a present. He'd fixed up some old bashed camera for me.

'There you go, Goblin,' he said. 'You capture your world with that.'

I was speechless as he slung it over my neck. Ma and da usually forgot my birthday. If ma did remember she'd just go on about how I never should have been born, so I avoided being at home on my birthday and spent it with Mac and Stevie and I'd sleep in our den.

'Come meet me at my work at five,' said David, 'I have a special treat for you.'

I was so excited I got there early and just sat in the street with Devil for half an hour until David came out.

'What's the treat?' I said.

'You'll see. C'mon.'

I followed him, all antsy and asking him where we were going every few minutes. He thought it was funny at first but eventually told me to shut up or we'd be going home so I shut up and kicked a stone along the pavement until we arrived at the cinema.

'This is it,' he said. *'Bride of Frankenstein.'*

'I don't wanna see some film about a boring old bride.'

'Look at the poster, you idiot.'

I looked – *The Bride of Frankenstein* in electrified letters; a woman with strange big hair, white zigzags at either side; lightning striking at a huge frightening face - all heavy brow, hooded eyes and dark shadows.

'It looks amazing.'

'I saw it when it came out, when you were too young to come with me. You're gonna love this, Goblin. I know it.'

I nodded, gawping at the poster.

'We'll have to leave him out here, though.'

'What?' I said, pulling myself away from the poster.

'We'll have to tie him out here. We can't take him in.'

'We can't leave Devil.'

'C'mon, Goblin, don't make a fuss. Dogs aren't allowed.'

'Why not?'

'Because they'll bark and shit and piss everywhere.'

'You know Devil won't do that. You *know* he won't.'

'They won't let us in with him. I can't do anything about it.'

He looked down at Devil and I could tell he was feeling bad.

'Look,' he said. 'There's maybe a way. Just let me get the tickets.'

We sneaked Devil in through the toilet window. I gave him a bunk up and David leaned out, got him under the shoulders and pulled him in. He hid him under his jacket and waited for me inside. Devil was no bother. He made some huffy snuffling noises as he explored some of the seats and smelled all the new smells and I glanced nervously at the usher, but he was up at the back talking with a girl. More people arrived and I worried they'd make a fuss, so I quietly called Devil but he ignored me.

'C'mon,' said David. 'Get him over. I don't want to be thrown out.'

'He's on important sniffing business – he's got to feel comfortable,' I said, but eyed the new arrivals all the same.

'David?' I said.

'Mh-hmm?'

'I heard da say we should go to war. He said Chamberlain is a pansy for letting Hitler take Checksvakia.'

David didn't say anything, his eyes fixed on Devil who was sniffing his way along our row.

'Do you think we will go to war?'

'I don't know,' he said. 'It's complicated.'

'Complicated how?'

'It just is.'

'Would you and da have to fight?'

'No. I don't know. Just drop it, okay?'

'Can you show me where Checksvakia is on one of your maps?'

'Sure,' he said.

'Hey, boy,' I said to Devil, who had finished his sniffing undetected. I ruffled his head and told him to stay put and he lay down under my chair. During the film he fell asleep and at some of the quiet bits I could hear him snore.

I loved being in the cinema. I loved the darkness and the smell of stale sweat and old furniture. David had bought me sweets and I sat slouched in my seat, stuffing them in my mouth, staring up at him. He looked beautiful and pale, the light from the screen casting shadows across his face.

Elsa Lanchester as the bride was the most beautiful thing I'd ever seen. When the film had finished I walked up the aisle, arms outstretched, hissing at everyone as they left. David lumbered after me. 'Friend?' he said, and I drew back, baring my teeth, hissing. He scooped me up, throwing me in the air. I scowled at him, indignant, but he lightly dropped me to the floor and did his best Dr Pretorius. I threw my head back, laughing like a banshee, almost despite myself, still bugged a bit by how easily he threw me around.

We'd forgotten all about Devil. He woke up at all the noise and barked and jumped up at us. He ran rings round the usher who came and chased us into the street.

'That was the best!' I said.

'Did you see his face, eh? When Devil was nipping at his feet?'

'Yeah!'

As we walked home David told me the story of the first Frankenstein film and said he'd get me the book.

'If you're good,' he said, and winked at me.

We fell into silence. I was lost in my head, reliving the film. I hissed quietly now and then.

'David?'

'Huh?'

'I wanna be Frankenstein. I wanna make a monsta.'

He smiled at me and made to say something, but he didn't.

'Look, it's Conchie and Pick 'n Chew.'

The idiot bastards Jack Alexander and Simon Mayhew were walking towards us. There were a half a dozen more, but I didn't know them.

'Whadya want, Jack?'

Jack walked right up to us and punched David in the face. Before I could do anything I was pulled from behind by one of the other idiot bastards. I was on the ground, my cheek pushed into the grit, one of them sitting on my back. I could barely breathe. I couldn't see David, but I could hear them beating on him. Two of them were chasing Devil, but he ran rings round them, always just ahead. I knew they would kill him if they got a hold of him, but he had them beat, he had them tripping after him and he'd feint, nipping the arse of the one who sat on me, then off he'd go again. When Devil whipped out of reach so fast that one of the bullies fell over, I smiled. Then David hit the concrete right in front of me, blood spattering across my face. I could see he'd lost some teeth. I struggled for breath and blacked out.

When I came to, he was holding me, half-dragging me home because he couldn't lift me anymore, Devil whining at my side. I felt bad that David had got the pummelling and he was having to carry me home. I struggled to my feet and managed to walk the rest of the way, holding onto his hand. I was too old for it and I had to pretend it was okay that we didn't hold hands anymore but that day we held hands. Ma made a fuss over David. He said for her to check on me too, but she ignored him and kept on fussing, so I went to bed. I got up in the morning and went out with Devil and Mac, still with David's dried blood on my face. I took them to where David had been pummelled and picked up his teeth to put in my treasure box.

David hardly looked at me after that night. I told him it didn't matter and he told me to shut up, Goblin-runt. He still looked handsome with his face all bashed up. We didn't speak much after that, even though we shared a room. He'd just listen to his records and smoke. One time I couldn't get in and I waited outside and a girl came out later and then I got in. He started to speak to me again. Just 'How you doing, Goblin?' and I'd say about going to the cinema again but he'd just grunt and I'd go play with Mac and Stevie instead.

Edinburgh, 12 July 2011

'I remember his face. In the cinema. I remember the light from the screen flickering across his cheeks, glinting in his eyes. I remember him smiling at me. That's what I remember. The smell of stale sweat and old furniture. The feel of the ticket crushed in my hand. That's what I remember and nothing else matters.'

'I'm glad for ye,' Ben says. 'I'm glad ye had someone. I didnae have anyone. At least ye had David, eh?'

I nod and watch as spectre-Monsta climbs over Ben's back

and on to his shoulder. All I can see are the worm tentacles, feeling their way across Ben's shoulder, up his neck. The shrew head appears, that pointed nose quivering as it sniffs at Ben, the beautiful dark eyes reflecting the light. I could lose myself in Monsta's eyes.

'You're my family now,' I say to Ben, Sam, Mahler, and the spectre of Monsta.

'Ah, c'mon, old lady. Dinnae make us cry.'

'It's true.'

'Aye, well. The weirdos always find each other, eh?'

He strokes Mahler's head.

'I dinnae want to outstay ma welcome, though. Now yer feeling better I'll be out yer hair.'

'I'd like you to stay.'

'I dinnae want to take advantage.'

'You know I've always wanted you to stay. I don't like you being on the streets.'

'I'm used to it.'

'I know, but you're family. And we need you.'

'Well, I think Sam would be pretty sad to no see Mahler all the time.'

'I'm back at work tomorrow and I'll need you to take Mahler for walks. It would be easier if you just stayed.'

Ben looks down at the dogs and strokes Mahler's nose, frowning, as if the stroking takes intense concentration.

'Aye, alright,' he says, not looking at me. 'I'll stay. For the sake of these two.'

'Good,' I say, feeling a warmth in my belly, the same warmth I felt when James and Mad took me in. 'This was my dad's flat,' I say. 'Before it was mine.'

'Which dad?'

'My new dad, James. He moved here after the circus ended. This is where he settled while I was living in Venice.'

'I've never been to Venice. Or London.'

'I never want to go back.'

'Why not?'

'It's best to leave the past in the past.'

'That's not what that Detective thinks.'

'I don't care,' I say. 'He can keep phoning. I'll never go back.'

Chapter 3

I was in Kensal Green Cemetery the morning war was declared, oblivious to Chamberlain's voice on the wireless.

I knew war was brewing after Germany had invaded Poland. We were all just waiting. There was a weird atmosphere at home and war was the only thing Mac would talk about, so I went to the cemetery to get away from it all. I'd stayed over, sleeping in my mausoleum. There'd been a thunderstorm the night before and Devil and I ran down the paths, dancing like maniacs in the rain. I climbed up a mausoleum and crouched on the roof, the rain slithering down my face. I watched the storm clouds envelop the city and saw lightning strike one of the silver slugs. It burst into flames, straining on its wires as it was buffeted by the wind. I clambered down and ran between the gravestones, mimicking Dr Frankenstein – 'It's alive!' I yelled, laughing as the lightning crackled through the black clouds and Devil hunkered down, ears back, barking at the sky.

We retreated to my mausoleum for shelter. I had hidden a bag of clothes and other supplies and I added to it each time we came. I dug out the old rag for drying Devil after his swims in the canal. I hugged him close to me, rubbing him with the rag as he licked my face. I changed into dry clothes and lit candles, keeping them near for some warmth. We curled up in my old blanket and I told Devil ghost stories until we both fell asleep.

*

The morning was crisp. The storm had cleared the air. We had breakfast and I gathered my things as Devil sat in the morning sun. We wandered lazily through the cemetery, on our way to the Underground when the siren smashed through the in-between realm. Devil barked at the snaking high-pitched moan.

'War!' I yelled.

I searched the sky for planes as we ran back to the mausoleum. There was a chamber below and I broke the old rusting lock with a stone. I coaxed Devil down into the darkness and he whined and slunk down on his belly, following me.

I lit candles and listened for bombs, but there was nothing. I traced my fingers across the coffins in the crypt, all covered in dust and scuttling insects. I wanted to break them open to see a real skeleton but I was afraid and pretended it was really respect for the dead because goblins shouldn't be afraid of anything, especially dead things. I sat with Devil, his head on my lap, and read some of *The Time Machine* again. I don't know how long we were in there. I hadn't heard the all-clear but I lost patience and crept back to London above. I searched the sky again, finding nothing. I climbed up on a mausoleum and looked out over the city. No planes or flames.

We left the in-between realm and found people in the street, everyone carrying a gas mask. Some of the kids still had them on. A group of toddlers were sat on the pavement playing marbles, all wearing adult gas masks, heads lolling, absurdly large and insect-like. Some girls wore their masks as they played with a skipping rope. The two holding the rope looked like sentries, standing still apart from a flick of the wrist. The two girls skipping in the middle were like little monsters, nimble and silly-looking, their ponytails sticking out the side of the masks. Devil ran under the rope, back and forth, but the girls didn't stumble. I pretended to shoot them, bang bang bang! They ignored me. One of the sentries turned and stared at me with her huge glinting bug eyes, still turning the rope. I called on Devil and ran off down the street pretending we were being chased by giant Martian insects. We arrived at the Underground and threw ourselves dramatically onto a train, lying on the seats as we caught our breath. I stared suspiciously at everyone, confused by the sudden camaraderie as strangers talked to each other. It was the same back home. Neighbours we hardly spoke to were round at our house, sitting by the wireless, a drink in their hands. David stood in the corner, away from everyone else. He smiled at me, beckoned me over.

'Where you been, G? You're always disappearing.'

'I was in the in-between realm.'

'Yeah? Is there war there?'

'When did it happen?'

'This morning. Eleven fifteen.'

'Are you going away? Are you going to fight?'

'I'm not going anywhere,' he said, looking over at da. 'I'm staying right here.'

★

The house was stifling and boring, with our neighbours everywhere and all the adults droning on. I found Mac and Stevie and we played war at the worksite. As darkness fell we sat eating our apples, watching the searchlights, listening to the hum of the barrage balloon wires. I was bloody and bruised all over. Even Stevie had got in a few hits.

We crept back home in the dark. The streets were deserted. When someone walked by, their footsteps echoed. They'd brush past us, a shadow, an apparition, except for some drunk old man who mumbled to himself and tripped over his own feet. I sneaked up on him and whispered some made-up German in his ear.

'Huns!' he yelled, losing his footing on the edge of the kerb. He half-sat, half-fell, his arms flailing. Mac hit him with a stick, Devil nipped at his feet and we ran off, leaving him rolling on the pavement.

I got home to find ma, da, and David in the sitting room. All the neighbours had gone. The wireless burbled in the background. The windows were covered, and the light was dim. Da sat next to ma, leaning back, smoking, looking relaxed except for his hand that gripped the side of the chair, his knuckles white. Ma was perched. Her nose was red, her mascara had run and was caked across her cheeks. David was sitting opposite them with his elbows on his knees, head bowed, palms pressed to his ears, his fingers sticking up through his hair. I thought maybe he was sick.

'David?'

Ma jerked towards me as if about to get up, but she stayed, perched. Her dark brown eyes looked black.

'I want you home before blackout from now on. You got that?'

'You never cared before.'

'Don't you answer me back, Goblin-runt. You've been running wild for too long, you and that Devil-dog.'

I nodded.

'You hear me?'

'Yes, ma.'

Da continued to smoke. David didn't move. I went into the hall and paused, listening.

'I'm not having a fucking conchie living in our house.'

Da wasn't even shouting. His voice was low and I strained to hear. There was no response. Just silence. I went to my room.

'They're idiots, Devil. Idiots.'

We curled up in bed and I flicked through *The Time Machine*, reading bits of it aloud to Devil.

David came in, took off his clothes and got in bed. He had a red welt on his cheek, just below his eye. Dried blood crumbled across his temple.

'What happened?'

'Nothing.'

He lit a cigarette.

'Mind if I put on a record?'

He'd never asked before.

'It's fine,' I said.

We lay there, listening to Liszt. Devil fell asleep, twitching and making little noises as he dreamt.

'We don't need to stay here,' David said. 'Do we?'

He turned on his side and looked over at me. I shook my head.

'We'll leave. How about that? We'll leave together and go to the west coast. We'll live by the sea. I'll get a job and we'll live by the sea.'

I nodded. I'd never been to the sea.

He turned off the record.

'Night.'

'Night.'

I sank into my bed and drifted, dreaming dreams of the ocean, of ships and pirates, of treasure and krakens and mermaids and adventures to shimmering glittering foreign lands.

Edinburgh, 16 July 2011

Holding the newspaper, worrying the edges, I stare at the photograph. It's blurry. There's very little light. At first glance, all you can really see is an indistinct mound, a jumble of old clothes maybe, rubbish, junk, just waiting to be tipped over into a pit where it would rot away. Light comes into the right of the photograph, an overexposed glare, melting, pushing back the darkness. Some of the bodies are in sacks, but others are piled on, legs in a tangled mess, heads drooping. Smoke was emerging from behind the mound and I remember the stench of burning hair and skin. Devil had been by my side, sprinting in short bursts, back and forth, barking and whining, but I'd ignored him as I stared at a dog that was pushed deep into the mound, its head sticking out. It looked comical, its front paw offered up. I'd taken the paw in my hand, feeling the pads, staring at its lolling tongue. There was a cat next to it and I'd lifted its head with the palm of my hand, pushing up the chin. I'd stroked it, poked into its strange ears, feeling the shape of the cartilage. The eyes looked fake. It was just a rag doll cat. I'd sniffed its head. It smelled cold.

I must have left the camera. Mac had picked it up. It was always round my neck. I can't remember anymore, can't recall why I left it. Maybe it was the shock of seeing all the dead bodies in our den.

Mac had raised the camera. At the time I didn't know whether he'd taken a photo or if he was just playing, just pretending. And here I was, walking towards Mac, emerging from the smoke, the dead animals barely visible in the background.

I had my brother's old shorts on. They were too big for me and I'd tied them round my waist with string. My spindly legs were covered in bruises from our violent games, from running through the streets in the blackout. I was reaching towards Mac. I didn't like anyone else touching my camera, even him. I'm frowning, about to speak, about to demand it back. You can see the scar on my arm, from the spike. And more bruises. My gas mask was propped on top of my head, my shorn hair sticking out in tufts.

It's a beautiful photograph.

London, 6 September 1939

I was about to snatch the camera away from Mac, but instead I was sick. It was mostly bile. Devil sniffed at my sick and I pushed him away.

'It's been happening all over,' said Mac.

'What?'

'This,' he gestured to the mound of dead bodies. 'It's been happening all over.'

'Who's doing it?'

'We are. Freddy from next door took his pup to the vet yesterday and the pup just followed him all excited like it was an adventure. Freddy said it was for her own good. That she'd be afraid of the bombs, that she'd go crazy. Freddy said they'd have enough to worry about without this pup causing them trouble and being another mouth to feed.'

'I don't believe it.'

'It's right there,' Mac said, pointing to the bodies. 'What's there to believe?'

'People won't just go and kill their family for no reason.'

'They're pets, you idiot. They're just pets.'

'Don't you think Devil's family?'

I punched him on the arm, he punched me back and we ended up in a scrap. He gave me a bloody nose but I pinned him down, pulling his arm behind his back and sitting on him. Devil yapped and nipped at me.

'See,' I said. 'Devil loves you. Devil matters.'

'I love the little bastard too, just get off me.'

We sat in silence for a while, staring at the bodies. Mac rubbed his arm and I wiped at the blood dribbling onto my lips. Devil nuzzled into me, trying to lick me clean of blood. I took his face in both hands and snuffled just behind his ear, breathing him in, smearing blood on his fur. I kissed his head.

'I wasn't saying he doesn't matter, I was just saying how it is. Yesterday I found Charlie from across the road sat in the gutter snotting all over himself and I flicked his ear and called him a cry-baby. He cried even harder so I shoved him and he fell and lay there in the road. I didn't know what to do, he was shaking and making this godawful noise. I dragged him out the gutter and put him in his garden and just left him there. Turned out his dad had taken all three cats to the vet to be killed. You know Charlie, won't speak to anyone except those cats, and he had that one he put on a lead, the one that would sit on his shoulder like some parrot. All the adults say it's for the best. All the adults say, "There's a war on."'

'People won't kill all the animals just because there's a war on.'

'But they have.'

Devil wandered over to the mound of bodies, sniffing round them, whining. I called him but he ignored me. He got down, flat on his belly, burrowing into the mound and pulling at something. I called again but he just pulled, dragging out a cat, causing the mound to collapse. The bodies fell on top of him and we ran to the rescue. The bodies shuddered as he struggled beneath them; a monster of heads and limbs shaking and lolling, paws reaching out to us, glacial eyes staring as we scrambled through the bodies searching for him. When we found him he had the cat held firm in his mouth and he growled at me when I tried to take it from him. He jumped clear, knocking Mac, leaving us in the pile of bodies. Mac was sprawled in a cushion of fur, cat and dog legs sticking out, giving him new limbs, heads sprouting from his shoulders.

'You look like a monster,' I said. 'A three headed catdogboy with belly paws like an insect.'

'A woodpig,' he said, kicking his legs in the air, taking two paws in his hands and waving them, 'a woodpig on its back.'

I laughed at him and he said, 'You have feathers.' I looked down and saw a dirty parrot by my knee. I picked it up, stroking it. It felt soft. Devil whined and I looked over. He'd let go of the cat and was sat flat in front of it, whining, scraping at the ground, pawing at its head. He circled it, got down flat again, pawed it, circled.

'We should get away from here,' I said.

I pushed myself up, feeling a crunch beneath my hand. I'd cracked a dog's skull. I looked over at monster-woodpig-Mac and it wasn't funny anymore. I felt sick again, drowning in bodies, no breath, no breath, trying to move, trying to get to Devil, my hands and feet crushing bodies. I couldn't get free of them, they cracked and groaned and burst beneath me, tumbling after me as I tried to move away. I was sick again, sick onto the animals.

When I reached Devil I recognised the cat. Ruby was a year old ginger that belonged to my neighbour Mrs Summers. Devil had wanted to be friends with her, but she'd only hissed and scratched at him, until one hot summer's day Devil was lying in our garden and Ruby came along and sat on top of him like they were best friends. Devil lay there like it was all normal, letting Ruby lick his ear.

I picked her up and Devil barked at me. She was damp and smelled of pee. She must have wet herself when she was killed.

'It's Ruby,' I said to Mac. 'I'm taking her home, giving her a proper burial.'

'Who's Ruby?'

'Mrs Summers' cat. She was friends with Devil.'

Devil stood on his hind legs and licked her dangling tail.

'I don't believe it,' I said. 'I bet it's Nazi spies infiltrating us, telling everyone to kill the pets, telling everyone it's for the best.'

'Maybe.'

'It is.'

'Probably.'

'It's Nazis.'

'Oi, you! Get out!'

I turned, spitting out of the side of my mouth. A man stomped towards us, carrying a shovel, sweat dripping.

'What're you up to, eh?'

I squinted up at him.

'The Nazis have come,' I said.

'Get lost, boy. And you. That your dog? It'll end up in here soon enough.'

I kicked his shin and spat at him, my saliva still mixed with sick. He took a swipe at me, but we ran, Mac swearing at him, calling him a fat German bastard. He just stood there, rubbing his leg, watching us run off.

★

'The Germans have come.'

That's what we told Stevie.

'They're spies. They'll kill all our animals. You heard what he said about Devil, Mac. They'll burn and bury them. They'll release millions of rats and there won't be any cats to eat the rats and they'll spread a plague, like before, like back in the olden times.'

Stevie looked frightened.

'I'm sick of your stories,' he said. 'Sometimes I'm just sick of them.'

'It's not a story,' I said. 'Look,' I said.

I held out Ruby. I shook her, as if that proved something. Stevie backed off.

'Get it away from me!'

'It's Ruby,' I said. 'The Nazis killed Ruby and all the other pets. It's real, we saw. Eh, Mackenzie?'

Mac shrugged and said, 'He looked like an ugly German but he didn't sound it.'

'I know, he's a spy. He'll have practiced our accent.'

'Yeah, probably a spy.'

'We'll go back and we'll take pictures and show everyone the Germans have come.'

'I dunno,' said Stevie.

'They have our den. We can't just let them kill animals and have our den and bring plague rats.'

'Yeah,' said Mac, 'but who wants pictures, Goblin? We'll capture him instead. How about that? We'll go in and we'll capture him!'

'Ayaiaiaaaai!' I yelled.

'He sure looked a fat German bastard, a stupid rubbish German spy and we'll get medals for finding him out, eh Goblin?'

'For definite, Mac. Come on, Stevie, you gotta come. We'll get medals, the three of us, and we'll meet the king and eat in the palace, a huge feast for capturing the Germans and stopping the rat plague.'

Stevie still looked uncertain, but smiled. He joined in our war cries and bowed down before me as I laid a stick on each shoulder.

'Sir Knight Stevie, Saviour of the Realm, Preventer of Rat Plague and Capturer of Fat German Bastards.'

He puffed out his skinny chest.

'I salute thee,' I said.

They both stood to attention.

'I salute thee,' they chorused.

'But first we'll leave Ruby at old Mrs Summers' house.'

'I thought you were going to bury her.'

'I'm going to leave her on Mrs Summers' step so she sees what the Nazis have done to her Ruby.'

I went into Mrs Summers' garden, Mac and Stevie keeping Devil outside the gate so he wouldn't make a fuss. I laid her down on the top step and said a short lizard prayer.

'We'll get those Nazi bastards,' I said to Ruby. 'I promise.'

I joined Mac, Devil and Stevie and we raised our sticks and ran for the worksite, yelling. On the way I saw my neighbour Miss Campbell in her garden with her dog Betty. I ran up to her gate.

'Keep her safe, Miss Campbell!' I yelled. 'There's Nazis killing the pets. You keep Betty safe.'

Miss Campbell looked startled as we ran by. The streets were emptying as the blackout darkness approached. By the time we reached our den we were tired out and the fat German bastard was gone. The fire had been extinguished and most of the animals had been thrown into a pit. Stevie looked sick.

'I thought it was a story,' he said. 'I thought Ruby had been hit by a car or something.'

'We told you the Germans had come,' I said, and he nodded, looking up at me like he was just a little frightened kid. And he was. That's all he was, all we should have been.

'Come on, we'll hunt the fat German bastard, we'll hunt him down.'

I persuaded Stevie but I was deflated. I wanted to be back home, curled up on my bed, watching David smoke, listening to his records. I knew the fat German bastard must have gone and we should be gone too but I turned it into a game, another adventure story.

'C'mon, Stevie.'

We heard voices coming from beyond the animal pit, behind a mound of rubble.

'The Nazis,' I said. 'They're still here.'

Stevie fidgeted, looking over to the worksite exit, barely visible as the sky darkened.

'Creep,' I said. 'We'll creep and sneak! Like spies, we'll sneak up on the Nazis and we'll capture them.'

Mac nodded, clasping his stick.

'Ssssshhh!' I said to Devil. 'We're being spies.'

He got down on his belly, mimicking us.

I knew Stevie wouldn't come, so I said, 'Stevie, you be lookout, okay? You just stay right here and you be lookout.'

He nodded, and we hunched down flat, creeping along the ground, Devil huffing by my side. We crept past the animal pit and round the mound and there they were, five Nazis.

I raised the camera and we fell like Alice down the rabbit hole tumbling in the darkness hail thee O lizards in the darkness in the depths hail thee who art in the darkness. In a moment, in a second, with a click, it was over.

Edinburgh, 16 July 2011

The phone rings and rings and rings and there's Queen Isabella but she isn't there she's in London you're in London not here not here in this room all shadows and dim orange light. I search the whole house on my hands and knees checking under beds in cupboards no whisky no whisky here or there and I lie on the floor watching spectre-Monsta, kerlumpscratch, kerlumpscratch, pretty monsta dead thing but you're not here you're in London buried dug up tagged and filed. You're not here, Monsta, you're evidence. I spy with my little eye in the darkness in the depths red wine buried in a cupboard and I feed myself one glass two and three. Back to my desk and here I sit and here I say I'm sorry Devil I'm sorry I'm sorry I'm sorry.

London, 6 September 1939

I was trying to stem the blood flow and I needed to get away.

As I'd clicked the shutter there was a loud bang and I fell back as if slugged, unsure what I'd seen, unsure what had happened. Devil barked furiously and there were two bangs one after the other, a strangled whine on the final blast. I scrambled up and saw Devil on the ground. I thought it was the sound that had sent him flat and was about to call him and run when I saw he was leaking red. I heard yells and the sound of rubble scattering, but the muddy light made it difficult to see and all I knew was that I needed to get Devil somewhere safe.

I hoisted him into my arms, holding him tight to my chest and I floated like the Martians, with ease and precision. The rubble was no obstacle. I knew my way through this land in the darkness. I knew it better than anyone. It was Devil who had given me our way out the day we played Frankenstein's monsta, Martians and Nazis with Mac and Stevie. He'd disappeared, following the rat as I lay impaled on that spike.

I found the spike and I twisted round, falling on my arse and sliding feet first through the hole I'd seen Devil disappear into that day.

You saved us, I said. You've saved us both. It'll all be alright.

I laid him down and pulled off my shirt, my hand gliding across his body, sliding through the blood. I tied the shirt around him, laying my hand across it, willing the bleeding to stop. I could feel his faint heartbeat. We were in the darkness, our protection, our realm, the kingdom of the lizards. Hail thee O lizards hail thee in thy kingdom down below.

You can't leave me, Devil.

The heartbeat stopped and I laid my head on his chest. I felt the blood on my skin, still warm; it soaked into my hair. I lay there until his body was cold. I held onto his paw and stroked the pads.

Hail thee O lizards carry upon thy river thy servant, hail thee O lizards carry upon thy river thy servant. In repetition

I fell into sleep and woke into a pointless rage. It was useless, I was useless. Everything was gone from me.

I held him in one arm, hooked around his neck, his body flopping like Ruby. I was taking him to Kensal Green Cemetery. We broke out into the early morning light, bloodied monsters from below. I didn't look at him, I just held him to my chest. I didn't look to where the Nazis had been. I didn't need to see anything more, for everything was gone from me, everything was to be buried, disappeared.

★

I found him a corner in the cemetery. It caught the sun in the afternoon. He used to sit there until the heat was too much and we'd clamber over the wall and he'd cool off in the canal.

I dug a hole. I kissed his head, nuzzling in behind his ear. He didn't smell of anything anymore. I placed him in the hole and showered him with pennies and sweets and ma's old lipsticks, treasures and gifts for the lizards below. I emptied out the treasure box and put the camera inside, placing it next to Devil. I covered him with earth, saying my lizard prayers. I lit candles. I cried for hours and fell asleep on the grave.

★

I woke up, pulled David's bear out from amongst the discarded treasures and cut its head off. I cut off its stubby arms and legs. I cut the head off the shrew Pigeon had given me and I carefully sewed it on to the bear body. It was squint and too small for the body but it was done and my sewing was good. I rummaged through the rest of the treasures and found the dried worms and the crow foot. I sewed the worms into both arm sockets and attached the crow foot into one of the leg sockets with wire and thread. I found a doll's leg for the other side of the body. With wire and thread I sat hunched, attaching pigeon wings to its back. The wings were joined by part of the spine, each wing still beautiful with perfect feathers. When I finished I inspected my creation and wrapped it in bandages.

The day had gone. My belly was growling. I chewed on sweets and walked deep into the cemetery, finding apples and berries. I held the bundle, looking for the perfect spot. I found a grand gravestone, sheltered by trees, and I knelt, lighting two candles at the base. I laid the bundle down and began to dig.

I didn't have Dr Frankenstein's science. But I had magic.

Hail thee lizards down below in the darkness in the depths hail thee O Lizard King I consecrate unto thee this creature of beauty made in observance of your law O Lizard Queen and King of the deep O guardian lizards I consecrate unto thee this gift the word shall be made flesh and this flesh shall be given lifeblood Holy Holy Holy which was and is and is to come I pour forth my blood I beseech thee O lizards of the depths by this passion I bring unto thee a gift and unto me I ask for a resurrection of these pieces I have sewn with diligence. I eat this heart for thee.

I placed the bundle in the hole, wrapped up like Frankenstein's monsta. Flicking open my penknife I cut my arm and drip-dripped blood onto the white bandages, watching it seep. I sank my teeth into an apple, dripping the juice onto the blood, imagining my teeth were sinking into a human heart, the heart of he who stole from us, giving back what he has taken. I poured earth over the creature and sat through the night.

The darkness began to recede and I pulled back the earth, lifting out the bundle. I unwrapped the blanket and out tumbled a monsta, spiral spiral wheeeeeee, with waving worms like beautiful tentacles, grasping and feeling and swaying in the breeze. Monsta lay fallen, the crow foot scratching at the earth, the worms feeling up the side of the gravestone, a stunning undulation. I caught my breath at the beauty of this creation. I caught my breath and crawled back, watching.

It's lopsided, said Amelia.

I twisted round. Amelia, Queen Isabella, Scholler. All three stood in waiting.

Don't ruin this, I said.

I'd forgotten to cut the doll foot so it would be even with the crow foot, so Monsta was lopsided and walked kerlump-scratch, kerlump-scratch.

He's lopsided, said Amelia.

It's not a he, I said.

Then what is it?

It's a monsta, I said, a pretty monsta dead thing. And dead things can't die.

Soon it was up and kerlumping through the earth and the grass, all lopsided like Amelia said, all lopsided and perfect. The pigeon wings spread, creaking, stiff and awkward. Monsta hovered then fell.

Now you're beautiful, I said.

Now you're ugly, said Queen Isabella, puffing her chest, causing her grotesque brooch to quiver.

Now, I said emphatically, you're a pretty monsta dead thing.

Monsta kerlumped to me, scratching at the earth. The black eyes roamed here and there, seeking me out, observing, considering. The worm-tentacles crawled through my fingers, pulling, slithering, climbing.

*

What happened to you?

Nothing.

You look a mess.

I'm going to the sea, ma.

I don't have time for your stories.

I'm really going.

You are? About time your school evacuated the lot of you.

My school's already gone. I'll go with another one.

As long as you're going. Go clean yourself up.

I will.

And wear a dress, for god's sake. Don't want the people by the sea thinking bad of me, do I?

I don't have a dress.

You can have an old one of mine.

I didn't want to wear a dress but I thought it would be a good disguise in case the Nazis saw me, so I got cleaned up the best I could and I put ma's dress on. It was yellow, with flowers. It sagged at the chest and bunched up on the ground. I cut off a bit at the bottom, but didn't manage the back, so it trailed, picking up the mud and dust, but it was a good disguise. I propped my gas mask on my head and stuffed my schoolbag full of treasures and books, mismatching socks, and shorts and shirts. I pulled on my old boots, raggedy boots that used to be David's that had been mended a hundred times. I wrote David a note: I'm going to the sea. I'll write and you can join me. Mermaids, krakens, pirates! I'm going on an adventure. Love, Goblin.

Monsta climbed into the bag, making a nest amongst the clothes, bits of worm and feathers and crow foot sticking out the top. We're escaping, Monsta. The shrew eyes blinked sleepily. I hiked the bag onto my shoulder and went downstairs. I climbed out the back window in case the Nazis were watching at the door, waiting to kill us. Amelia, Scholler and Queen Isabella led me through the backstreets and alleys and I sang songs of the sea to Monsta, whose worm-arms flopped and swayed.

We're going on an adventure, Monsta. An adventure to the sea.

Chapter 4

'How'd it go with the doc?' says Ben.

'She signed me off for a couple of weeks. I stopped off at work and chatted with my boss. She's been pretty good about it.'

'It's good if ye have a decent boss.'

'Can't fault her.'

I sit down at my desk and slip off my shoes.

'Are ye going to keep writing?' says Ben.

I nod.

'Why'd ye write on that beat up old typewriter when there's a perfectly good laptop.'

'The laptop's for work. I prefer a typewriter.'

I go to the kitchen and get some wine. I shout down the hall, asking Ben if he wants a glass.

'It's too early for that, old lady. I'll have a cuppa, though.'

I come back through with the wine and tea to find Ben reading one of my pages.

'What's this about Martians and Nazis?'

'Don't read that,' I say, hurriedly putting down the wine and tea, snatching the page away from Ben. 'That's private.'

'Then dinnae leave it lying around.'

'This is my flat,' I say.

Ben looks as if I've just slapped him.

'Aye, well if ye dinnae want me here just say so – yer the one who wanted me to stay.'

I hold the page tight in my hand, crushing it, not caring that Ben feels hurt. I put the sheet of paper with the rest on my desk. They're all crumpled, strewn everywhere. I bunch them all together and sit on the floor, drinking my wine.

'I must bring order,' I say, sorting through the papers. 'I must bring some order.'

'While ye bring order by drinking yersel intae oblivion me n Sam'll be on our way then.'

I look up at him, confused for a moment, watching him pack his few belongings into his rucksack.

'On your way where?' I say.

He ignores me and I feel panicked.

'On your way where? Are you leaving? I said you could stay.'

I stand up and clutch at him, and he makes to brush me off but he looks at me and stops.

'Alright, old lady, alright.'

He puts his hand on mine.

'You're not leaving?'

'No,' he says, 'we'll stay right here.'

We stand there for a moment; Ben looking at me, his hand still on mine. I shake my head, feeling sick.

'Hey,' he says, leading me to the couch, 'It's alright, sit down. I didnae mean to upset ye.'

We sit on the couch, Ben's arm around me. Mahler jumps up and lies down, his head on my lap. Sam sits at the door, expectant. Ben calls him over and gives him one of his toys to chew on.

'I'm sorry, Ben.'

'Dinnae worry, old lady.'

Monsta walks along the floor, kerlumpscratch, kerlumpscratch. A flutter of the pigeon wings and Monsta is up on my writing desk, worm-arms prodding at the typewriter keys. I laugh.

'What's so funny?'

'Monsta – The Life Story.'

'What's that?'

'My life story. That's what I'm writing. And it's private, that's all, it's private. I didn't mean to hurt you.'

'I know. It's okay. I shouldnae have read it without yer permission.'

'Ben, I want you to stay. I don't want that to ever be a question.'

He puts his arm round me, pulling me close. We sit there quietly for a while then Ben says, 'How about a film, old lady? Before ye get back to yer writing. I'll make some breakfast and we can watch some old film, eh?'

'Sounds good.'

Ben goes through to the kitchen, Sam and Mahler following. I hear him giving them some food as I go over to see what Monsta has written: 'I learned to swim in the sea.'

'That's too far on,' I say. 'I'm not there yet, Monsta.'

Monsta sways. The smell of toast reaches me and I say, 'Later, Monsta. Writing can wait.'

I join Ben in the kitchen, listening to Monsta's stilted typing.

Cornwall, September 1939 – September 1940

Piss and shit, I reeked of it. We'd been travelling for hours, crammed in, no stops, no toilets, no food. It smelled like a pit in hell.

I'd made it to the station without the Nazis seeing me, so I'd taken off my disguise. I shimmied my shorts on under the dress and pulled it off over my head, replacing it with a crumpled shirt. The station was a mess of children, all bustling and chattering and crying. I pushed my way into the crowd and eyed some kid's label, remembering the school in case anyone asked, but no one did. I headed over to the train before I realised Queen Isabella, Amelia and Scholler weren't following. I stopped and a kid bashed right into me.

'Aren't you coming?'

'You're in the way,' said the kid.

'I'm not talking to you,' I said, and he shoved me, walking round.

'Aren't you coming?'

'We can't leave London.'

'Why not? I thought ghosts could do anything.'

Other kids gave me confused looks and squeezed past me.

'We belong to London.'

Kids kept pushing at me and I staggered backwards towards the train, my eyes on the ghosts. I was caught up in the flow as the kids surged onto the train, so I turned away and climbed up the steps. I tried to catch a glimpse of the ghosts before disappearing into the train but I couldn't see over the heads of the other kids. I moved down the corridor looking for a seat by the window. Finding one, I knelt on it and pressed up against the window watching the ghosts standing serene in the crowd. Three boys sat next to me and I glanced at them before turning back. I waved goodbye as the train started to roll its way to the sea.

'Who're you waving at?' said one of the boys, looking out the window.

'Ghosts,' I said.

'Ghosts aren't real,' he said.

'They are. So are lizard people,' I said.

'Don't be stupid,' he said.

When I couldn't see the ghosts any longer I sat down properly and faced the boy.

'Underground is where the lizard people live,' I said, and I told them stories as London disappeared.

By the time we arrived I was all out of tales, all of us thirsty and hungry and stinking. The doors opened and out we tumbled, spreading across the platform like a plague. The waiting adults were expecting little angels with bouncing hair and rosy cheeks and there we were, flat out on the platform, a stinking mass. Realising these monsters were the children they'd come to greet, one of the women snapped her fingers: 'Water, food. Now.'

Without hesitation, the others scurried, following the Snap-dragon's orders. They went to a local shop a few minutes from the station and trudged back, laden with supplies. By the time they returned the Snap-dragon had already sorted us into an order of priority. Most of the tiny kids were dealt with first but there wasn't much of a wait as the Snap-dragon had everything in such perfect control that everything was done efficiently.

'Well, isn't she a Queen Bee?'

That's what Isabella would have said if she'd been there. She would have been impressed but jealous and uppity too, I was sure of it. I would have told her, 'She's not a Queen Bee. She's a Snap-dragon.' And to placate her I would have said, 'You're the only queen here,' because I wouldn't have wanted any trouble. Then I would have kept quiet, not wanting to stand out as the kid who talked to ghosts right on the first day of arriving. But I didn't have to worry about that because they were in London where they belonged and here I was making a plan already in my head to be as normal as I could so I'd get good pretend parents who would look after me.

The only thing I had that I shouldn't really have was Monsta but I wasn't about to give up my best friend, not now Devil was gone. I just had to hide Monsta the best I could and hope the pretend parents weren't the kind that were nosy parkers who liked to rake through all your things like Stevie's parents used to do, because then I'd definitely be in trouble and if I wasn't in trouble exactly, they were still sure to throw Monsta in the rubbish or make use of all Monsta's body parts for something else because we don't waste anything in wartime. But I already thought Monsta wasn't wasting things, Monsta was Monsta and was making good use of all the parts. I pushed Monsta further down in my bag and drank the water I'd been given.

The child picking had started and the Snap-dragon wasn't in control anymore. The adults already had in mind to go for boys, especially the strong boys, though none of us looked strong at all, just a dirty mess collapsed on the platform, shovelling food in our mouths. Some of the adults were walking off with boys and the Snap-dragon just about threw a fit when she saw that. Some had already managed to sneak away with their choice boy, but others hadn't quite and she gave them a bollocking. She already had a list of who needed boys, all those that needed hard work done.

'Slave labour,' is what Amelia would have said. She wasn't there, but that's what she would have said. 'Slave labour is all they're after,' and she would have been pleased because she didn't like children anyway so she would have nodded her approval.

As the Snap-dragon was shouting at someone for stealing a boy I thought about whether I wanted to be a boy or a girl – maybe I should have kept ma's dress on so I wouldn't be breaking my back doing hard labour, but then girls would be made to do cleaning and sewing and cooking and breaking their back that way. I'd decided being a boy was better because I'd probably get to go outside and there'd more likely be adventures outside and the sun and animals and even the rain but being stuck inside cleaning up after people would be like being trapped in a cage.

'Come here, boy.'

I stood up and shuffled over to her. She squinted at me before lifting my arms, yanking at them like I was some rag doll.

'Hey!' I said, but she ignored me, squeezing my arms then turning me round and round until I got dizzy.

'What's in your bag?'

'Clothes and books,' I said shoving Monsta's head and tentacles right to the bottom and showing her a sock and an H.G. Wells. She looked at the book and was about to say something when a man came over, dragging a boy, and said, 'This one will do, Margaret.'

'This one too, Tom,' she said, and gripped my arm, pulling me over so he could see me. He nodded and she let go and patted me twice on the back.

'C'mon then,' she said, 'get going.'

They ushered us off the platform. A girl stood ahead of us, face all a-storm.

'Jesus!' she said, 'I can do just as good as any boy can.'

Tom and Margaret walked on as if they were going to ignore her but as they passed Tom took a swipe at her, hitting her across the face with the back of his hand. Her head hit the station wall with a crack.

'Don't you take the Lord's name in vain, lass,' he said.

I stared back at her. She lay on the ground, dazed. I walked on, following the couple. I could hear the girl swearing again and I smiled.

'That girl has no good sense in her,' Queen Isabella would have said. 'I hope you do.'

I nodded. I knew how to look after myself.

'I'm Goblin,' I said, and held out a dirty hand to the kid next to me.

'I'm John,' he said.

We shook hands and followed Tom and Margaret, our pretend parents.

★

When we got to the pretend house we were marched straight past it. Margaret disappeared inside and came out a moment later, throwing something at us. Tom barked at us to pick it up. We both scrambled for it. It was soap and it slid out of our hands, falling back into the mud. We kicked it along the path, back and forth, until Tom barked at us again. I took a hold of it and Tom shoved us into the river, throwing our bags on the bank.

'Get clean, get dressed and get back to the house.'

We stripped in the water, scrubbing our clothes with the soap and throwing them onto rocks to dry. It was freezing but we warmed up as we pushed and splashed each other, fighting over the soap. When John almost fell over into the water he panicked and refused to get the soap when we dropped it. I ducked down, sweeping it off the river bed. I saw John's willy all shrivelled up against the cold, bobbing in the current.

'I can't swim,' he said, when I emerged.

'I can't swim either,' I said, contemplating the water burbling past my belly.

'I don't want to drown,' he said.

'Do you think we'll see the sea?' I said. 'Do you think we will? My brother was gonna take me to live by the sea and we were gonna fight with pirates and swim with mermaids.'

'I can't swim,' he repeated. 'Mermaids don't exist.'

We scrubbed ourselves clean, washing away the journey, washing away London. John got out and got dressed. He waited on the bank, shifting from one foot to another.

'You coming?'

'In a minute,' I said, not wanting him to find out I wasn't a boy. 'You go on up.'

He hesitated then turned and walked back up the path. I watched him disappear and pulled myself up onto the bank, shivering. I shook like a dog. Monsta crawled out of my bag as I dried myself.

'You want a bath too?'

Monsta's tentacle arm swayed. Kerlumpscratch, kerlumpscratch, down to the water's edge. Monsta dipped in an arm and retreated instantly. Kerlumpscratch, sway, Monsta came back to me.

'Ha! Monsta, we're both shaking like dogs.'

But Monsta had an elegance. The black shrew eyes looked up at me as the water snaked down the worm-arm, disappearing into the grass.

'Don't worry, Monsta. Water won't hurt you. We'll go to the sea and we'll learn to swim, eh?'

Monsta shuddered. I laughed and put on my shirt and shorts, propping the gas mask on my head. I dried Monsta off and we walked back up the path.

*

Luke was what they called me, because they were all religious and didn't like 'Goblin' at all, not one little bit.

'What's your name?' asked Margaret.

'John,' John said.

'Goblin,' I said.

'What?' she said. 'What was that?'

'Goblin.'

'We'll have no foolishness here,' she said, all put out. 'What's your actual real God-given name?'

'God didn't give me a name,' I said.

'God gives everyone a name.'

'I've always been Goblin. It's what they called me from the beginning. Except most of the time it was the long version, Goblin-runt, but my friends just call me Goblin.'

I got a skelp across the head.

'There's no swearing in this house,' she said, and I took a minute to think what she meant and thought maybe she thought 'runt' was a swearword, so I thought of putting her right, but thought of Isabella and David and their advice and just stayed quiet.

'You must have a Christian name.'

I shook my head.

'Then we'll give you one. I'm not having any goblins in this house.'

That's when they called me Luke, like in the Bible, and I just thought fine why not – a pretend name for pretend parents.

'How old are you, Luke?' asked Tom.

'Nine, sir. I'll be ten in March.'

He nodded.

'And you?'

'Ten,' said John.

'Ten what?'

John looked confused and said, 'Years old.'

I nudged him in the ribs and whispered, 'Sir!'

'Ten years old, sir!' he said and Tom nodded.

'Right. Let's get you to work.'

Every morning we were up at dawn. Eggs for breakfast then off to milk the cows and feed the pigs and the chickens. I soon learned that John was a real pain – he'd fiddle around, making it look like he was doing things but mostly he'd be letting me do all the work, and when I asked him for help he'd get all haughty and act like he was the one doing the most. He wasn't worth the bother so I just got on with things and enjoyed being with the animals. I loved watching them. The chickens had shiny feathers and amazing feet. I'd stay with them long after feeding and stare at those feet, the way they curled in on themselves when they lifted them, the way they splayed out, claws scratching at the earth. Tom would yell over at me to stop dreaming and get on over to the pigs and off I'd trot and feed the pigs and muck them out and all morning I'd be sweating it out on the farm watching the animals eat and shit and play.

'You're not a bleedin' dog,' I'd say, as one of the pigs followed me round like I was the kingqueen goblin of pigland. 'You'll be on our plates soon enough,' I'd say, but along he'd come, snuffling at my legs. I'd go about my work, this pig by my side the whole way until Tom yelled at me and I'd swot at it and I'd get grunts and a nip on the calf. Soon it was all round the town: 'London rat and his pig pet.' It came with me to the shops, it followed me to the forest, but got caught in the bracken and made a helluva fuss and I'd have to turn round and go back home again.

'That pig gets lost, you're paying for it,' said Tom.

'Pigs like the stench of rat,' said old Wendy and I spat at her and she harrumphed at me, her ugly face all set in an ugly scowl.

'You've got a face just like a chicken arse,' I said to old Wendy and me and my pig, we went on our way, our arses wiggling, our noses up in the air like we were the rulers of the town.

Then there we were, seeming just like it was back in London, walking right up to that reverend and standing all defiant: 'Can pigs come to church?'

He looked down at me and he looked down at my pig and he said, 'I don't see why not. Pigs are God's creatures too.'

I stared at him, my mouth hanging open, feeling foolish with nowhere for my stored up swearing to go.

'Just make sure it doesn't shit all over the place.'

With that, the preacher turned and off he went.

'As if you'd shit in a church,' I said, all indignant. I scuffed at the ground and stared at the pig.

'Corporal Pig. That's your name and don't you forget it.'

Monsta liked Corporal Pig. Monsta rode on CP's back, worm arms swaying with excitement as CP trotted along.

★

When we started up at school I didn't like being cooped up but I behaved and did my work (Miss Hallows praised me for being 'diligent' and 'clever' and I puffed my chest out all proud at that). Turned out the Snap-dragon was the headmistress, which made a lot of sense. I didn't like her all that much and I was thankful we didn't see her all that often. I did like Miss Hallows and I liked when we got to read books, but we never read books as exciting as *The War of the Worlds* or *Alice's Adventures in Wonderland*. The town kids stayed away from the London rats and I was doubly scorned for being diligent and clever. I didn't need any friends, though. I had CP and Monsta. I sometimes saw that girl who Tom had hit at the station. She was in the class above me and she was so beautiful I could hardly look at her and she didn't look at me at all.

I was pretty damn tired in term time; up at the crack of dawn to look after the animals, then there was school and straight into chores when I got home, then supper and homework. After homework, when I was in bed, I'd sometimes write stories. Some I made up, but they were mostly the stories Pigeon told me about the ghosts and the lizard people, so I would never forget them. I didn't have much paper so I'd write them really small in the front and back pages of *The War of the Worlds* and *The Time Machine*. Once or twice a week I'd write letters or postcards home, to ma and da and David. I always wrote my address on them and asked them to write, but they never did. I figured they were busy with the war in London. I told David

I was at the sea, I told him he should come and we could live together by the sea. I wrote less and less. Tom complained about the cost of the stamps and the wasting of paper and I had more and more chores to do anyway.

On top of all that Tom taught us to shoot. I took to it like I was born for it. John wasn't any good. 'John,' I said, 'you're shit-bollocks at this,' and he shoved me so that I fell over in chicken shit. His head snapped back when he laughed and I was up like a shot, punching his face. He wasn't laughing then, but spitting blood into the chicken shit, one of his teeth floating in the shit-blood mess. It glistened like a jewel.

'I was just saying it like it is,' I said, my anger gone. 'I can teach you to do it better.'

He was crying by now and Tom came over and didn't even ask what happened, but just took me by the ear. I'd seen what he'd done to that girl at the station so I expected a beating, but he just dragged me by the ear and shut me in the shed. He let me out in the evening, sat me down and said, 'No one damages my property.'

Just like that. Not even pretending. I kept my mouth shut. I'd said to Isabella, who wasn't even there at the station, I'd said to her I knew how to look after myself, so I had to be smarter and not mess things up. I understood Tom. As soon as he said what he said, I understood. He would look after us and treat us well as long as were useful to him, as long as we didn't take the Lord's name in vain and knew how to be good property. I knew how to work hard and I knew all about churches and God and I could play the hardworking God worshipper if it meant a good life.

'You've got to compromise sometimes, Goblin,' David had said to me. 'You have to allow a little leeway,' and I knew now what he meant. I knew he had given me that advice so I wouldn't go and mess up and just be stomped on. 'You're clever,' he said. 'You'll figure it out.'

So I nodded when Tom said no one damages his property and I said, 'It won't happen again, sir.' I could tell at once that

I needn't have even said that because it didn't need to be said, it just *wouldn't happen again*, he was that sure. I could tell too that by saying it I might as well have written in my own blood that it wouldn't happen again. John was a pain and not being able to pummel him was going to be hard work, but then I thought maybe it would build character. Maybe I shouldn't just pummel people all the time. It's not as if I have anything to prove. So, I thought, right. I'll do this. I'll build character and be all stoic-lipped.

But I did ask for our work to be broken up between us, saying that we'd get things done quicker if we each had our own tasks instead of doing things together. Tom thought for a moment, then nodded. He sat us both down later that evening and told us what tasks we'd each do and I could tell John wasn't happy but at least he didn't know it was my idea and he had to obey Tom so that was that. I got my chores done a lot quicker since he wasn't in the way and I didn't have to do absolutely everything.

John was still useless at shooting, though.

'Luke,' Tom said. 'You sort him out.'

So I had to teach the idiot to shoot, but he was terrible and he was pretending to be even more terrible just to provoke me. He'd worked out that I'd had some kind of warning and couldn't hit him, no matter what, so he called me names, telling stories where horrible things happened to me, stories about my origin as Goblin and how my parents must have hated me, how everyone hated me. Sometimes all this rattled my stoic cage, but I just thought of Isabella and David and their advice and mostly managed to ignore him. I'd go into my head so that I didn't even hardly hear him, he was just a drone, like the insects, except I liked insects.

That was another thing – he didn't like insects so he killed them and tortured them and left them alive all messed up and broken and I can't even begin to tell you how badly I wanted to pummel him. I was stoic-lipped and tried my very best to make sure he didn't see how much it bothered me, made sure he didn't see how much I loved insects, because then I knew he would get worse, I knew it would be another thing for provoking me and more insects would get hurt so I stayed quiet even though I wanted to rescue the insects and pummel him and I got thinking that this compromising wasn't as great as David had made out because the insects were still getting hurt and I was still getting hurt because it made me so damn sad and angry so what was the point if I was sad and angry anyway and I was thinking maybe I'd be better off out of this situation away from the pretend parents and the Idiot.

That's when I met her.

Though, I'd met her before. I'd seen her get her head cracked against the station wall and I'd seen her a couple of times at school and in the town. She looked like some kind of angel, that's what she looked like, with her bouncing curly black hair that sparkled in the sun. She had rosy cheeks and green eyes and she was the most beautiful thing. I don't know how adults know when they fall in love, but I thought that was maybe what it felt like, the way I felt when I saw her, and between my legs I was all a-tingle like when I played with myself, and I imagined her, I imagined what she looked like playing with herself, and then she said, 'You fucking shits.'

I squinted at her, confused.

'You fucking stinking shits.'

I turned and saw John torturing a spider, pulling all its long legs off. She barrelled towards him and punched him and I reached out to stop her, thinking he's property and I needed to protect the property and bloody hell was she gonna be in all kinds of trouble but then I realised she didn't belong to Tom so maybe he couldn't touch her and maybe she'd be okay. I smiled. Weeks of anger just melted away as I watched her punching and kicking John. When she finished she stomped right on that spider, putting it out of its misery because it was just all messed up beyond repair. She ground that spider into the dirt and looked at me with the most vicious look anyone has ever given me, even more vicious than ma, and she said, 'You goddamn son of a whore stinking shit.'

Then she was off, before I even had a chance to explain, before I even had a chance to tell her I thought she was some kind of angel, like you get in the Revelation book, all powerful and beautiful and you just don't mess with those angels and I wanted to be on her side. I wanted her to love me.

But she was gone, and she thought I was some sort of spider mutilator. It really ate away at me, right down in my belly, that she thought I would have anything to do with the Idiot if I had a choice. I wanted to explain. I played it out in my head over and over, changing small things here and there, but she would always listen, listen quietly to my whole story and then she'd take me in her arms and she'd kiss me on the head with those rose red lips and I would melt away, drifting. 'My angel,' I'd say, 'my angel.'

The Idiot got up out of the dirt where he lay next to the crushed spider and I wished he was the one that had his legs pulled off and was all crushed, but he wasn't, he was alive and telling me how he'd see Tom and tell him I'd pummelled him, and you know what? I didn't even care.

'I don't care,' I said.

It was true. At that moment, I'd stopped caring about having pretend parents, because the love of my life hated me and thought I was an idiot just like this Idiot in the dirt. I was about to kick him until he was all broken when old Mrs Bellhaven came over and said, 'I saw it all. That girl is trouble.'

She helped him up and marched him off.

'Don't you worry,' she said. 'I saw everything.'

I just sank into the dirt with the spider, stupefied, not knowing what was what anymore.

'My angel,' I said and stroked the spider corpse, covering it with dirt like it was a grave.

It was then I started reading Revelation like mad. I was all fire and brimstone, I was all little goblin plague and blood.

★

I learned to swim in the sea.

But not for months yet, and not a word was said to my Revelation angel. Winter was hard. Knee deep in snow and my chores became doubly difficult. We got through the winter with only a couple of deaths, a chicken and an old sheep, and I worked hard at home and at school and Tom was pleased with me, I could tell he was, but I can tell you something for certain – I was glad for spring. Long warm evenings playing with Corporal Pig in the woods and a summer holiday stretching out ahead with no schoolwork, only chores and roaming here and there when I'd done my bit.

In April we had an Easter gathering in the church hall after the service and it was then I realised I'd missed my birthday in March. I was ten-years-old and I hadn't even noticed, so to mark it I got a hold of a big slice of cake and said, 'Happy very belated birthday to me myself,' and I was just minding my own business stuffing cake into my mouth when I heard the words 'Greedy London rat.'

That's what the old Snap-dragon called me. I pushed all the cake in, trying to chew, crumbs spilling on the floor.

'No manners.'

I knew she was right, I knew I couldn't swallow the cake, I knew I was choking and I knew she had no manners either so I spat the cake on her feet and ran like I had a spitfire up my arse.

That was the day I learned to swim in the sea and became best friends with Angel.

I ran to the back of the church hall, poking my head round the corner to see if the Snap-dragon was following me, but she wasn't. I knew I'd be in all kinds of trouble later, but right then I didn't care. It was worth it to see the look on her bloated snooty face.

'Hey, London Rat.'

I almost jumped right out of my goblin-skin with fright. When I turned round and saw who it was I was so embarrassed that I almost fell over but I stood straight as can be and stared at her with my eyes narrowed, trying to pretend like I was oh-so-cool but inside I was churning, my tummy growling with nerves.

'Well, that was a disaster,' is surely what Queen Isabella would have helpfully pointed out and I could just see Amelia nodding in agreement.

'You really stuck it to that stinking old Mrs Carter, didn't you?'

She thought I was some kind of hero, spitting that cake at the Snap-dragon. She cocked her head at me.

'You'll get a hiding for that, for sure.'

I gawped at her. She was tiny and her hair was as black as the midnight Cornish sky. When it shone in the sun, her hair sparkled like glittering stars.

'Are you dumb or something?'

I said, 'Maybe you're an angel or a Martian.'

Her eyes popped wide and she said, 'You're daft.'

I said her name was Angel. She said I was a silly London rat. I said I'm not a rat, I'm a goblin and anyway, you're a London rat too. She said, 'Angel is a stupid name.' I said, 'But you're not like some boring old angel all in white on a cloud playing a harp. You're one of those angels like in Revelation who doesn't let people away with sins like torturing spiders, an angel who rains fire and blood down on people.'

She looked at me, cocking her head again, narrowing her eyes. She didn't say anything and I felt uncomfortable, so I just said, for no reason really, just for something to say, '"Rats" backwards is "Star",' and she shrugged and she said, 'Goblin-Rat-Star? Let's go on an adventure.'

'Angel?' I said, 'I was born for adventure,' like some terrible Hollywood line out of a cowboy film, and I blushed, but I was pleased. She was my friend. We walked through the forest and I said, 'Where're we going?'

She looked at me with hooded eyes and said, 'Stupid Rat, we're going to the sea.'

I got huffy and said, 'Well, how would I know?' though

inside I thought I might explode. I was going to the sea with my Angel. What could be better than that?

She said, 'This is the path to the sea, stupid. How long have you been here? You not been to the sea yet?'

I thought, who you calling stupid, and was about to say 'Who you calling stupid?' but I didn't because I was trying to be all good and nice and not mess things up and I thought I could impress her later with all my stories, all the stories from Pigeon and the bible and the books I'd read and I could scare her with stories of Queen Isabella and her pulsing heart and I thought in my head how we would be on the beach and it would be getting dark and I'd scare her and she'd cuddle into me to stay safe and I liked that thought even though I knew it probably wouldn't happen because she was some sort of angel of death or war or pestilence and I'm sure they don't get scared by ghost stories.

I said, 'I've not been to the sea. Tom keeps us working on the farm or hunting in the woods and he wouldn't take us. But he said we'd be going fishing soon.'

She didn't say anything. She just hit at the grass with a stick, like she hadn't even heard me. I was going to tell her how I was good at hunting, 'I'm a shit-hot shot,' I was going to say, but I thought it might not impress her if she didn't like the killing of spiders maybe she wouldn't like that I shot rabbits but we have to eat and I have to help Tom or I'd be out on my ear but I kept quiet just in case. I was getting all in a tangle in my head and not appreciating the walk at all, my palms all sweaty and my mood turning so that I was frowning like mad and suddenly she turned to me and was about to say something and stopped, seeing me look like I was crazy angry about something, my face all twisted up. I tried to turn all happy but turned contorted and probably looked like I was grimacing. It was exhausting being in love.

'What's eating at you?' she said. 'Don't you want to go on an adventure?'

'I do! I'm just—'

'I'm not wasting my time on some old misery guts.'

I thought I might just collapse then and there but I thought, Goblin-runt, get out of your bloody head. Stop thinking so much. That's what David would say. Getting all caught up in tangled thoughts and look how it turns out, all back to front.

So I came out of my head and I said, 'I've never been to the sea. Are there mermaids and pirates? My brother said there was.'

She looked at me, laughed and ran off ahead.

'Mermaids and pirates!' she shouted back. 'Let's find out!'

I ran after her, yelling a battle cry.

*

There it was, sparkling in the sun. Angel had already kicked off her shoes and was splashing around. I just gaped. There weren't any pirates or mermaids, no anyone except us. Cliffs slanted up into the afternoon sun, gulls floated overhead and trundled along the beach, squawking. Angel ran back onto the sand and threw off her clothes. She ran into the oncoming waves and disappeared. I was anxious and jealous. Her head bobbed up and she waved at me.

I took off my shoes and shirt, but kept my shorts on. I stuck close to the shore, just splashing around, enjoying the feel of the warm water on my skin. I sat down, feeling the pull of the sea. Angel waved at me again, and I shook my head. She swam for shore.

'What're you doing?'

'I can't swim.'

She took me by the hand, dragging me up. I stumbled after her, staring down at our joined hands, water dripping between our fingers like we were melting into each other.

She took me past an outcrop, letting go of my hand so it was easier to scramble over the rocks. I followed obediently and we came to a rock pool. I wasn't sure how deep it was, but the water was clear and you could see to the bottom. Seaweed swayed when the waves came in, the water gently entering the pool, flowing over the top of the rocks, causing only a slight ripple. I stared in awe at the starfish at the bottom of the pool. Angel lowered herself in and I followed.

'I'll teach you,' she said.

⋆

It took about three weeks, mainly because my chores took up so much time, but also because the Idiot had noticed I was always going off somewhere, and he would tag along, pretending like we were friends. CP and I would just lead him to the woods and we'd stop there so CP could forage – he loved collecting branches and leaves and making a nest, so I pretended that's all we did and after a couple of evenings of this the Idiot got bored and left me alone. Tom didn't care where I went in the evenings, as long as I'd finished all my chores and as long as I was up at dawn to do my morning duties. Angel's pretend parents were the ones who'd shown her the path to the sea when she'd first arrived. They were happy for us to go out in the evenings as long as she told them where we were going. She usually had to be back by nine, but at the height of summer they let her stay out until after sunset.

By the end of three weeks I was swimming pretty good. I stuck to the pool. I wasn't ready for the sea, and Angel seemed fine with that. She didn't even tease me for being a coward and I felt bad because I thought of Stevie and how if I had been him and I was Angel I would have given him a hard time and he probably would have swam in the sea just to prove to me he could and he probably would've drowned or got eaten by sharks and I'd be all twisted up with guilt. Angel was a real angel about it, not one of those Revelation angels, but those angels who give you a break.

I liked the rock pool better than the sea in those first days. It felt more private, like the whole world had disappeared and it was just me and Angel. Corporal Pig would come along most days too. He couldn't get up to the rock pool and he'd make a godawful noise when we left him behind but he'd soon amuse himself, snuffling about in the sand. He would swim in the sea too. The first time I saw him I scrambled out of that rock pool, ran across the beach and into the sea to rescue him before I even realised he was swimming as happy as can be. I stood with the water lapping at my chest, feeling like a fool.

'You're making me look bad in front of my girl, CP. Look at you, swimming in the sea and swimming better than a Goblin could.'

I went back to Angel who was watching from the rock pool.

'Who knew pigs could swim?'

'How did you think you could rescue him? How could you drag that fat pig out of the sea?'

'I dunno,' I said, annoyed, wanting her to drop it.

'I like that you'd try,' she said as I swam off, still feeling that ache in my belly, that fear of losing Corporal Pig.

I practiced hard that week, listening to Angel's advice, determined to get good enough so I could swim in the proper sea with CP. After I'd done practicing we'd flip onto our backs and just float. Sometimes we'd reach out and hold each other's hand and we'd float in silence or we'd chat about this and that, sometimes about what was going on in the town, about old Mrs Carter and her stupidness, or I'd complain about the Idiot but mostly I didn't mention him because I didn't want him messing up my happiness with Angel. Sometimes we talked about before, about London and who we were then and what we did and who our families were. I told Angel about how Devil used to swim in the canal next to Kensal Green Cemetery, but I was too afraid to go in.

'Who's Devil?'

'My dog.'

'Where is he?'

'Buried. In Kensal Green.'

I didn't tell her what really happened to him. I just said about how the Nazis had come to London without people knowing and killed all the pets so that we would feel all demoralised and not be as happy about being at war and we'd give up.

I said, 'I don't really want to talk about it. I want to know about you.'

She said how she lived not far from me and I wondered how I'd never seen her before. She said she was happy in London and her parents were nice, but her dad had gone off to fight and her mum was sad. 'My mum loves me, so she sent me away. She didn't want to risk me being killed by a bomb so she sent me off on that hellhole train and now here I am.'

I told her about my ma and da and about David.

'He was in a row with my parents about the war. He didn't want to fight.'

'He a coward?'

'He isn't a damn coward. He's a conchie. He hates fighting, thinks it's a waste of time. He wants to travel the world, sail on the seas. That's pretty brave, when you don't know if there's going to be pirates or krakens.'

'Uh-huh,' she said, 'that's pretty brave.'

'He was being made to go to the war. My parents were making him, but he said to me we would just leave. "We'll leave all this madness," he said. "We'll go to the sea." I dreamed it. I knew it would happen, but when I left I couldn't find him and I had to go.'

'Why did you have to go?'

'The Nazis who killed the pets were after me, so there was no time to wait for David. I write to him but he doesn't write back – I think he must have gone to the sea too. I'll keep writing anyway, just in case. C'mon. I want to swim in the sea proper now.'

I swam to the rocks and peered over them, looking out to sea. I climbed up, pulled myself over and slipped into the ocean-proper. I became like liquid. I became emerald green, with seaweed hair. Angel came in after me, and we met beneath the surface, smiling at each other, blowing bubbles and chasing them to the surface. We swam over towards the beach and joined CP. I dived beneath him, his massive form blocking out the sun, his legs gently kicking. I came up by his side, planted a kiss on his head and followed Angel further out. The sea was cold, losing the concentrated warmth of the sun-drenched rock pool. It froze me blue.

As twilight fell, we sat on the beach and made a small fire from wood collected in the nearby forest.

'The planes will see us. We'll be bombed.'

'They never come this far. Anyway, we're sheltered. Hardly anyone can see anything down here.'

Corporal Pig lay on his side, snoring by the fire as Angel and I dried off. I told her about how at home I had washed in a shallow tin bath.

'The water was cold. Ma scrubbed my skin raw. Sometimes she forgot, sometimes she forgot to scrub me raw and I'd go without a bath for weeks until David said I stank and locked me out our room. "You stink, Goblin," is what he'd say. "You stink worse than old Mr Fenwick and he hasn't washed for a hundred years."'

'You don't stink now,' she said.

It was true. Pretend parents made me and John wash every day in the river because God's children had to be clean and pure. It was cold in the river. It turned me blue.

'I was born blue,' I told Angel. 'Like the sea.'

'Ha!' she said.

'It's true,' I said. 'I was born blue and dead and they had to slap me alive. I was so ugly, ma said, that the midwife died of fright. "Goblin!" was the last thing she said. The first thing I did when I was born was commit murder.'

'It wasn't your fault you were so ugly.'

'No.'

'But you're not ugly now.'

I shrugged, still not really sure if I was ugly or not and I hadn't looked in a mirror since that time I'd sneaked into ma and da's room.

'I grew out of being blue. David said I was only blue because the umbilical cord had tangled round my neck. Ma said she wished my da hadn't slapped me to life because she thinks I would have been better off dead.'

'Why would she say that? Why would your ma say that?'

'Because I'm a monster, a demon, a goblin.'

'A goblin isn't a demon and I think your ma is a monster.'

I smiled at her, my heart aching as I watched the way the warm glow of the fire turned her skin golden. Her eyes looked like black pools, her pupils a flickering flame.

'Your ma's an idiot. Just like John. You're handsome and goblins are magic.'

*

She showed me all the sea creatures. We didn't know what they were called so we made up names. We didn't know if they were a he or a she so we called the creatures 'em'. It was that day I showed her Monsta and we three lay in the sun.

'This is Monsta.'

'It's good to meet you, Monsta.'

'Monsta, this is Angel.'

She reached out and held a tentacle arm. Monsta swayed and hummed before kerlumpscratching, up up up, crawling across my arm, tentacle worms wrapped round my neck.

Angel stared, and circled, hovering behind us. She stroked the pigeon spine, and Monsta hummed in my ear.

'This is beautiful. Did you make it?'

'Not an it, not a she, not a he. A Monsta.'

'An 'em',' she said, 'like the sea creatures.'

Monsta crawled down and sat in the sun with us. Monsta's bear body was wearing away, bald patches spreading across the torso like a rash.

'You're still pretty,' I said, 'pretty Monsta dead thing.'

The black shrew eyes rolled in their sockets, the nose twitched. I watched the wings unfurl and stretch, beating for a moment; Monsta hovered, the crow foot flexing. The tentacles swayed on the breeze, the doll foot stuck out, a little squint, inert. The wings neatly folded across Monsta's back.

*

I swam to the surface and saw Angel disappear. A wave pushed me back under and she was beneath me, glinting white skin, a flurry of hair. She was sea serpent supreme. I flailed and panicked as I gulped down water. I was engulfed by a mess of bubbles, sand and seaweed. Angel took my arm and pulled me up, swimming to the shore, dragging me behind her, vomiting up the sea.

It was a stormy day. I'd insisted we swim, convinced I knew the sea so well that it couldn't surprise me but it had pulled me under. Angel didn't even say anything. We just lay on the sand. I knew what she was thinking, and Queen Isabella, I knew what she would say. 'Trying to impress a girl by drowning, are we?' and Amelia, with that cruelty, 'trying to impress a brother who isn't even here.'

I lay there and I was glad Angel didn't say anything. She knew I'd learned my lesson. She was never cocky like the Idiot, there were no I-told-you-so chants.

The next day was calm and warm, even early in the morning when I got up to do my chores and go hunting. I met her in the evening and it was still hot. Before the sun disappeared behind the woods we lay on the sand basking like lizards.

We swam to cool off, but even the sea was warm. I swam with my shorts on. Angel swam in her skin. She said to me later, before all the trouble, 'I knew you were a girl. It didn't matter either way.'

Before the trouble there was just me and her and the ocean. There was CP snoring in the sand, and the summer sun on Angel's white skin, turning her gold. We lay on the beach and I watched the sea water dribbling over her ribs and the mound between her legs. I held her hand. I held Monsta's tentacles.

She was my first kiss.

'You're handsome,' she said. 'You're like a film star.'

'Do my teeth shine?'

I grinned at her, a wide, manic grin. I gnashed my teeth.

She held my hand firmly and said, 'You're beautiful and you're mad.'

We swam and we kissed and we made up names.

★

We made a fire on the beach. We roasted fish, their eyes popping. We watched the sun sink beneath the sea.

'The kraken is pulling it down,' I said. 'Its tentacles reach up and drag the sun into its mouth and it glows in its belly. It keeps it safe until morning. When it wakes up it spits the sun into the sky.'

The sky was like velvet, layers of yellow, emerald, deep blue dotted with fuzzy twinkling stars. The sea turned to blood. The sea turned black. The sky was a mottled blanket of shimmering lights. We listened to the crackle of the sandhoppers as they threw themselves into the flames. They hopped and popped, like disembodied fish eyes. We sat for hours, poking at the glowing branches, encouraging their angry fizzing, drifting off to the sound of the waves. We lay side by side, pressed in against each other to keep warm. I said a lizard prayer for the troops at Dunkirk. I didn't know it then, but my dad was one of them. Not my current da, or my pretend one, but my dad-to-be. If I'd known it then, I would have prayed harder to the lizards below, but instead we stared at the stars and I told Angel stories. I told her about *The War of the Worlds* and the Martians, *The Time Machine* and the Morlocks, *The Island of Doctor Moreau* and the Beast Folk. I told her about the secrets beneath the streets of London.

'Underground is where the lizard people live.'

Angel shooed a sandhopper away from the flames and we heard the pop of a dozen more.

'The Lizard King shoots poison from his eyes. There was

one time, in human form, that he cried, and his skin peeled away as if burned by acid.'

I dragged my fingers down my face.

'When it healed, he had silver scars from his eyes to the corners of his mouth, to his chin. Half of his lower lip was burned away.'

'What made the Lizard King cry?'

'The Lizard Queen, she'd become trapped in human form and she couldn't descend to the lizard realm. When people saw her they thought her eyes and skin were made of jewels and they turned mad with greed. They wanted to possess her, and they did. They ripped her to pieces and they each took a part of her body to keep for themselves. The next morning they awoke, as if from a spell, and they remembered their frenzy. That was the one time the Lizard King cried. He hunted down every person responsible for the Lizard Queen's death and he tore them apart the way they'd torn her apart. From each person he kept a token, just as they had, and he strung the body parts in his palace and lived the rest of his days in mourning.'

I told her the story of Queen Isabella, of Scholler, and Amelia. She told me stories of Cornwall, ghost stories her pretend parents had read to her.

*

'Did you hear about Scotland?' I said, poking at our beach fire with a stick.

Angel didn't answer.

'Well, I heard from old Bob who heard from Elspeth who heard on the wireless that Germans have landed. Parachutes were found. Then dead bodies were found in villages and towns nearby, all charred to a crisp. The Germans have landed,' I said, pausing for dramatic effect, 'and they have electro-magnetic death rays.'

I stopped and looked over at Angel. There was no response. She just sat hunched over, staring at her hands.

'My mum was bombed,' Angel said. 'She's dead.'

The excitement leaked out of me. I felt sick.

'I'm staying here now. Ann and Bill said they'd keep me.'

'That's good,' I said.

'Uh-huh,' she said. 'I like Ann and Bill.'

We stared at the flames.

'I'm sorry,' I said.

'Tell me the story about the man who was eaten,' she said. 'The one where he turns into a dog. Tell me that one again.'

I glanced over at her. Tears glinted on her face, streaking through the dirt of the day. She didn't make a sound, just quietly cried. I couldn't look at her, I couldn't do anything, so I told her the story.

★

The government were asking for donations to build a Spitfire and I so badly wanted to own a piece of a plane. I didn't have any money but when I found sixpence in the street I sent it straight to the fund, buying myself a rivet. I wasn't sure he would appreciate it, what with being a conchie, but I wrote to David: 'I own a piece of Spitfire. I prayed to the lizards down below and kissed that sixpence. I know my bit of Spitfire is going to help win the war.'

A rivet wasn't enough. I wanted more, so I decided to raise the money. There were regular fundraisers in the town hall for the war effort; concerts, cabaret nights, plays. So Angel and I, we did a play with Corporal Pig and the chickens. We worked for weeks to get it right and John was jealous. He'd hang around as we rehearsed and I knew he wanted to join in but I didn't want him ruining our fun and Angel hated him so much she didn't even let on he was there. He tried to disrupt our rehearsals by scaring the chickens or messing up his chores so that Tom would make me help out, but we managed to get it done despite him and his jealousy.

On the night, I was dressed as a girl; hair made out of straw and grass, a daisy crown threaded through it, and berry juice smeared across my lips as lipstick. Everyone laughed when they saw me because they thought I was a boy being a girl, but me and Angel, we knew I was a girl being a boy being a girl. I made my voice high and people laughed some more. We acted out the story of a girl and her pig and the three evil chickens who came and stole her away. The chickens they came out a-clucking right on cue and they were terrifying. They whisked me away to the Dark Kingdom of the sun-eating kraken and Corporal Pig had to find his way to rescue me and off he went trotting through the forest of the audience, waddling between the seats, chewing on skirts and trousers and snuffling at shoes. There were yelps and heys and oi kid this ain't funny I'm no forest I'm a person and everyone laughed and yelled at him to shut up because they wanted to know what happened next. Corporal Pig came trotting back to the stage and sat slumped, his head down, and people shouted, 'Aaaw, c'mon, Corporal Pig! C'mon, you lazy bugger, there's a maiden in distress!' Then there was quiet as Angel came in dressed like a knight and she nudged CP on his behind and up he stood and off they went to the castle of the evil chickens. The ending was a bit of a mess as CP snapped at the chickens and they snapped back and there was a flurry of snorting and clucking and feathers here and there, but I was rescued and we kissed and I said to the audience, 'And they lived happily ever after.'

We were the belles of the ball, we were pink with happiness having raised enough to pay for a bomb and a whole bunch of rivets, but John hated us being belles of the ball and not long after, that's when the trouble started.

Edinburgh, 1 August 2011

Mahler thunders through from the hall, chasing a ball. He skitters, trying to stop, but bashes into my leg before bouncing off and running after it. He lunges on it, clasps it in his jaws and looks up at Ben as he walks in the room.

'Well done, boy,' he says, holding his hand out. Mahler drops it and Ben throws the ball down the hall, Mahler chasing after it.

'He's a bit hyper, should probably take him out for a walk. Still writing, old lady?'

I nod and say, 'About Cornwall.'

'What about it?'

'I was evacuated from London. I stayed in Cornwall for a bit with pretend parents and a pretend brother.'

'The ones with the circus?'

'No, the circus came later.'

'Hang on… Three lots of parents?'

'That's right.'

Ben takes the ball from an impatient Mahler. He throws it down the hall again and says, 'That's just greed.'

I laugh.

'I hadn't thought of it that way.'

'And now ye have us,' he says, watching Mahler run back up the hallway.

'I do.'

I look down at what I'm writing and say, 'Ben, you ever shot someone?'

'Yer kidding? I've never even seen a gun nevermind shot someone. Why would ye even ask that?'

'I shot someone.'

'Jesus. Yer batshit, old lady.'

'I was ten, living in Cornwall. He sure as hell deserved it.'

'Is that why the Detective keeps calling?' Ben says.

'No, he wants me for something else.'

'Jesus, ye killed someone else too?'

'No, not me.'

'I'm harbouring a bloody murderer.'

'What the Detective wants – it's not me.'

'Who are ye anyway, old lady? So many secrets.'

'Not anymore,' I say. 'I'm writing it all down.'

Chapter 5

Cornwall, September 1940 – February 1941

Angel had stacked and threaded branches together. She'd propped them against two trees which had fallen against the side of the gully, offering firm support. The afternoon sun scorched the gully, but it was dark inside our den. Slivers of sunlight broke through the gaps in the branches, falling across Angel's face.

'Where'd you get that?'

'It was in the junk yard. I stole the battery from old Al and borrowed his wheelbarrow. Can't get it to work, though,' she said, bashing the wireless. 'Guess there was a reason it was junked.'

'I can look at it,' I said. 'I used to fix things with my da. The neighbours would come to us if they ever needed their wireless looked at.'

I came back the next day with some tools I borrowed from Tom. I opened it up. It wasn't anything complicated, just a couple of loose wires. I tightened the last screw and said, 'You can have the honour, Miss Angel.'

She turned it on and it was all fizz and crackles.

'The Martians are trying to speak to us,' I said.

She tuned it as I put away the tools.

'I'm glad you could fix it. I got it for you, because you said how you liked the wireless…' She trailed off, her tongue sticking out slightly as she tuned it.

Tom didn't have a wireless, said something about it being a sin, but he still asked Mr Moore everyday about the news. I guess secondhand sin isn't as bad, but if you ask me it's cheating. 'Compromise,' I could hear David say, and I guess that was Tom's version of compromise. Maybe he scrubbed himself clean that bit longer just to make sure the secondhand sin was all washed away.

'You said how you listened to it at home and I know you miss David's records. We can listen to music and we can dance.'

'Thanks,' I said, feeling pleased but embarrassed. I poked at some old toy Angel had brought and said, 'You know, the Idiot's been giving me a hard time, ever since the play.'

'He's a shit.'

'I know. He's just been more of a shit. He said he was gonna hurt CP.'

'That shit. What'd you do?'

'I just said he better not or I'd shoot him, right through the heart.'

'Yes!' she yelled. She'd picked up reception. We sat chewing on wild berries, listening to the news then Glen Miller's *In The Mood* came on and Angel got up and danced out the entrance of the den, shimmying her shoulders and wiggling her arse. I laughed and clapped and followed her out. We danced liked mad things, possessed creatures of the forest. I grabbed a hold of her, spun her round and pulled her close, kissing her before letting go and dancing a circle round her. When the song ended we collapsed onto the grass, laughing and trying to catch our breath. *We'll Meet Again* came on and Angel hummed along. It made me feel sad, but not bad sad, just kind of quiet and caught up in my thoughts. I took hold of her hand and held it tight, listening to her as she sang along to the chorus.

We met every evening at the den. We'd eat our berries, play cowboys and Indians in the gully, listen to the wireless. One night we both fell asleep there, waking up curled up together, freezing. We walked home in silence, leaving each other at the fork in the road just after we entered the town. I watched her walk away in the dark.

Angel wasn't allowed out for a week but all I got was a slap across the face and told never to do it again. Tom wasn't much bothered, as long as I did my work.

The week without her was strange. I didn't go to the den the first couple of days. I went to the beach and went swimming and caught some fish to take home. The third day I went to the den and listened to the wireless but it felt wrong without her there so I didn't go back. The week after was a strange kind of bliss. We swam, we went to the den, we had a fire on the beach. Apart from Angel having to be back by nine sharp every night we did what we'd always done. But it didn't feel the same. We knew it could all be taken away. It was taken away the day I shot John.

★

Tom didn't believe I'd shot him. But I had. Only it wasn't through the heart.

I was out hunting. John would sometimes come with me, even though Tom had given him other tasks after he realised how useless he was at it. John tagged along and I put up with him. Ever since my threat he wasn't so annoying. He was mostly quiet, which gave me the creeps, but it was still better than his taunts.

I had a rabbit in sight, waiting for the right moment, when I heard a shot just beyond the hillock, followed by a whooping. I cursed the Idiot; my rabbit had gone.

I went to look for John, finding it hard to believe he'd managed to hit anything. When I found him, he was crouched down, hunched over something and there was a horrible noise. I circled and saw what it was. He'd shot a rabbit, but badly. It was wounded, and he was shoving a stick into its wound. I shot it in the head. Blood spattered on John. Barely thinking, I swung the gun over and shot him in the foot.

I walked away. That was that. The beginning of the end of my life in Cornwall.

Tom didn't believe him. And I lied. When I left John I was so angry that I was ready to barrel on in to the house and confess with pride, but as I walked through the woods and past the den, all I felt was fear.

I walked in and said to Tom, 'John shot himself in the foot. I need help to get him home.'

John accused me the moment he saw us, but Tom said nothing. John had stemmed the flow with his shirt and we removed it, putting a temporary bandage in its place. I lifted John onto Tom's back and the Idiot pinched my arm. I bit on my lip as he kept pinching and pretending he couldn't get onto Tom's back because I wasn't helping properly. He let go of me and climbed onto Tom, piggybacking the whole way home, ranting about how I'd shot him. Tom didn't say a word.

We dropped him off at the doctor, who fixed him up. He kept him there overnight and told us he could return the next day, but that he'd be laid up for a good few weeks. Tom, who still hadn't spoken, grunted.

I knew my workload would double and there'd be no more evenings with Angel, but somehow I felt that was right. I had to pay for what I'd done. I'd have to pay for my lie.

It was in the evening after supper that Tom sat me down and asked me.

'Did you shoot him?'

'No.'

He nodded. Just like that, he believed me. I knew if I confessed I'd be sent away, maybe be locked up, and I would never see Angel again.

'You'll need to cover his work while he's recovering,' Tom said.

'Uh-huh.'

'What was that?'

'Yes, sir.'

'And you'll look after him. Serve him his food, change his bandages, whatever's needed. We're not having our lives disrupted by this.'

The thought crossed my mind that I should have shot John dead.

'Yes, sir.'

I expected taunts, for him to make things difficult for me, to be smug as I changed his bedpan and brought him food, but there was nothing. There was no expression on his face and he wouldn't look at me. I did what I had to do and I left. Doing double the chores was exhausting, but Angel helped when she could. Tom didn't believe it was right for women to do manual labour, but when he wasn't supervising, Angel would help me out.

It was much later, back in London when I was telling Queen Isabella what had happened that she said to me, 'Goblin, are you telling me you hadn't even thought about revenge?'

'I was busy,' I said, 'with the extra work and looking after him and getting away from him as soon as I could. I never thought about his revenge.'

Weeks had passed, he was back on his feet, using a walking stick, doing the chores he could and avoiding me as much as I avoided him. I just wanted things to be as they used to be, with me and Angel swimming in the sea every evening, hiding in our den. I didn't see it coming.

'Well,' Queen Isabella said, rolling her eyes at me like I was the biggest fool there was, 'what doesn't kill you makes you stronger.'

★

I came in from mucking out the pigs, covered in mud and shit. I dumped the potatoes I'd collected and said to Margaret, 'I'm going to wash up then I'll be in for supper.'

I glanced around the kitchen as I turned to leave. A reverend was there, but not the one from our local, and several others I didn't know. Supper wasn't on. I knew something must be up, but I thought it was just adult stuff and I'd do best to get out of there.

'You're not going anywhere, Luke. You'll be staying right

here.'

'But I need to clean up.'

'Sit,' Tom said.

There was an empty chair right in the middle of the room. I shuffled over, thinking I was clearly in some deep trouble if they'd let me traipse through the kitchen covered in dirt and smelling like the pits of hell.

I hesitated at the seat, glancing at Margaret. They'd trained me well and I didn't want to get dirt on the chair.

'Sit, demon.'

I looked at Tom and sat. I saw John standing behind him, leaning on his walking stick, his hair slicked back like on Sundays for church. He smiled slightly. My chest tightened.

No one said anything. They just sat, impassive, staring at me. I looked from person to person, licking my lips. I looked over to the door, wondering if I could make it, but the group had closed in, forming a circle, blocking my exit. I waited for someone to say something and looked over at Tom and Margaret. Tom was holding my *War Of The Worlds*.

I frowned and said, 'What's this about?'

'Hold your tongue, demon.'

I turned to the reverend who held a bible up at me. I thought, that John, he's sank me down into a whole heap of shit. I eyed up the reverend to try and figure out who I was dealing with, but didn't figure out much of anything. I squinted at his lap. There was some sort of dead animal on it. I couldn't make it out until he shifted it a bit so he could put the bible on his lap and it was then I could see. It was Monsta, all broken up. It was then I lost sight of trying to figure out the situation, like David would have said. 'Sit back, Goblin. Assess the situation, figure it out, then act. You're too impulsive, and that's gonna get you into all kinds of trouble one day.' Up until that moment I'd thought that pretty good advice, even if I didn't always heed it, but now for certain was a time for war. 'Goblin,' I could hear David say as I stood up like a piston and kicked back my chair, 'there's never a time for a war.'

I lunged for Monsta but didn't get near, everyone likely thinking I was about to eat that reverend's soul or whatever it is that demons do. I didn't stand a chance. I was pinned to the floor, yelling, sobbing, 'Monsta, Monsta!' but I think they thought I was casting some demon spell because pretty soon there was an old rag shoved in my mouth and tied tight with rope right round my head. Then it was my arms and my legs and there I was all parcelled up, and up up up I went, the demon ascending, raised on a throne of bony old hands as they took me to the attic room.

★

Holy holy holy lord have mercy trap trap trapped in chains in ropes bound in bound down lord have mercy christ have mercy hear us o lord o god the father have mercy on us in the shadow of this cross pressed down bound down bound in holy mother holy virgin of virgins have mercy have mercy sisters and saints the holy holy martyrs the angels above all holy angels o blessed revelation angel in holy holy water drip drip dripped in chains in ropes bound in bound down holy patriarchs and prophets saint john the baptist no head hahaa hahaa saint sebastian punctured and bled and bled in rivers of red deliver us from evil deliver us from deliver us from evil ring the bells saint agatha hahaa cut off cut from and bled and delivered from evil you have no power over me bound in bound down unclean spirit unclean unclean I command you the children of god the child of god this child of god blessed be blessed be glory glory glory the way the light the truth I cast you out from this creature of god devil begone no devils here not here no devils never to return no devils no devil amen.

★

'There's rabbits,' he said, his face right up against mine. I stared at the ceiling, at the peeling picture of the Virgin Mary.

'There's rabbits, five of them, down in the larder, hanging, waiting to be eaten. I shot them and I hurt them until they died. Every one. I can tell you all about it. Would you like that? Would you like me to tell you a bedtime story?'

I closed my eyes and drifted on dreams of Angel and the sea.

'Devil worshipping scum,' he said, and spat in my face. His saliva dribbled down my cheek.

'I'm the favourite now,' he said.

*

'Luke, they're not giving up on this. They believe you're possessed. Are you listening? Can you hear me?'

I rolled my head to the side and looked up at Miss Hallows.

'You need to repent. Do you know what I'm saying? You need to repent.'

She gave me a drink and helped me sit up. I stuffed bread in my mouth.

'Not too much, you'll be sick. Luke, they think you shot John.'

I did shoot the son of a bitch.

'They showed everyone the devil you made. John said you were going to bring it to life. He showed them your scribblings in those blasphemous books – cannibalism, shapeshifting, worshipping serpents.'

'Lizards,' I said. 'Lizard people.'

'They think you're evil.'

I was born blue. Dirty little goblin-runt.

'You're not getting out of here until you repent.'

She meant it. I hadn't figured it out until she said it. She was on their side. They were tired, they were weary. They wanted me pure.

'I'll bring the reverend,' she said, 'and this time you have to repent.'

She was gone and Isabella was there holding the heart, blood dripping between her fingers.

'You can't be here,' I said. 'You're in London.'

'Do you remember your prayers?' she said.

'I remember.'

'You can't fake it.'

'I don't have to,' I said. 'You need to leave. The reverend is coming.'

★

I was demon child covered in shit and piss stained in pig pig piggy shit and piss stinking and stinking and rotting. The stench of evil tied in ropes tied down in the attic on a bed in the attic with mary and jesus and the cross for friends all stuck on the wall eyes on me and in my mind in my closed eyes the revelation angel of the sea far away drifting as the reverend in the attic was all rat-a-tat-tat! Begone begone holy holy holy rat-a-tat-tat london rat bound down cross pressed close down hard bruised down rope shapes cross shapes body bruised body razed body bound down bound in behind the eyes floating in the sea with the revelation angel drip drip drip devil begone amen. No devils here, sir. No devils ever again. All gone all clean all pure.

★

Margaret untied me. Tom was behind her, carrying a tin bath, a bath for me to make the unclean clean. Inside outside scrub scrub scrub. She peeled off my clothes and I thought, shit, this is it – no more Luke all gone all gone, a Miriam instead? A Holy Holy Holy Virgin Mary? An Esther, whatever you please, who am I to choose? She didn't say a word, but turned her head away sick with the stench of me and lifted me into the water, scrubbing and scrubbing turning red turning the clean and pure water black with sin.

I climbed out, wrapping myself in a towel, dripping sin across the floor. I watched it roll off me and I felt cleansed. I was good and clean and pure.

Tom took away the bath. Margaret didn't say a word to Tom, not then and not ever as far as I can know so I stayed a Luke for then for them and Margaret brought me food. Bread and water bread and water the body of Christ the body of Christ.

★

They paraded me down the aisle, made me stand on a platform. Praise the Lord, for I was saved.

The reverend had come up to the attic and I dazzled him. I remembered my prayers well, and the hymns, and passages from the bible I'd learned off by heart. I picked wisely and reeled them off. I was pure, I was holy, I was saved.

They let me out of the attic, dressed me up smart and took me to a church on the outskirts of town, showing me to the congregation, showing what the power of the Lord could achieve. Holy holy holy.

Angel had been outside the house when we left. Margaret invited her to the church. 'Your friend has been saved,' she said.

The whole service I stared at Angel. Everyone closed their eyes and bowed their heads in prayer but I stared at Angel. She unclasped her hands and looked up at me, turning her palm to face me. 'I love you' was scrawled across her hand. She held it there, as if in salute. At first I thought I'd choke just from wanting to go and touch her, to feel her fingers in mine. She winked at me and I smiled, I thought I'd start snorting with laughter, I thought I'd choke on misery and laughter, and I smiled. It was then I decided to gut the rabbits.

★

Old lady Taylor had herbs that would send you into a deep sleep. It was easy for me to get a hold of them and slip them in John and pretend parents' dinner.

Then I cut out the rabbit eyes and I sliced open their bellies. The house was still. The oil lamp flickered. I carried the rabbits upstairs and laid them across John. I pulled the guts out of the bellies and scattered them over his body. I placed the eyes on his eyelids. He didn't stir.

I left the house, picking up my bag and a shovel by the door. I went to the pig pen and Corporal Pig came trotting out. We walked through the town. The buildings looked unreal in the moonlight. John had told me Monsta's remains were buried at the crossroads on the edge of town, and I saw the mound of earth next to the wall. I dug up Monsta, stuffing the broken pieces into my bag. I dumped the shovel and doubled-back into town.

I climbed the fence into the Tremayne garden and threw stones at Angel's window. Her washed-out face appeared then vanished, and there she was in front of me. I touched her face, and I held her.

'I have to go,' I said.

She nodded, her lips pinched. Corporal Pig snuffled at her feet.

'What'd they do to you?'

I shrugged.

'John told them I had a demon in me.'

'That shit. He'll suffer, I'll make sure of it.'

'I put rabbit guts on John. I said a lizard curse. He'll stink of rabbit guts forever.'

'Good,' she said. She held my hand and we kissed. She tasted like the sea.

'You could stay,' she said. 'With us. Ann and Bill will take you in, we can share a room—'

'I can't. Not after everything.'

She couldn't look at me. She scrunched up her face and stared over at the fields, up at the moon. She scuffed at the dirt.

'I want to ask you to come but I'd only be taking you to bombs and ma… She won't let you stay. I know she won't.'

'You shouldn't be going back to that either.'

'I don't belong here.'

'You belong with me.'

'Always,' I said, crying despite all my effort. I wiped at my face with my sleeve and said, 'I'll write you. About Queen Isabella, Amelia and Scholler. I'll tell you about the bombs.'

'And the lizard people.'

'And the lizard people.'

'You better,' she said, frowning at me.

'I will. Promise.'

'Wait here,' she said, and went back into the house. She emerged a moment later and pressed some coins into my hand and gave me a map.

'Won't they be mad? I don't want you to get in trouble.'

'I'll be fine.'

I put the map and coins in my bag.

'I'll give you my address,' I said, taking her hand and writing across the back of it. 'You can write to me while I'm travelling, so it arrives before I'm home. It'll be like you're there, waiting for me.'

She didn't say anything, just made a choking hiccup noise, kissed me, and ran off, disappearing into the house. I stared up at the house and she appeared at the window. The moonlight made her skin glow.

Chapter 6

Cornwall, February 1941

We walked along the main road out of town, a skip in my step as I thought of John and those unholy bastards.

'Holy, Holy, Holy!' I sang. 'Corporal Pig, sir! Those fools don't know what holy is, but we do, we do, CP. All hail the lizards down below. Yes, sir!'

I laughed, thinking of John waking up covered in rabbit insides. I jumped into the air, 'Yee-hah! We're on an adventure, CP!' CP took fright and skittered off the road, half-falling into a bush.

'Ah, CP, c'mon, c'mon. There's a war on, CP. How are we supposed to win if you're all dirty milky?'

We stuck to the main road through the night, but took a sheltered route through the forest as dawn broke.

'I'm sure they're glad to see the back of me, CP. But you never know, you never know, and I'm not going back in that old attic, that's for sure.'

We were well past the outskirts of town and I marked on the map where I thought we were and plotted where we would be heading. Signs had been removed in case of a German invasion, which made finding our way more difficult. I didn't have much of a plan past getting as far away as possible, and once we were far far away we would hitch lifts, hop on trains.

'I'm tired out, CP. Some breakfast and a nap is what we need.'

We walked deeper into the forest and settled down at the base of a tree. I rummaged in the bag for food, pushing aside the remains of Monsta. 'We'll fix you soon, Monsta,' I said. 'You'll be good as new.' I gave CP some feed and I had a slice of bread. CP fell asleep and I used him as a pillow, drifting off to the rhythm of his breath.

★

I had a nightmare. I was back in that attic, tied to the bed, unable to breathe as they tore Monsta apart. Angel was there and she was one of them.

I woke to the gloaming. I felt sick, unable to shake the nightmare. Corporal Pig had wandered off and I panicked before I saw his pink bulk through the trees. I went to fetch him and found him snuffling amongst the undergrowth, gathering sticks for a nest. 'I'll need to tie you up, CP. You can't go a-wandering. There's beasts in the forest that will gobble you whole.'

We set off again, trudging along, moving back to the main roads. The sun set in the west and I knew we more or less needed to head north-east, so on we went and I hoped for the best.

★

A week into the journey and our supplies were running low.

'CP,' I said. 'If I die, if I starve to death, you can eat me.'

'Why, Goblin,' I said, putting on a hoity-toity voice I was sure CP would have if he could speak human, 'why Goblin-runt-human-child, if *I* die *you* can eat *me*.'

'Never, CP. Never.'

'And I'd never eat you Goblin-runt-human-child. It'd be like sucking on a mummy's corpse all decomposed and gnarled and rotten and skin and bone.'

'Why thank you, Corporal, thank you *very much*. Eating you would be much the same. Look at you! Empty fatty folds hanging off your bones. A pig should be rotund, a pig should waddle, head held high as their humongous behind sways this way that way.'

'Why, thank *you* very much, Goblin-runt-human-child. So

what are we to do about it?'

'A mission, CP. Into enemy territory.'

That's when I took the risk of leaving the forests and the fields and headed towards a small village. I tied CP to a tree. I didn't want the villagers thinking they could eat him for their tea.

'Look, CP,' I said, 'I need to go this mission alone, but there's danger that lurks round every corner and if a monster or a tiger or a wolf or a fox tries to chew on your skinny bones you do just like you did back home and give 'em a kicking. Right? Just like you used to, CP. I'll be mighty mad if I come back and you're a bloody mess. Mighty mad.'

*

'Where's your ration books?'

'I lost them.'

The old grocer man looked me up and down.

'I don't know you. You one of those refugees?'

'Evacuee. I live with the Frys,' I said, remembering a name on one of the doors I passed as I walked through the village.

'The Frys didn't take on any refugees.'

'I can assure you, sir, they did. I am me, I am they, the refugee, evacuee. They took me in. The *authorities*, sir, said they must. "Don't you know there's a war on?" is what the authorities said, and the Frys they had to do their bit or be shamed.'

'Well, I haven't heard news of this. When'd you arrive?'

'Sir,' I said, 'you have to help me out,' I sidled up to him and lowered my voice. 'The Frys are reluctant guardians, sir, poor parents to I am me the refugee evacuee. Poor parents indeed. But it's a roof over my head and a bomb-free sky over that roof, so who am I to complain? No, sir, not one to complain. But they'll give me a thrashing, sir—'

'I doubt that, young lad. Unless you deserved it.'

'Well, sir, you see, I lost the ration books.'

'So you said.'

'It takes an awful lot of time and fuss to sort that out, sir, and if I go back empty handed... well, you don't want us to starve, sir. I'm sure you don't.'

He let out a snort.

'They got themselves a right one in you, didn't they? I can tell the likes of you. Weaving tales, spinning words into nets. One day you'll get in trouble with that mouth, boy. Starving, indeed!'

He shuffled over to the shelves, picking out various bags and tins.

'The usual, then? I'll be making a note of it, mind. I'm not getting in trouble on this one.'

'Yes, sir, of course, sir.'

I watched him and could see there was too much for me and Corporal Pig to carry, so I said, 'Well, sir, why don't you make it half the amount. We really don't need all that, just a bit to tide us over 'til new ration books come in.'

I smiled sweetly and nodded as he paused.

'Just half?'

'That's right. That'll tide us over.'

I came away with a good supply that would keep CP and I going strong and I hurried past the Frys' house with my loot, glancing nervously at their door as if they might sense I was off with half their rations.

'There's a war on,' I said to CP, 'and the Frys are just doing their bit for the thing I am, a refugee, evacuee, a holy holy holy escapee.'

★

Travelling by foot was taking its toll, feet all blistered, weight falling off me and the Corporal before we could put it back on with the rations. We were weary, me and CP, the spirit of adventure sucked out of us by the reality of day upon day upon day of trudging. The more miserable I felt, the more I thought of Angel, the more I wished I'd brought her with me. But I was just feeling sorry for myself – I knew it was selfish, I knew I couldn't take her away from a home where she was cared for and subject her to my ma.

I tried to keep spirits up by talking with CP, telling stories, singing songs. Less wary of humans now that I'd put a fair distance between us and the unholy bastards, I greeted fellow travellers on the road and trotted through villages head held high, CP kept close.

'Which way to London, my fine man?' and off we went, trudging, trudging.

★

Trucks went by in a succession of khaki and indistinguishable faces. I trotted after them.

'Oi! You got room for a kid and a pig?'

The faces came to life, laughing and sneering. One of the soldiers flicked his cigarette from one side of his mouth to the other and gave a squint smile.

'Where you going, kid?'

'London.'

'Most kids go the other way.'

'I'm going home.'

'You running away?'

'What's it to you?'

He laughed. 'You got balls, kid. Throw us the pig.'

I tried to lift Corporal Pig, floundering under his weight, even in his skin and bone state. He wriggled, all legs and flapping ears and snorting. I loped along, but couldn't keep up. The soldiers gathered at the back of the truck to watch, cheering and whooping. A lit cigarette hit me in the face.

'You sonsofbitches, you goddamn bastards I'll bash you, I'll bash the lot of you.'

They cheered and the squintsmiler jumped out, grabbed CP, threw him on board, took a hold of me and threw me straight after CP, before jumping up like it was easy as pissing in a pot.

There was chaos. CP was snorting and squealing, running round the truck in a panic beneath the soldiers' feet. They kicked at him and he squealed some more and they laughed. I ran after CP but they grabbed at me, all hands. CP bit one of them and the soldier flicked out a knife and I went for him, bashing his face. He fell back and took the pummelling as his comrades dragged me off, yelling and foaming at the mouth.

'Yerasorrybunchosonsobitches,' I said. 'Stay away from Corporal Pig, you shits.'

'Corporal Pig! Corporal Pig!' they chorused.

'Leave the kid's pig alone,' said Squintsmiler, 'It's his only friend in the world. That right, boy?'

He winked at me and I scowled, getting a firm hold of CP, who was shaking and wide-eyed. I stroked him and whispered in his ear and I stroked his ear too and rubbed his snout and patted his back and he calmed down. I eyed the one who had flicked open the knife. He stared at us, using the knife to pick dirt from under his nails.

'Sons of bitches,' I said every few minutes, chewing on gum Squintsmiler had given me, but soon no one was really listening. They went back to their card games and nude magazines.

'Don't mind us, kid. We were just playing.'

'Sons of bitches.'

'You've got some mouth on you, kid.'

I chewed on my gum, stroking CP. I looked around, just daring any of them sonsofbitches to come near us.

'You're a wild one, boy. Whatcha running away from?'

'Sons of bitches.'

'You're trouble. You'll give the girls a hard time, won't you? I can see it in those eyes. You like pussy, kid?'

He showed me one of the nudey pictures, and I said, 'Sure. Sure, I like pussy.'

'The kid likes pussy, boys!'

They cheered. I was patted on the back.

'You can keep that kid. For the lonely nights.'

He winked at me and I stuffed the picture in my pocket.

'How old are you, boy?'

'Ten.'

'That right? You not too young to be travelling on your own?'

'I'm not on my own – I have Corporal Pig. He's a trusty companion.'

'You look after each other?'

'That's right.'

He smiled at me and nodded and I shifted as close to CP as possible, laying my head on his side. I fell asleep, curled up practically wound right round CP to protect him. I woke to Squintsmiler shaking me and I almost strangled CP in panic.

'It's alright, I don't want to hurt your bleedin' pig. It's your stop, kid. You're getting off here.'

He lifted me and Corporal Pig like we were nothing and set us down on the road.

'Here, kid, take some of these.'

He threw me sweets and cigarettes.

'You got any money, comrade-sir?'

'Have I got any money?'

'Yes, comrade-sir, we're weary from walking. We need money for train fare.'

The truck was pulling away, too fast for us to keep up. Squintsmiler disappeared, moving back into the throng of soldiers.

I could hear them chanting. 'Corporal Pig! Corporal Pig!'

'You hear that, CP? The soldiers, they love you, CP. They really do.'

I saw something fall from the back of the truck as it rounded the corner and I waved, but they'd gone. I broke into a run, hoping it was more cigarettes or candy I could use to barter for a ticket or some food, but when I got to it I saw it was just a piece of the nudey magazine. I picked it up, unfolded it and found money nestling between the woman's legs.

'I sure like pussy, CP,' I said, shoving the money in my

pocket. 'I sure do.'

*

No pigs. That's what he said. Dirty animals. Show some respect to the Corporal, I said. I'm not having that animal shitting all over this train, he said. I protested, I cajoled. I pleaded with my fellow humans. London, I said. I miss my family, I said.

'Look,' he said. 'Leave the pig behind and we have no problem, but that animal isn't staying on this train.'

'I can pay extra,' I said, holding the remaining money in my hands. 'I'll clean up any shit.'

'There will be no shit to clean up. No pig, no shit, and no you. Now get lost.'

I thought for a moment then pulled out the packet of cigarettes. I smiled.

'Huh? What do you say?' I shook the packet, raising my eyebrow.

'Get!'

CP trotted in front of me, half falling onto the platform. I started after him, cursing my way down the corridor when I felt the nudey picture in my pocket.

'Wait!' I said, turning back to the conductor. I unfolded the picture, holding it up.

'You like pussy, eh?'

He barrelled after me, crushed the nudey picture in his hand and grabbed a hold of me by the back of my shirt, manhandling me right off that train. I lay on the platform, bruised, wielding my ticket and yelling 'I paid good money for this, sir! Comrade-soldiers paid good money for this. I've got to get to London. We're refugeesevacueesescapees.'

'Then you're going the wrong way!' he yelled at me.

I rubbed my bruised knees as I watched the train pull out of the station.

*

'You're going the wrong way,' the man said.

I told him my story of woe, adding here, taking away there. I didn't get in trouble at all, not this time, but elicited pity from the stationmaster, or more like he just wanted me to leave him be, but he took my ticket and returned my money and I bought food for me and CP. We stayed there a day and a night and I stuffed CP full, as full as can be, then off we trudged, but this time CP had a spring in his step.

'This time, CP, we're sticking to the roads and we'll hitch a ride. No more weary fat-stealing walking for you and me. We'll hitch a ride and be fat as kings.'

Many passed us by, or stopped when they saw I was a kid, but like that evilsonofawhoreticketmaster, wouldn't take me with CP, not until one kind man who after listening to my story of woe and a litany of CP's strengths, stopped me mid-sentence. 'Boy,' he said, looking as weary as us skinny walkers, 'I don't need a story, just get in the car.'

'Yes, sir! Yes, sir, in the car! C'mon CP, stop that loitering. Quick march, in the car!'

The man sighed and I pushed CP into the back. I climbed in and we were off.

'Thanks, mister, sir!'

He gave me the side-eye and said, 'You're going the wrong way, boy.'

I told him the story of how we were escaping unholy bastards and he listened, not saying a word. I dropped off to sleep, still trying to talk, still trying to tell my story, but me and CP we were weary and off to slumberland we went.

When I woke I didn't start back on my story. I just watched the clouds, dreaming of London.

London, March 1941

'This is as far as I go,' he said, dropping me off on the outskirts of the city. I dragged a snoring CP out of the car.

'I had pigs when I was your age,' he said to me. 'Good animals. You watch out for him, you hear me?'

'Yes, sir!' I said, standing to attention and saluting. 'Me and Corporal Pig, we're comrades, friends for life.'

'I'm glad to hear it,' he said, and started up the car. 'Good luck, comrades.'

'Thank you, sir.'

He drove off and I had some trouble waking up CP to restart our weary walking. He'd resumed his snoring on the pavement and I pushed and shoved him and flicked his ear.

'Comrade, CP! You get up! You've slept an age in the back of that car. We're back on our mission. There's a war on, CP. Look lively!'

With a bit of prodding, ear flicking, tail pulling and a ration of oats, CP was soon on his feet and sleepily shuffling along by my side.

'We're almost there, CP. You can sleep all you want when we're home.'

We wandered through the suburbs of London. It was a glorious day; baby blue sky and gossamer clouds. Not knowing the way through my city I felt like a foreigner, a Martian, a German spy. Street names had been removed or obscured. I asked directions, not a single person suspecting me of being a German spy, everyone saying, 'You're going the wrong way, boy.' The last person I approached, I berated them, 'Don't you know there's a war on? Don't you know I'm a German spy?'

I could see the familiar landscape in the distance, my heart aching for the silhouettes of my neighbourhood buildings. It was peaceful here. The sun cast long shadows and turned buildings a warm orange. Birds fluttered and sang. I passed open gardens, their fences requisitioned. As the sun set and darkness descended, the distant sky was lit up with searchlights. The sun had melted into the landscape, setting it alight. The East End was on fire.

I felt sick at the thought that our home might not be there

anymore. All the time I was travelling home I felt like I was travelling back in time. But I wasn't. This was the future. The months had gone by, but I thought of London frozen in time. I'd heard reports of the bombs, but it was a fantasy, a story.

I could see the Luftwaffe, but they looked unreal; little slivers of silver circling London, caught in the searchlights. Smoke roiled in the sky, a black mass, blacker than the night sky. Dark clouds billowed, cut through by beams from the ground, illuminated by flames. My home was being obliterated as I returned. Those familiar streets, those familiar silhouettes, razed.

I could hear nothing. It was like watching a silent film.

'The Martians have come,' I said to CP, who was hoovering up insects. 'We're going home and the Martians have come.'

Edinburgh, 6 August 2011

London is on fire. I pick up the phone.

'Detective?' I say, watching the flames flicker across the screen. 'I'm coming home.'

Goblin and Monsta and Corporal Pig. Off we trotted to London, and here I am, returning too, and it's time travel. My home is being obliterated. Those unfamiliar streets, those unfamiliar silhouettes, razed.

Now's not a good time, he says. Wait until the rioting has passed. We have our hands full, he says. 'What happened to needing me, Detective? What happened to the court order?' London is in flames, he says. I know, I say. I'm coming home.

Chapter 7

'Hail thee lizards down below in the darkness in the depths. O Lizard Queen and King of the deep, O guardian lizards, the word shall be made flesh and this flesh shall be given new life blood. I beseech thee O lizards of the depths bring forth this monsta-child who was struck down by servants of all that is corrupt and evil, struck down and pulled apart and desecrated. Resurrect these hewn pieces, I beseech thee. I offer thee blood.'

'So you're back?'

Amelia, Queen Isabella, Scholler. All three stood in waiting.

'I'm back,' I said.

'Things didn't go so well for Monsta, I see.'

'A nasty little bastard ruined it all. But I put rabbit guts on him and I became a vice-versa refugee, evacuee, escapee.'

'Is that hideous beast yours?'

'That's Corporal Pig and you should salute him.'

'I'm not saluting anyone. I'm a queen. And you should be having that beast for dinner – you're all skin and bone.'

'Why don't you open up that pig instead of yourself?' said Amelia as I rolled up my sleeve and held the penknife over my arm.

'You're ruining the ceremony,' I said. 'Don't you want Monsta back? And you'll treat Corporal Pig with respect. He's an adventurer, an explorer and a sure and steady comrade.'

Scholler sniffed at CP's behind before nuzzling into his snout.

'That's more like it. You two should take a lesson in politeness from Scholler.'

'Well, I'm certainly not sniffing a swine's behind,' said Queen Isabella. 'Come, Amelia, it's obvious when we're not wanted.'

'Wait!' I said. 'Wait.'

I turned to them, gesturing with the penknife.

'I missed you.'

Queen Isabella looked down at me, her eyes narrowed.

'Is that so?'

'You know it, you snooty old queen. I missed all of you.'

I watched her expression soften.

'I saw you in Cornwall, you know.'

'We weren't anywhere near Cornwall,' said Isabella.

'No, nowhere near,' said Amelia. 'We don't leave London.'

'You were. You were in the attic and you helped me. But that's all in the past. This is the present.'

'Monsta has sunk into the past,' said Amelia, 'Monsta is over.'

'This is the past,' I said, pointing at Monsta's broken body. 'And Monsta's resurrection is the future.'

I cut my arm and my blood drip-dripped onto Monsta's corpse. I sank my teeth into four apple-hearts, dripping the juice onto the blood. I could see Monsta's eyes rolling beneath the lids, the tentacles twitched, the crow foot stretched.

'Holy, Holy, Holy,' I said as Monsta's eyes opened.

I cradled Monsta in my arms and we all went to the mausoleum where I fell asleep telling Queen Isabella, Scholler and Amelia about Cornwall and Angel.

*

In the morning, I awoke to find Monsta asleep on my chest, tentacle arms wrapped around my fingers. CP was making a godawful noise and snuffled at the door.

'Alright, you old foghorn, I'm getting up.'

Monsta sleepily crawled onto my shoulder and sat snoozing against my head, tentacles threaded through my scraggly hair. I let CP out and he was off, crushing flowers and searching for insects.

'We're going home, CP,' I said as I led him through the cemetery and out into London's streets.

When we got to the East End the ARP were still putting out fires. Some people were making their way to work, walking past the smashed up buildings as if it was normal. Some stood and stared at their lost home. One of the houses was spliced and there were framed photographs still hanging on the wall, a fireplace with a mirror above and vases on the mantle. A door remained intact but opened out on to nothing but the rubble below. Beams criss-crossed, leaning against the crumbling building as if supporting it.

A woman was bent over, rummaging through the rubble, rescuing a cooking pot. She stood, clutching it, staring at the building, mesmerised by the insistent embers that glowed and crackled beneath the onslaught of water.

I spotted a camera and picked it up.

'This yours, Mrs?'

She looked at me blankly and shook her head. The camera was a bit bashed but I knew David could fix it if it didn't work. I shoved it in my bag and walked further on, reaching my street. A jagged hole hunkered down into old Fenwick's home, revealing my house behind it. I wasn't ready for this homecoming, I wasn't prepared for this absence. I wanted to burrow down into the earth, into the Kensal Green crypt, into the underground tunnels with the lizards.

I picked my way around the rubble that was Mr Fenwick's house, not daring to clamber through the new thoroughfare. I circled round it, as if the emptiness would suck me in. I wondered if he'd died, or moved on. I wondered what had happened to Groo. I saw no sign of her now, but old Fenwick's two chickens were pecking round the rubble in the garden. Their run was smashed open but they looked unharmed.

I rounded them up, Corporal Pig snorting at their arses to keep them in line and there I stood, on my doorstep, with a pig, a monsta, and two chickens. That terrible absence pulsed at my back, pushing me to safety through the door, pushing me back to David, back to ma and da.

London, 7 August 2011

'So you're back?'

Amelia, Queen Isabella, Scholler.

'I'm back.'

I stand in Kensal Green Cemetery looking at the crime scene tape around Devil's grave.

'It's almost as if they're treating Devil's death as murder.'

'You look old.'

'Yes, very old.'

'It *was* murder, you know.'

'We know.'

'But it's the photo that matters, not Devil's bones.'

'They've set fire to London. Is that why you're back? Drawn to the flames?'

'Like a moth,' I say. 'But I won't burn just yet.'

London, March 1941

'Ma?'

'So you're back? Didn't they want you?'

'They said I was possessed by a demon.'

She nodded, rocking a little, holding a pen like it was a cigarette.

'Ma? Can I take your picture?'

'So you can steal my soul, demon?'

'I forgot what you looked like. When I was away, I forgot.'

'Well, you're here now, no need for pictures. I thought you'd died. I told everyone you'd likely died and they all said what a shame it was.'

She looked away and her head swayed from side to side as she said shame, shame, shame, in a sing-song voice.

'And here you are, Goblin-runt born blue. Nothing can kill you.'

'No.'

She looked me in the eye.

'You're like a cockroach,' she said.

She chewed on the end of the pen and stared at the fireplace.

'I got you cigarettes.'

Her head snapped up, her eyes narrowed.

'Where'd you get those?'

'Soldiers.'

'Give them here.'

She lit up.

'Where's da?'

She sucked on the cigarette and closed her eyes.

'Ma?'

'He's dead.'

I stared at the floor and scrunched my fingers into the folds of my shirt.

'Died months ago, leaving me, just like that.'

'How'd he die?'

She exhaled and said nothing.

'Why didn't you tell me, ma? Why didn't you write me?' I gestured back into the hallway. 'All my postcards and letters are just lying there. Ma?'

'What?'

'Why didn't you read them? Why didn't you tell me about da?'

She waved her hand through the smoke and said, 'No time for that. I've been working so hard, day in day out, while everyone just leaves me.'

I stared at her, clenching my fists.

'Where's David?'

'Where's David, where's David?'

'Where is he, ma?'

'No one's seen David. Here I am on my own, everyone just leaves and I've got to run this house alone.'

'He'll come back.'

'He better. What use is it otherwise?'

'I'm here, ma.'

'What use is it?'

'I'll help out.'

'What use is it, huh? Just me alone.'

She cried with the cigarette in her mouth, tears and snot and saliva slithering over her lips and down her chin.

I found Corporal Pig in the hallway, fast asleep, making huffy noises. I looked down at all my postcards and letters piled behind the door. I got down on my knees and searched for something from Angel – it was a postcard with a picture of a beach and she'd drawn me, her, and CP basking in the sun. I turned it over and read her words aloud: 'My handsome Goblin, I miss you. I didn't eat for two days but Ann and Bill were worried and made me. Your pretend parents told everyone your ma and da had wanted you back so you'd gone. The Idiot was being a shit and saying things about you at school so I punched his face. He's got a broken nose and I was kept in for two weeks but I didn't care becos I don't go out anymore anyway. Write and tell me London stories, your Angel forever xxxx.'

I sat for a few minutes reading it over and over again, looking at where the ink was smudged by her hand, before turning it over and staring at the drawing of us on the beach. I put it in my pocket. I shooed the chickens out into the back garden so they could eat insects and have dust baths. I dragged my bag and a half-asleep CP up the stairs into mine and David's room, and there was Groo curled up asleep on my bed. Without even realising, I was crying. I was smiling and laughing and crying and I called her name and she meowed at me, little plaintive confused sounds I'd never heard her make before. I gathered her up, hugging her and staining her with tears. She struggled and I let her go, dropping her back on the bed. She meowed and meowed and meowed.

'I missed you, you strange wee terror,' I said, hiccupping through the tears. 'There's no Devil-dog to groom, you skinny wee thing. No Devil dogs at all.'

I hoisted CP onto my bed and Groo looked startled, backing away, her fur standing on end.

'It's just CP, Groo. Just good old CP, trusty weary walker. We're a fine scrawny bunch,' I said, petting her and feeling her ribs. 'You two wait here and I'll get you some food. Don't you touch CP, mind.'

When I returned, CP was snoring and Groo was keeping her distance, sat on my pillow, pressed up against the wall.

'You'll make friends soon enough.'

I gave her food and she was so excited about it she got most of it on her face and my bed. I looked around the room. Some of the Dietrich pictures had fallen off, so I pressed them back onto the wall. The note I'd left for David was still on his desk. I traced my finger across it: 'I'm going on an adventure. Love, Goblin.'

It felt like so long ago I'd written it. And he hadn't read it. He hadn't read any of my postcards or letters. I scrunched up my note and threw it on the floor. I crushed it under my foot. I crawled into David's bed, pressing my face into the pillow. I could still smell him. Monsta climbed from my bag and lay on my shoulder, tentacle-worms stroking my head. Groo hopped up and sniffed at Monsta, sneezed, then licked my hair.

'I sure missed you,' I said, falling asleep to the sound of her rough tongue on my hair and skin.

*

I slept through the week, only getting out of bed to feed Groo, Corporal Pig and the chickens. I'd let CP out to rummage for insects in the garden, then I'd climb right back into bed and disappear into darkness, ignoring the air raids.

When I emerged at the end of the week I bathed myself and bathed CP and I ate a feast and was almost sick. I played David's records and I tidied our room, scooping out the shits CP had done on my bed and the floor, scrubbing everything clean.

'CP, I'll need to make you a home outside. You'll be happier in the garden and I won't have to smell your stink anymore.'

I sent a postcard to Angel – it was a picture of Trafalgar Square and I'd drawn CP, Angel and I swimming in one of the fountains.

'My beautiful Angel,' I wrote, 'I made it home, CP and I all skinny from weary walking. We have a cat called Groo, and chickens – Billy Bones and Dr Kemp. They were our neighbour's family, but he's been bombed out so I took them in. How are things? I hope you're happy and the Idiot isn't being a shit. I'm glad you broke his nose. I miss you and I miss swimming in the sea. Love forever, your Goblin xxxx.'

I didn't bother telling Angel about da being dead, and David being missing and ma being ma. I only wanted to write about happy things so she wouldn't worry about me. And mostly things were happy anyway, especially when ma wasn't around and she hardly ever was – she worked at the factory and went out at night, drinking. She'd come home and sob and fall asleep on the floor. I'd wake her up with tea and a cigarette and she'd sit up, her make-up all run down her cheeks, snot all crusted on her lips, and she'd drink her tea and smoke her cigarettes and I'd watch her wash off all the grime and put a new face on.

'Ma,' I said, 'Where's David?'

'I told you. He's gone.'

'Where?'

'It's your da's fault.'

'Da? Did he make him go to war?'

She shook her head. 'He pushed David too hard and now he's gone.'

'Gone where, ma?'

'Just gone.'

I went through some family photos and found one of David, taken almost three years before when ma and da took us to get proper photographs of us all. There was one of the family together, one of me and David and photos of each of us on our own. I took out the one of me and David and put it on our bedroom wall. I shoved the one of him in my pocket. Everywhere I went I brought it out, 'Have you seen this boy? I think he went to the sea, but maybe he's still here. Have you seen him? He'll be older now, older than this, but he'll look much the same. Have you seen this boy?'

I got a reply from Angel saying she was glad I had a family of animals and even though she's sad I left she's glad for the family I'm looking after. She said she's doing fine, that Ann and Bill are good new parents and they took her to the beach for a picnic at the weekend which was nice but she felt a bit sad because she missed me.

I wrote back and said maybe her and Bill and Ann could come to London for a holiday one day and she wrote that Bill and Ann said they'd come visit after the war so I prayed like mad to the lizards below that the war would end that very day but it didn't.

I settled into a routine at home. Ma didn't bother me. I was free to do as I pleased and she didn't even notice CP snuffling in the garden, she didn't even notice the brand new palace I made him out of scraps of wood I'd found. She didn't notice anything. Until one day she did, and I came home from scootering around the city with Monsta and found her slitting Corporal Pig's throat, but the knife was blunt and she was drunk and CP was too strong. She only managed a few small cuts, but from then on I made sure CP was with me when I knew she'd be home. I would stay in and keep an eye on them both, or I'd put a lead on him and keep him close, growling at anyone who came near.

Ma worked all hours at the factory and had no time to queue for food, so I took the ration books and spent hours getting food in. I didn't mind so much. I had Corporal Pig and I'd put together a show. Some people even gave us money, but you had to watch out for people who wanted to steal CP for their stew, so when I was sure ma wasn't home I'd leave him behind where he'd be safe.

I had to drag ma into the Andersen shelter when the siren went. She'd yell at me, but usually she'd come. There were nights she didn't, when she'd just sit and rock and sob, and she wouldn't come at all, so I left her. I left her to get bombed, but she never did.

Then one day she never came home. Sometimes she came home late in the night, but this night she didn't come. I waited, but she didn't return, not for days or weeks. I asked some of the neighbours, but they hadn't seen her and I soon stopped asking when they started snooping on me – 'You on your own, Goblin?' I lied and said David had come back. I said everything was fine.

I thought she might have died in a bombing. Or maybe she'd found a brand new family and gone to live with them because she had nothing here. I didn't care much at all, except I was worried about the rent. I went to old Martha to pay her what I could out of the tin in the kitchen where ma and da kept money for food, but old Martha and her house were gone.

'Bombed,' said her neighbour. 'A few weeks ago.'

'Where is she now?'

'Up there, boy. Or more likely down there, to be truthful.'

'She died?'

He nodded. 'Remains sent down south to her son. He got special leave on account of her death. I suppose he'll be up to deal with her affairs at some point. What you want her for anyhow?'

'Nuthin',' I said, 'She was just a friend of my ma.'

'Well, if you ask me, it's no big loss,' he said, staring at the rubble. Then he looked at me and said, 'Condolences to your ma, though.'

'Right, thanks.'

There was a spring in my step as I headed back home, feeling as rich as can be with all the tin money in my pocket, and pleased that old Martha was dead and gone. I just had to hope her son was too busy being a soldier to bother with Martha's affairs as I had to keep a roof over the head of my ever-growing family.

There was CP, and Mr Fenwick's Groo, and his chickens, Billy Bones and Dr Kemp (I asked around the neighbourhood about Mr Fenwick, but no one knew where he'd gone). I sometimes looked after Betty, an old dog belonging to my neighbour, Miss Campbell. She asked me to take her out for walks, as she was working long hours, doing her bit for the war effort, and poor Betty was lonely. I wasn't too happy about it at first because I thought she'd remind me of Devil and I didn't want to think of Devil anymore, but I felt bad for Betty and she wasn't like Devil at all and I was glad for that. She was old and slow and liked to sleep a lot. She got on well with CP, but she didn't like the chickens. She didn't much like Captain Flint either. I found Captain Flint, a baby raven, after a bombing. I'd taken him to the vet who said Flint was just stunned and the vet gave me advice on how to feed him until he was old enough to make his own way. I'd collected them all and taken them in and it was so much trouble to get them in the shelter when the siren went that I eventually stopped going. We all stayed. 'If you lot die,' I said, 'I may as well too.'

They mostly didn't bother at the sound of the siren or the sound of bombs exploding nearby, but Captain Flint would sometimes get all het up and flap about making a hideous noise, which made Groo shake with nerves and caused Billy Bones to join in with the flapping and skittering. CP would just sit and snore, adjusting to the war noise better than any of the city animals.

I wrote to Angel and told her about Captain Flint and Miss Campbell's Betty, but I didn't tell her I didn't go to the shelter anymore – I pretended they were good and obedient. She replied saying she looked forward to meeting them one day and told me she was happy because Ann and Bill were going to adopt her. That made me feel sad, even though I should have been happy for her, so I didn't write to her for a few days.

I just got on with looking after my family. Groo became attached to CP. She'd groom him like she used to do with

Devil, except CP didn't mind at all. She'd follow him around and soon she was riding on his back, lying stretched out, like she was trying to get her legs all the way round him in a big hug. I saw her riding backwards once; she watched CP's curly tail jiggling and swiped at it.

'Claws in!' I warned her, but I didn't need to. If she hurt CP at all, he'd snort and roll over and she'd leap off before he crushed her. She'd meow at me, all put out, when it was her own stupid fault.

Sometimes the chickens ran through the house, shitting everywhere, and I'd chase after them and curse them and tell them, 'Do your pooping outside, ya vagrants! This is a respectable household! Here I am looking after the house all alone, and there you are pooping on the upholstery.' That's what I said to those chickens, and I'd chase them and they'd flap and cluck and not give a care. Groo would ignore the chickens, turn her back on them like they weren't even there, like they were beneath her. She only had eyes for CP.

Then CP went and vanished. Now ma was gone I thought it was safe to leave CP in the garden, snuffling and rolling in the mud, but he went and vanished. My comrade, my friend for life, he was gone, throat slit for sure, bubbling away in someone's stew, in someone's bloated belly.

'I tried to look after him, mister,' I said, thinking of our kindly stranger who liked pigs. 'I tried. But there's a war on, and people get nasty in a war, mister. They steal your best friend and boil them in a pot. That's the war for you, mister sir. That's the bleedin' war for you.'

We held a ceremony in memory of Corporal Pig, Comrade in Weary Walking, Friend for Life. Queen Isabella, Amelia and Scholler came along, and I could tell they could tell I was really grieving for that old CP so they didn't give me any trouble. Queen Isabella said, 'We're sorry about your hideous beast,' and I know she was trying her best so I just nodded and let them stay. I gave a speech and put a stake in the ground, tying a plaque to it that read 'Here does not lieth Comrade in Weary Walking,

Corporal Pig, Friend in the Highest Esteem, for he lieth in the belly of a bloated son of a whore. A salute to Corporal Pig, the finest friend for life, may the lizards below keep thee and curse the bloated belly of the murderous bastard. Salute!'

Groo wailed and wailed after CP vanished, and I cried with her and I said, 'I'm sorry, Groo, I'm sorry I didn't look after your comrade. And I'm sorry I let Devil die. I'm sorry,' and she wailed and wailed and started chewing on my hair again.

From then on I looked at my neighbours with suspicion, checking their bellies, looking to see if they'd gotten suddenly fatter. 'Good morning, Goblin!' they'd say. 'What's good about it?' I'd say and walk on, eyeing their bellies.

From then on the chickens were only allowed out when I was there. All the animals lived in the house with me and they pooped wherever they pleased.

I wanted to ask Angel to come, but I didn't. I wanted to tell her about CP, but I didn't because she'd only worry, so I wrote to her and said everyone was happy and everything was fine.

London, April 1941

Trundling and bumping and falling at times, Monsta and I.

I'd made a scooter from wood, scraps here and there, and it was rickety and squint. Still early, still quiet, people stooped and tired, bending to the rubble, searching and searching and finding crushed food and clothes and toys and photos and bodies and parts of bodies and burnt up bodies that didn't look like anything at all. We flew through the streets, turning and feinting, once here, once there, avoiding rubble and people and holes but a brick we hit and over we go, Monsta and I, head over heels in the air. Oi kid! Stop messing and help, don't you know there's a war on? Let the kid play leave him be, it's good to see them play. Bleedin' kids think it's all a game, eh?

I lay in the rubble and stared and blinked. There was a hand on the ground; roughly severed, bone protruding, two fingers broken, twisted back.

I pulled myself from the rubble, hunkered down and inspected it. I placed my hand on the ground next to it and saw how small my hand was. I crawled my hand over the rubble and onto the hand and I felt it. It was cold and hard, like plastic. I turned it over. The palm was blackened. The fingertips were torn. I pulled off a dangling shred of skin. I took the hand. I locked my fingers between its fingers and I took it, I picked it up and shoved it in my waistband, tying my string belt tight so it stayed put so it was hidden so the man couldn't see I had treasure. The treasure was mine. Cold and plastic, it's mine.

I picked up my scooter. It was still working, but scratched and squint, so I had to work out all over again how to ride and not fall head over heels, and off I went home with Monsta and treasure. On our way I saw a bunch of kids crowded round a water tank.

'What's all the fuss about?' I said, pushing my way in. 'What's all the fuss?'

This little runt of a kid, even runtier than me, he said, 'There's a body in the tank.'

I looked down at the kid, all aloof, rolling my eyes, and I said, 'Kid, there's dead bodies everywhere.'

I pushed in further to have a look, just to see the kid wasn't lying, and there it was – the truth of it – a girl, a dirty white dress face down just floating, a tiny thing, her dirty blond hair all raggedy and tangled floating out like a messed up halo, a dirty little holy girl with no shoes and sores on her feet and bruises on her legs and a homemade boat bobbing through her tangled hair. I stepped away and said, 'What's all the fuss? Dead bodies everywhere.'

I pulled the severed hand out from my waistband and said to the crowd of kids, 'But this, this is special.'

They gathered round me, forgetting the girl in the tank as I held the hand aloft and said it would cost them if they wanted to feel it and hold it.

'This is the hand of a monster. Look at the black skin, black as night, and there's flaps of skin hanging off the fingertips. When the monster was alive, the skin would open up and it would ooze poison. The monster would grab you and put poison in your body, in your blood, and you'd die and it would eat you but maybe it would eat you even before the poison made you die, it'd eat you alive.'

Some of the kids made noises of disgust, others pushed in and said, 'Let's see it then, let's see the monster hand.'

'You can touch it, you can feel it,' I said, 'and I'll tell you the terrible story…' and I filled my pockets full of coins, buttons, and battered sweets, until along came Doris who clipped me round the ear. Old Doris was so enraged she couldn't get out any words, her face just puffed up as she hit me round the side of the head, snatching the hand from my hand.

She held it, her rage turning to disgust and she let out a startled yelp, dropping the hand at her feet. It rocked for a moment, like an upturned crab. The kids all scattered and before I could run off, Doris had me by the arm, pinching, hitting at my head again, my ears ringing.

Old Doris was a tank. She always could give a good hiding. She'd beat off the Germans single-handed, I thought to myself. She'd beat them off even if she had her hands all cut off. She pinched harder and I squinted at Monsta who lay fallen next to the hand.

'Don't you know there's a war on?' she said, pulling at me by the ear, forcing me to look at her big tank of a face. 'Have some respect.'

She let me go and I dropped to the ground next to Monsta, who swayed, unconcerned.

'I can't count,' I said to Monsta, 'how many times people have said to me, "Don't you know there's a bleedin' war on?"'

'What's that?' Doris said. 'You giving me cheek?'

'I said I know there's a war on.'

'You don't act like it. You get home and you behave like a proper girl, you hear me? You wait till I see your mother.'

'Yeah, I'll wait, you can wait, we all can wait.'

She leaned down, her big face right at mine.

'You've always been an oddball. You know that?'

'I know, I know, of course I know, we all know, and doncha know? There's a bleedin' war on. We all know.'

'Get!' she said, and I pulled myself up, grabbing Monsta, grabbing at the hand. I scrambled over to the water tank, where I'd dropped my scooter but it was gone, one of the kids had taken it, so I was running instead, running like I had an incendiary up my arse.

'I know where you live!' old Doris yelled after me. 'I'll be having a word with your mum, you devil!'

'No Devils here,' I said to Monsta, and I ran and ran until we got to our house and I collapsed at the door, the money and buttons and sweets weighing heavy in my pockets and I thought of the number of times people have said to me, you're an oddball, you're a strange one, you really are a queer one, the number of times I've lost count and I said, breathing heavy, 'Monsta, we don't belong here. I don't know where we belong, but not here.'

I crawled my way into the house and turned my pockets inside out and out sprayed all the treasure. I rummaged through it. I thought of old Doris and her threats and I thought, I'm free as a bird, with no parents to tell anything to. I'm free as a bird and who cares about that old tank Doris.

I hadn't eaten all day, except some bread at breakfast and my stomach growled like a monster.

'I could eat the whole of London, Monsta, I truly could,' I said, looking at my treasure. 'But sweets won't do it, I'll make us a feast to end all feasts!'

I made us all dinner, me and Monsta, Groo, Billy Bones, Dr Kemp, and Captain Flint. Monsta and I had boiled potatoes, corned beef and some cheese, which we shared with Groo. I gave the chickens lettuce and cereal. Captain Flint had some of the corned beef and a bit of apple too, but he was mostly good at catching his own dinner – worms and insects from the garden – so I usually only fed him as a treat. We feasted like kings that night, sick and fat and roly-poly with our dinner in our bellies, like big fat barrage balloon slug-kings.

'Ugh, I'm stuffed. I'm full to popping.'

I slapped my belly and you could still see my ribs from when I travelled back from the sea.

★

The next morning I got on with making a new scooter and took the hand to Kensal Green Cemetery. I took it there to bury it and on my way I stopped and charged all the kids for a look making sure I kept a hold of my scooter to scooter away if trouble was in sight. The older kids, the ones I couldn't pummel, they looked at me all squint-eyed oi boy whatcha doin? and I got on my scooter with my pockets full of treasure and went to the in-between realm where I dug a hole for the hand.

I put some pennies on the hand and said our lizard who art in the darkness below hallowed be thy name consecrate this hand unto the earth and may it rest in peace, amen.

I got more food in, but this time I was careful. I kept some locked away instead of having a feast and being fat like a slug on the floor and we, me and Monsta and the rest of the family, we ate together every day, just us, until the police came and they said about the river. It was finished. Our life in this house was over. No more just me and the animal family. Our lizards who art in the darkness below why hast thou forsaken me? Boy, they said. Boy? You hear what I'm saying? It must be a shock, but we can help. Hallowed be thy name, hallowed be thy name. Boy, it's going to be alright. Can you hear me? It's going to be alright. But it wasn't. They were going to take me away.

Chapter 8

'We're dealing with the riots. Hundreds of arrests. Are you hearing me? Your case will have to wait.'

'It waited this long. What does it matter?'

'Don't disappear on me. Stay in London and I'll be in touch. This is murder we're talking about, however long ago. We're taking this very seriously.'

'I won't disappear. I'm here now. Queen Isabella won't let me go.'

'Good. You catch up with your friends and I'll call you when all this is under control.'

'What did he say?' asks Isabella.

'He said it can wait.'

I call Ben. I'd asked him to stay at my flat and look after Mahler for me. I didn't want to bring Mahler to London. I wanted him to be safe, and he would be, at home with Ben.

'How are you?' I said. 'How's Mahler?'

'We're all good, old lady. Everything's fine. How's London?'

'On fire.'

'Ye better watch yersel. Keep safe.'

'I am safe.'

'Where ye staying?'

'Some cheap hotel. It's far away from the riots, so don't you worry. How's Mahler and Sam?'

'I cannae move right now, can I? Mahler is stretched out on my legs. Sam is snoring by the fire.'

'That's good, Ben. I'm glad Mahler has you.'

'Did ye see that Detective yet?'

'Not yet. He's busy with the riots.'

'He harasses ye and now he doesnae even want to speak to

ye?'

'I can wait. I hope you'll be alright looking after Mahler a bit longer.'

'Aye, he's nae bother. Though, I dinnae ken why ye didnae take him with ye.'

'I wanted him to be safe.'

'He's safe as can be, dinnae worry.'

'Good. What have you been up to, Ben? Are you still smelling books?'

'I don't do that anymore. I've gone back to reading – I've reached K.'

'What K book are you on?'

'*The Palace of Dreams* by Kadare. It's about some totalitarian government that monitors people's dreams. Just like living under a Tory surveillance state, eh?'

'It sounds good.'

'It is. I've had to read a lot of rubbish first, though.'

'Life's too short for bad books – why don't you skip them?'

'Then I wouldnae be reading from A to Z. It wouldnae be right.'

'I miss you, Ben,' I say.

'Are ye laughing at me, old lady?'

'Maybe. But I like your dedication.'

Ben doesn't reply.

'Ben? You still there?'

'Aye, sorry. I better go – Mahler's woken up and wants his walk. Not sure I can get Sam moving, though.'

'Give Mahler a hug for me.'

'Aye. And take care of yersel, mind. Dinnae go out in the streets.'

'I'm fine, Ben. You don't need to worry about me.'

★

CCTV, cameras, mobiles. Everything is recorded. News channel helicopters circle. Rioters and looters film each other.

I walk the streets and see the ghosts of the buildings that haunt this city. We erase the past and the present, but it all stays, hunkered down.

A car is crumpled beneath flames. A rioter stalks past, beer in one hand, a stick in the other, their face covered by a scarf, hood pulled over their head. Joining others outside a supermarket, they smash a window. I watch the glass cave in. They hop through the window and emerge with anything they can carry. In and out they go. Some stock up trolleys and wheel them off.

I once said to Ben, what would you do if these buildings disappeared? If they went up in flames? How would you feel? I'd dance in the flames, he said. I'd dance. So I close my eyes and I dance. 'Stay safe, old lady,' he said to me, but London burns and I sway, feeling the heat. When I open my eyes, I see the looters have joined my dance. Some dare each other, dancing close to the flames. I weave my way through them and walk away from the fire, my feet crunching on smashed glass.

Time has collapsed, and we are there and here. London is burning, the headlines scrolling in a flurried panic across the screen. BREAKING NEWS. A capitalist warzone of burning cars and stolen flat screen TVs.

The pet massacre has been wiped off the page of every newspaper. What does the past matter when London is in flames now?

London, April 1941

'It was an accident,' they said, 'we're sure it was an accident.' Sure, I thought, sure, we all know it wasn't any kind of accident. Ma was dead, drowned herself in the Thames. Ma was dead and I was gone. I didn't go with the policeman. I slipped through that door, jumped on my scooter and I was off. They weren't taking me to some orphanage. They weren't putting me on a train to the sea and the attic and the unholy bastards. I was my own person now and I had a family to look after. I waited, watching until they'd gone and I crept back and I gathered my family and blankets and food and off we went on the Underground to Kensal Green and our new home in the crypt.

'It's only temporary,' I said to them. 'It's only until the heat is off.'

Captain Flint sat on my shoulder. Groo prowled round the crypt, sniffing and peeing and scratching.

'Get!' I yelled, 'Don't go stinking up this crypt. Do your peeing outside.'

'Well, this is a fine situation.'

Queen Isabella, Amelia and Scholler were standing at the entrance, looking down on us all.

'Yes,' said Amelia, 'a fine situation.'

'Don't you two start. I'm doing the best I can.'

'It's the orphanage for you,' said Amelia, looking very smug indeed.

'No, Miss Amelia, I'm not going to some orphanage to be murdered by the likes of you,' I said, collecting some leaves for the chickens, 'I'll get our house back. I will.'

'We'll see,' said Amelia.

'Come,' said Queen Isabella, 'I can't stand the stink of these beasts.'

'A lot of good you lot are,' I said, watching them walk off amongst the gravestones.

I got some more leaves and put them in the corner and the chickens scratched around and clucked and seemed content, but then Dr Kemp started pecking at Billy Bones. That Dr Kemp would peck Billy Bones' feathers right out so that he'd be all patchy and his arse was as naked as could be. That naked chicken arse looked like a chicken arse you'd eat, just like you'd get from the butchers, except this chicken was walking around and if you so much as tried to shove it in the oven for the Sunday roast it would peck your eyes out for certain. It made me think of Cornwall and that old Wendy who really did have a face like a chicken arse and I started to think about that and about Angel and the sea. I wrote to her and told her all my woes, but I didn't send it. I read it over then ripped it up. I was going to write to her after she told me Ann and Bill were adopting her but I didn't and she sent me another postcard saying she'd made a friend, one of the town kids. She said I'd like him, he was almost as crazy as me. I didn't reply. The next few postcards she was more worried and I liked making her worry, making her wait. And anyway, I had more important things to think about, I had problems to solve; a home to get back and a stressed out chicken I needed to keep from bullying Mr Bones.

I went back to the neighbourhood every day, keeping an eye on the house. The policemen returned, looked round the house and talked to some neighbours. No house, and ma's money was running out. We'd no longer have rations for a whole family. We'd starve, we'd die from cold.

I went back to the family and we discussed our situation and I said, 'Chickens, you've got to earn your keep.'

Not long after CP disappeared, I trained the chickens to come when I called to make sure I could keep them from danger. I pretended they were my crew on the good ship Goblin. I'd call 'Crew!' and shake their food and they'd come running. I decided to see if they'd still come if I only called and didn't shake any food for them and they did but they'd fuss and cluck around me, expectant. When I saw how they thought the word crew meant they'd get food I decided to see if I could teach them tricks.

I held an old walking stick horizontal just above the ground and in the other hand I held their food. If they sidled round the stick to get to the food I wouldn't give them anything. If they jumped the stick I made a clicking noise with my tongue and gave them a reward. They were clever those chickens, they caught on pretty quickly. I raised the stick higher and higher until I thought it looked impressive enough. I worked with them every day, trying out different ideas.

'We'll be an Underground hit, me and my chicken crew,' I said to Groo, who yawned at me. 'We'll be a sensation!'

Off we went, busking on the Underground, collecting pennies. We always went to the same station, taking the same route every day. We'd get funny looks from people but I'd pretend like I didn't notice, nose in air, marching along, calling 'Crew!' if they stopped to gobble some insects or roll about in the dust. And off we'd march, people turning to look at us, laughing and calling me Chicken Boy.

We soon had regulars watching our show at the station, laughing and clapping, oohing and aahing when the chickens jumped the stick or jumped through a hoop. I took my scooter apart, leaving only the board with the wheels and tied on a bit of string. When I called Billy Bones he'd jump on the board and when I clicked my fingers Dr Kemp picked up the string in his beak and pulled Billy along the platform. I got cheers and laughter for that one and the chickens got their treats as I was showered with pennies. I worried I might have some trouble with chicken stealers but the regulars soon saw to anyone who tried it on.

'We're the breadwinners now,' I said to the chicken crew, pouring the coins onto the floor of our crypt. 'Now I need to figure out how to get our house back.'

*

I went back to our neighbourhood with Monsta every day, leaving the rest of the family in the cemetery. On this day, I stood at Miss Campbell's gate, all lost in my head, staring at my house. I didn't know what good just staring at it would do, but that's what I did, keeping my distance in case the police came back. I was all lost in my head and almost fell in the road with fright when Miss Campbell shouted, 'Goblin!' I dropped Monsta who looked all put out and was moody the rest of the day, but it turned out to be a good thing me loitering at Miss Campbell's. I'd forgotten about poor Betty what with all the troubles I'd been having and I thought Miss Campbell would be mighty mad but she wasn't, she was just glad I was alright because the police had been round all the neighbours and she thought something had happened to me. Betty came ambling out the door, but when she saw me she trundled down the path and I bent down and she barked in my face and slobbered all over me her tail going like crazy. I ruffled her head and told her I was sorry and I told Miss Campbell my story of woe and tribulations, telling her that no way was I going to an orphanage and losing my family and who would walk Betty, miss? Who? Miss Campbell eyed me for a bit before saying, 'Don't you worry, Goblin. I'll get the authorities off your back.'

'You serious, miss?'

'I am.'

'Why would you do that, miss?'

'I'll be straight with you,' she said, 'I don't like kids and I don't much like adults either.'

'I know,' I said, 'Ma said you were gonna die a withered old maid.'

'She did, did she?'

'Yeah, but what did she know?'

'She's probably right. I like to keep to my own company, but you're different.'

'That'll be cos I'm part-goblin, miss.'

'Even so,' she said, 'I don't want responsibility for any children, part-goblin or not. But we can help each other out, can't we?'

'Sure, miss.'

'You can move back to your home with your family and as well as walking old Betty you can do some chores for me, you can get in the food so I don't have to waste my free time standing in queues for hours. I'll pay you, Goblin, and you can come round here for your dinner now and then.'

'So you'll get the authorities off my back, miss?'

'Just leave it all to me, Goblin.'

'Hail the lizards!' I said to Monsta as I skipped back along the street, back to Kensal Green Cemetery to tell the family the good news. I couldn't wait to rub it in that Amelia's smug face.

Miss Campbell told the authorities she'd be my guardian and that a relative would come over from the U.S. to look after me in a few months. So we all moved back home and every day I walked old Betty and did some chores and Miss Campbell paid me. She had me over for dinner sometimes but she was so busy working I didn't see her all that often. The money she gave me helped feed the family, and I thought I could do chores for the whole neighbourhood as well as fix anything that needed fixing and that way I could pay the rent when old Martha's son came to sort out her affairs.

The family was happy and me and Monsta, we were busy – we became death-defiers, animal rescuers. At night we'd scooter round the city watching the parachute flares glowing all amber and green, casting spooky colours and shadows across the buildings. Ping ping ping, incendiaries littered the road, fizzing and sparking, lighting up Monsta all strange with their green-white flames.

'The Martians are here,' I said to Monsta, sure that I saw their giant insect legs pick their way through the streets, slicing through the smoke and dust. I put on my gas mask and walked through the devastation, Monsta clinging to my neck, peering over my shoulder. Flames erupted amongst the rubble and I skipped between them, watching the insect-Martian disappear to the sound of a distant explosion. People were scattered around the street, plunging their stirrup pumps into buckets, drenching the bombs. I got water from tanks for people who were having a hard time of it, fetching and carrying until those demons were dead then off we'd go, scootering round the street looking for animals. Monsta and I, we'd sneak sneak sneak round the ARP wardens and cordoned off bomb-filled streets picking up any pets we could find, searching for hours, peering in windows, breaking into houses, picking them up right off the street, chasing them, coaxing them if they weren't of the disposition that would make them so inclined to come near us pet-napping bomb-defiers. We'd make trip upon trip upon sneaky trip in and out of the danger zone with cats, dogs, rabbits and birds.

We rescued as many as we could. It was our job, me and Monsta, and we worked round the clock.

Sneaking done and dusted our work was still tick-tock tick-tock all hours, feeding, rehoming, taking them to the vet and I couldn't even pay the bills. I couldn't trust those vets, those no-money-no-way vets who would 'dispose' of my rescued pets. I found a vet I could trust with their lives and who would patch up any old beast for me but then the family got too big and chaotic and there was a complete lack of harmonious niceties when cats screeched and scratched and dogs chased the chickens. All this only went and caused more trips to the vets and a hardship of looking out and keeping them apart and inspecting every room and every creature and feeding them all and cleaning up shit and dirt and stink and there I was all collapsed exhausted, no longer able to stand up and call myself a bomb-defying rescuer, instead I was a shit-wallowing stinker.

I had to reduce the family, so I went on a mission, going round the neighbourhood to rehome them. I'd go round every room, inspecting as any good inspector would, making sure their home would suit the cat or the dog or the bird or the rabbit, and I rat-tat-rattled through my list of questions keeping the sharpest of eyes out for any suspicious motives.

'Sir,' I said to one shifty-looking neighbour, 'you thinking of boiling this dog in some stew? I can see it in your eyes – "this fella would be damn tasty with our potatoes." Don't lie to me, sir.'

I didn't have much time for the animal charities. I didn't like being ordered around and I didn't like how many animals they killed. Our Dumb Friends' League really got my goat.

'What's dumb about 'em?' I said to that trusty old vet. 'Humans are dumber if you ask me.'

'It's because they can't speak, Goblin,' he explained to me, like I was dumb.

'They can speak,' I said. 'They never shut up. I'm lucky if I get a good night's sleep. Just cos they can't talk English like we do, people think they're stupid.'

'Goblin, it's about their lack of voice. It's so that we have some compassion and speak up on their behalf.'

'What right do we have to speak for them? If I couldn't speak, I wouldn't want someone pretending to say things for me like they'd even know what I'd say without even asking.'

'You do it every day. You do exactly that.'

I scowled at him and said, 'I'm just trying to give them a good life.'

I couldn't take them home anymore. I couldn't keep them, my neighbours couldn't take them, the charity homes were all filled up. If they were injured I'd get the trusty vet to patch 'em up, feed 'em, then send them on their way. If they were uninjured I'd feed them and just let them be. The house was packed full and the ration books stretched as far as they'd go. I was twitchy as hell – there were fines for feeding animals food fit for human bellies, so I pretended like I had hardly any animals to anyone who asked. I'd keep them all in the house during the day, only letting them out in the garden at night so the neighbours wouldn't see how many I had. I told the neighbours I hardly had to feed those chickens at all, as they'd hoover up the garden insects and Groo caught mice and rats. Mostly the neighbours let me be, but I still worried I'd be reported to the authorities by some nosey busybody.

I had a veg patch in the garden to bring in extra food. It took a good few months, but I was proud as proud could be when it turned out so well I was able to sell some and I got more money to help look after the family.

But I was worried and I was tired.

★

I kept on busking with the chickens and one day a soldier came

156

up to me after our show and took hold of my hand. I frowned at him and was about to punch him when he pressed money into my hand and squeezed my fingers round it. He stood for a moment, just looking at me.

'Are you here every day?'

'Most days,' I said.

He let go of my hand and wandered off into the crowd. I opened my hand to find I was rich. 'Jesus,' I said, 'That'll feed us all for two weeks, maybe more. What's his game?'

There was no need for another show that day so I packed up. We needed a rest and it meant we could go home and be content and maybe practice a new routine for when we needed to get back to work. As I was packing some idiot tried to run off with Billy Bones, but she pecked the hell out of him and Dr Kemp got under his feet and flapped and screeched and I yelled 'Murder! Murder!' and everyone turned to see what was going on. When they saw what was happening they gave the thief a hard time and he ran off, embarrassed.

I was so angry and scared I was almost sick. We'd had people try to steal the chickens before, but this was the closest it came to losing one of them, and the thought of losing Billy Bones or Dr Kemp had me in a sweat, so I explained to them on the train home that our performance days were over.

'You'll stay at home,' I said, 'and I'll make my own routine. I'll be a clown, I'll use ma's old make-up and I'll make my own clothes, and you'll all be safe at home.'

That's what I did. I only went exploring with Monsta after that, and I let the chickens out into the garden at night so they could get their worms and all the neighbours were hidden away in their houses on account of the blackout so they wouldn't think to try and kidnap my family and put them in their bellies.

'You can't trust humans,' I said to the chickens. 'Apart from me, but I'm part-goblin so I don't count.' Then I thought of the man who'd given us all that money and I said to myself, 'What's his game?'

I thought how it would be good if I had a performance

partner, but I didn't have anyone. Miss Campbell wouldn't have time and I didn't think she'd want to anyway. I knew David would have done it, but he was gone. Maybe he'd gone to the sea like I had. Maybe he escaped to the sea and he was swimming with a girl just like I did, and maybe he'll come back just like I did. I had to earn money and feed the family and get money for rent if I ended up needing it, so that I can be here, waiting for David. If he were here I know for sure he'd come busking with me. But he wasn't here and I needed a partner in busking, and it was then I found the Lizard King.

★

'Get lost, ya wee cunt.'

A pale orb emerged from the darkness. It moved closer and I raised my torch, the features falling into place. His skin was white. His lips were shrivelled, dry and cracking. I expected his lizard tongue to flick out and taste me. His eyes were as black as the tunnel. Silver rivulets were painted on his cheeks, flowing from his eyes down to his neck. They shimmered in the torchlight.

'Hail thee, O Lizard King.'

I prostrated myself before him.

'This is ma spot, ya wee cunt.'

I looked up, squinting. His face was right next to mine, the stench of his breath intolerable.

'I dinnae ken what yer game is, but ye can get!'

'Mr Lizard King, sir, I've come to live with the lizard people.'

He snatched my torch and shone it in my face.

'I remember you,' he said. 'Used to run wild, you and two others. Right little cunts ya were.'

I shielded my eyes from the light and sat up.

'Mr Fenwick?'

'Ye cannae live wi me. This is ma spot. Where's yer ma and pa?'

'Gone.'

'That right?'

I'd heard about what happened to Mr Fenwick from Miss Campbell. He was too old to serve, so he stayed living on our street but he'd been bombed out, his face scarred by the blast so he looked just like the Lizard King who'd lost his queen and cried tears of acid that burned away his skin.

'I have Groo,' I said.

'Eh?'

'Your cat.'

'Issatright? She still alive? Wily wee thing.'

'She misses Devil and Corporal Pig, but I look after her. She chews on my hair.'

'She always wis an odd one. I expect ma chickens are long gone by now.'

'They're alive and well, Mr Fenwick, sir. They live with me.'

'Ye 'ave a habit of kidnapping people's animals?'

'They were on their own. I rescued them and they're my family now.'

'Family, eh? They'd be better off in your belly. Or in mine.'

'They're not going in anyone's belly. I'm looking after them and I'll guard them with my life.'

He eyed me.

'Aye, well, ye better be getting back to 'em then.'

I looked round and said, 'What you doing down here in the tunnels, Mr Fenwick?'

'It's ma home.'

'You seen any lizard people?'

He pushed me and said, 'Get lost like I told ye.'

'I brought you offerings,' I said.

'What's that?'

'Offerings... for the Lizard King. You may as well have 'em.'

I poured the offerings on the ground and he rummaged through them. He sat chewing on some bread. I took my torch back and looked around. It was a dump. Junk everywhere, and a makeshift bed.

'I'm the Lizard King,' he said. I shone the torch in his eyes.

'And we dinnae like light,' he said, putting his arm across his face.

I lowered the torch.

'You're no Lizard King. You're just Mr Fenwick.'

'That's ma pseudonym, lad. No one wants tae think their neighbour's a lizard person, eh?'

I shook my head.

'I accept yer offering,' he said, sweeping all the food into an old box by his bed. 'But what Lizard Kings really like is cigarettes. Ye can get some of those, can't ye?'

'Uh-huh.'

'Get, then. I'll see ye the morn.'

I made my way out of the tunnels, Queen Isabella, Amelia and Scholler guiding me back.

'That man was definitely not a king,' said Isabella. 'There isn't an ounce of royal blood in him, lizard or not.'

'I know,' I said, 'it was just Mr Fenwick, but—'

But he could be the Lizard King if I wanted him to be. He could be my partner in busking: The Lizard King and Goblin of the Realm Below. We'd dazzle the crowds, that was certain.

*

He mostly said nothing. I'd give him food and cigarettes and he'd eat and smoke and shoo me out with a gesture, but I'd stay and talk and tell him my plans for us both.

'I like your face,' I said one time. He looked like he would stab me with his fork but he kept eating and I kept talking. I told him who he was. I knew what I was doing – seducing him with a new identity, a new way of being in the realm above.

'I'm Goblin-runt born blue,' I said. 'And you're the Lizard King. You cried tears of acid for your loved one who died in the realm above and now you hide away, but I'll take you above and tell your story. People will love your story,' I said. 'I'll paint you green and people will love you. I'll tell your story and people will love me. We'll make a fortune.'

He chewed and he smoked, not even looking at me.

'A fortune?' he said.

'We'll dazzle 'em!'

★

We were an instant hit.

Sitting underground, piled on top of each other, both scared and bored all at once, everyone appreciated a distraction.

'Roll up! Roll up!' I yelled, 'Come see the tragic Lizard King of the Realm Below.'

In my da's old coat I was disappeared but for my fingertips and my monster head made out of bits cut from ma's nightdress. I'd cut out holes for my eyes but they were squint, my face all lopsided with a huge clown grin scrawled across with lipstick. My short hair stuck out all angles in-between the bits of bunched up wool I'd tied into it and all the Lizard King had to say was that we were supposed to be entertaining people not scaring the holy bejeesus out of them. What do you know, Lizard King old man all hiding in your cave? I clutched a stick, holding it aloft, shuffling toward him all clumsy in da's old shoes. I'd tied Monsta to the stick, my trusty companion in entertainment. I'm being *mysterious*, I said to that Lizard King. People will be all interested in us in their curiosity. Lizard King stood looking uncomfortable in a smart-as-can-be dinner jacket I scavenged from a bombsite, his face all painted green apart from his scars. He nudged me out the way and looked in the mirror.

'We look a right coupla cunts.'

'We'll be an instant hit,' I said and handed him the mask I'd made him.

We were already in the Underground as the bombs fell and the crowds gathered.

'Roll up! Roll up!'

People shuffled over, gathering round, mumbling grumbling, what's all this then what's he supposed to be some sort of clown you from the circus let's see a trick then!

'I'll tell you a story,' I said. 'The tragic true story of the Lizard King.'

What'd he say a story about the king sshh!

'Underground,' I said, pausing, 'underground is where the lizard people live.'

Lizard people what a loada bollocks shut up let 'im tell the damn story will ya.

'Underground is where the Lizard King lives and he shoots poison from his eyes. There was one time he cried when he was in human form and his skin peeled away as if burned by acid.'

I dragged my fingers down my masked face.

What kinda story is this lizards and poison nonsense he'll scare the wee uns shut up I wanna hear the rest shut up will you?

'When it healed, he had silver scars from his eyes to the corners of his mouth, to his chin. Half of his lower lip was burned away.'

What made the Lizard King cry yeah why'd the sissy lizard cry anyway shut up sshh!

'The Lizard King cried because of the Lizard Queen.'

It's always some woman's fault hahaa yeah shut up already or I'll shut you up.

'The Lizard Queen had gone to the Realm Above, the realm where you and I live and work and play. The lizard people can take on human form and walk amongst us.'

My landlord's a lizard person that's for sure ssh! all cold hearted shut up as cold as can be shh let her finish!

'The Lizard Queen was in the Realm Above and a human man fell in love with her. He kept her in the Realm Above beyond the witching hour and she became trapped in human form. She could no longer descend to the Realm Below. The only signs left she was a lizard person were her red glinting eyes and her shimmering skin. When people saw her they thought her eyes and skin were made of jewels and they turned mad with greed. They thought if they plucked out her eyes and picked the jewels from her skin they'd be rich. So they plucked out her eyes but they were only eyes and they ripped at her shimmering skin but it was only skin. The Lizard King came to the Realm Above to search for his queen and that was the one time the Lizard King cried. He hunted down every person responsible for the Lizard Queen's death and he plucked out their eyes the way they'd plucked out hers and he skinned them alive the way they'd skinned her. From each person he kept a token and he strung the body parts in his palace and lived the rest of his days in mourning.'

Throat clearing and shuffling and grumbling and what kind of story is that horrible disgusting it's a parable like Jesus tells what does it mean it means don't be a greedy bastard doesn't mean nuthin pile of nonsense thought he was a clown do some tricks it means don't steal people's eyes that's the moral of the story don't steal no no no it's don't judge by appearances don't covet someone else's Lizard Queen do some tricks make us laugh what kinda clown are you anyway?

'This,' I said, talking over them, 'This is the Lizard King.'

What was that what'd he say shut up I can't hear he said that's the Lizard King.

'This,' I said again, 'is the Lizard King.'

They all turned and stared at old Mr Fenwick who'd been all hunched up swamped by the dinner jacket, hidden by the mask. He stood up all tall and slowly slowly slowly just like we practiced raised his hand to the mask and now no one was talking you could hear the bombs dropping ping ping up above all held their breath as his bony green hand clasped at the mask and slowly slowly slowly just like we'd practiced he lowered it. His eyes were closed. I'd painted red lizard eyes on his eyelids, the rest of his face painted green but the scars, the silver-red scars weaving down his face from his eyes like tears. There was a collective intake of breath from the crowd.

My god it's true a lizard he's scarred look he's scarred from his tears half lizard half human it's true my god don't be silly it's a story he cried for his loved one it's sad so sad just a story a good story it is poor old lizard man.

People jostled, trying to see.

What happened what really happened that poor man daddy is his skin really green it's just a story am I a lizard mummy I want to be a lizard.

'Ladies and gentleman! We are the Lizard King and Goblin of the Realm Below, and we thank you!' We both bowed, and I took my gas mask through the crowd, seeking pennies, sweets, and cigarettes.

I was proud of our success so I wrote to Angel to tell her all about it. She'd sent a few more postcards asking for news, worried I'd been hurt in the bombs, so I finally told her I was okay, just busy because I'd met the Lizard King and we were professional performers now, doing lots of shows, bringing in the money for my family. I didn't hear back for a while, then she wrote that she was glad I was happy and she was happy too and she'd been going to the beach with her boyfriend and swimming in the sea with him all summer. I read it over and over before dropping it in the rubbish. I tore up all her other postcards and punched and kicked the wall, frightening Billy Bones who'd been scratching around in the leaves I'd collected for the chickens. He clucked and ran into the hallway and I collapsed into the leaves and stared at my scuffed knuckles. Angel wrote to me twice after that, but I didn't read her postcards. I never wrote to her again.

The Lizard King and I passed the weeks of the war travelling the Underground, performing, telling stories. I'd tell the tragic story of the Lizard King over and over, changing things here and there, more dramatic, less dramatic, sad, gruesome, even more gruesome until mums complained and clasped their hands over the ears of their children. I told the stories of Queen Isabella (who puffed her bloody chest out with pride), Scholler and Amelia. I told them of the kraken who eats the sun and the Crazy Old Pigeon Woman who kept birds in her hair.

That's when our lives changed, that's when my future was written; my future in lights. It was all mapped out. I saw the soldier who'd given me money and made me rich for two weeks,

I saw him in the crowd many times until one day he came up to us and said, 'How would you like to join the circus?'

London, 5 September 2011

Alone in my hotel room, shut in, writing, missing home. I miss Mahler's smell and his huffy noises as he sleeps, the way he sits by the fire with his paws in the air, his belly exposed.

'Ben?'

'Morning, old lady.'

'I miss you, Ben. And I miss Mahler, the feel of his fur and his smell.'

'Aye, but I bet ye dinnae miss his farts. They're lethal.'

I laugh.

'I even miss that.'

'Ye all homesick, old lady? Ye got anyone there? Old friends or something?'

I eye Isabella, Amelia, Scholler and spectre-Monsta.

'I do,' I say.

But they don't smell of anything.

'But it's not the same.'

'Ye seen the Detective yet? Once yev seen him ye can come back home, right?'

'I don't think it'll be that simple.'

'We could come visit.'

'No. It's not safe to bring Mahler here.'

'The riots are over.'

'I just think he's better off at home with you. And I'm doing okay. My friends here aren't so bad.'

Isabella harrumphs.

'Not so bad? Did you hear that, Amelia?'

'I did.'

'Ssh!' I say, covering the mouthpiece. 'You know I love you, you uppity queen.'

'Old lady? You there?'

'I'm here, sorry.'

'Still writing?'

'I am. About my new dad when he rescued me. Him and Mad. They took in me and the Lizard King and—'

'Lizard people again, eh?'

'That's what I called him, that's all. They took us in, all of us. I was so happy then, Ben. You would have loved them, you really would.'

'I'm glad, old lady. Your other parents sounded like right cunts.'

'That's what the Lizard King used to call me.'

Ben grunts.

'He was just an old curmudgeon. He was alright. I better go, Ben. You give Mahler a kiss on the head for me.'

'That's minging.'

I laugh.

'A snuffle behind the ear, then.'

'Yer batshit, old lady. I'll think on it... I've kissed worse. Look after yersel and if ye need us, we'll come down, drop of a hat.'

Chapter 9

London, 16 March 1943

'I was down in the tunnels minding my own business, hiding this messed up face from the world, when this weecunt comes down and starts calling me Lizard King and bringing me offerings like I was some sort of god.'

'Is that right, Goblin?'

I nodded, blushing, letting my hair fall over my face. I'd let it grow out, just that bit longer than a bob. Mad was always getting at me to style it, but it was too much fuss and bother. She got me to wear some of her old dresses, though, as I'd grown out of my clothes. She showed me how to sew so I could take up the hem and take them in a bit. She said I looked pretty, but I thought I looked skinny and awkward, shifting around underneath this new feminine skin, not sure how to hold myself.

I fiddled with the hem of my dress where my sewing hadn't been so good and the thread was coming loose. The Lizard King pointed his cigarette at me, ash falling all over Adam the Flipper Boy who was sleeping on the floor with Groo on his chest. Adam was called Flipper Boy because he had no arms but he had hands that just kind of jutted out of his shoulders. He was a couple of years older than me and I had a crush on him. Seeing as he was asleep I took the opportunity to stare at him without him noticing and I thought about maybe asking him out.

'Aye, I feckin hate weeuns, the weecunts that they are.'

'I'm a grown-up now, LK,' I said, watching Groo rise and fall with the rhythm of Adam's breathing, 'I'm all grown up.'

'Issatright? Yer still runty ifyeaskme, eh?'

'I'm with you, Fenwick,' said Potato Pete. 'Kids get away

with murder these days.' We called him Potato Pete because he had a face just like the Ministry of Food's potato propaganda cartoon. I was sick of potatoes and I was sick of Potato Pete. All the while LK went on I manoeuvred myself so that I could tie Potato Pete's shoelaces together, aware I was confirming their opinion of me as an immature weecunt.

'So down she comes all the while, however much I tell 'er to feckrightoff, and she brings me 'er rations, eh? So I think I'm onto a good thing, getting free food, so I humour 'er, ken? And she spins this piece of nonsense story about how I got my scars and tells me this money making scheme idea, and like a fool I go along wi' it.'

Potato Pete tutted and I said, 'We were a success, LK.'

'Aye, well, if ye can call it that. It isnae my fault people are easily entertained, eh?'

Potato Pete snorted and I sidled away from him, my work done. Old Louise, who'd been reading a leaflet, said, 'Bloody conchies.'

'Eh?' said LK, 'What was that?'

'Bloody conchies and their protests. They handed me this.'

'What they protesting?'

'British internment camps.'

'German lovin' conchie bastards. Do they wanta be overrun by Nazi scum?'

'I wouldn't start on this,' said Adam, who wasn't asleep after all. He sat up, Groo tumbling onto the floor, and he cocked his head towards Matt. I didn't know what any of this had to do with Matt. I wondered if he was a conchie.

'Aye, well,' said LK. 'Jus' sayin', eh? Jus' sayin'.'

'My brother's a conchie,' I said. 'Sometimes,' I said. 'Sometimes a pacifist is a good thing. He's a good person. Sometimes that's just how it is.'

Old Louise, delight in her eyes, turned on me.

'You a pacifist?' old Louise said. 'You a coward?'

'No, ma'am! I'd shoot any Nazi who set foot on our shore.'

I meant it. I wanted to protect our British way of life, like all the papers said. I wanted to protect our existence in the flat with James and Mad and LK and the artists, the performers, and the writers who came and went.

'I'd shoot them dead,' I said. 'I'd shoot those Nazis dead.'

Old Louise laughed.

'I bet you would,' she said. 'But you won't have to. Our troops are leading us to victory, you mark my words.'

'I didn't know you had a brother,' said Adam.

'Uh-huh.'

'He in the army?'

'No, he went to the sea.'

'What sea?'

'The sea.'

'He a sailor?'

'He joined the pirates. He fights krakens. He married a mermaid.'

'How,' said LK, 'can he be a conchie bastard if he's a pirate and fights krakens?'

'He doesn't kill humans. Just krakens.'

'See what I mean,' said LK, gesturing with his cigarette, 'a weecunt.'

'And you're just a boring old fart,' I said.

LK doubled over coughing, spewing out smoke. There were snorts of laughter, some cheers and claps, and a chorus of 'Weecunt! Old fart! I'll drink to that,' and they did. They drank to anything. I looked round, embarrassed, not realising so many people had been listening. Adam winked at me and I blushed some more. The excitement died down, with only a few mumbles here and there as LK heaved in air.

I saw something was going on at the other side of the room; a raised voice and a knocked over chair. Fights were always breaking out, so I wasn't much surprised. I saw it was Matt causing the fuss. He was crying. James took a hold of him, almost forcing him into an embrace and that just made him shake and cry all the harder. I'd never seen a man cry before.

'What's up with Matt?' I asked.

'His friend,' said Adam. 'His friend was taken to an internment camp.'

'Ha! His friend. That's a way of putting it,' said LK.

'Why's he in a camp?'

'He's German,' said Adam.

'If ye ask me, all fruits should be locked up.'

'What's a fruit?'

LK was about to reply but Adam said, 'A German. That's all. He was German.'

'Good riddance to Germans,' I said. 'He's probably a Nazi spy, that'll be why he's locked up.'

'He killed himself,' said Adam, looking over at Matt.

'Who did?'

'The fruit,' said LK. 'Those perverts are better off dead if ye ask me.'

'Nobody asked you,' said Adam. 'No one fucking asked you.'

A hush fell over our small group and LK looked down at his hands, mumbling, glancing up at Adam who'd gone over to Matt, taking him out of James' embrace and leading him out of the room. I watched them walk off, worried I'd said the wrong thing and Adam would hate me for it.

'Dinnae ken what's wrong with 'im. There wis no need… No need. Only saying what should be plain to all, that's what. Only speaking ma mind.'

'I'm with you, old man,' said Potato Pete, raising a glass to him. 'Don't you worry.'

The music stopped and the lights went off. I thought there'd been a power cut but then I saw Mad standing in the doorway with a cake, the candlelight shimmering across her face. She sang happy birthday and the rest joined in, quietly at first as if they didn't want to drown out her beautiful voice, then they got louder. Arms fell across my shoulders, hands patted my back and ruffled my hair.

I didn't know this party was for me. I thought it was just another party, like all the others. No one had ever made me cake before and it must have taken a lot to pull together all those rations. I felt sick and pleased all at once.

Everyone cheered and Mad told me to make a wish, and I couldn't decide. I had a million wishes to make.

'World peace!' someone yelled, and it echoed through the room before LK damned them all with, 'Now who's a boring fart, eh? All of ye. World peace ferfecksake, we all know she's gonna wish to be a pirate or some such nonsense, eh ye weecunt?' They all laughed and yelled 'Pirate! Pirate!' as I wished for David back. I figured it was the same difference as wishing to be a pirate because David for certain was a pirate by now and he would make me a pirate and we'd sail the seas together and we'd find treasure and I'd marry a mermaid too. I pictured him in my head but he was fuzzy and black and white, smudged at the edges like the faded photograph I carried. I decided it didn't matter. He was a pirate now and he'd look different; swarthy and all muscle, wielding a sword. There he was, on his ship, in glorious technicolour.

I blew out the candles and Potato Pete stood up and fell on his face.

London, 1944 – 1945

People always came to the flat, hanging around, drinking, staying the night. I called them the Army Rejects because most of them were from the Freaks and Wonders troupe in the circus days and most of them had deformities. There was old Louise and her dwarf brass band; Betsy, Frank, Holly and Lester. Old Louise's singing was really something but their musical abilities were what old Louise described as 'Avant-garde, dahling,' and everyone else described as a godawful racket.

Then there was Lenny the Giant but I called him Lenny the Spider because his limbs were so long he looked like a spider, especially when he was sat down and he was all legs and arms. And there was Adeline and Ariadne, the beautiful conjoined twins. There was also Maisie. She had growths coming out either side of her neck. Adeline told me that they found Maisie in the street and she would charge people who wanted to touch her growths but when I flipped her a shilling and went and felt them she pushed me off and slapped me. The growths felt all rubbery and she was a snooty bitch so I told everyone she was a faker and that they were just glued on to make herself seem more interesting.

Then there was Adam. We hung around together and I eventually asked him out. He was telling me that when he was in the circus he wrapped his fingers up to make his hands more like flippers and he'd hide his legs and paint his whole body a silvery grey and during his act he would make seal noises and balance a ball on his nose. When he told me about painting his body I thought of him with nothing on but the paint and I went to my room and played with myself as I thought of painting him, stroking him slowly all over. It was after that I asked him if he would go with me, though it was a while before I saw him with nothing on. He was a good kisser and he taught me to play poker. He didn't have any parents either; they'd sold him to a sideshow in Brighton. The sideshow owners kept him locked in a cage until James rescued him. I heard the story from James, from Mad, from Adam and from anyone else who would tell it. Each time it was different.

'James broke in at night,' said old Louise, 'he was attacked by a monkey and poisoned by a snake but still he saved Flipper Boy, even while he fought off a ten foot giant.'

'It's true what old Louise said,' said Adam. 'I watched from my cage as he wrestled with that snake. He didn't have to fight off the giant, though. Lenny was a right softie, he only roared and beat his chest for the show. James had him in the palm of his hand the moment he walked in.'

'I'd heard about the boy locked up in the cage,' said James, 'so I paid the sideshow a visit and paid a hefty price for Adam. Lenny simply followed me, leaving of his own free will. That's all.'

'Don't listen to him,' said Frank, one of the dwarfs who played the tuba in the brass band. 'He's just down-playing it all because he doesn't want to get caught after stabbing the sideshow proprietor and stealing Adam. It was in all the papers.'

'James killed a man?'

'So they say.'

'Who's "they"?'

'The papers. He will have killed plenty more by now, eh, Goblin? But it's for King and country. God save the King.'

I asked Mad if James had killed a man but she just said, 'Don't listen to those gossip-mongers and storytellers, G. There's nothing controversial here apart from that bastard who locked up Adam.'

There were many stories like that; tales woven by so many different people that no one knew what was true anymore and the tales flowed when the wine flowed. People came and went, an old circus family stayed for months after being bombed out, others just dropped by, sleeping on the couch, in the bath, in the hallway. The circus men who weren't freaks were drafted. Everyone else worked, even the freaks.

'No one wanted us before,' said old Louise. 'But now there's a war on they can find work for us. Now there's a war on we're worth something.'

'Not me,' said Adam. 'I'm not worth anything.'

No one would give him a job – they just took one look at his hands and turned him away.

'You are worth something,' I said, 'They're just idiots.'

We retreated to my bedroom where I kicked out Holly and Lester who were sprawled out on my bed having some drunken conversation. Adam lay down on my bed and I curled up next to him, my leg over his, my arm around his waist. I burrowed my head into his neck, smelling and kissing him.

'You're my first girlfriend,' he said. 'Girls can't see past these. Not like you.'

I pulled back and looked at him for a moment.

'Why would I see past them?' I said.

I kissed him on the lips and pressed myself into him, rubbing myself against his thigh. I flicked my tongue out, like a lizard, tasting him. His tongue met mine and pushed into my mouth.

'Goblin!'

I jumped, pulling away from Adam.

'Goblin?' said Mad. She knocked on the door. 'You in there? You've not done your chores. The kitchen's a mess.'

I rolled my eyes at Adam and said, 'I'll do them later.'

'You said that yesterday. Now, Goblin.'

'Okay, okay. I'm coming.'

I kissed Adam and said, 'There's never any peace here.'

He came with me and helped with my chores. Old Louise was sat at the kitchen table, drinking beer and singing to herself. Adam and I swayed to the sound of her voice, bumping up against each other, giving each other love-eyes as we tidied and cleaned.

★

One morning after one of our parties I woke up with my stomach all cramped up and I thought I was dying, but then I bled from between my legs and I knew I was okay. When I felt the wetness I put my hand in my pants and my fingers came away bloody. I looked at myself in the bathroom mirror and smeared the blood across my cheeks like I was a warrior.

I went to my room and tore up an old shirt, stuffing it in my pants. I was worrying about what ma had said about the curse and having babies so I went to find Mad. She was having breakfast in the kitchen with old Louise. I sat down and helped myself to toast. Mad poured me some tea.

'What's that on your face?'

'The curse.'

'What?'

'The curse came.'

Mad and Louise looked at each other, eyebrows raised, then laughed. Old Louise had quite the cackle and Lizard King shouted through from the sitting room for her to keep it down.

'So you smeared it on your face?' said Mad.

I shrugged, looking from her to old Louise.

'It seemed the thing to do,' I said and stuffed the toast into my mouth.

'How old are you now, G?'

There was a pause as I chewed and old Louise said, 'She's a woman now.'

I shook my head and said 'Still a goblin. Always a goblin.'

'A fourteen-year-old goblin?' said Mad.

I nodded.

'You're growing up so fast.'

'Well,' said Louise, 'She might be growing up fast, but she's got a thing or two to learn.'

'Why'd you call it a curse?' asked Mad.

'That's what ma said it was.'

'It's not, G. And it's nothing to be ashamed of.' She looked at me a moment, then laughed. 'Though, I don't think you have a problem with that,' she said, gesturing to the stripes of blood across my cheeks. She offered me more toast and said, 'What do you know about it?'

'Not much. Ma said the blood makes babies.'

'Is that all?'

'Mostly,' I said.

'Do you know anything about sex?'

'A bit. I've done some things with Adam.'

'With Adam?' Mad's eyes widened. 'What things?'

'Just… You know, kissing.'

'Is that all?'

I nodded.

'But how do you think the blood makes babies? How do you think that all works?'

'Oh, please,' said Louise, 'are we getting all birds and the bees? It's too early for this.'

She stood up, shuffled over to the cupboard, pulled out a bottle of whisky and shuffled back to the table, grabbing two glasses on the way.

'Is it not too early for *that*, Louise?'

Old Louise ignored her and poured herself a glass. Mad placed her hand over the other glass and Louise snapped, 'It's not for you.'

'Louise!'

'It's to take the edge off for the poor girl.'

Louise poured the whisky and slammed the glass in front of me. Mad pursed her lips and shook her head at me.

'I can see you, you know.'

'She's my daughter, Louise.'

I was pleased that Mad called me her daughter.

'You don't have to drink that, G,' said Mad, pouring me more tea.

I sniffed the whisky, took a sip and screwed up my face.

'So what do you know? What did your ma tell you?'

'She just said babies came from the blood, so I thought that if you kept the blood in a jar and if you looked after it, kept it warm, a baby would grow, like a plant.'

Louise slammed her hand on the table, making me jump, and cackled.

'It's silly,' I said, blushing, looking from Mad to Louise and back. 'I was just a kid.'

Old Louise, slowing down to a chuckle, nodded at my whisky and said, 'Knock that back, child. You're going to need it.'

I did as Louise said, feeling it burn my tongue and throat and warm my belly. Mad whisked away my glass as old Louise tried to pour more. She lit a cigarette and said, 'I think that's kind of beautiful. Growing a baby in a jar of blood.'

'It's morbid is what it is,' said old Louise.

'I like it,' said Mad. 'It would make a good story.'

She got up and went to the stove to make more tea. When she sat down she explained it all to me. I'd pieced some of it together already but now it all made sense, no gaps for my imagination to fill. Mad even showed me how to use a condom and I was relieved I didn't have to have children. I didn't want them, ever.

'You might change your mind,' Mad said.

'I won't,' I said.

'Children are only trouble,' said old Louise.

Mad rolled her eyes at her.

'If there's anything you need, G,' said Mad, 'if you need to talk about anything, you come to me, okay?'

'Okay,' I said.

She stubbed out a cigarette and said, 'So you gonna wear your blood every month?'

I smiled and said, 'It'll be the new fashion.' I struck a pose, head tilted, hand under my chin. 'I'll be on the cover of Vogue. Lee Miller will take my picture.'

Mad laughed and old Louise grunted, frowning at me.

'You've got a lot to learn, child,' said old Louise.

'You said I was a woman.'

She shook her head dismissively.

'Better get on,' said Mad, standing up, 'my shift starts soon.'

She squeezed my shoulder as she walked past and suddenly it was just me and old Louise.

'You gonna wash that muck of your face?'

'It's not muck.'

'If you want to be a woman you need to act more ladylike.'

'I don't want to be a woman. I'm Goblin.'

'That so?'

'Through and through.'

'Mad and James have their work cut out with you, that's for certain.'

'Old Louise?'

'Enough with the "old".'

'Miss Louise, what happens if I like girls as well?'

'As well?'

'As well as boys.'

'You can't like both.'

'But I do like both,' I said.

'You can't. You'll find that out soon enough.'

She pushed her chair back and stood up, taking the bottle of whisky with her. As she went to the door she turned back to me.

'You be careful,' she said, wagging her finger at me. 'You be careful who you talk to about things like that.'

★

When James and any of the other men came back from leave there'd be a party. It would start off small but soon everyone would gather and the party could last for days. James let me drink beer. I remember the adverts in the papers: 'Guinness Is Good for You' with a smiley face on the beer foam. I liked the foam moustache it gave me. I liked the dreamy feeling and it wasn't as harsh as whisky. James wasn't so impressed when I had my first cigarette, though. I hung around with the clowns a lot, bugging them for stories, asking them to show me some of their routines, but when Marv gave me a cigarette James banned me from going near them anymore.

It wasn't just the circus crowd who came to the parties; there were writers, actors, singers and hangers-on. One of the hangers-on was some lord or other who was a patron of the circus. He'd come to the parties with his wife and he'd usually get thrown out for something. His wife would get drunk and follow me around, trying to fix me, telling me I was beautiful but, 'You should use make-up, brush your hair and wear a dress that fits for godsake.' I didn't know if I was beautiful or not and I didn't care either way and I told her that.

'You should, little Goblin. People love you if you're beautiful and you need to save all that love for when the beauty is gone.'

When I managed to shake her I came across Lord whatshisname kissing Betsy on the kitchen counter, his penis dangling out of his pants as he slobbered over her and told her how much he loved dwarves. Betsy just cackled and poured beer over his head. I felt bad for his wife after that but I didn't want to be her personal little Goblin to do up all pretty like a doll, so I avoided her if I could, even if I felt a bit bad about it.

Captain Flint loved the parties – he would perch on a lamp, observing, joining in any singing with some squawking while Groo slinked around looking for someone to sit on. Most of the animals wouldn't fit into the small flat and there was no garden so I spoke to Mad and James about rehoming the animals that weren't part of my immediate family. I'd cut down on my rescuing because I couldn't take any more creatures, but I still had three dogs, five cats and a rabbit, as well as Billy Bones, Dr Kemp, Groo and Captain Flint. I'd said the chickens had to stay but I knew I was being selfish what with there being no garden for them to rummage in and have dust baths. Mad and James said I should at least go and inspect Colin's place to see if they'd be happy there. Colin had looked after a lot of the animals in the circus, so he was sure to take care of them, but I was still all reluctant. I went round with my nose stuck up in the air as if his place wasn't any good at all, but the house and garden were big and I could see how happy the chickens would be. I questioned Colin like I'd questioned all of my neighbours but it was no good, he was perfect. I could tell he'd care for those chickens but I just said all haughty, 'We'll think about it.'

I gave him three of the cats and one of the dogs. I hadn't been as close to them, so I didn't mind as much as I would if he was to take my chicken crew. We rehomed the others no bother with more of Mad and James' friends. I eventually gave in on giving away the chickens when they pooped and scratched all over the flat and started pecking at each other, both showing off ugly bare arses.

I got on with Colin. He didn't say much, but he seemed interested in my stories and he was really good with all the animals, I could see that. He was only a few streets away so I visited all the time. I showed him the tricks I'd trained the chickens to do and he was impressed, saying I could help out when the circus started up again. I was proud as anything at that. He spoiled those chickens rotten and Dr Kemp lived to a ripe old age. But Billy Bones died in early '44. I buried Billy in Colin's garden and we had a funeral, just me, Colin and Dr Kemp.

It was just as well Billy Bones wasn't around on 6 June '44. He hated the sound of planes and would start plucking out his own feathers. 'You stupid chicken,' I'd say. 'Nobody wants to see that pink skin of yours. You peck yourself anymore and I'll put you straight in the oven.' But he wasn't there for me to tell off. I thought of him, though, as the planes roared overhead.

'We're going to destroy those Nazi bastards,' said old Louise, who was curled up on the couch under her tattered fur coat. 'Do you hear it? That's the sound of victory.' She sat up and swayed gently, humming along to the sound of the planes, humming along to the sound of victory and destruction.

There'd been a small party the night before and people had stayed behind; old Louise slept on the couch, Adeline and Ariadne shared Mad's bed, an old man I didn't know was on the floor in the sitting room, Betsy was in the bath using her coat as a blanket, and Adam had slept in my bed. LK was snoring away on his camp bed behind the couch; he'd moved in with me when James and Mad took me in and he never did much of anything other than drink and gossip with Potato Pete. He was oblivious to the roar of the planes, but everyone else had been woken by the noise and knew something was up. We had breakfast huddled round the wireless waiting for any news. When the news came that our troops had landed in Normandy, Mad sat nodding as everyone cheered and old Louise started up on the national anthem. LK's head bobbed up from behind the couch, grumbling at us to shut the hell up and get out of his bedroom but we hushed him and turned up the wireless. We didn't know if James was involved. He wasn't able to tell us where he was going to be stationed last time he left. We'd had a few letters, but they were all brief and he wasn't allowed to write much about the war.

Mad wandered off and came back with a bottle of sherry, doling it out to everyone. She gave me some too and I sipped it. She sat on James' chair, still in her nightdress, everyone else crumpled in yesterday's clothes, all of them bleary-eyed but with a glimmer of alert expectation.

People came and went throughout the day and by the evening the flat was packed with people, drinking and singing. I sat with a small group listening to the king on the wireless: '… none of us is too busy, too young, or too old, to play a part in the nation-wide vigil of prayer as the great crusade sets forth.' I prayed. I prayed like mad. O lizards down below I beseech thee, may the German bastards be destroyed, Holy Holy Holy, Amen.

★

James came back poisoned. A wound had become infected.

'He was lucky to survive,' Mad said.

He was poisoned in other ways, I thought. He wouldn't speak to me anymore. If I got under his feet, he'd snap at me. He was only on leave three days and him and Mad holed up in their room. I could hear them. LK would just look at me and roll his eyes and put a record on to drown them out. I listened at their door and got a clip round the ear from LK. 'Ya dirty weecunt,' he said, and dragged me away.

I was reading in the kitchen when Mad came out in her silk nightdress, her hair all a mess. I stared at her heavy breasts, the curve of her hips and her rippling muscles as she rummaged around the kitchen. She spent the mornings exercising to keep her pre-war circus fitness then spent the day hauling heavy equipment at the factory. Her thighs were solid muscle. Her body made me feel secure. I thought she was invincible. She rifled through the kitchen, a cigarette dangling from her lips, bouncing up and down as she mumbled to herself. She piled food onto plates, and shoved a beer under her arm, staggering back through with it all. The bottle slipped and rolled on the floor.

'Hey, G, get that will you?'

I scurried after her. James was lying naked on the bed. I

stared at him, putting the beer on the table. I stood, uncertain, just looking at his body. His penis was like a strange creature nestled amongst the dark hair that spread up to his belly button in a thin line. He was covered in fading bruises. The wound on his leg was still an angry red. I watched his muscles flex as he reached for the beer. He didn't look at me. It was as if I wasn't there. Mad dropped all the food in a heap on the table. He pulled her into bed and she half fell, half sat on top of him. She slid off him and curled up by his side, his arm around her. They shared the beer.

'Alright, Goblin,' she said, realising I was still there. 'Thanks.'

She gestured to the door and I left.

There were sudden outbreaks of yelling, something I'd never witnessed between them before. They'd tease each other, but never fight. This was new. LK shrugged as we heard furniture being upturned. James came out and a beer bottle came after him, just missing his head and smashing on the wall. He didn't even flinch. Groo scurried away, hiding under the table, and Captain Flint shrieked and didn't stop. James threw his clothes on, lit a cigarette, grabbed his jacket and left, leaving me to calm Flint and comfort Groo. James came back in the middle of the night and I couldn't sleep for the noise of them making up. In the morning he was gone and the house was quiet again.

I used to miss him when he left. It was a horrible ache that brought back nightmares about Devil, but this time I didn't have nightmares. I didn't miss him at all. It was as if he'd never been.

'He's poisoned,' I said.

'There's nothing wrong with him,' Mad said. 'Everything's going to be alright.'

When he came home next time, it was for good. He'd lost half of his left arm. He didn't speak to me, Mad, or the Lizard King. Mad and James didn't make love or fight. He was just silent. He drank his beer and smoked his cigarettes.

'He's going to be alright,' Mad said.

*

There was a small gathering in the sitting room; Colin, LK, Potato Pete and a few others. I was playing poker in the kitchen with Adam and the brass band dwarves when we heard a V1 buzzbomb. The V1 rockets got under your skin, a creeping fear. That moment you heard the buzzbomb buzz, you'd feel sick and pray to the lizards below it wasn't you it got. The V2s were different – they were silent and you didn't hear them until they hit and I decided that was better than the V1 fear.

When we heard the buzz we all froze, gripping the cards in our hands, silent, waiting. The buzz stopped, we counted, and I prayed like crazy to the lizards. When it hit, we dropped our cards, running outside. Four doors up, a building had been obliterated, now existing only as rubble, dust and flames. Smoke rolled down the street in slow motion waves. We pressed ourselves into doorways, holding handkerchiefs to our mouths. It rolled on by, like a monster in search of prey.

We formed a line, dousing the flames with the water from the tanks. Neighbours scrambled amongst the rubble, looking for survivors and pulling out bodies, parts of bodies, some crushed or charred, others looking like they were sleeping. We laid them out in the street and put sheets over them. As I stared down at the sheets, Mad grabbed me.

'You shouldn't be here,' she said, 'Get back to the flat.'

'I'm helping.'

'You don't need to see this. Get back home.'

'I've seen worse.'

She looked at me for a moment and said, 'Goblin, you go home. Now.'

I didn't argue. I went back to the flat to wait for them and found James sitting in the dark. All I saw was the light from his cigarette and my stomach tightened. When I turned the light on he said, 'Turn it off.'

I turned it off and said, 'I thought you were a demon.'

He didn't say anything.

I made my way to him in the dark and curled up next to him on the couch, my feet touching his thigh. I lay there, staring at the crackling light of the cigarette, drifting off to sleep.

When they returned to the flat it was close to dawn and everyone was blackened with dirt and dust and blood, stinking of smoke. James was gone, probably back in his room. He spent most of the day in there when Mad was at work.

A few people gathered in the sitting room, listening to a record, nursing a beer. I heard squealing and swearing coming from the bathroom so I went to see what was going on. The brass band dwarves, Adam, Adeline and Ariadne were all piled into the bath, yelling and splashing. Maisie looked on, disgusted. She reminded them of water rationing and poured her beer over them. There was more swearing and a scramble to get out of the bath, bodies falling to the floor, a scrummage for the towel. I helped Adam out of the bath and took him to my room, giving him some fresh clothes. I turned my back when he took off his wet clothes and he asked me, 'Why so shy?'

I turned and saw he was lying naked on my bed, as beautiful as I'd imagined. I went over to him and traced my finger over his body as if I was painting him. I ran my finger across his chest, down his stomach, down down down. I stopped and curled his hair around my finger. I watched his cock harden.

'Kiss me,' he said, sitting up, reaching for me, but I backed off and just looked at him. I stood up and left.

'Goblin?'

I went to Mad and James' room. I rummaged in their drawer, found what I was after and came back, closing the door behind me, pushing a chair up against it.

'Goblin, I'm sorry if—'

I threw the condom on the bed and I took off my clothes, dropping my cardigan on the floor, pulling my dress over my head, standing there for a moment in my knickers. I walked over to him, peeling my knickers off, and sat next to him on the bed. I ran my fingers across him again, then I stroked his cock. I straddled him, rubbing myself against him as we kissed. I reached over for the condom.

As I opened the packet he said, 'Where'd you get that?'

'Mad and James. Mad showed me how to use them.'

I rolled the condom over his cock and I climbed on top of him, my fingers in his. Lowering my hips slowly, I gasped and stopped. A moment, a glance, my hand pressed on his chest and I moved down, down, down, not stopping this time; feeling the pain and the pleasure and the liquid warmth. I kissed him and breathed him in, his smell of smoke, beer and sweat. He wrapped his legs around me. I wanted to open him up and feel under his skin, I wanted to disappear inside him. I sucked on his tongue as my cunt closed around his cock. I pressed his head against my chest. He licked my breast, biting my nipple, the gentle pain accentuating the heat spreading inside me, up, up, up, like golden bubbles. We heard a scream and we came together as Maisie walked past my door, yelling curses at the dwarves. We collapsed on the bed, laughing, still entangled in each other.

'This isn't how I meant it to be,' he said.

'You'd thought about it?'

'Of course. Hadn't you?'

I nodded and said, 'What was wrong with it?'

'Nothing, G. Jesus. It was being here, that's all, with all of them.'

I sat up and Adam leaned over, kissing my hip. He looked at my arms and said, 'Did you injure yourself? What are all those cuts?'

'They're nothing,' I said, 'Just scratches from scrambling around on bombsites.'

I felt between my thighs, sticky with blood. I looked at my fingers and rubbed my thumb over them. I pressed my fingers on his lips, smearing them red. He smiled and flicked his tongue out, licking. I walked over to the window.

'Someone will see you.'

'I don't care.'

He joined me as I opened the window. He pressed up against me and we leaned out, feeling the cool air on our skin. The city was cast in a strange blue light as the sun struggled up, obscured by the billowing smoke. In the distance, a barrage balloon was caught in the flames of a building. The fire circled it, as if gently stroking its skin.

'James is sick,' I said.

The balloon collapsed under an invisible weight, like a giant had squeezed its tail. The ripple of the impact spread through the body, transforming it into a fiery fish streaking through the sky.

'His arm will heal,' said Adam. 'He'll be alright.'

'He's different,' I said. 'He's changed.'

As the balloon headed for the ground it exploded into flames, all form lost, shards bursting out and floating down after the fire ball. The flames were striking against the deep inky blue of the buildings and the black smoke. I looked out across the rooftops, smoke rising in pockets all across London. I could see tiny flickering flames in the distance. The landscape was breaking up, changing every night.

*

I crept into James and Mad's bedroom one morning when Mad had left for work and LK was still snoring in the sitting room. It was one of those rare days when no one else was around.

James was still asleep. I opened the curtains a little and placed the worms next to James' stump. I couldn't sew them on, but hoped a prayer would do. I was nervous. I wasn't sure the lizards would listen because I hadn't given any blood to Monsta since I'd come to live here; I'd left Monsta tucked away in a box under my bed, forgotten.

I cut my arm and held it over the stump and the worms before closing my eyes and saying the lizard prayer. When I'd finished I opened my eyes and saw the worms were just lying there, covered in my blood. James was in the same position but he was awake, watching me.

'I'm trying to give you a new arm,' I said. 'Like Monsta.'

He reached over and held my arm, his hand sliding a little in the blood. He didn't move, just held me like that. When he let go he stared at the blood on his hand, flexing his fingers. I gathered the worms, holding the bloody bouquet. He got up and pulled his trousers on before placing his hand gently on my back.

'We'll get you bandaged up.'

He ushered me through to the kitchen and sat me down. He cleaned me up and tied a bandage round my arm.

'It's what I do,' I said. 'I mean, it's what I did. To keep Monsta alive.'

He sat across the table from me and lit a cigarette. He exhaled and looked back at me.

'I don't need a new arm.'

'But, I thought—'

'You thought wrong.'

'I'll pack,' I said.

'What?'

'I'll leave.'

'Why would you leave? I don't want you to.'

I fiddled with a loose bit of bandage. I couldn't look at him. He reached over and put his hand over mine.

'We love you, you fool. We don't want you to leave.'

He sighed, and leaned back in his chair. The cigarette dangled from his lips, dropping ash onto his chest. He didn't seem to notice. It mingled with his chest hair and disappeared.

'I'm a bit fucked up,' he said. 'I'm sorry.'

I squirmed in my seat.

'It's not about the arm, so much. And it's not about you, or Mad.'

He scrunched up his eyes.

'You've seen things you shouldn't,' he said. 'You haven't told us, but we know.'

I looked down at the table.

'The world is fucked up, Goblin. We've got to make the best of it. Someone like you, you bring light.'

I started poking at the wound beneath the bandage without even realising. He reached over and stopped me.

'Hey,' he said. 'I'll sort myself out, okay? Look at me. Everything is going to be alright.'

I nodded. He got up and pulled some chocolate out of the cupboard and handed me a piece. He sat down next to me.

'What happened to your family? Your old family.'

I squinted up at him.

'David went to sea to fight the pirates. Or to be a pirate, I don't know which. Da went to fight the Nazis, but he wasn't just any ordinary soldier, but a spy. He was tortured but he didn't give up anything and they shot him dead. Ma fell in love with a merman and drowned in the Thames.'

He didn't look at me. He placed a new cigarette in his mouth and held a lighter, flicking it on and off, on and off. He stared at it.

'Is that right?' he said, really quiet, like he was talking to the lighter and not me.

'That's right,' I said. 'And David was supposed to take me with him. We were both going to go to the sea. To escape. David was a conchie so da hit him and David said, "Goblin, let's go to the sea." He left without me but he sends me letters in bottles. There's hundreds of them floating in the sea, buried on beaches, framed in pubs above the bar, all the locals wondering who the mysterious Goblin is.'

'How old are you now, Goblin?'

'You know how old.'

'Tell me.'

'Almost fifteen.'

'You're growing up.'

'I am.'

'You're a dreamer.'

I tensed and I waited, but he didn't say it. He didn't give me the speech about being a grown up, about responsibility. He just lit his cigarette finally and put away the lighter.

'Don't let anyone crush it out of you.'

He put his arm around me.

'We're your family now,' he said. 'Me and Mad. And all our friends, they're your friends too.'

I lay my head on his shoulder.

'What do you say to adoption, Goblin?'

'Yessir,' I said, my voice muffled.

'What was that?'

'Yessir!'

He placed his hand on the side of my head, holding me for a second before letting me go. He pointed at my bandaged arm.

'But you need to leave that behind, Goblin. Leave it behind. You can't save anyone with your blood, you're no Jesus. Martyrs are boring, Goblin.'

He stroked the scars further up my arm, and I pulled away, embarrassed.

'Yessir.'

'You got any problems, you come to me and Mad. And no more running round London like a wild thing. No more helping at bombsites, you've seen enough. And you've got classes to go to.'

'I don't want to go to school,' I said.

'Circus school,' he said. 'When this war is over you'll be travelling with us and you've got to pay your way. You've got to make yourself useful.'

'I want to be a clown,' I said, straight off.

'Well, we all know you're good at clowning around, G. But let's wait and see what else you're good at.'

'I can tell stories,' I said.

'For sure,' he said. 'That's how I found you, remember? You're a little raconteur.'

'Yessir,' I said, puffing my chest.

In the evening we sat at the kitchen table, Mad and James drinking beer and smoking as they put together a timetable for me; clowning, acrobatics, animal keeping, animal training. When it got to maths and English I rolled dramatically on the floor as if I'd just been poisoned, but all they did was laugh at me and flick ash in my hair.

'Goblin,' Mad said, 'the circus is a business and you need to chip in.'

'I can read. I can write.'

'You know all there is to know at age fourteen? What about your sums?'

I lay on the floor and recited my times table at the ceiling to show I knew it all already but all Mad did was say, 'Well, aren't we clever? We'll need more advanced classes for you.'

I shut my mouth after that.

'We'll get the adoption process started. You just leave it to us.'

It was then I had to tell them about Miss Campbell as I knew that could cause all sorts of complications but they told me they'd handle it and not to worry.

'You don't need to call us mum and dad. You can go on calling us by our names if you want. We can't ever replace your parents.'

'I want you to,' I said. 'I want to call you mum and dad.'

They tried not to, but they both smiled at that.

*

I enjoyed being at school again, or a kind of school if that's what you can call sitting in the kitchen with whatever teacher happened to be available. My timetable was fragmented at first, due to the war and my teachers' availability. When Marv was on leave he'd teach me some clowning. 'The trick is, G, it has to look effortless. But it's not, it's carefully choreographed. There's a lot of work goes into looking clumsy and falling on your face. You seen any of those Chaplin films? You get yourself along to the cinema when they're on – he'll teach you a lot.'

Mum and her partner Matt taught me some acrobatics, though it was difficult without much space. We'd sometimes go to the park if the weather was good. They'd hook a rope up between two trees and I'd practice tightrope walking for weeks until I got it just right. A lot of the work I did was about timing, balance, discipline and focus. I didn't think I'd have the patience but I loved it and worked every chance I got.

Leo, a writer, came round and taught me English. We did lots of boring work on grammar but we also read a lot of books and he gave me advice on writing stories. I started writing on everything I could get my hands on – in the margins of books, on the walls of my room, on dad's handkerchief when it was the only thing to hand. My head was bubbling with stories and Leo taught me discipline; he taught me about structure, setting and character. When I gave him a mess of a story he'd give it back to me and say, 'Edit. Edit, edit, edit. And tell me why you're doing what you're doing. Justify it.' I'd groan and whine and say it's fine as it is and he'd say, it isn't. You know it isn't. Dazzle me.

Dad told me about the history of the circus and showed me photos, posters and newspaper clippings of their heyday. I loved the photos of mum's aerial act; a sparkling blur in the air, a triumphant pose in the ring. Her red hair was pinned up and crowned with feathers, her face a strange mask of make-up. One of my favourite photos was of the clowns, lined up like a class photo, looking serious in their eccentric costumes.

I was awed by the photos of the lions and elephants. When the war started mum and dad couldn't afford to keep all the animals. Lord whatshisname, the one who slobbered all over Betsy, had estates all across the country and provided sanctuary for all the circus horses, chimps, elephants, lions, tigers, giraffes and camels. He didn't charge rent, only for the food and the wages of the keepers. Even with the savings from the circus boom years it wasn't easy for mum and dad. They'd pore over their finances and got me to help as part of my maths schooling. They made it work, mostly through the help of pre-war patrons, and the rest of the animals made it through the war.

Colin had been an animal trainer during the circus days, working mainly with elephants, horses and camels, and he travelled round that lord's estates when he could, making sure all was well. Colin was a different person with the animals; awkward with humans, but at ease around any other creature. He took me to one of the estates to see Mitzi the elephant. We stayed for a couple of weeks and worked with the keepers, helping them look after her. I'd seen elephants before when Pigeon took me to the circus but I'd never seen them close-up. The enclosure smelled of shit and that warm musty animal smell, just like at Pigeon's.

'Hey girl, hey girl,' Colin said, stroking Mitzi. She knew him, it was obvious. Her ears flapped and her trunk knocked into him, nudging him, almost pushing him over before wrapping around him and pulling him close to her.

'Mitzi, this is Goblin. Goblin, this is Mitzi, one of our superstars. Eh, old girl?'

I looked up into her eyes and I stroked her. I loved the feel of her body. I ran my hand over the skin, feeling the tiny hairs and the busy lines. I tried to follow their trail with my finger and got lost in a myriad of folds.

'They skinned them,' I said to Colin.

'What? What did you say?'

'The demigods, the lizards down below, they skinned the elephants and scrunched up their skin like paper, then they clothed them again, and now they feel like this.'

He rolled his eyes and shook his head.

I helped Colin and the keepers muck out and feed Mitzi. Colin wasn't much for talking so I talked on and on until I ran out of things to say. We worked in silence until Colin said, 'When the war ends, we'll bring the circus together again.'

I nodded, pleased he was talking to me. I decided to be quiet and maybe he'd talk some more but he was silent after that and I was bursting with things to say so I said, 'When the war ends I'm going to be a clown and I'll travel with you and all my new family, and I'll find my brother and he'll travel with us too, telling tales of pirates and mermaids. That's what'll happen when the war ends, everything will be right.'

London, 8 May 1945 (VE Day) – 2 September 1945 (VJ Day)

I made a crown like for a king but cardboard with trailing ribbons from old-ma's old clothes and I dressed like a clown, painted my face white with a big red smile and black round my eyes with a tear at the side, just one tear for the lost the dead the forgotten, floating in the past in the ether down below. I fall into victory above, a tea party where the wine flows, I wear my crown like for a king but cardboard with trailing ribbons and I clutch my flag arm in arm with new-mum new-dad. Swept up in a Trafalgar Square ocean of people swaying back and forth and buffeted here and there, surging and waving, waiting for Churchill chanting and waiting for him to appear and tell us what we wanted to hear. We'd dip down sullen and silent just waiting with clutched white knuckles, flags drooping crumpled, my smile false and tired, drowning in the crowd, pulled out by mum and dad following a surge moving with the flow pushed up up up climbing Eros encased in concrete up up up perching waiting above the sea above the swarm and Churchill is there – victory in Europe! 'Londoners, I love you all!' and the ocean explodes a deafening thunderous stamping roar an explosion of flags and hats, a tide of V's. Drinking late into the night on our street jam jars lit up shimmering flames flittering flies wine and rivers of V's and hugs and kisses floating away from sadness, entranced by the fire in the street the piano in the street singing and dancing with the flames, fireworks in the sky, wine in my belly, the glow of the fire on my skin, drunken soldier kisses and laughter closed eyes closed eyes sway and listen and feel until dawn a flickering path of jam jar flies leading us home through the twilight, in bed with Adam curled close, Groo licking my hair. I rub my tear, smearing it gone, no more war, the certainty of bombs stripped away. I fell into sleep and woke above to liberated Nazi camps, the emaciated diseased. The Lizard King says, no love lost for jews, gypsies, commies, homos, but those Nazis are inhuman. Animals, those Nazi bastards, he says, animals. Corpses piled on corpses, buried in liberty, V for victory.

I fell into sleep and woke above to 6 and 9 sixandnineoftheeighth Hiroshima nine Nagasaki six atom bomb six and nine and gone. I woke above to VJ Day and I was glad. V for victory and the end of an era.

I dug out Monsta from under my bed. Dead things can't die but Monsta was inert; bits of old worms, worn bear body, plastic doll foot, dried up crow foot, stiff pigeon wings and a shrew head with eyes closed to me. I'd stopped feeding Monsta, stopped needing Monsta. Now Monsta was gone.

I made my way through the city, through the pockets of VJ Day celebrations. I went to Kensal Green Cemetery and dug a small hole above where Devil lay. I wrapped Monsta in a blanket, said a lizard prayer – Holy, Holy, Holy – and down Monsta went with Devil and the camera.

I was fifteen years old when Monsta was buried and I was glad. It was the end of a childhood born blue.

Chapter 10

Detective Curtis has everything spread out on the table. Evidence tags hang from each item. I pick up the camera and examine it.

'It still works,' he says.

I lay it down and lift Monsta's shrew head.

'What is all this?' he asks, gesturing to Monsta's remains. 'Voodoo?'

'Something like that.'

'Tell me.'

'He was my friend, after Devil died.'

'Voodoo and devils, huh?'

'He was my dog.'

'Devil?'

'It's from the comic strip, *The Phantom*. My aunt would send them to my brother and I read them all.'

'What happened to your dog?'

'He died.'

'Did he end up here?'

He brings out the photo.

'No. He was shot. I buried him in Kensal Green. These are his bones.'

'Who shot him?'

I pick up a photo of Devil. Detective Curtis leans back in his chair, considering me. I know what he's thinking; is it too soon to bring out the photograph? He makes a huffing noise as he pulls it out and places it in front of me. It's the first time I've seen it.

'Is this anything to do with your devil dog and the voodoo?'

'No,' I say. 'Not really.'

'Either it is or it isn't.'

'Have you ever been to the sea, Detective?'

He sighs. I stare down at the photograph.

'Right,' he says. 'Before we go any further, I have to warn you that there's going to be some press interest in this. For now, if they approach you, the only thing you can talk about is the dead pets. Okay? That's all. If I was you, I'd avoid the tabloids completely and don't say a word about devil dogs or voodoo.'

'My lips are sealed, Detective. As they have been for seventy-two years.'

'And why is that?'

'Who lives in the past, Detective?'

'Did you take these photographs?'

'Yes.'

'And you buried the camera. Why did you do that?'

'Who wouldn't?'

'How old were you when you took this?'

'Nine.'

We both look at the photograph.

'It turned out well. The light was fading.'

He nods.

'You're a storyteller, aren't you, Goblin?'

'Yes.'

'I want you to tell me the story of this photograph. Of all of these photographs.'

He spreads them out across the table, but he keeps the focus on the one in front of me.

'Let's start with names. Who are they?'

'I don't know, Detective.'

'Who is this?'

'I don't know. I don't know who any of them are.'

'Who's responsible for this, Goblin? Don't you want them brought to justice?'

'I'm responsible,' I say.

He sighs.

'I was born blue,' I say. 'I could have died. Could've,

should've.'

'Give me their names.'

'There is no justice. There can never be justice. It's too late.'

'Where was this? Where did you take the photograph?'

'I don't remember, Detective. It was a long time ago.'

He looks at me, taps his pen on the edge of the table and stands up. He leaves the room and I stare at the photos, a few minutes passing before he returns.

'You know who this is, don't you, Goblin?'

I look at the man standing in the doorway next to Detective Curtis. He rubs his grey beard nervously before taking off his cap to reveal a balding head. I was about to say no, no I don't know him, when he smiles tentatively. I know that smile, I know those eyes. He sits down in front of me.

'Yes, Detective,' I say, looking at Mac. 'I know who this is.'

'You can catch up. I'm sure you both have a lot to talk about.'

He closes the door, leaving us sitting in silence.

★

'The detective said you were in the circus.'

'Yes.'

'Makes sense. How long?'

'Several years. I retired in Venice, where I wrote articles, busked, ran history tours. You?'

'Teacher. Not as exciting as you.'

'A teacher is good.'

Mac looks at the photos, spreading them out, pinning one down with his finger.

'I pretended it never happened. But I had nightmares about it,' he says. 'For years.'

'I didn't.'

'No?'

'No. Only dreams of the sea.'

'I heard you came back, you know. From evacuation. I knew you were back in the city when I came home, but I couldn't face you. We moved away, shortly after. We moved.'

'You took this,' I say, holding up the photo of me standing in front of the mound of animal corpses.

'I threw up. When I saw it in the paper, I threw up.'

'Then you went to the police.'

'Not straight away. I looked them up first,' he says, drumming his fingers on the photo. 'Do you know they're war heroes?'

'I found out.'

'It was then I picked up the phone,' he says.

'What good is it now?' I say.

'I couldn't take this to my grave.'

'Why not? It's where it belongs. Buried.'

'You don't believe that.'

'They're going to exhume the body,' I say.

'You think it's there?'

'Where else would it be?'

'I'll come with you,' Mac says. 'If you want me to.'

'You think it will stop the nightmares.'

Gathering up all the photos, he piles them on top of one another, burying the one depicting what we were going to unearth. He looks up at me.

'Tell me about the circus. What did you do?'

'I was a clown. And I helped look after the animals.'

He smiles. 'Of course.'

I know how it felt for them; like disappearing into another world. Greeted at the entrance by the guardians of the realm, ushered in to the sound of music, enveloped by an intoxicating medley of scents, surrounded by laughter and yells as they jostled for space and made their way down the aisles, finding their seats. I'd peer out at them, looking at the faces of the children, remembering my first experience of the circus with Pigeon. Now I was one of them. I was a clown, a fantasy, a freak.

The thing I loved the most about circus life was the feeling of anticipation and excitement when we arrived in towns. We'd set up camp on the outskirts before travelling into town to parade through the main street and in some cities thousands would turn up to watch us. The animals were the star attractions. As the elephants lumbered by with the glitter girls astride them you could see the sense of wonder in everyone's eyes, even the adults. It made me feel that this Goblin-runt born blue was meant to be. In the circus I was a bringer of joy. I was no longer the travelling Goblin with her Devil dog or her Corporal Pig or her Monsta. I was travelling Goblin-clown-freak with a family of hundreds, humans and other animals.

I was with the clown troupe, Marv, Ali, Paul, and later on there was Horatiu who we picked up on our travels. I loved clowning and took it very seriously. We trained with the acrobats – learning the rules before breaking them; it took a lot of grace to look clumsy. I came out of it mostly unscathed, with lots of bruises and aching muscles, though Paul was laid up for a while with a sprained wrist.

We teamed up with Milly, the tiger trainer, devising an act where Ali's Jack Russell, Rusty, was replaced with a tiger cub but he pretended not to notice. This was a real hit with the audience – they'd yell for him to watch out and he'd feign deafness, shrug and continue on with this tiger cub at his side. The tiger 'mum' would enter the ring and the audience went wild. Ali just looked confused for a moment, shrugged and continued walking round the ring. The tiger mum padded up behind Ali, took the tiger cub by the scruff of the neck and exited the ring – there was an audible sigh of relief from the audience every time. Ali turned round, saw his Jack Russell was gone and started searching, lifting up women's skirts and looking under men's hats. The audience, distracted, laughing at Ali, didn't see the tiger mum at first – she'd re-entered the ring, carrying the Jack Russell in her mouth. There was a gradual ripple through the crowd, followed by yells. Ali turned, saw his dog and stomped his way back into the ring. Two pats on the head of the tiger – a collective gasp from the audience – and Ali had his dog back.

It was one of my favourite acts – the whole troupe had devised it and it was always a success – but I ended it. The trainers had trouble breeding tigers; it wasn't successful whatever they tried, so they bought cubs from traders or zoos. I didn't know much about zoos, but I didn't like separating the cubs from their mums, and I felt uneasy about cubs from the wild. It took me a while to persuade mum and dad, but I got them to effectively kill our best act. The clown troupe never knew it was me; mum and dad took full responsibility. I felt pretty bad about it and did all I could do make it up to them; working harder, helping other acts, doing more than my share if we needed extra hands for the erection and dismantling of the tents. Mum and dad reassured me, telling me they understood – 'We know how much you love animals, G' – but I decided I wouldn't rock the circus boat from then on. The clown troupe bitched and moaned about Mad and James' decision, saying, 'Sorry, G, but it's just—' and I'd nod and say, it's fine. I get it.

'We don't need the cub anyway,' I said. 'We can stand on our own clown feet.'

And we could. The audience loved us and I loved being a performer. Sitting in front of that mirror each night, Goblin becoming clown. I wasn't as skinny as I was during the war but no one could tell I was a woman as my body disappeared beneath my costume; layers of blue and white stripes with ruffles at my neck. I wore a pointed hat with blue pom poms down the front, and we all had our signature make-up; I whited out my face, my dark eyebrows and my big lips disappearing, giving me a strange otherworldly look. I then exaggerated my lips to the point of grotesqueness, smearing lipstick over my philtrum and chin, each side curling high up on my cheeks. My eyebrows were thick black triangles, high on my forehead, giving me a look of permanent surprise and I drew in vertical lines at each eye. The other clowns coloured their noses, but I left mine white – from a distance it looked like I didn't have a nose at all.

Other than the tiger cub and occasionally Rusty, we didn't perform with the animals, but I loved to be with them so when I had time I helped Colin and his workers muck them out, wash them, brush them, feed them, whatever needed done. The menagerie was one of my favourite things about the circus. I'd try to get my costume and make-up done in plenty time before the show so I could go out and watch all the people, seeing their reactions to the animals. I moved through the crowd, selling a few clown toys, watching the people mill around taking photos of the animals. I took a photo of a family with two of our elephants, the little kid not wanting to look at the camera, too busy staring up at Mitzi and her flapping ears. A click and a flash and I caught her sense of wonder.

The menagerie weren't the only animals in the circus. Captain Flint and Groo came with us. Captain Flint would fly off when we pitched, disappearing for hours, returning with prey he'd eat on my bed. I'd come in from a performance to find a corpse, half-eaten. I remember when he brought a corpse and a diamond bracelet, almost as if it was an appeasement. We were pitched in York when he didn't return one evening. I didn't fret, sure he would make it back before we left. Four days passed and he didn't return; I was anxious for him, but hoped he was enjoying his freedom and not injured or dead. I missed him and his gruesome meals.

Groo took a while to get used to circus life and mostly stayed in my caravan on my bed. Eventually she ventured out, exploring the new terrain in each town and city we stopped in. She would bring me mice and small birds until my caravan was a grisly menagerie of corpses. Groo would sniff out the other animals in the circus, fascinated by all the new smells. Trotting in front of the cages, she held her head high in a haughty display of her freedom in contrast to the mighty big cats behind bars. She made friends with one of the performing dogs, Ali's Jack Russell, Rusty, and I'd find them curled up on my bed together, making huffy noises in their sleep. Groo groomed him and he enjoyed it. I tried not to think of Devil, I tried not to think of the past at all. Except for David; I used our travelling as an opportunity to look for him. We travelled for eight months of the year, all across the UK, everywhere we went I would put up posters of David, keeping an eye out for him in seaside towns. I'd also get tattoos in almost every town or city we stopped in. I asked the publicity troupe to scout out a tattoo artist for me and book me in before we arrived. I'd get waves, ships, pirate flags, mermaids and mermen, krakens, sailors, anchors, lizard people, Mary and Jesus. I had 'LOVE' tattooed across the fingers on my right hand and lines from *Alice in Wonderland* and *The Time Machine* across my back and my legs. Each year we'd return to the same towns and cities and I'd return to my favourite tattoo artists. They'd be waiting for me with a shot of whisky, vodka, gin or a pint of beer and it was like I'd never left. The last tattoo I got was a small lizard on my ring finger.

At the end of the tour the circus would return to London to do a few shows there, then we'd have a short break before coming back together and repairing and repainting our carriages and props, working on new acts, bringing in new performers. I'd return to letters, people telling me they'd seen David, but they were all from cranks, lonely people looking for someone to rescue them. I kept all the letters and some of them I replied to, keeping up a correspondence with an old woman who lived in a cottage near the coast with her two dogs. She had so many stories to tell and I'd get lost in them, pretending her past was mine.

Adam and I split summer of '52. We'd been taking each other for granted, being together out of habit, not really connecting anymore. And he hated when I was drinking.

'You get drunk and maudlin, talk *around* your past – never about it.'

'Don't pry,' I said, 'leave me be.'

'You need to talk about it.'

'Don't tell me what I need.'

I ended it before he could. He didn't speak to me for weeks after, but I hardly saw him anyway, as he was involved in Freaks and Wonders and I was busy clowning. It was strange going back to my caravan in the evenings now he wasn't there. I met up with mum and dad for a weekly evening drink, and I started going round to Marv's with Ali and Paul and drank with them a couple of nights a week. They were all about fifteen years older than me and they'd fought in the war – Ali and Paul had been in the army with dad, and Marv was in the RAF. Ali and Paul barely spoke about it, but Marv regaled us with tales of derring-do and womanising. When Marv wasn't with us in the evenings he was off wooing one of the glitter girls and he'd tell us all about it the next day, 'That Laura, she was something else – kept me up all night.' He didn't seem to care I was a woman. At first I thought their easy acceptance was because of Mad and James, but we hit it off and they enjoyed my crazy stories about the London ghosts and my collection of animals.

I wasn't with anyone for the next few years; just brief flings here and there. Mum and dad had rules, the main one being that we weren't to fraternize with any locals when we stopped off, though I know many did. The second rule was that if we had affairs, it wasn't to affect our work. The third was that there were no unplanned pregnancies; contraception was provided and every child was given sex education. If any performers wanted children, they informed mum and dad, giving them time to plan so that performances didn't suffer. The circus was one big family and mum and dad encouraged everyone to help with the children.

It wasn't until '55 that I was in another serious relationship, when I fell for another angel. Angelina was a glitter girl, one of the aerialists who worked with mum. Everyone called her Glitter Queen when she became one of our big stars with fans clamouring for her autograph after shows. When she took part in the parades through the towns she'd wear wings. She was a dream.

I went to watch her rehearse whenever I had the time. She was another fiery angel – all temper and expletives when practice didn't go well, no patience if anyone dared to disagree with her. I must have been watching her work for weeks when she came over to me after rehearsal.

'Jesus!' she said. 'You saw that, right? If he doesn't pull his fucking weight the whole act will fall apart. I need a drink – you coming?'

I went back to her caravan and sat on her bed as she told me about her trouble with Dave.

'He's got a problem with me just because I turned him down. What are we – school children? Jesus!'

She didn't seem to mind that I was there as she peeled off her tights and unclipped her bra. She stood naked in-front of the mirror, taking her hair out of a bun, brushing it and tying it back. She pulled a towel around her and said, 'Just getting a quick shower, hang around will you? Help yourself.' She pointed to the whisky on her dresser.

We lay on her bed, drinking late into the evening. She finally moved on from the trouble with Dave and told me about growing up in poverty in Manchester, said her parents had tried to marry her off to an old man with money, 'so when your circus came I stowed away. I'm lucky your parents took me on.'

'We're the lucky ones – you're our star.'

'All thanks to your mum,' she said raising her glass, 'taking a chance, taking the time to train me.'

'Mad knows potential when she sees it,' I said, clinking glasses with her.

I took a drink, but Angelina just looked at me, eyes narrowed and said, 'How long have you been watching me for?'

I swallowed the whisky and coughed. 'I don't know,' I said.

'It's been weeks, right?'

'I was just—'

'Were you ever going to make a move? Or just watch me from a distance?'

She leaned in, kissed me and that was us – Goblin-clown and Glitter Queen, the gossip of the circus.

We met up every evening, talking about our childhoods, discussing rehearsals, drinking and fucking into the night.

'My first love was an Angel,' I said. 'Just like you – all fire and brimstone.'

But our relationship was more tempestuous; I'd get jealous as she flirted with her fans, convinced I was going to lose her to one of the men who showered her with gifts. She did interviews for magazines, telling them she was single and just waiting 'for the right man.'

'Are you ashamed of me?' I said.

'Of course not, G. It's all publicity – I'd lose my fans if they knew we were together.'

The clown troupe changed towards me when they found out I was with Angelina. They didn't do or say anything overt, but I could see there was something up the way the glanced at each other whenever I mentioned her, and when I joined them for drinks I could tell they didn't want me there anymore. I didn't know what to do; there was nothing I could point to that had really changed and I knew they'd just deny it, so I went on as if everything was fine. Our work didn't suffer – we were still a great team, so I decided to leave it, thinking it would eventually all work out.

Dave, the aerialist who'd been giving Angelina trouble, called me over one morning. He waved a magazine at me, pointing to one of her interviews.

'Are you man enough for her, Goblin? Do you have what it takes?' he said and grabbed at his groin, grinning at me. I wanted to hurt him, but I didn't stand a chance, so I clenched my fists and stalked away, listening to him laugh.

I told her and I thought she'd be on side, given the trouble she'd had with him, but all she said was, 'Ah, just ignore him, G, he's a child.' And when I wouldn't let it go she said she had no patience for my 'neurotics'.

I can't count the times we'd fight and split up and be back together again by morning. I enjoyed the drama of it at first, but we were together for over four years and it started to wear me down; whenever anyone in the circus glanced my way I would prickle, already defensive, sure I knew what they were thinking about me, about us. It was too much to be in the fishbowl; I loved when we went home over the Christmas period. Angelina and I would hole up together, enjoying being away from the noise and stress of circus life. Over Christmas and New Year '58 and '59 we watched *Quatermass and the Pit*, gripped by the unfolding story of Martians and genetically modified humans, but then Angelina teased me when I had to stop watching because it gave me nightmares.

She gave me *Frankenstein* by Mary Shelley for Christmas. When I opened it I wanted to throw it back in her face. It's David who should have given me the book. He had said he would and Angelina had ruined it.

'What's wrong?' said Angelina.

'Nothing.'

'You told me you loved the films. You said you'd never read it, so I thought—'

'I loved the films when I was a kid, that's all.'

I apologised later, telling her it reminded me of the past and I didn't want to think of the past anymore. She kept on about it, though, just like Adam – grilling me about the past, about David and why I was searching for him. She couldn't just let it be. And I was growing tired of things always being so uncertain, sad that I no longer felt at ease in the circus, so I ended it, spring of '59. There was a hubbub just after we split, but it died down and it felt like things were back to normal – no more eyes on me, no more razor tongues.

Angelina and I became friends after a month of her telling me to go fuck myself. She turned up at my caravan with whisky and said, 'This is stupid, G. We can be friends, right?'

We met up off and on, but mostly I retreated to my caravan, devouring books – Wilde, Saki, Nesbit, Woolf, Orwell – and writing; I'd kept a diary for years, only sporadically writing fiction, but now I wrote down many of the stories Pigeon had told me. I changed them, elaborating, expanding. And I wrote a semi-fictional account of the adventures of Corporal Pig and fragments about the circus.

Before Angelina and I had hooked up I used to meet mum and dad once a week for dinner or an evening drink, catching up, telling stories, singing, but Glitter Queen had consumed me and we'd only met up sporadically when I was with her. Mum and dad didn't say a word; they welcomed me back as if nothing had changed.

We sat outside their caravan, next to a small fire, drinking beer. I read them my favourite Saki, *Sredni Vashtar*, which they loved. And we chatted, catching up. Mum told me she was learning Polish – we'd ran auditions when we were in Newcastle and Ania Przybylski had wowed us with her acrobatic skills. She'd left Poland with her family in 1937, but she'd never felt settled. She fit in with the circus like it had been her whole life. Mum and Ania became close and Ania would teach her Polish songs. Mum loved the language and spent every spare minute she had learning and practicing.

Mum sang us a Polish song and I watched dad watching her, still so very much in love all these years later. I asked them about when they met.

'It was love at first sight,' said dad.

Mum laughed and said, 'Is that right?'

'Of course that's right.'

'The way I remember it you didn't even notice me – you

were going out with Booby Betsy at the time.'

I laughed and watched dad squirm.

'You know it,' said mum, nudging him.

'I fell for you. I just didn't want to let Betsy down.'

'Oh, sure.'

'I'd been going out with Betsy for three weeks,' he said to me. 'What kind of man drops a girl so quickly? But I was smitten with your mum.'

Dad came from a family of circus folk – his granddad had started a small family circus which James' dad took over. It passed to James when his dad died in The Great War. Mum's dad worked at the London docks, expecting his two sons to follow him.

'He planned to marry me off as soon as possible,' said mum. 'He'd say to people: "One less mouth to feed." I didn't hold a grudge – it was difficult for him to provide for us all on his wage. But I knew I'd make my own way. I started dancing at the local theatre and it was there I met your dad. He came back after the show and outlined then and there what the circus could offer me. I snapped it up without a thought – packed my things, said goodbye to my family, who were relieved to see the problem of a daughter solved. I kept in touch as I travelled – sending postcards, sometimes money. And your dad asked me out a week after I joined the circus.'

'What about Booby Betsy?' I asked.

'She threw wine in my face,' said mum.

'No!'

'She did. I got off lightly, though – she dumped camel shit in your dad's bed.'

'I like the sound of her,' I said, and laughed with mum as dad just sat there, smiling and shaking his head. He put his arm around mum and said, 'It was worth it. I'd suffer a whole caravan of camel shit for you.'

Mum pulled away and hit him across the shoulder. He pulled her back to him and kissed her.

'C'mon!' I said as the kiss went on.

They broke apart and dad said, 'The most amazing woman in the world and she's all mine.'

Mum, blushing, smiled and looked over at me, 'And what about you, Goblin? Your life is all drama.'

'Aah,' I said, looking down and taking a drink, 'Angelina and I are over.'

'You okay?'

I shrugged and said, 'Yeah. Things are getting back to normal.'

'If you need to talk, we're here,' she said.

I was about to tell her about the clown troupe being awkward around me, but I shook my head and said, 'Things are fine now.' I smiled at her, 'Really. I'm good.'

I finished off my beer and said, 'How about a song before I turn in?' And I watched dad watching mum as she sang *I'll Be Seeing You* – 'I'll find you in the morning sun, and when the night is new, I'll be looking at the moon, but I'll be seeing you.' She swayed, looking into the dying flames of our fire and I watched him, wondering if one day someone would love me the way he loved her.

*

The clown troupe thawed after I split with Angelina, but I was pissed with the way they'd treated me and Marv got all weird again when I was in another relationship – summer '61 I fell in love with Tim, one of the freak-boys we picked up on our travels.

'I thought you'd turned queer,' said Marv. 'Adam, Angelina, now Tim. Can't you decide which side you play for?'

I gawped at him for a moment, unsure what to say. He wouldn't look me in the eye.

'I'm not on any side, Marv. Fish Boys, Glitter Queens... What does it matter?'

'You just better be careful, that's all I'm saying.'

'D'ya have a problem with me, Marv?'

'Nah, G. I'm jus' jealous. Glitter Queen...' He whistled. 'Plenty woulda wanted to be in your shoes. Can't believe you dumped her for Fish Boy.'

'I didn't dump her, Marv. It just ended. And Fish Boy came later.'

'I heard you dumped her.'

I shrugged and said, 'It was mutual.'

Marv grunted and didn't say anything else about it after that.

We'd picked up Tim in a seaside town in the south of England. I was helping out at the ticket booth when he wandered up and said, 'You looking for any freaks?'

I looked him up and down, this Montgomery Clift dream, and said, 'Sure, you know any?'

He held up his left hand, fingers splayed to show me the webbing. I whistled. This sure was love at first sight.

'I've worked at a sideshow in this shithole for years. I'm looking to see the world.'

'You'll need to speak with James and Mad. I don't know if they're hiring right now. Money is tight.'

'I can earn my way.'

'I'm sure.'

He stared at me and said, 'I like your tattoos.'

'I collect them,' I said. 'Every town and city, I get a new one.'

'You're beautiful,' he said.

'You're a charmer,' I said. 'I'm not the one you should be charming. James and Mad will make the decision whether you can join us or not.'

He painted himself blue and green and called himself Fish Boy, the Wonder of the Deep. He joined me when I went for tattoos, adding to his fish scales – he had scales tattooed on every inch of his body, including his face. He looked beautiful, a stunning merman. It was the only time I didn't join him; I didn't want face tattoos because I didn't like the idea of always being on show. I was sure one day I'd want to hide, to disappear in a crowd. Maisie said that was a luxury that most of the freaks didn't have.

When I had time I'd go and watch the Freaks and Wonders performances. Ariadne and Adeline were first; Ariadne would play the accordion as Adeline sang a song. They were on a rotating platform so people could look at where they were joined together. The main stage in Freaks and Wonders was for the dwarves, Old Louise and her brass band; she'd mesmerise the audience with her beautiful voice. Lenny the giant would play the tambourine but he was a terrible musician and was only there to emphasise the extremes of stature. As the dwarves performed people would stand in line for Morgana, The Fat Lady fortune teller. She'd wear a skimpy outfit, usually a homemade bikini embellished with sequins, so that people could ogle her curves and folds of fat as she told them their fate.

Fish Boy and I were next up. Clowning and the animals were my priorities, but after hooking up with Fish Boy I helped him with his act and did some stints as The Tattooed Woman. I'd flex my muscles and tell stories of pirates and sea monsters. I'd tell the story of a Goblin-child hunting for her long-lost brother only to find he was enchanted, turned into a merman, the memory of his previous life lost.

Fish Boy played his part in my story, becoming my merman brother. We made his fish tail together, matching the blues and greens of his tattoos. He'd swim in a tank of water, sometimes hovering at the glass, his webbed hands pressed up against it for the kids to see. When our story was finished he'd flick his tail, splashing the kids who would run off screaming, straight to the Lizard King who was waiting to tell them the story of how he cried tears of acid.

I watched the kids watching him as he told the story we'd told in the Underground during the war. The kids were spellbound; he was a real hit. On their way out after the show Morgana would be waiting, selling rubber lizards with glued-on crowns.

France, Spain, Belgium, Czechoslovakia, West Germany, 1961 –
1964

Dad took the circus further afield, travelling through Europe.
As we travelled, we picked up people along the way. Over fifteen
years since the war had ended and people were still trying to
escape; memories, loss, poverty. They were the displaced, the
dispossessed, those with no family, uprooted by the war and
unable to settle back into their old lives. We'd picked up many
people who'd been persecuted by the Nazis, but no one talked
about it. The Eichmann trial was on everyone's lips everywhere
we went, but we hardly mentioned it. We were in Belgium the
day he was hanged. A small group gathered together and sat in
a circle, each with a glass of whisky. I watched them. No one
spoke. They drank their whisky and the group dissolved.

Our clown troupe had been myself, Marv, Ali and Paul for
years, but Horatiu joined us in 1963. We picked him up in a
small town in France on our way back home. He'd been working
as a mime in theatre and in the streets. He was from Romania
but had fled when the post-war Communist Party arrested
and tried his father as a collaborator, threatened the rest of the
family, and killed his friend. This was what mum had told me,
but Horatiu wouldn't talk about his time in Romania when Ali
quizzed him, and I let him be; there was a quiet understanding
between us both. The past should stay in the past. He freely
spoke about his time in France; he was queer and didn't hide it,
regaling us with tales of his affairs. I thought the clown troupe,
especially Marv, would bristle at his sexual exploits, but they
enjoyed his stories.

'Why so easy on Horatiu, Marv?'

'What's that, G?'

'You had a problem with me and Angelina, but not Horatiu.'

He continued applying his make-up then said, 'That's
different.'

'How so?'

'Horatiu is honest.'

I didn't respond and stared at myself in the mirror, Goblin disappearing, becoming clown. I smeared on the lipstick, going over my fake smile again and again until it was a deep obscene red.

'I told you – I don't play for any side,' I said, looking into my eyes.

He grunted. I closed one eye and drew in a vertical line, a black scar.

★

I'd sometimes spend the night in Fish Boy's caravan. When I returned, Groo would be waiting for me, complaining. The morning she wasn't there, I called for her and heard her faint voice. I got down on my knees. She was lying under the bed, lifting her head to meow at me.

'Hey, Groo. C'mon out, whatcha doin' under there?'

She half-stood, half-fell her way out from under, her back legs not working properly. She collapsed in front of me, on her side, breathing heavily.

'What's wrong, old thing? You've gone all lopsided like Monsta.'

A tumour, Colin said. She won't have long to live, Colin said. Best to let her go.

'I can't let her go, she can't go. She's all I have left.'

'You have me,' said Fish Boy, 'you have us.'

'I should have looked after her more. I should have stayed here every night with her. I neglected her and now she's dying.'

'G, there's nothing you could have done. She's old. She had a good life. You loved her.'

'It wasn't enough.'

Fish Boy and I holed up in my caravan and lay on the bed with Groo. We stroked her and spoke to her and tried to get her to drink and eat, but she only lay there, her breathing more laboured. Fish Boy went for Colin and I put Groo on my lap, my arms around her as Colin inserted the needle. I kissed

Groo's head. I smelled behind her ear like I always did, but she didn't smell of anything anymore. I watched her slip away. She peed on me, the warmth seeping through to my skin, and she was gone. I said I was sorry over and over, so so sorry. I kissed her head again and held her paw. My tears and snot darkened her fur.

★

Before we buried Groo, I let Rusty see her and smell her. I don't know if it was the right thing to do but I thought maybe he would understand and I wouldn't have to deal with him plaintively following me around, wondering where she'd gone.

He sniffed her, licked her, growled, circled her and barked at me before running off. He turned up at my caravan a couple of times, sleeping at the bottom of the bed, then I didn't see him again apart from the performances and I was glad.

After Groo died I stayed in bed for a week. Mum and dad, Fish Boy and Angelina all came to see me, but I couldn't get up. I had nightmares again, about Quatermass and Martians, about Devil and old-ma. I stayed in bed until one afternoon I woke up and felt like a weight had fallen from me as I slept. I had all the energy in the world and the first thing I did was print posters of David. I'd let it slide, so wrapped up in work and Angelina and Fish Boy that I'd only put up a few here and there. But now I had hundreds and I'd put them up in every town and city we stopped in.

★

We didn't usually get much time to sight-see as we travelled, but when we were in Prague I walked down Charles Bridge and touched St. John of Nepomuk's five stars, hoping the silent saint would grant my wish. When we were in Paris mum and dad gave us all a couple of days off and several of us went up the Eiffel Tower. Two of the acrobats were arrested for doing dangerous stunts on the top level and mum and dad had a hell of a time getting them out of jail, which gave us all a few extra days in Paris. I visited Père Lachaise Cemetery with Fish Boy, mainly to see Oscar Wilde's grave, but I loved it there and we stayed until late afternoon. It reminded me of the days I'd spent in Kensal Green, but it was a soft, melancholy feeling, only a tinge of sadness as I remembered Devil leaping after bumble bees.

In the evening after we'd returned from the cemetery I sat on the steps of my caravan with Fish Boy, basking in the glow of the fading sun. I thought of the times I was entertaining in the Underground and I thought of meeting dad, how lucky I was. I was where I belonged. End the story here. The past be damned.

London, 25 November 2011

I try to cancel the exhumation.

'It's not there,' I say. 'I've forgotten. Mac doesn't know, don't trust him. It's all forgotten.'

But it goes ahead and I go along. The old worksite is a worksite again; it was all sct for new development when the bankers failed us.

The media are here. Only a handful of them, the few that are after something different to the Eurozone crisis, something different to riots and phone hacking. They stand around behind the police line. I can't imagine they'll last long; there's nothing to see.

'Where's Mac?' I ask Detective Curtis.

'He helped us. Told us where he thinks it's located, then he left. He wasn't feeling well. What do you think? Does this look about right?'

'I don't know. It's hard to get my bearings. It's all changed.'

'We'll start here,' said the detective. 'Maybe we'll be lucky.'

'Lucky?'

'I'm sorry, I didn't mean that. It would just make things easier if this was quick.'

'Did Mac tell you everything?'

'Yes.'

'You know it all?'

'I do, but I'd like to hear it from you.'

I say nothing.

'You can tell me when you're ready.'

I nod.

'This is going to take some time,' he says. 'You don't need to stay. I'll call if we find anything.'

I stare at where they're digging.

'I'll call you,' the detective says and walks over to talk to one of the workmen.

I hover, still staring. It's difficult to see the past here, hard to see this as the place where Mac, Stevie, Devil and I used to come and sit by a fire telling stories.

'You're Goblin?'

A woman stands next to me, one of the reporters.

'You're Goblin, right?'

'I am.'

'I'm Belinda Cartwright. You can call me Linda,' she says, offering her hand. I take her hand and she says, 'Mind if I record?' She holds her phone up, nods and smiles as if I responded and says, 'What's your real name?'

'Goblin.'

'You don't look like a goblin. In fact, you're awfully pretty for your age, if a bit skinny. I need your real name.'

'My name is Goblin.'

'You changed it?'

'It's been my name since the day I was born.'

'Do you have something to hide?'

'No.'

'Then surely your name won't hurt.'

'I'm Goblin.'

'Your surname?'

'Just Goblin.'

Linda smiles and says, 'Is it true you used to pretend to be a boy?'

'You spoke to Mac?'

'Mr Mackenzie? I did.'

'I didn't pretend. I just wore my brother's hand-me-downs and had short hair.'

'So, this is where all the animals are buried?'

I look at her for a moment and she prompts me, 'The pets killed in World War Two?'

'Some of them, yes.'

'And you saw it?'

'I did.'

'How old were you?'

'Nine.'

'That must have been a horrible thing to see.'

'It was.'

'Why do you think people did it? Killed them in such vast numbers?'

'I thought it was Nazis,' I say, remembering when we played Nazis, Frankenstein's monsta and Martians. I look across the worksite, searching for our den, trying to imagine it as it used to be. 'Stevie was the Nazi.'

'Who's Stevie?'

'No one. Just a friend.'

'He was a Nazi?'

'We used to play a game, that's all. He pretended to be a Nazi. At the time we thought it was Nazi spies who'd killed the pets. I couldn't believe we were responsible.'

'Why would Nazi spies kill pets?'

'To demoralise us.'

'And what do you think now?'

'There was worry about how animals would react to bombing, so people thought it was a mercy killing. Animals weren't allowed in public shelters, weren't allowed on evacuation. There were laws against feeding your pets food humans could eat and you'd be fined if you did.'

'But why euthanize them so soon after war was declared? In such vast numbers when there hadn't been any bombing yet?'

'It wasn't euthanasia,' I say. 'There was nothing wrong with them. They weren't ill.'

'"Kill", then. Why were so many of them killed so soon?'

'I don't know… Worry about what was to come.'

'Why did you bury the camera?'

'What?'

'The camera. You're the one in the photo, aren't you? The camera was found in a graveyard with some old bones, doll parts and a rat head.'

'Shrew. It was a shrew head.'

'Why did you bury those things?'

Queen Isabella stands next to Linda, the pinned heart dripping blood.

'Yes, Goblin, why did you bury those things? Are you going to tell her?'

Linda looks to where I'm staring, then back at me.

'What is it? Do you remember something?'

'No. I just… What was the question?'

'Why did you bury things in the graveyard?'

Spectre-Monsta appears from behind Linda, slowly climbing up her arm.

'It was like a time capsule,' I say, watching Monsta's ascent. 'That's all.'

'So you meant it to be found?'

Amelia walks along the worksite with Scholler, joining us.

I shake my head and say, 'I need a drink.'

'You'd like a drink?' asks Linda. 'It's a bit early, but I'd be happy to take you for one. We could find somewhere nice, have a good long chat.'

'No, forget it,' I say, scowling at Amelia and Scholler. 'I think I should—'

'The camera, the things you buried, you meant people to find them?'

'I don't know.'

'You said it was a time capsule. You meant for people to find it in the future.'

'Not really,' I say, looking at Monsta, now sat on Linda's shoulder.

'Not really?'

'I don't know. It was just a game. That's all.'

'Why don't you just tell her,' says Amelia, crossing her arms. 'It's all going to come out anyway.'

'They might not find him,' I say.

'Find who?' asks Linda.

'No one,' I say, 'I'm sorry, but I need to get going.'

'How did you feel when you saw the photographs in the papers?'

'How did I feel?'

'Were you happy to see them?'

'No.'

'Why not? Why didn't you come forward?'

'Leave the past in the past.'

'So you didn't mean for it to be found?'

'No, I don't know. I didn't expect it. I'd forgotten. It was all forgotten.'

'Why are they digging up the animal remains?'

'They're going to relocate them, give them a proper grave with a marker.'

'Seems like a lot of time and money just for animal bones.'

'It's right that they should be remembered,' I say. 'It's right that we pay tribute to them.'

'But wouldn't the money be better used for an animal shelter? Isn't that a better tribute?'

'I don't... I'm not...'

'She'll find out soon enough,' says Amelia.

'She will,' says Queen Isabella.

'I need to go,' I say. 'I need to get back home.'

'Where's home?'

'A hotel.'

'What hotel? Give me your details so I can get in touch and clarify anything.'

'I'd rather not.'

'It's in your interest. You can make sure I have everything right.'

I walk away.

'Wait! Here's my card. You can call me, Goblin. If there's anything you want to add, give me a call.'

I take the card and leave the site, followed by Queen Isabella, Amelia and Scholler. I leave spectre-Monsta perching on Linda's shoulder.

★

I lie in bed with the papers, Red Queen snoring at my feet. I'd found her in the street, a skinny and dirty ginger cat. I took her to the vet. They kept her in a couple of nights then I sneaked her into the hotel. She peed everywhere but in her tray and I tried to clean it up the best I could. This can't last. I have to find somewhere else to stay.

I flick through the papers and find the pet massacre stories buried underneath all the articles on phone hacking and the financial crisis: 'Pet slaughter shame for nation of animal lovers', 'WWII Pet Holocaust', 'Pet massacre grave in central London'. I glance over the articles. A WWII RAF veteran said 'all this fuss over some pets is an affront to all those who lost loved ones in the war. It's disgusting, it's sentimentality gone mad.'

I find the article written by Linda. She'd discovered the name that's on my birth certificate and uses it throughout the piece so it feels like I'm not reading about myself. Linda describes not-me as 'frail and easily confused'. Queen Isabella, who's reading over my shoulder, snorts. Linda concludes the piece saying that in this time of financial crisis it's a waste of money to dig up the pets and give them a memorial.

Ben calls and says, 'Are ye eating properly, old lady? Are ye staying off the drink?'

'I'm eating like a queen,' I say. 'And I haven't touched a drop. Don't believe everything you read, Ben.'

'I'm just worried about ye. I know how confused ye get when ye drink and I know when ye drink ye dinnae eat.'

'You don't need to worry, Ben. I'm fine.'

'Aye well, ye better be looking after yersel.'

'I am.'

'Take care, old lady.'

'You too, Ben.'

I put down the phone and stare at the paper. I should have refused the interview.

'Wait,' says Queen Isabella, right next to my ear, making me jump. 'Just you wait until they find out you covered up a murder.'

'I didn't cover it up.'

'Wait until they find out you were arrested for murder yourself.'

'I was innocent.'

'Just you wait,' she says. 'Just you wait.'

Romania, Hungary, Austria, Italy, France, 1964 – 1966

After a show, the clown troupe would get together for a drink, to unwind and dissect our performance, discuss what we could improve, but when we travelled through Romania Horatiu would go straight to his caravan. The other clowns didn't say anything so I let him be, except when he was late for rehearsal one morning and I went to fetch him. I barged into his caravan, not even thinking, just all breezy, all 'C'mon, Horatiu, you had too much to drink last night? Look lively, you're late for rehearsal.' But there he was sat on the edge of his bed, tears and snot streaming down his face. He was holding a photograph.

'Hey... You alright?'

He looked up at me, saying nothing, and I backed out of the

caravan. I wanted to be as far away from him as I could, away from his scrunched up tear and snot-stained face. I returned to the clowns and told them Horatiu was ill and we got on with rehearsals.

After putting up posters of David in the town that evening I sat with Fish Boy, having a drink in my caravan.

'I found Horatiu crying today, holding some old photo.'

'He's not happy being back in Romania, and it happens to be the anniversary,' said Fish Boy.

'What anniversary?'

'His boyfriend was shot. Horatiu witnessed it.'

'How do you know?' I said. 'How do you know what's going on with Horatiu?'

'We got to talking recently, that's all.'

'What kind of anniversary is that anyway?'

'One he can't forget.'

'Well, he should. What's the point in holding onto that?'

'What's wrong with you?'

'Well, tell me – what's the point? He should let it go, leave the past in the past.'

Fish Boy knocked back his whisky and said, 'Maybe you should take your own advice.'

'What's that supposed to mean?'

'What's with all the posters, G?'

'You know I'm searching for David.'

'I'd thought you'd given up. Then Groo died.' He looked at me for a moment, then said, 'She was an old cat who loved you and now she's gone. It's just the way it is. You need to move on.'

'I need to find him.'

'Why?'

'I can't let him go.'

'You always skirt around the past, you always say, "Let the past stay in the past", but you cling onto this. Why won't you let him go?'

'Because I'm his family. He's my family. Because he was supposed to take me with him to the sea.'

'We're your family now.'

'I know.'

'Then why not let him be? Why are you chasing a different life, a future that didn't happen? Maybe he doesn't want the past – you – catching up with him. Maybe he has a new life and he's happy. Even if he isn't, who says he wants to be found? He disappeared for a reason.'

'I've always searched for him.'

'Maybe if you stop, he'll come to you.'

Fish Boy put his arm around me.

'Goblin, just let it go,' he said. 'The past be damned.'

'The past be damned,' I said, and drank my whisky.

*

I went to Horatiu's trailer and knocked on the door. There was no answer. I walked in. I searched through his belongings until I found the photo he'd been holding. I sat on his bed and stared down at Horatiu and his boyfriend. I imagined him being shot, I imagined it and I thought, what's the point? What's the point in holding on to that? I threw the photo on the floor, stepping on it as I left. I changed towards Horatiu after that. I shot him down any chance I got and his look of confused hurt made things worse. I started to hate him. He should burn it, I thought. Burn it, bury it. Be rid of it.

*

We stopped in a small town in southern Austria where mum and dad were running auditions, trying to get some new blood after two of our acrobats had left to settle down. I was chatting with Matt when a scrawny teenage boy disappeared into the audition tent. Matt had been one of our star acrobats but there was an accident in one of the rehearsals and he'd broken his spine. He was in a wheelchair now; couldn't feel his legs but could still use his upper body so he worked the wheelchair into the show. He was a spectacular showman. Matt would come over to my caravan in the evenings, bringing his guitar, and we'd drink whisky and sing with Fish Boy and Angelina.

We were chatting, about to head off to rehearsals when the scrawny teen stomped out of the audition tent. I looked up, squinting at him.

'Another reject, I guess.'

'Seems that way.'

The boy made to leave but he spotted us and headed over.

'Who the fuck is this?' he said, gesturing at Matt. 'I get sent away, but this cripple-leech can stay? You belong in the gas chambers, you waste of fucking space.'

He stabbed his penknife into Matt's leg. I hadn't even seen it in his hand. Without thinking I flew at the boy, knocking the air out of him. Pinning him down, pushing on his lungs, I punched his face to a bloody mess before Matt had me by the neck and pulled me off him.

'I can fight my own fights, Goblin, and that wasn't worth it.'

'He stabbed you. He just came right up to you and stabbed you.'

Matt looked down at the forgotten knife.

'And I didn't feel a thing.'

'The things he said to you.'

'I didn't feel that either.'

'I did. I fucking felt it.'

He pulled the knife out and grinned at me.

'I could join Freaks and Wonders. The human pincushion.'

We both laughed, laughing so hard we cried as the boy rolled over, pushed himself up on his hands and knees and spat blood and teeth onto the ground. This is how mum and dad found us, laughing as this boy dribbled blood.

Mum and dad had Matt's wound seen to, making sure it didn't get infected. The boy reported me to the police and I spent the night in a cell. We paid a huge fine, all of it coming out of my wages. I explained what had happened but mum and dad still had me mucking out the animals for the next three months. No clowning, no Freaks and Wonders, just piss and shit.

London, 29 – 30 November 2011

I need an anchor. Queen Isabella, Scholler, Amelia and Monsta are keeping me safe but I need more than those old ghosts. I avoid Mac because all I can think of when we're together is the last time I saw him when we were kids and I can't be reminded of that all the time.

I'd kept in touch with Tim over the years; no real details about our lives, just sending each other postcards of art we liked, sending holiday greetings. I never thought I'd see him again, but here I am, going to see Tim, my Fish Boy.

It isn't a shock to see him. He looks much the same. My imagination had exaggerated his age so much that the actual changes don't matter. His scales have faded. They emerge from beneath the collar of his shirt, flow up his neck and disappear into his grey beard. It was all polite niceties all hello how are you can I take your coat would you like a cup of tea, weren't the riots a blast.

'I danced amongst the flames,' I say.

He laughs and I laugh and I spill my tea I'm shaking so much.

'You haven't changed a bit,' he says.

'I'm old.'

'We're both old.'

'We are.'

'Did the rioters join you?'

'They did,' I say. 'They danced too.'

'Of course they did.'

'What…' I say, trailing off and looking down at my tea and back at him again, 'What have you, I mean, all these years, what have you done with yourself?'

'This and that,' he says.

'Me too. This and that.'

We both smile.

'Is that your wife?'

I gesture to a photograph on the mantle.

'We were never married.'

'No?'

'Together for forty-one years, though.'

I nod.

'It's strange being on your own after that,' he says. 'Almost ten years now and it's still strange. What brings you here?'

'The police. Dead animals.'

'That right?'

'You know me,' I say, smiling.

'Repeating patterns.'

'It can't go as badly as last time,' I say. 'The dead are already dead.'

I stare at his hand clasped around his mug and I look at the faded scales and half-smile before I notice what's missing and I'm sure I'll be sick. I put my mug down clumsily, spilling, shaking with grief. Grief for skin.

'G? What is it?'

I find myself at his feet, kneeling, taking his mug away and holding his hands in mine, inspecting. I weep, his old scaled hands wet with my tears.

'G, it's okay. It was a long time ago, after the circus.'

Finally crying and it's for missing skin. He wraps me in a blanket, like I'm some old lady, frail and pathetic. I wake up on the couch. I squint into the gloaming, unsure where I am. I open the curtains and I look round the room, taking in the strange objects illuminated by the orange light from the street. I find my way to his room and I climb in beside him. I put my arm around him and fall asleep to the sound of his breathing, the sound of his heart. In the morning I run my fingers over his scales and his wrinkles. We fuck away our loneliness; there is only us. The world disappears.

I tell him over breakfast that I don't mind. 'It was just a shock. I'd imagined all kinds of ways in which you'd changed but I never thought that.'

'It was practical. After the circus I retrained in joinery and the webbing was an annoyance. It got in the way.'

'It wasn't even that,' I say. 'It wasn't really about that.'

'Tell me then, tell me why you're here.'

'I'm a witness. They're dragging me all the way back to 1939. How am I supposed to remember that long ago? But I do. I've been holed up in my hotel, writing it all out.'

'What do you remember?'

'Cinema tickets. Devil. Scrumping with Mac and Stevie.'

'You can stay here, you know. You can stay here as long as you need.'

'I have a hotel.'

'We'll go today and pick up your things. You're staying.'

'It's not just me. There's Red Queen, a ginger cat I found. I shouldn't have left her alone all night.'

'You can stay. You and your strays. You can all stay.'

★

We go to the hotel to get my things, to get Red Queen, and there's Ben, Sam and Mahler at reception. Mahler runs to me and I kneel, letting him slobber all over me as I breathe in his smell and ruffle his ears. Sam joins in and there I am, bowled over on the hotel floor.

'Yer hard to pin down, old lady.'

'What are you doing here?'

'I wis worried about ye,' Ben says, eyeing Tim. 'But maybe I didnae need to.'

'It's good to see you,' I say, extricating myself from the dogs.

I hug Ben, holding him tight, then introduce him to Tim. Ben, Tim and the dogs sit together and I watch them from the reception desk, trying to hear what they're discussing.

There's a message for me from Detective Curtis asking me to call back. I go up to my room, feed Red Queen, and I call him. He tells me they've found human remains amongst the pet bones.

'I want you to tell me your story, Goblin.'

'Mac told you.'

'I need to hear what you have to say.'

'I don't have anything to say,' I say, petting Red Queen.

'Goblin, I know it's a shock. You take some time, okay? But I'll be in touch. We'll need to talk this through eventually.'

I give him Tim's number and when I hang up, the phone rings.

'Detective?'

'You lied to me.'

'Excuse me?'

'You said you had nothing to hide.'

'Who is this?'

'They found human remains in the pet pit. It was murder. Was it you? Did you kill someone?'

I say nothing.

'I know your real name.'

I sigh, realising who it is.

'It's not real,' I say to Linda. 'I'm Goblin through and through.'

I hang up.

★

We all pile into the kitchen and I feed the dogs and Red Queen as Tim makes tea. Red Queen is first to finish her food and goes over to sniff Mahler and Sam. I watch her, ready to snatch her up if it looks like a fight will break out, but they just sniff her too before going back to their food.

'I hope ye dinnae mind, old lady. I know ye said ye wanted Mahler to be safe, but the riots are over and he wis missing ye like crazy.'

'Don't worry. I'm glad you're all here,' I say. 'I really am. No tea for me,' I say to Tim before turning back to Ben. 'I'm sorry, Ben, but I'm tired. We'll catch up later, okay?'

'That's alright. Get some rest.'

I scoop up Red Queen in one hand, dragging my bag in the other, and retreat to Tim's room. Mahler follows me through. I get into bed, pull the covers over me, trying to block out Detective Curtis, Linda Cartwright, the discovery of the 'remains'. Red Queen pads around on me, turning in circles until she's comfy and settles. Mahler jumps up, sniffs at Red Queen who ignores him, then settles down next to me, his head on the pillow. We sleep away the morning and when I get up I pull my typewriter out of my bag, setting it up on Tim's desk.

Belgium, West Germany, Poland, 1966 – 1967

Despite the piss and shit, I enjoyed spending time with the animals. I hadn't helped much with the camels before, so there were many times I ended up pushed, kicked and spat at before I got to know them. There were five of them, all named after Colin's ex-girlfriends; Veronique, Julia, Mary, Betsy and Lou. Veronique was the most friendly, Julia had a habit of spitting at people. Mary, Betsy and Lou liked some attention but were mostly only interested in people for food. I loved the feel of them, the smell of them. I felt safe. When I returned to clowning and Freaks and Wonders I continued to visit the camels every evening when my work was done. I'd sit by candlelight and read them stories as they huffed and snored. One night I fell asleep with them, curled up next to Veronique and I got hell from Fish Boy who thought I was off sleeping with someone else. We'd been drifting apart for months and my absence from Freaks and Wonders made that drifting easier. The stupid argument over my night's absence finished us, even though he believed me, even though I smelled of camel. I ended it and things were strained between us, but eventually we were back to meeting some evenings with Angelina and Matt when I wasn't with the camels.

While I was mucking out the animals I'd take a break and watch Milly practice with the big cats. I was in awe of the care she took, the endless patience. She loved them, that was clear. During one of her training sessions one of them scratched her. I say scratched like it was a kitten, just a regular cat. I wasn't sure exactly what I was going to do, but I stood to intervene. She held her hand up: stop. Three handlers stood round her, but didn't approach. They waited as she spoke to the tiger in whispers, stroking its head. It had its paws around her, holding her close. It licked her face. She whispered and it set her loose, padding off to its chair.

'Are you okay?'

'Don't come near me during practice,' she said. 'Especially suddenly. They might think you're trying to attack me.'

'But it hurt you.'

'It was play. This is nothing. I know them well and I know how to control them. Introduce an outlier and there could have been trouble. If you watch, you don't move. You don't come near us. I don't want to lose you or one of the cats.'

'But if one them attacks you? Really attacks?'

'Then it's my fault and I pay the price, and *you don't move.*'

'I don't do anything? Are you serious?'

'What do you think the handlers are for? And this gun?'

'You'd shoot the cats?'

'It's just blanks to scare them. It shouldn't happen, though, not if I'm doing my job properly. They know me, respect me. We have our own language.'

'What happens if they really do attack someone? What happens to the cat?'

'They're euthanized.'

'What do you mean "euthanized"? There's nothing wrong with them.'

'Put down, however you want to say it. They're a danger.'

'They can't be rehomed?'

'It's too risky.'

'What about a zoo? Surely—'

'Is living out their days bored in a cage really any better than death?'

'They already live in a cage.'

'They have me, the ring and the performance. They'd rot in a zoo. I love these cats, Goblin. I'd do anything for them. What do you want? What are you after?'

'I'm just not sure we should have animals performing.'

Milly rolled her eyes and turned away.

'Are you kidding me? Jesus.'

'I just think—'

She turned back to me and said, 'Look, Goblin, they've only known the circus – they're happy here.'

'How do you know they're happy?'

'Because when they're not happy they don't play ball. I've known some rotten trainers who've beaten their animals to get them to perform and it always ends badly. They won't do a thing if they don't want to and I know when not to push it, I know when they're sick or when they need a break.'

'I just feel they should have more.'

'More what?'

'I don't know… Freedom… Maybe their enclosures could be bigger.'

'It's not practical, not if we're to be able to travel the way we do.'

'I know.'

'Look, Goblin, the animals here are well cared for. You know that. I agree, though, that the travelling can put too much stress on some of them. I don't think we should have elephants but there's no way James and Mad are going to lose their star attractions. It'd sink the circus.'

'Don't you think an all-human circus would work?'

'No way, Goblin. We take away the animals and we take away the audience. It's as simple as that. And I love my job. You want me to lose my job?'

'No, I just… It's just a thought.'

'The animals would be put down or trapped in some zoo. You wouldn't be doing them any favours. They're better here with us.'

*

'Time,' I said to mum. 'More time, for the animals to get out of their cages when we travel. More workers to look after them.'

'No,' said mum. 'We can't afford to. Things are tight, Goblin. We're competing with TV and cinema. We can't afford more time or workers, we're stretched as it is. The animals are happy, G. It's in our interest that they're happy. Don't worry, they're well looked after.'

*

Read all about it – life in the circus. TV and cinema were taking over, but the circus still intrigued people. There's always an audience who want to know more about the circus life. They want to know what's behind the fantasy. They want to know about the people who perform such feats, who travel with elephants and tigers, who descend upon towns in a flurry of glitter and music, trumpeting and roars.

I used my initial 'G', and 'Bradfield', my new surname after Mad and James adopted me, and I pitched to UK newspapers. I had several rejections before a tabloid accepted my pitch, but they wanted sensational stories and more focus on the freaks. I talked to my Freaks and Wonders friends over a drink and they said, 'Sure, G. If it gets more people in, write whatever you want.' We sat for hours, laughing as we made up sensational stories of infidelity and freak fetishists. In the cold light of day I had to hold back on the outlandish tales as I didn't want to get in trouble in my first journalist job for making up articles. I based the columns on real life experiences and framed them with rumour and hearsay: 'It's been said that the Lizard King killed the mob who murdered his wife...'

I gave the money from the weekly column to mum and dad for the animals. We hired more workers to help with the animals and we hired a full-time vet. As we travelled, we had an extra few minutes to check on them, to let some of them out of their cages. The circus started to make more money too – there was an increase in audience numbers as we toured, with fans clamouring for autographs from the freaks whose stories I'd told: 'Is it true that—?' 'Did you really—?'

I wrote my columns, I sold my photographs; life in the circus – read all about it.

★

When my column came to an end I was approached by a broadsheet; they wanted a more serious one-off piece, so I wrote about the animals.

When it was published it was seen as a betrayal. I used a pseudonym and changed all the names of my circus colleagues, but they still saw it as a personal attack. I'd proposed that circuses only use domesticated animals, such as horses and dogs, and I called for stronger regulation on the trade of 'exotic' animals. I also wrote with admiration of trainers like Milly, and how they loved the animals and treated them well. I thought it was even-handed. I thought I'd argued my point about animals in the circus without demonising anyone, but mum and dad stopped speaking to me. When I tried to speak to them they'd pretend I wasn't there until mum turned to me and said, 'No more articles.'

Colin, Milly and the other animal trainers wouldn't let me near the animals anymore. Some nights I'd sneak in to sleep with the camels but I slept in one morning and Colin discovered me. He changed the locks on their enclosure.

Angelina still talked to me, but wasn't happy. 'People don't trust you anymore, G. Milly said you were asking awkward questions. There's rumours you're pressuring your mum and dad to get rid of the animals. No one wants to lose their job, G.'

Things were already difficult with the clown troupe; when I returned after the months spent with the animals they'd devised a whole new act that didn't include me, and now they wouldn't speak to me, except for Horatiu.

He came round to my caravan with a bottle of whisky one evening and we sat outside watching the sunset, drinking and talking like we were old friends.

'The whole community treats me like a pariah, but not you,' I said.

He shrugged and said, 'Personally, I don't give a shit about the animals. Travelling would be a lot easier without the dumb bastards. They draw all the attention. We'd make a fortune if we got rid of those spotlight whores.'

I laughed. 'I like your perspective.'

I nursed my whisky for a moment then said, 'But I wasn't trying to get rid of them, I was just—'

'Making a point?'

'Starting a discussion.'

I drank my whisky and looked at him. He continued staring at the sunset.

'Why are you being so nice to me?' I said. 'After how I treated you?'

'Tim said what it was about, and I understand your feelings about the past.' He looked at me and said, 'You just took it out on me.'

I felt myself blush and looked away, down into my whisky glass.

'I'm sorry,' I said, glancing at him, 'I'm sorry, Horatiu.'

'It's all in the past,' he said.

I looked up at him and smiled, shaking my head.

'Yeah,' I said, 'all in the past.'

'I'll drink to that. More?'

When he reached over for the whisky bottle his sleeve rolled up and I saw the small faded tattoo on his forearm. He glanced at me, pulled his sleeve down, and poured me another glass.

'To the past,' he said, raising his glass. 'To leaving it behind.'

I met his glass with mine and we knocked back the whisky, sitting in silence. I recited the numbers on his arm over and over in my head until they became meaningless.

'Did you travel much, Horatiu? Before the war?'

'Not before the war.'

He didn't elaborate and we sat in silence until I said, 'You think it's okay not having a home? Do you think we're missing something?'

'You carry your home with you, G. Modern living is an illness. Those people, settled, with their comforts – they're never happy, never truly alive.'

★

Eventually things returned to normal. Mum and dad talked to me again after a month or so. They never brought it up, just got on with things as if it had never happened. A few of the other circus folk thawed too, but there was still an awkwardness with some of them and Milly wouldn't speak to me at all. I stopped writing articles on circus life and put more time into fiction and photography, getting several short stories and photographs published. I didn't go back into clowning or looking after the animals. I spent my time in Freaks and Wonders, taking photographs, and writing. Creating a different future for myself.

Then the dog was found hanging from one of the candy-striped circus poles, neck broken, tongue lolling. I couldn't look at his eyes. I was a murderer and I was being arrested.

Chapter 11

Who's responsible for this, Goblin? Don't you want them brought to justice?

I'm responsible. I was born blue. I could have died. Could've, should've.

Just give me their names.

There can never be justice. She was tied up and dragged down until she drowned. There's red in the river and it's too late.

Poland, 1967

We should've moved on. When we rolled into the town it was clear we weren't welcome, but we performed to a half-empty circus tent. Dad cancelled the evening performance and we stayed on to do repairs and get some tools and food. I went into town with Blake and Laura to help get the supplies.

We were loading everything into the back of the truck when I heard yelling and laughing. I looked over at a small crowd in the square.

'What's the entertainment?' I said.

'Who knows,' said Blake, not bothering to look.

We finished loading the supplies and Blake went back into the store for something we'd forgotten. Laura sat in the truck and I went over to the crowd, edging my way through. There was an old man on the ground, crying. He was speaking, but I couldn't make out what he was saying or what language it was. A dachshund was running from one side of the crowd to the other, looking for a way out but only finding the force of a boot.

The dog whined when they kicked him but continued running, this way and that until I kneeled down and grabbed a hold of him. I held him to my chest and walked through the crowd, who parted in surprise.

I made my way back to the truck, the dog uncertain of me, wearily trying to bite. I heard yelling and shouting. A couple of people caught up with me and tugged at my arms. I placed the dog on the seat of the truck, handing Laura my coat.

'Wrap him in this.'

'Goblin, what—'

I closed the door and turned to find the crowd were coming towards the truck. A man dragged the sobbing old man by the collar of his coat.

'Why were you kicking the dog?' I said, looking round the crowd.

'It's German. We don't like Germans.'

'And we don't like gypsies.'

'Give the old man his dog back.'

The man who had been dragging the old man dropped him in front of me. The old man babbled at me in what sounded like German.

'I don't understand,' I said, repulsed by him snotting and shaking at my feet. 'I don't speak Nazi.'

'Please, help me,' he said in English. 'They beat me, spit on me. They think I'm German but I'm from Austria, I'm an Austrian Jew. Let them have the dog,' he said. 'Let them have him then they will leave me be.'

Laura got out of the truck and joined me.

'What's going on, G?'

'These scum were kicking the dog.'

'Give the old man his dog back, gypsy,' said the man who had held him.

'I'm not a gypsy,' I said.

'Give the German bastard his dog.'

'For what?' I said. 'For you to kick to death?'

'Please. Give him to them,' said the old man, pawing at my

legs.

'Goblin, you can't just steal someone's dog,' said Laura.

'They're going to kill him,' I said. 'The old man can come with us too. You can come with us.'

'Look,' Laura said to the crowd, hands out as if in surrender, 'we'll give the old man his dog back, just calm down, just everyone calm down.'

A man pushed her and she fell against the truck. I punched him, sending him into the crowd. I was grabbed at either side and held as the man who had dragged the old Austrian punched me in the stomach. As I doubled over I heard Blake shouting and I was dropped. Blake was over six feet and made of muscle; the crowd backed off.

'What's going on, G? What the hell's going on?'

Blake pulled me up and helped me into the truck. I sat next to the dog who was hidden under my coat, not making a sound. The crowd started to gather round again.

'Let's just go, Blake,' said Laura. 'Let's get out of here.'

I put the dog on my lap as we drove away. He made a small huffing noise and settled.

When we got back, Colin took a look at him. He was malnourished and badly bruised. We fed him and he slept. I took him out briefly late in the evening, a short walk around the caravans. He peed and fell asleep where he was standing. I carried him back to my caravan and placed him in a box with a blanket at the end of my bed. The next morning he was hanging from a tent pole and I was being arrested for stealing and damaging property.

'He's not property,' I said. 'This is murder. Tell them, mum. Tell them it's murder.'

But she didn't translate.

'Don't make it worse than it is,' she said.

'Those murderous sonsofbitches,' I said, when I saw the jeering men. They'd all come to watch, to point me out.

'To ona,' they said. 'Ukradła psa starego mężczyzny i zabiła go dla zabawy.'

'What are they saying?' I asked mum.

'They said you took the old man's dog and killed it for fun.'

'Those sonsofbitches.'

They spat on me as the police led me away.

'Sześć miesięcy i grzywna,' the police said. 'Six months and a fine.'

'When I get out,' I said, 'I'm gonna kill 'em. Every one of them. Tell them that.'

Mum didn't translate.

★

The circus left to finish the tour and mum stayed. I told her I'd be fine, that six months wasn't that long, but she insisted. Dad didn't want to leave me either, but mum spoke some Polish so it made sense that she was the one to stay. Dad held me in his arms until the policemen pried us apart, barking at us, with mum translating that no touching was allowed. We ignored the policeman, as if coming out of the embrace was our choice, as if we couldn't hear him.

'I'll miss you, G. I love you. I'll write to you.'

Then he was gone.

It was a small town and the prison only had two cells, each with two beds. Both were empty when I arrived and mostly stayed that way apart from the regulars. Two men dressed in layers of ragged clothes were dragged in most nights, drunk, stinking and singing. I was sure they got themselves arrested just for a roof over their head. The only time we had any new prisoners was a couple of months into my stay and it seemed like they'd arrested all the men in the town. I could hear them before I saw them; it felt like the prison was under siege. They filed past me, all of them beaten up and bloody. Eight of them were squeezed into the cell next to mine and that still left half a dozen more. I searched their faces, looking for the men who killed the dog, but I didn't recognise any of them. The police officer eyed me for a moment then opened the cell door, snatched up my blanket and pillow, shoved them into my arms and pushed me out. I spent that night on the main office floor, my wrist handcuffed to a desk despite my protest, not able to sleep for all the noise the new prisoners made.

Other than that night, prison wasn't so bad and I settled into an imposed routine based around meal times and visiting hours. Mum took a room in the only hotel and came to see me every day. We'd sit across the table from each other, sometimes taking furtive moments to clasp hands. Until prison, I hadn't realised how much I'd become used to touch. It was so easy, hugging mum and dad and my friends. I'd taken for granted the presence of Fish Boy or Angelina when we were going together. In prison, I'd think back on when I was with them and fantasise about the smallest things; running my fingers through Fish Boy's hair, the way Angelina used to stroke my eyebrow and trace her finger down my cheek. I'd lie on my bed, arms by my side, eyes closed, and I'd think of Angel. I'd think of us holding hands, floating in the rock pool, watching the clouds coagulate and break apart. I'd float on those memories until I was back in London and dad had pressed those coins into my hand. I'd think of dad's embrace and remember how lucky I was, looking forward to being back with my family.

When mum came to visit she'd read to me; letters from dad, Angelina, Horatiu and other circus folk, and books by Kafka, Dostoyevsky, De Beauvoir, my favourite Saki stories over and over. As she settled into her life in the town, she'd tell me about some of the people she met. One of the local shopkeepers had warmed to mum and always asked after her 'córka kryminalistka'.

'I told Aleksy your name many times, but he still insists on calling you my "criminal daughter". You'd like him – mischievous, with a gift of the gab, just like you. He told me yesterday that the hotel owner is overcharging me just because he knows I have nowhere else to go. He said I should come stay with his family, said he wouldn't charge me a penny. I told him I didn't want to impose, but he was adamant, said I'd be doing him a favour because he has a long-running feud with the hotel owner and would get a lot of satisfaction to be taking away his custom. How can I resist an invitation like that?'

She was laughing, but I just stared at my hands.

'G? You okay?'

'Mum, I'm glad you have friends,' I said, looking up at her, trying not to cry like some baby. 'You've put your life on hold because of me.'

She didn't respond for a moment, just stared at me, her lips pursed.

'Goblin, my life isn't on hold. You're part of my life. And I choose to be here.'

'I know, I just... I dunno. I just want you to know I'm sorry.'

'G, there's nothing to be sorry about. You did the right thing.'

She held my hand.

'I'm still sorry—'

'Nie!' the policeman yelled and I jumped at the sudden intrusion, yanking my hand away like I'd been shocked. 'Nie dotykać.'

Mum had a short talk with him before turning back to me and rolling her eyes.

'What did he say?'

'He said we have to obey the rules or visitor privileges will be taken away.'

'Why can't we touch?'

'He said we could be exchanging contraband.'

'Are you serious?'

'It's just power, that's all. That's all it's ever about, isn't it? Power and money.'

I fiddled with the edges of a book and said, 'Mum?'

'Mm-hm?'

'I never thanked you and dad for taking me in.'

She huffed and said, 'G, c'mon, you're our family. Simple as that.'

She reached for my hand again, but stopped herself and

glanced over at the policeman who was glowering at us. She smiled, shook her head and raised her hands in mock surrender. The policeman grunted.

She looked at me for a moment then said, 'Goblin, what happened to your old family?'

It tripped off my tongue before I could even think how to reply, 'Pa was killed by Nazis, ma became a mermaid, and David went to the sea to be a pirate.'

I stared back at her and blushed, realising how childish it sounded.

'What really happened?'

'Pa died in the war. I don't know how. Ma drowned herself in the Thames. David disappeared. I think he went to the sea – that was his plan.'

Mum nodded.

'What were they like?'

I shrugged and said, 'Pa hardly spoke to me, but we fixed things together – neighbours always came to us with their wireless. I liked working with him.' I picked at the cover of the book, peeling it away at the edge. 'Ma hated me.'

'What?'

'She said I should never have been born.'

Mum put her hand over her mouth.

'Why would she say that?'

'She said I was born blue and I was so ugly I killed the midwife. She called me Goblin-runt. David looked out for me, though. I had him, my dog Devil and my friends Mac and Stevie.'

Her hand still across her mouth, she said, 'I'm glad you had some people who cared about you.'

'And Devil.'

'And Devil. What happened to him?'

I was silent for a moment and said, 'Mum? Can we talk about something else? Or you can read me a letter if there's any? Or more Saki?'

'Of course, I'm sorry,' she said and picked up her bag. 'I

have a letter from your dad.'

As she rummaged in her bag I said, 'Maybe I can talk about all that some other time.'

'Whenever you're ready,' she said.

Shortly after that visit, mum moved in with Aleksy and his family. She'd update me on the feud with the hotel owner and tell me about Aleksy's kids. She helped look after them and taught them acrobatics. She stayed fit, with a daily regime of exercise and practice. She told me she'd rigged up a swing between two trees by a river just outside of town and the children took picnics and they'd watch her fly. Mum seemed happy, so I no longer felt guilty about her staying. I no longer thought of the dog or the old man. I simply enjoyed my time with mum – with no circus distractions I had her all to myself. She was soon bringing bread and biscuits every day, a gift for her 'córka kryminalistka', freshly baked by Anastazja, Aleksy's wife. The policemen made a fuss at first, but when she gave some to them, they let it pass. It wasn't long before the bureaucrat was turning the other way when we held hands or even hugged.

We settled into the routine, waiting for the day I'd be free and we could go back to the circus. Instead, the day came when mum didn't return.

I asked about her, but the policemen pretended they didn't know what I meant. They spoke English when it suited them and when it didn't they'd say they didn't understand me, they'd pretend they couldn't find the words.

I knew some basics – I'd asked to learn 'bastard', 'son of a bitch' and 'fuck you' but mum had just laughed and taught me niceties like 'please' and 'thank you'.

'Where's the lady?' I said. 'My mother?'

They frowned at me.

'Pani?' I tried. 'Szalona – moja matka. Gdzie?'

They shrugged and shook their heads saying something in Polish I didn't understand. I needed her to translate, but she was gone. Two days passed and Aleksy and Anastazja came by, but

I couldn't understand them and they couldn't understand me and the policemen were amused by our failed communication. They gave up trying to speak to me and had a long discussion with two of the policeman, who glanced at me now and again. The conversation became heated and Aleksy shouted at them before leaving, dragging Anastazja with him.

Aleksy and Anastazja stopped by to see me every day. We didn't speak, but they'd sit with me and Anastazja would sing. They continued to bring me food but I barely ate.

Almost three weeks had passed with no news of mum. I was with Aleksy, sitting side by side in silence when dad walked into the police station and I felt the bars fall away. I thought of when dad first found me and the Lizard King, of the time he held my bloody arm, of our last hug when he left. I waited as the bureaucrat let him into my cell, Aleksy giving him a nod as he left. I waited for my dad to hold me in his arms.

He removed his hat, sweeping his hair from his face. He was pale, his eyes pink and bloodshot.

'She's dead,' he said.

My legs buckled, but before I fell he pushed me and I stumbled back, knocking my pile of books, hitting the wall, crumpling, falling to the floor. As I made to get up, his hand was around my throat, his knee pressing on my chest. Everything was muted; just a buzzing in my ears. I felt the weight of him crushing me, and looked into his eyes. He was crying, his tears falling onto my face. I saw Aleksy and the bureaucrat grabbing at him. Their mouths were moving but I couldn't hear them. The bureaucrat had his arm around dad's neck, pulling him off me. I heaved in air and blacked out.

*

When I woke I didn't remember what had happened, not at first. And when I did, nothing was worth anything anymore. I spent my days sleeping in my cell. Aleksy and Anastazja came by. They brought me bread, but didn't stay. I didn't eat so the policemen took it.

Tim visited, with Ania in tow to translate. He told me mum had been found in the river, tied up in her makeshift swing.

'They're insisting it's an accident. James is enlisting legal help from the UK.'

Tim held me and fed me. We talked. Or he talked and I listened. I liked the sound of his voice. He said that dad had taken the body back to London, the funeral had been attended by hundreds.

Then he said, 'I know he attacked you, Goblin. He told me.'

'I don't remember,' I said.

'You do. I know you do.'

I nodded.

'He blames me,' I said. 'And he's right.'

'That's not right at all, G. He's your dad—'

'It's my fault.'

'It's not your fault. It's the bastard that killed Mad. Ania helped me speak to Aleksy and Anastazja. Aleksy said your dad attacked him and the policeman, they had to restrain him. He was lashing out, G. He didn't mean to hurt you.'

'She wouldn't have been here if it wasn't for me.'

'G, you can't think like that. What use is it? Your dad will come round – I know he's ashamed of what he did. Now listen – you get released tomorrow. You'll be free.'

I looked at him.

'I'll take you back. The circus is going to Venice. We're doing a show in Piazza San Marco.'

'I can't do it,' I said. 'I can't face him.'

'He won't be there. James is in England for now.'

Tim laid his hand on my shoulder. He leaned in and kissed me on the cheek. He whispered in my ear.

'We love you, Goblin.'

★

We sat in the train carriage watching the landscape slide by, disappearing into the past.

'Those years with her – I want them back. I'm not ready for her absence.'

'I know, G,' Tim said, putting his arm around me.

'I thought she was indestructible, but I killed her.'

'It wasn't your fault.'

I breathed on the window, blurring the world outside.

'You know it wasn't your fault.'

I nodded to let him know I believed him.

'You can't carry that with you, Goblin. It's a poison.'

'It doesn't feel real. That she's gone. What did she look like?'

'She was cold and her lips were dry. I put lipstick on her lips and a flower in her hair. I gave her one of the stories you wrote, her favourite about the lizard people. I put it in her hands.'

'She was indestructible.'

'I know.'

'It doesn't feel real.'

'Matt, Colin, Angelina, Horatiu and Adam – they all give their love. They're looking forward to seeing you.'

'No, I don't want to see any of them.'

'We'll get you settled, then we'll see.'

We arrived at the train station and went to catch a vaporetto. I knew little about Venice, and at first I didn't have any interest in it. All I wanted was a place where I could curl up in bed and disappear, but as we chugged our way down the Grand Canal I couldn't help but feel curious.

'How does this place exist? Am I dreaming?'

Tim laughed and put his arm round my waist.

'I knew you would love it.'

'It's an impossible city.'

'I read that to make the impossible possible the ruler of Venice, the Doge, would be taken out into the lagoon where he'd drop a gold ring. He'd marry the sea, protecting Venice from floods.'

'Of course,' I said. 'This city could only be built on myths and magic.'

'And blood, empire, and the money of tourists.'

I stared down the Grand Canal, looking at the water. For the first time in a long time I thought of David. I knew. I could feel it physically; a knot in my belly.

I remember what he told me: 'I'll sail around the world. I'll meet a girl and we'll make our home by the sea – a place where the sea is everything, where it changes people.'

I knew there was no other place he would be other than this floating city.

'You knew what you were doing, bringing me here,' I said.

I smiled. For the first time in weeks I smiled, and he smiled back and took my hand.

'I knew you would love Venice,' he said.

But at that moment, it wasn't Venice I loved.

Chapter 12

London, 30 November 2011

I emerge from Tim's room in the early evening and join Tim, Ben, Sam, and Mahler, who had already been through for his dinner. Mahler rushes to greet me as I sit at the table.

'Have a good sleep, old lady?'

I nod and laugh as Mahler puts his paws on my lap and licks furiously at my face.

'I missed you too,' I say.

I snuffle into Mahler's fur, breathing in his smell. Tim makes me some tea and Ben tells me about his journey down. I sit at the table, listening to Ben's voice, glad to feel part of a big family again.

'Aye, so it wis a right bastard of a journey. I'm no saying she wis an actual Nazi, but she definitely had fascist leanings.'

'What?' I say. 'Who's a Nazi?'

'That woman on the train.'

'What woman?'

'Have ye no been listening?' Ben says, rolling his eyes and turning to Tim as he sits down, placing biscuits on the table. 'Away wi' the fairies – has she always been like that?'

Tim laughs and says, 'She was always in her own world.'

I look at them both, past and present coming together, so I say, 'The woman was a fascist?'

Ben looks at me, then says, 'Aye – she didnae like it one bit when Mahler and Sam were up on the seats. It's not as if anyone else needed them, she wis just being snooty and said they were dirty and should be on the floor.'

'You're not dirty, are you Mahler?' I say, ruffling his ears.

'She made a big stink about it and the conductor said they had to go on the floor or we'd have to get off at the next stop. So

I made that woman's life a misery – I let off some awful farts, then I blamed her, saying she wis the one causing a stink, which wis the truth of the matter. She just tutted. There's nothing worse than a tutter. I bashed into her as I went to the loo and she spilled her drink on herself. She got the conductor again, but I pleaded persecution, saying she wis a nasty dog hater and wis trying to get me thrown off. Eventually he just took her to a different carriage – upgraded her to first class, so I bet she wis happy with that.'

Tim laughs and says, 'Good for you.'

'Aye, it wis good, until hordes got on the train and then the delays. A bastard of a journey.'

'I'm glad you came, Ben,' I say. 'I really missed you.'

'It wis boring without ye. Though, these two kept me on ma toes.'

'I bet they did.'

'How did you two meet?' asks Tim and I clatter my mug onto the table.

'She stole ma spot,' says Ben.

'He doesn't want to know about that,' I say.

Ben frowns at me, 'Well that's how we met and that's what he asked – I had a begging spot and I came back to find she'd stolen it. So I told her tae get tae fuck but she wasnae listenin – too busy hugging Sam, the wee traitor.'

I get up and go to the kitchen counter, turning up the radio.

'She wis crying and snottin all over him', says Ben, 'but he wis lapping up the attention so I just sat next to them and let her cry into his fur. She dried up and Sam fell asleep in her arms.'

'I remember,' I say, swaying to the music. '"Look, lady," you said, "we've all got our sob stories, but this is ma spot."'

'Aye, that's right. But ye just ignored me and asked about Sam. Before I knew it I wis telling ye our sob story. She wis deflecting,' says Ben, turning back to Tim, 'away from the situation of ma spot.'

'I wasn't there for long,' I say.

'Aye, ye had tae go get medication for yer wife.'

I nod, looking down at Mahler who'd followed me. I stroke his head.

'Her wife wis sick,' says Ben to Tim, 'but I didnae find that out till later. From then on, though, we were pals. Eh, old lady?'

Red Queen wanders through, jumps up on the counter and meows at me. I scoop her up and hold her, swaying together.

'She'd bring me coffee and her freshly baked banana cake – that wis the good shit, I'm telling ye. And I helped her too, taking old man Monty – that wis her dog before Mahler – for walks when she had to stay in with her wife.'

'I couldn't have managed without you, Ben,' I say, listening to Red Queen's purring.

'Dinnae get soppy on me, old lady.'

I smile and look over at him. He winks, raising his mug to me.

I put Red Queen down and scoop some food into a bowl for her. I sit back at the table and Ben shifts round in his chair, stares at Tim, and says, 'So, what's yer story, lizard man?'

'He's not a lizard,' I say, 'he's a Fish Boy.'

'Not anymore,' says Tim.

'They're some tattoos,' says Ben. 'Got them all over?'

Tim nods and says, 'Goblin and I would get tattoos in every city we stopped in.'

'What circus tricks did ye do?'

'I was "Fish Boy, Wonder of the Deep" in Freaks and Wonders. I'd swim in a tank and show people my webbed fingers as Goblin told my story.'

'She's a good storyteller, our G.'

'That she is.'

'How long did ye work together?'

'Until we split up.'

'Ye were a couple?'

'We were.'

'I thought ye were a lezza, old lady.'

Tim and I laugh and Ben says, 'What's so funny?'

'Nothing,' I say.

'So did ye turn lezza after him?' says Ben. 'No offence,' he says to Tim.

I laugh and shake my head.

'I'm not gay,' I say, stroking Mahler's ear. 'Or straight.'

'Bi then?'

I shrug and say, 'Maybe.'

'Maybe? What kinda answer is that?'

'What does it matter what I am?'

Ben looks at me for a moment then says, 'Dunno, old lady. I guess it doesn't.'

Red Queen slinks over to me and jumps on my lap. Ben feeds Sam a biscuit under the table and says, 'So how long were ye in the circus?'

'I left in sixty-seven. I went to live in Venice.'

'Why'd ye leave?'

I say nothing and stare down at Red Queen, stroking her head, her eyes half-closed in contentment.

'She was seduced by Venice,' says Tim.

'I've never been to Venice,' says Ben.

'It's beautiful,' I say, 'but full of tourists. All the residents are being driven out.'

'Aye, it's getting that way in Edinburgh.'

I nod and say, 'I'm going to take Mahler for a walk.'

'Sure, old lady.'

'You alright?' asks Tim.

'I'm fine.'

'I was going to rustle up some pasta.'

'Sounds good. I won't be long.'

I take Red Queen off my lap and place her on my chair. Turning to Ben I say, 'Do you want me to take Sam?'

'Aye. Thanks, old lady.'

As I walk down the hall with Mahler and Sam I hear Ben say, 'So what wis old G like when she wis young?'

Venice, 1967

I didn't watch the performance. I didn't see anyone else from the circus. Tim had arranged a lease on an apartment for me and the first few days I stayed inside. He'd gone to the market to stock up on food for me, so I managed. On the third day, he came to see me.

'You haven't been out? At all?'

'No.'

'This beautiful city, and you've been cooped up here. What did prison do to you?'

'It isn't that.'

'Angelina came by. She said you weren't in.'

'I was in. I heard her.'

'So why didn't you—'

'I don't want to see them. That life is gone.'

'Goblin, we love you.'

'I can't face them. I can't go out until the circus is gone.'

'Are you going to be alright?'

'You don't need to worry.'

'But I do.'

'I know you do. I'm fine.'

'You'll go out when we're gone? You promise me?'

'I'm looking forward to seeing the city.'

'You'll love it, G. I know it.'

He hugged me.

'You'll keep in touch, won't you? You'll write?'

'I will. I appreciate everything you've done for me.'

'I want you to be happy. You'll be okay, won't you?'

'You don't need to worry.'

We kissed and he was gone, the circus was gone, and the next day was the start of my new life.

★

The sky was light blue, the sun was blinding. I wandered the labyrinthian streets without a map, getting lost, reaching dead ends, doubling back. I weaved my way through the city, finding myself in wide open squares and busy thoroughfares. I sat outside cafés, sipping coffee and listening to the lively gabble of tourists and the rapid-fire Venetian dialect of the locals. Continuing my walk, I wandered down dark narrow streets that led to small canals that were hidden from the sun. Only minutes away from the bustle and noise, I was enveloped in the mystery of dark, crumbling buildings and the gentle lapping of water.

I stopped for lunch at a café hidden down one of these narrow streets, before making my way to San Marco. The mid afternoon sun scorched the square as it heaved with tourists. I joined the long queue to the Campanile. From the top of the tower I could see right across the jumbled rooftops of the city and out across the lagoon to the other islands. Seeing the city from above, it felt even more impossible, vulnerable to the sea that surrounded it.

After the Campanile I bought a map and made my way through the streets to the vaporetto stop that serviced Burano. I sat at the back of the vaporetto and looked across to San Michele, the cemetery island. I watched Venice recede, listening to the sound of the engine and the churned-up water.

I wandered through the streets of Burano, admiring the brightly coloured houses, petting the many cats. I bought a lace bookmark to send to Tim. I watched the sunset over the lagoon; the boats bobbing past, the birds dipping and diving for fish. I thought of Cornwall and the story I told to Angel about the kraken who reached up for the sun, pulling it down, swallowing it whole, nursing the warmth in its belly before spewing it up in the morning. I watched the sun disappear and sought warmth for my own belly; a glass of wine, a hot meal.

I found a restaurant full of rowdy locals. I took a table outside, enjoying a simple seafood dish for dinner. Each table had a candle and I watched the warm light dance on their faces.

The group burst into song off and on, little fragments.

I knew if I was to stay here I'd need to learn Italian, but I was happy in my ignorance – no small talk, nothing expected of me. I was silent, observing. This was the first time I'd ever been alone, properly settled and alone. When I travelled to Cornwall I had Monsta. In Cornwall I had Monsta and Corporal Pig and Angel. On the journey to London I had CP. When ma disappeared I had a family of animals.

I was afraid, as I sat there listening to the locals. I was afraid I wouldn't be able to be truly alone, but I knew that I wouldn't be alone for long.

I said, 'I am alone and I am home,' raising my glass to no one, to the locals, to the island, to Venice, to the moon that was creeping up above the buildings. All those years of travelling, all those years on the road, I never thought I could feel at home in one place, but here it was; these people I couldn't understand, this magical crumbling land that was sinking into the sea. I couldn't imagine belonging anywhere else. I knew if that's how I felt, then David would too. If he'd been travelling the world by sea and found Venice I knew he couldn't leave. He had to be here and I would find him.

On the vaporetto journey back to my apartment, I watched the moonlight shimmer across the black lagoon and I thought of David, lying on his bed, dreaming of escape, dreaming of the sea. I thought of the creatures beneath those waves – fish monsters, mermaids, krakens, sunken treasure.

'I'll find you, David,' I whispered to the sea.

*

Tim had given me my circus earnings to get myself settled and I got by for a couple of months. I bought some language books and tapes, teaching myself some basic Italian, embarrassing myself at the local market as I stumbled through fragmented sentences. The stall holders would laugh and shake their heads at me, replying to me in Italian that was too fast to follow. I was tempted to forgo these regular humiliations and shop exclusively at the supermarkets, but I always went back. After almost three months, the stallholders would greet me warmly and they were soon helping me, teaching me new words. One of the fish merchants, Benito, could speak English all along.

'What's Italian for "asshole"?' I said.

He smiled, raised his hands in supplication. 'I was helping you,' he said.

'You enjoyed laughing at me.'

My Italian was hesitant and fragmented for the first few months and while I was able to make myself understood I found it hard to follow replies and couldn't hold a conversation. My circus earnings were running out and I wasn't able to get a regular job with my poor Italian, so I started busking as a clown. Our circus acts were all developed for a group, so I had to adjust to being solo, adapting some of Horatiu's mime work. I kept up with my writing, but my pitches for articles on everyday life in Venice were rejected by UK newspapers and magazines and I had little success with short stories. I was still running short, so I asked Benito to help me write a poster advertising myself as a dog walker. This was a real success and I was soon breaking even.

I had my routine. I had coffee at home then picked up the dogs I was looking after. As I walked them I put up 'missing' posters of David, layer upon layer as previous posters were defaced, torn, weather-beaten.

I was soon picking up strays and injured pigeons and my apartment quickly filled with dogs and cats and birds. The first dog I rescued, Montgomery, was the only one I named. I said to the others, 'You can have your own names that only you know.' It was partly to keep me from becoming too attached – I couldn't afford to keep them all and there was always more to pick up. Monty stayed with me but I tried to find homes for the others, so there was a constant stream of animals coming and going. A number of the animals were rejected several times – too small, too big, too old, not the right colour, too much work, too ugly, too ill. I liked to think it was us who rejected them; I vetted the potential people thoroughly and anyone who wasn't suitable was promptly ejected, often followed by a stream of my well-practiced Venetian swearing: 'Chi ta cagà! Col casso. Ti xe via de testa. Va a cagar sule ortighe! Ma va' in mona.'

In the evening I'd go to a local bar, where I'd write. Gio, the owner, would come in now and again, checking in with the manager, ordering a drink and talking with the regulars. His English was basic, but much better than my Italian, which was still fragmented. He was small, corpulent, with a genuine warmth and a mischievous curl of the lip. Gio soon learned of my collection of animals and my love for pigeons. When I told him my name he looked disgusted and said, 'What kind of name is Folletto?'

'Folletto?'

'Si, Folletto – Goblin.'

'Ah, what's wrong with it?'

'A folletto is an evil thing.'

'Maybe I'm evil.'

He shook his head, 'No, you're no folletto. La Pazza dei Piccioni is what you are.'

I looked at him blankly and he said, 'Crazy Pigeon Woman.'

I laughed and almost cried as I hugged him. He looked disgruntled and said, 'I don't know why you're happy – that name's no good. Pigeons are horrible dirty things.'

But he smiled, pleased I liked the name, and a couple of weeks later he brought me an injured pigeon.

'I should have left the dirty thing where it was, but I didn't want to be cursed by an evil folletto,' he said, handing over the bird.

I needed to earn more to feed the animals and for vet bills, so I read books, studying the history of Venice and set up my own business, running macabre history tours for the tourists. I cut back on dog walking, as the tours paid better and between that and looking after the strays I didn't have as much time. Gio supported me, putting up adverts in the bar for my tours, telling everyone I was the one to go to. I'd lead the tourists through the labyrinthian streets and scare them with tales of Biagio Cargnio and the cursed Ca Dario.

London, 5 December 2011

I return from seeing Detective Curtis to find Tim and Ben waiting for me, sitting at the kitchen table. I look at them, suspicious of their ease with each other.

'How'd it go?' asks Tim.

I shrug and shake my head.

'I don't know why he wanted to see me,' I say, bending down to greet Sam and Mahler. 'Mac had already told him everything.'

'And what's that then?' says Ben.

'Don't you start in on me too,' I say, ruffling Mahler's ears. 'I don't want to talk about it.'

'You might find it easier talking to us than the detective or reporters,' says Tim. 'You need to talk about it eventually.'

'Don't tell me what I need.'

'We're here, that's all.'

I glance at them, annoyed by the look of concern on their faces.

'I'm just tired, okay?'

Tim gets up and hugs me. I lay my head on his chest.

'I'm writing about it,' I say, listening to his heart. 'I'm still writing about the past. I think I'll be able to talk about it soon.'

'I just want you to be okay.'

He runs his fingers through my hair.

'I know.'

'Sit down and relax. I've made dinner. I'll get the wine.'

I slump into the chair and watch spectre-Monsta's tentacles come over the top of the table, followed by the shrew head. Monsta settles, looking at me with those beautiful dark eyes. Tim comes back through, hands Ben a beer and pours me some red wine. I sip it and feel myself unwind.

We have dinner together and tell Ben about the circus. When dinner's over Ben takes Mahler and Sam for a walk and Tim and I continue talking. He pours me another glass of wine, spilling some on the table as he tells me what happened to our friends after the circus ended. Monsta kerlumpscratches across the table, crouches down and licks up the wine. I smile, watching. A tipsy Monsta would be an entertaining Monsta. I tune back into what Tim is saying, feeling the warmth of the wine in my belly.

'Ariadne and Adeline had found it hard to get any work after the circus ended,' he says.

I nod as Monsta stands and sways before kerlumpscratching back to me.

'They appeared in a few B-movies and did stints in various striptease clubs. I was doing well so I'd send them money when I could. Ariadne got married but it only lasted a few months and I'm pretty sure they only did it for the publicity. They had to make a living.'

'It's hard,' I say. 'Trying to find your place in the world after you leave the circus. It must have been even harder for them. At least I could disappear into the crowd if I wanted to. What happened?'

'They gave up showbiz in the end and worked in a newsagent in Brighton. Ariadne died from heart failure in '89. Adeline followed her two days later.'

I wish I'd kept in touch, wish I'd brought them to Venice. We could have worked together. They could've helped with the tours. Could've, should've.

'Don't you have any happily ever after stories?' I say after a while. 'Don't you have any of those?'

'Does happily ever after exist?'

'I was happy once.'

'I'm glad,' he says. 'Tell me about your happiness.'

Venice, 1968

On the day of the 1968 Biennale opening, police ran through Piazzo San Marco. I was fascinated by the sight of these quasi-military men in the square. It looked like theatre. I took photos and stopped one of the men, asking in broken Italian what was happening but he raised his hand dismissively and continued running. I followed and caught up with them as they were dragging protesters away from a Biennale pavilion. I knew David would be disgusted by the police and their use of force, so I documented it with my camera; I was a witness and I'd tell this story. I captured the moment a policeman tore a banner – 'Biennale of capitalists, we'll burn your pavilions!' – from a protestor's hands. I took a photo of the banner as it lay crumpled on the ground, the protestor being hauled away in the background.

I walked over to the policeman, taking more photos as he carried off the girl.

'Ehi, ma io ti conosco!' she said to me.

I shook my head. 'I don't know you,' I said, and was about to reply in Italian when she said in English, 'Yes, I've seen you, every night, drinking and writing. I'll meet you there. Tonight, tomorrow, who knows? As soon as I'm free.'

She winked at me. I stood staring after her and as she disappeared I heard her yell, 'Le foto! Keep taking photos!'

I did as instructed, speaking to the protestors, a mix of students, intellectuals, artists. 'We're protesting the commodification of art. It's no longer about expression, no longer about experimentation, no longer about the art itself. It's all about money, the rich pigs buying culture and killing it.'

I took photos as artists covered or turned over their own work in support of the protest. By the end of the day all the protestors had been removed and the Biennale opened. I went home and developed the photos. I contacted the UK broadsheet that had published my circus article and was paid a decent sum for the photographs and a first person account. I felt guilty, making money from an anti-capitalist protest, but it all went towards looking after my ever-expanding family.

★

I woke up the next morning on the couch, covered in dogs and cats. I slithered my way out from under them and fixed myself a coffee, thinking of the girl. I had seen her before, at Gio's bar in the evenings. She'd meet her friends there. I liked listening to them, their raucous conversations and loud laughter. But they were background, merely a familiar comfort, and they seemed so wrapped up in themselves that I was surprised she had noticed me.

That evening I went to Gio's, waiting for her, but she didn't show. I wondered if I should go to the police, find out if she was in prison, but I didn't know her name. I went to the bar the next night, and the next. On the third night she turned up, sitting next to me, putting her hand on mine like we were friends or lovers.

'Sorry I took so long, those pigs kept me locked up.'

'They're not pigs.'

'No? You on their side?'

'No. I like pigs.'

'Aaah, yes, I've heard about you – the crazy woman who collects animals. La Pazza dei Piccioni.'

'You've been talking to Gio about me.'

'I have. I know all about you.'

'You know everything about me?'

She smiled.

'I will soon. Drink?'

We ordered wine and properly introduced ourselves. Juliana told me she was an artist and she worked at Ca' Pesaro, the gallery of modern art, to bring in more money.

'They weren't happy when I got arrested. I am lucky to still have my job but I charmed them and all is well.'

She raised her wine glass in a toast. I followed suit and said,

'To your charm.'

She laughed, a deep belly laugh that caused everyone to turn and look.

'To my charm,' she said, clinking glasses, 'may it forever get me what I want.'

She winked at me and finished off her wine.

'I like pigeons too, you know,' she said.

'You do?'

She nodded. 'Birds are my favourite animal.'

'Even pigeons? Most people hate them.'

'People are stupid. I like your tattoos,' she said, looking at my arms and chest.

'I travelled a lot,' I said. 'I'd get tattoos wherever I went.'

'But where are you from? Where were you born?'

'London.'

'I was born there too,' she said. 'My father was born in Venice but moved to London to study and met my mother at university.'

She was interrupted by Gio who hugged her like they were old friends. He greeted me and squeezed my shoulder as he chatted to Juliana. I couldn't follow their rapid-fire Italian so I sat and watched her. I watched her laugh that mischievous laugh, her whole face lighting up. Her long dark brown hair was tied messily up in a bun with strands falling about her face, stroking her brown skin. As she talked with Gio she poured us more wine and suddenly turned back to me, not missing a beat.

'We moved back to Venice when I was three,' she said. 'We would go to London for holidays and to see my grandparents and I stayed with them when I studied art history there, so I grew up knowing it well.'

I didn't want her to ask me about my time living in London so I told her of the years travelling with the circus. I painted a romantic picture.

'So I've fallen for a clown?' she said. 'You couldn't be more perfect.'

'Fallen?' I said, but she didn't hear me. Her friends had

arrived and she disappeared in a flurry of hugs, laughter and overlapping voices, all discussing the protest and arrests. I drank my wine and watched them together, catching parts of their conversation. Juliana turned to me, pointing, her friends all looking me over. I turned away, pretending to write but trying to listen to what they were saying.

'Did you miss me?' she said as she hugged me from behind, her arm across my chest, her head leaning gently on my shoulder. 'I'm sorry, but I haven't seen them all since the protest. I was telling them about my Goblin-clown.'

'Yours?'

'I'm hoping my charm will get me what I want.'

She leaned in and kissed me fleetingly on the mouth and said, 'Tomorrow, you and I. Dinner.'

'A date?'

'Of course a date.'

'How old are you?'

'Twenty-four. Why?'

'I'm older. A lot older.'

'I've dated older women.'

She ran her fingers through my hair, tucking it behind my ear.

'What does it matter? You're my Goblin-clown and I'm your criminal artist. We're meant to be.'

'Are we?'

'I feel it,' she said, placing her hand on her chest.

'Dinner,' I said, nodding. 'Tomorrow.'

'I'll meet you here at seven.'

She kissed me again and I held her this time.

Venice, 1960s/1970s

I fell in love with Juliana.

We went for dinner that night, talking for hours. Walking tipsily back to her flat, she whispered in my ear a mixture of

English and Italian, telling me what she wanted to do to me before throwing her head back and laughing that raucous laugh. Her flat was a mess of paintings and art materials and I negotiated my way through the flotsam, following her to the kitchen. I stripped for her as she poured us prosecco. She held the glasses awkwardly in one hand, spilling some as she led me through to the bedroom. I fell onto her bed and she poured her drink across my breasts and belly. I laughed as the cold hit my skin, as it rolled onto the sheet in rivulets, as it fizzed and pooled in the concave of my stomach. She parted my legs, kissed my cunt and licked from my belly to my breasts, her tongue flicking at my nipples. We kissed, her fingers massaging my inner thighs, moving to my clit and making me moan and then she was gone and I blinked up at her as she stood over me, removing her clothes. I pressed my hand between my legs as she slowly peeled the clothes from her body. Watching her, I came. She finished the prosecco as I knelt on the bed, my arm around her waist, pulling her to me. I kissed her stomach, breathing in her smell as her fingers threaded through my hair. I pulled her down. I kissed and bit her thighs as she put her legs over my shoulders. I tongued at her clit, tasting her, listening to her, feeling her body shake as she came.

We'd meet in the evenings at Gio's, we'd walk through Venice together in the middle of the night, enjoying the quiet. We'd sleep at hers or more often mine, feeding the animals, playing with them, taking the dogs for walks. I fell for her but I thought I was just a phase for her, a passing affair. I buried the doubts and let it be, I let us exist in the present.

I thought I was happy until the evening I was tired and I got talking about the circus, giving away too much. I told her about the posters, about David, that I was still searching for the brother who escaped to the sea, but she asked too much so I left the bar early, telling her I had to go home to feed the animals. Instead, I walked to the Grand Canal and lowered myself in.

I swam for a moment, then floated. I thought of the tourists finding my body. I thought what a story that would be. I thought it was a shame that I wouldn't be there to write about it. Goblin Drowns in Canal, no one mourns.

I let go, sinking. I thought of nothing at all. I felt cleansed in the dirty water. It wasn't deep. It was a struggle to stay on the bed of the canal, with the rubbish and the fish. I floated and I thought of the animals. Juliana will look after them, I thought. I closed my eyes.

I was pulled and jerked out of my garbage grave. A mermaid, a merman, a pirate, a monster. I was to be devoured and my bones were to be buried beneath the silt and junk. They gripped my arm, so tight it hurt. They pulled me, but not down. Up, up, up we went and I saw the black sky again, a bat's silhouette flittering across the bright stars. They held me round the chest as they swam for land. The canal spat me out and I spat out the canal.

What monster was this? Or guardian angel?

I heaved in air and rolled over, lying on my back, staring up at my monster-angel; he was small and fat, his face scrunched up and ugly. He shouted, limbs exploding out like pistons. He spat on the ground next to me and left. I turned onto my side and watched him barrelling his way down the street, disappearing into an alley.

I wondered how my monster-angel could just leave me. I could so easily roll over and sink back into the canal. But the moment had passed. My monster-angel knew that.

'The moment of my death has passed into the past,' I said and laughed. 'The past is the past is the past.'

I laughed so hard I shook. I got up and walked back to my apartment, leaving a trail of water, drip drip dripping like black ink.

*

The next day was the same as every day. I looked after the animals, I wrote an article, I did the history tour and I met Juliana. The only thing that changed was the posters. I had grown weary of replacing them, but on this day I printed hundreds and I put them everywhere.

I carried his photograph with me. It was crumpled and a tear was worrying at the right hand corner. If the tear went further it would rip right through his head. I took a copy and left the original at home.

'You seen this boy?' I'd ask people in cafes, in restaurants, in bars. I'd ask tourists who stopped me for directions. 'He'd be a man now,' I'd say. 'Imagine him in colour and not so pale. He'll be tanned now. Swarthy after being a sailor for so long, probably a pirate. You seen this man?'

'No,' they'd say. 'We've not seen him.'

'He's here for sure,' I'd say. 'I should have known it, you know? Of all the places. Where else would he settle? This fantastical realm made of water and glass and crumbling stone. Have you seen this man? Imagine him in colour.'

I put hundreds of missing posters all across Venice. They merged with the graffiti, fraying at the edges, spattered with paint. He had a moustache in one and in another a green penis grew out of his forehead, but mostly they were ignored; covered over, forgotten. Have you seen this man? In response I received smears of paint, tags, slogans: 'Love the lost'.

My phone number was on the posters and in return I received calls from lonely people and old perverts. Love the lost, and I embraced them all. The police fined me for fly posting and graffiti but let me put the poster in their station and in 'designated areas'. I'd go to the station every week to ask if anyone had seen him. The answer was always no, always 'we'll get in touch with you.' They huffed when I walked through the door each week but they'd ask how I was, asked how many more dogs and cats and injured birds I had collected. I stayed for coffee and they asked if I had found a proper job yet, they asked if I'd settled down with a good man. They warned me not to put my number on the posters, not to answer calls from 'perverts and crazies'.

'"Stay away from my son, whore!"'

'What? She said what?'

'"Stay away from my son, whore!" That's what she said. Her voice creaks, like old furniture. She sounds like she's a hundredbillion years old.'

Juliana laughed.

'The phone call after that, all I got was "Whore! Bitch! Who do you think you are?" That's all. That was it. She hung up. It's gone on like that for over a week now.'

Juliana raised her whisky, 'To the old lady! May she forever be crazy! May she stalk you to your grave.'

'To the old lady!' I said, and we downed our drinks.

'You need to find out who she is.'

'I can't get a word in.'

'You'll see, she'll be lonely. Soon she'll be your best friend. Soon she'll be your grandmother, offering advice, telling you you're all skin and bone and you need fattened up.'

'I've never had a grandmother. I never knew her.'

'Well, you have one now.'

'She'll stop calling. She'll get bored of it and move on to someone else.'

'I'm telling you,' she raised her glass. 'I'm telling you.'

She nodded and I shrugged.

'We'll see.'

★

I received a call every night from Maria. She told me her life story. She was rich, she said. Sure, I said. I live in a Palazzetto on the Grand Canal, she said. Sure, I said. Rattling around on my own, she said. Rattling, like my old bones. It's hard to get around now, she said. And now my son is gone, I'm all alone. What's your interest in him, whore? What's your interest in him? Stay away from Antonio!

Next time she phoned she was polite, talking to me like we were old friends, like we were family, like she was some long-lost, concerned relative. Then she said to me, 'If he wants to leave us, then let him, don't go shaming my family name all over Venezia!'

She called every night. Some nights it was 'Whore! Bitch! Who do you think you are?' and other nights we'd talk for hours and she'd tell me about her family, about her friends, about her glamorous life before she got old and was forgotten. She was a socialite, she said. 'All I did was go to parties, look pretty and slay the boys with my viperous tongue.'

'I can believe that,' I said, and she'd chuckle, a hoarse, dirty chuckle. 'You should have seen me,' she said. 'You should have seen me back then.' She'd grow maudlin. I heard the clink of ice in a glass, and she said to me, 'Come visit. Come visit, it's been so long. I miss you. I will show you all my photos from back in the day. I was beautiful then. I was everything then.' I wanted to say, 'You're everything now,' coming to realise that Juliana was right. Instead I said, 'You don't know me, Maria. I could be a serial killer. I could be in it to steal your fortune.'

'In it? In what?' she said, sharp, distinct. 'In what?'

'In this, our friendship.'

'I call the shots,' she said. 'I called you and I call the shots. Now you come and visit me. Come round and I will fatten you up.'

'How do you know I need fattened?'

'Anyone who sits on the phone all night talking to some old woman doesn't know how to cook themselves a proper meal.'

★

'He really does look like David,' I said, 'but older, olive-skinned, and in colour.'

'You can have the picture,' she said. 'Maybe you'll have more luck finding him if you have a more up to date photograph.'

'But it's not him,' I said. 'It's not up to date. It's someone else.'

'It could be him, and what does that matter? If it helps you find him?'

I posted photos of her son all across Venice: 'Have you seen this man?'

When Antonio came home that summer, we got phonecall after phonecall. 'I've seen this man, I've seen him.'

'It's not him,' I'd have to say, 'it's not him.'

I took an even more up to date photo, but didn't post it up, waiting patiently until Antonio left so we didn't get pointless phone calls from people telling us they'd found the man sitting right next to us.

Antonio took us out in the evenings and Maria would say to everyone, 'Have you seen this man? No, not him, not him *exactly*, stupid! Why would I be asking, when he's right here? Someone *like* him. My son is just like him, you see, but more up to date.'

I sat across from Antonio, watching him eating and drinking and talking. He looked just like David. His skin, his hair, his cheekbones, the shape of his nose. Even the same brown eyes, so dark they looked black. But his manner was different and it shattered the illusion, it ruined his face. You're not doing it right. You're not moving your lips the way you should. You're not smiling the way you should. You're not raising your eyebrow and giving me that look the way you should. You used to touch your lips, when you were thinking. You'd rub your fingers across your lips but now you pull at your ear, or tap your fingers. You've changed too much. If this was you, would you have changed this much? When I find you will I not know you?

*

'She really was beautiful.'
  'Who?'
  'Maria.'

Antonio didn't respond. He poured himself more coffee, stood up and gestured at me, to stay, to wait. He came through with her photo album.

'I've seen it so many times,' I said. 'She likes reliving her glory days.'

He opened the album and slid it over to me, pointing to a group photo. I'd seen this photo countless times, yet I still felt warmth when I saw her luminous smile, her delicate fingers curled round a glass, her husband's arm around her shoulder. I smiled. 'It's a beautiful photograph.'

I looked up at him and my smile froze.

'Look again,' he said.

I looked.

'This is Maria,' he said, drumming his finger on the woman she had said was her sister. 'This.'

I looked at the mousey girl, the one who stood slightly off, away from the others. I scanned across and my gaze fell upon the glittering centre of attention; she was pretty, she glowed. I traced a line between them.

'You didn't have to,' I said. 'You didn't have to tell me.'

'It's a fantasy. She has never been able to let her sister go.'

'It's her story. Let her be who she wants to be.'

'Don't you mind being lied to?'

'It's her story.'

'You're encouraging her to live in the past.'

'I'm her friend. I look after her.'

'If you want her money you won't get it.'

'Why would I want her money? She's helping me find David.'

'She said I look like him.'

'You do, but in colour.'

'Don't you have any friends? Move on with your life. I wonder, what makes you think he's here?'

'Where else would he be? There's nowhere else on earth. Only here.'

'You're both fantasists. Why don't you live your life?'

'I loved you,' I said. 'I loved David. Old-ma and old-da loved him but they didn't love me because I was Goblin-runt born blue.'

'Move on,' he said. 'Live your life,' he said.

He closed the album.

★

Maria, Antonio, Juliana and I walked to a restaurant in the early evening. Maria and Antonio walked ahead of us, arm in arm. They stopped, the way blocked. I heard some heated words; Maria didn't take well to having her routine disrupted. 'What's going on?' I asked.

'They're filming,' said Antonio, 'we have to go round.'

'What is it? What are they filming?'

I moved closer and saw the film crew and the cast.

'They're not even working!' said Maria. 'Just standing around, causing us trouble.'

'They're working,' said the man who was blocking our way. 'You'll have to go round.'

Maria let out a grunt of dissatisfaction and turned dramatically, pulling her son. As they walked back, I hovered.

'Is that Dirk Bogarde?'

'Who?' said Juliana.

'You'll have to go round,' said the man.

'What are you filming?'

'Visconti's *Death in Venice*.'

'That's Bogarde. I know him from the Doctor films in the fifties. He was a star,' I said, turning to Juliana. 'Before your time, he was a star.'

'Please go round.'

I lingered for a moment, watching Bogarde talk with Visconti. I knew Bogarde had been a soldier in the war, though it wasn't until later I found out he had witnessed the horrors at Belsen before being stationed in the Far East.

'He served in the war,' I said quietly, to no one in particular.

'Round,' the man said, raising his eyebrows and making a

circle in the air with his finger. 'Go round.'

Juliana took my hand.

'We better go,' she said. 'We don't want to lose them.'

'It was Dirk Bogarde,' I said when we caught up to them. 'That star from the fifties. They're filming *Death In Venice*.'

Antonio eyed me and said, 'I know that story, about an old man who can't let go of an illusion.'

I pretended not to hear and looked at Maria.

'Do you know him, Maria? Bogarde? He was a dream.'

★

We sat at a table outside the restaurant, waiting for our food. Maria and Antonio were talking and Juliana and I held hands and drank our wine, watching people come and go. I removed my cardigan.

'Why do you have those?' Maria said, abruptly breaking away from her conversation with Antonio. She stared at me.

'What? Why do I have what?'

'Those tattoos. Why do you have them? How do you expect to find a husband with your body all ruined like that?'

Juliana made an exasperated huffing noise. I stared at Maria, dumbstruck, before laughing and shaking my head.

'I don't want a husband,' I said. 'And I wouldn't marry anyone who didn't like my tattoos, so what does it matter?'

'You'll never find anyone respectable looking like that,' she said, ignoring me. 'You should cover them up.'

'Maria, you old witch. Sometimes you don't know when to hold that tongue of yours. You know I have someone.'

Antonio squeezed Maria's arm as she was about to reply.

'I'm sorry,' I said to Juliana.

'I just want you to be happy,' Maria said, brushing Antonio's hand off. 'You need a husband to look after you.'

Juliana let loose on Maria, a volley of Italian I struggled to follow. Maria blushed and laughed and said, 'Nevermind, eh? I'm just old fashioned. To me, a tattooed woman is a loose woman who will never make a good life for herself. I just worry for you.'

'I know, Maria. I know you do, but I'm happy.'

'You can't be that happy if you can't let go of the past,' said Antonio.

I could see Juliana was going to defend me, but I squeezed her hand and shook my head.

'It's okay,' I said. 'Antonio's right. I think I should let him be.'

'Let who be?' said Maria.

'David,' I said, looking at Antonio. 'I should just let him be. Wherever he is.'

'Yes,' said Antonio. 'You should let him go.'

'I should leave him in the past with everything else,' I said. 'I should let it all rot.'

I raised my glass and said to Juliana, 'To the future.'

Juliana hesitated then said, 'To the future,' clinking her glass gently against mine. We all toasted and Juliana leaned in and kissed me. I heard Maria make a disapproving clicking noise.

After dinner, we all staggered, talked and laughed our way through the streets. I saw posters of David, of Maria's son. We tore them down.

'To the future!' we shouted.

The next morning was the first day I received a postcard.

*

I didn't know who they were from. They were unsigned. He said he was living in Edinburgh. That he was well. That he hoped I was well. There was no return address. A postcard arrived once a week, sometimes more. Beautiful scenes of Edinburgh.

"Dear Goblin, I've lived here for many years now. You would love it here. I'm well. I hope you're well."

Of course, I thought it was David.

But I knew it wasn't. I knew who it was but I pretended it was this person or that person. It could be whoever I wanted it to be. Until one day he signed it and I ripped it to pieces.

He had attacked me, abandoned me, and now he was sending me postcards telling me he was well and he hoped I was too.

London, 16 March 1930

She died the day she was born. Goblin-runt born blue, not breathing, never to breathe. They buried her in Kensal Green and they lived happily ever after.

London, 16 March 1930

She died the day she was born. Goblin-runt born blue, not breathing, never to breathe. They buried her in Kensal Green and they grieved. They wept at her grave and rent their clothes and wailed. Their son David healed them, bringing joy. Only his love could keep them from clawing their way six feet under to join their baby blue. David became a musician and they were proud. He objected to war and they were proud. He lived until he was 102 years old, when he died peacefully, his wife by his side holding his hand, holding his dear true heart until the moment it stopped.

She was comforted by the lives he had touched, by the people he brought joy to. She was glad of the chance he got to live that his baby sister did not have. She was comforted that he would live on in the lives he had touched, in the music he had made. He would live on.

His baby blue sister was erased the moment she emerged from the womb. Erased and forgotten. She touched no one. No lives were touched, except with grief, which David healed and they forgot, baby born blue, six feet deep.

London, 1939

She told everyone I'd likely died and they all said what a shame it was. Shame, shame, shame.

London, 1930s/1940s

Goblin and Devil, Mac and Stevie. We played in our street, we made up stories, we made up plays. Da died in the war. Ma died in our home, bombed out. David and I went to the sea.

London, 1930s, 40s, 50s, 60s, 70s...

The Crazy Pigeon Woman of Amen Court flew home to her family, held by the pigeons' beaks clamped shut on her clothes. She flew and flew and flew until she was gone.

Goblin-runt moved in and became the Crazy Pigeon Girl of Amen Court. She learned taxidermy, she fed the baby pigeons and they followed her here and there and they slept in her hair. The local kids spat at her but she didn't care because she knew they'd get eaten by the lizard people down below. The Crazy Pigeon Girl of Amen Court lived out her days happy and content.

Prison, 1967

My legs buckled and I fell. He had me by the throat. He squeezed. I looked directly into his eyes, glad that someone was finally pushing me down that rabbit hole. Soon I'd be six feet under. Soon the mistake would be erased. But not my mistakes. There was nothing I could do about that now. I couldn't rewrite the story.

I let go, my breath gone.

The In-Between Realm

Goblin: a mischievous ugly dwarf-like creature of folklore.
Doesn't exist. A fairy tale.

Venice, 1972

I took the boat out to the Bone Island. I had several bottles
of wine. I was knocking one back, rowing, knocking it back,
rowing... drinking, drinking, drinking... the sun was high in
the sky and my cheeks burned with booze and heat. Chattering
and laughing and greeting the dead I leapt from the boat,
hoisted out my bottles of wine and clambered ignominiously
over the wall, falling, scrabbling, smashing a bottle of wine,
saving the others and spraining an ankle. I licked the sweet
red wine that dripped from the wall, spattered like blood. I
surveyed the land, disappointed to see bushes sprouting up
here and there and there and here and where are the bones? I
left my treasures by the wall, holding one bottle by the neck,
staggering across the uneven ground, pushing at the bushes,
peering between the branches and leaves. I found bones; the
bleached, the forgotten, the poor, the nobodies. 'You didn't
count,' I said. 'You meant nothing, you are nothing, and I join
you and I toast to that!' I took up a bone, wielding it like a
weapon, knocking back the wine, dizzy with booze and sun
and suicidal elation. 'My weary bones,' I laughed. 'My weary
bones shall rest with the dispossessed. Will you drink to that?'
I sprinkled the wine across this bleached bulbous land. 'Drink
this, my blood,' I said, and fell back, burrowing into the bones,
marking my space amongst the dead, baking in the sun. 'Drink
this, my blood,' I mumbled. I had a blade with me, hanging
around my neck on a silver chain, but I was tired, I was worn
out. All I wanted was sleep and I slept, for surely I would die

in this heat. Surely these bones would pull me down and down and down. My rotten flesh would feed these plants and I would be gone, disappeared, swallowed up. 'I am well,' I said, sinking into sleep. 'And I hope you are too.'

★

I swayed, gently. I woke and I puked. Someone tried to guide me, guide me to the edge, but I was still sick on myself and in the boat, the rest spewing out into the lagoon. I leaned over the edge watching the little fish hoover up my vomit. I swayed and swayed and I was sick and sick.

Hollowed out, I fell back into the boat, lying on the bottom, laughing.

'Feeding the fish,' I said. 'Feeding the fish.'

A hand gripped my face, clasped around my jaw.

'Get up. Sit up.'

I sat up, trying to focus.

'Drink,' they said. 'You're dehydrated. Drink.'

I took the bottle of water from them and knocked it back like it was wine.

★

The night after the Bone Island and feeding the fishes, I went out drinking with Juliana and her friends, laughing and dancing, ignoring my throbbing ankle. I passed out in the bar and woke up in my flat. I woke to the smell of burning. I pulled myself up, blinking into the smoke. I would rather drown, but this would do. I leaned back, waiting.

'You're not Catholic.'

'Who's there?'

Was this murder? Did someone want me dead?

'It's me, you idiot. It's always me, picking up the pieces.'

I looked over and saw Juliana, rummaging through papers, burning my things. She'd found my scraps, my fantasies, my what-ifs. I watched as her anger sent everything up in flames, dropping them into one of my cooking pots. Monty was whining, the cats scratched at the door.

'What are you doing? They don't like the smoke, you're upsetting them.'

'You're not fucking Catholic,' she said. 'You're not a martyr.'

I was weak, but I struggled up, opened the door for Monty and the cats to get into the sitting room. I lurched back and fell into bed.

'What are you burning?'

'You're not a slave to this pathetic self-hate. You need help.'

'You need help,' I said, curling up into a foetal position, pulling the covers up to my chin. 'You're burning my things.'

'What does it all mean to you? Tell me.'

'Fuck you.'

'Don't be a victim of your mother's hate,' she said, waving a sheet of my writing at me. 'She's gone and you're here with me in Venice. This is our life. You're an adult, not a Goblin-runt baby blue.'

'I tried to kill myself.'

'I know,' said Juliana, setting the paper alight. 'I know.'

'You know?'

'Giorgio told me he pulled you out of the canal. I've never seen him so angry.'

'Gio? I didn't recognise him.'

'He wouldn't let up on it. Every time I saw him.'

'You knew?'

'I knew.'

'Okay.'

'I assured him I was taking care of you,' she said, her face lost in a haze of smoke. 'That you were coming out of it.'

'It explains why he's been such a sullen bastard recently,' I said.

'Do you know how many people have died in those canals? Too many. And who wants to die there? In all that silt and dirt and tourist garbage?'

'No one,' I said.

'No one,' she said, holding her hand up to the flames, feeling the warmth.

'Me,' I said.

'No one,' she said, putting more paper into the pot.

'There's nothing wrong with suicide.'

'Are we getting philosophical now?'

'No. Maybe… If I lost you I would happily drown in the silt and the dirt and the tourist garbage.'

'That's the most romantic thing you've ever said to me,' she said, her lips curling into a half-smile.

'I'm glad I'm alive,' I said. 'Goblin-runt born blue. I'm glad I'm alive. I think I tried to kill myself after that too.'

'You think?'

'I think.'

'How can you not know?'

'It was lazy, a lazy death on the Bone Island. I was drunk, roasting in the sun. I was going to feed the plants and the lizards when another guardian angel saved me. No one will let me put myself out of my misery. Fall down that rabbit hole.'

She lit up my diary.

'You're going to set fire to my home,' I said.

'Marry me.'

'What?'

'I love you,' she said, 'marry me.'

I sat up and stared at her.

'You're burning my things!'

'I'm burning your past. You don't need it.'

'Everyone needs a past.'

'You don't need to hold it so close. Tell a different story.'

'It's not legal.'

'What?'

'Marriage,' I said. 'We're perverts.'

'We'll do it our way.'

'You can't fix me.'

'But I can love you,' she said. 'I do love you.'

'It's too late.'

'Then why are you here? Why are you even here? Why do you bother? You may as well just die.'

'I've been trying.'

'Not hard enough,' she said, standing back from the smoke. 'If you want to die, you'll die. But you're here. I know you want to be and I know you love me.'

'I do.'

'Well then, marry me,' she said and opened a window. 'Till death us do part.'

I watched as the breeze whipped the smoke round the room.

'You don't know what you're getting into,' I said.

'I do. I know exactly,' she said and set more of my things alight.

Venice, 24 July 1972

We got married on the Bone Island.

I wore one of mum's old dresses. It was really a nightgown, a long cream slip with lace panels. Juliana wore a silk red dress that belonged to her aunt. We travelled to the Bone Island in Maria's old motorboat, holding hands as we set off, our lace veils fluttering in the breeze. Our friends followed close behind us; the students I met at the bar and the protest, Juliana's parents, Monty, Maria, Antonio, Gio, two of my neighbours, and one of the policemen – 'I knew you'd attract a pervert and a crazy'.

Maria took the service. When she first found out we were getting married there was all sorts of fuss and histrionics. 'It's not real love, how do you even have sex? It's not right – a woman like you, you need a man to look after you.' I loved Maria like she was family, so I said to her, 'You old dragon, you old conservative bitch, don't tell me what is and isn't love.'

She grunted and refused to discuss it. Eventually Juliana charmed her. They talked in Italian, so fast that I couldn't keep up. They finished each other's sentences and laughed like old witches.

'What did you talk about?' I asked Juliana.

'This and that; art, love, life, Venice. She has a dirty sense of humour, that old woman.'

'Did you talk about us?'

'Yes. I said I loved you and she grunted and shook her head. I said, "Maria, you love Goblin. If you love her, you'll accept she loves pussy."'

'You didn't?'

'I did, and the old lady went crimson then laughed like a sailor. She pinched my cheek and said, "You look after her."'

'She accepts us then?'

'She accepts us, but you know Maria – nothing is ever straightforward.'

I spoke to Antonio, quizzing him about Maria's turnaround.

'She's just jealous,' he said.

'Jealous?'

'She lived a restricted existence – she wasn't as free as her rebellious sister. She obeyed her parents. She was a good Catholic.'

'She doesn't really hate queers?'

'She disapproves, but she'll make an exception for you.'

I smiled and shook my head.

'She's good at – what's the word? – keeping things separate, not seeing the contradiction. And she likes the late rebellion. She gets a kick out of it. "What would papa think?" she asked me. "He'd be scandalised," I told her and she laughed.'

We had Maria's mixed blessing and now the glorious old lady was our stand-in priest, our stand-in government official, and she loved every moment – it was just as much her day as it was ours.

We gathered on the island where I'd previously gone to die and we celebrated love, the present and the future.

I don't remember which part was in which language, but Maria, as agreed, took the service in a mix of Italian, Venetian dialect, and English. My difficulty remembering is partly due to Maria's liberal stretching of our instructions to mix it up. It seemed that every fifth or sixth word was in a different language, making the ceremony oddly fragmented, with the guests whispering amongst themselves, 'What did she say? I didn't catch it,' before simply accepting the disjointed flow. I don't remember all that was said, but I remember fragments, I remember the feel of it. The warmth, the sea breeze, the scent of jasmine from the plants Maria brought, the tinkling of the little bells that hung from the leaves. I remember the feel of Juliana's skin as we held hands.

'Carissimi, oggi siamo qui riuniti,' said Maria, 'par tacare in maridauro promiscolo these two beautiful and perverted creatures.'

She winked at us and our guests cheered. 'Do you, Goblin, take Juliana Sophia Acciai come tò mojere proibio?'

'I do.'

'E tu, Juliana Sophia Acciai, vuoi Goblin to be your unlawfully wedded also-wife?'

'Si, lo voglio.'

'Vi dichiaro moglie bella e perversa and beautiful perverted also-wife. Voaltri vivarete na vita de amore e de sganassade finamente al dì che vu morìa e anca dopo – your love and laughter will echo down the generations, in the lives you touch, in the stories they tell.'

Maria was crying, struggling to get the words out. A tear slipped down Juliana's cheek.

'You may kiss the brides.'

We kissed and I licked the tear from her cheek. There were cheers, laughter, clapping, and singing. We hugged Maria.

'Thank you, grandma,' I said, and kissed her, but this – the first time I called her grandma – only set her off sobbing. 'You old dragon, craving all the attention as always. This is a happy day.' I grabbed hold of her and swung her round, dancing, making her laugh. Antonio swooped in and danced her away, wiping at her face with tissues and I fell into the embrace of

Juliana.

We had a lavish reception at Maria's, where the prosecco flowed and a banquet was laid out with waiters on hand. As the sun set, the room was bathed in an orange glow. One of the waiters went round the room lighting dozens of candles, enclosing us in a flickering warmth. Maria had set jasmine on her balcony, the breeze carrying the scent. A bat flew in the window; confused, it circled the room over and over before disappearing into the hall, returning, spinning round the room then back out into the night.

'A good luck bat,' said Juliana.

'Is that a Venetian thing? Bats are good luck?'

'It's our thing.'

Gio lured us out of the room on some pretence. When we returned, the wedding cake was on the centre of the table, our glasses re-filled with prosecco, and our guests had transformed into Beast Folk, each of them wearing an animal mask. Some of the masks had been decorated to resemble the animal as closely as possible, others simply had the shape of the animal's head but were painted bright colours, adorned with plastic jewels. We were each presented with a mask. Juliana's was a colourful bird with a huge orange beak, crowned with rainbow feathers. I was given a dog mask, covered in soft synthetic fur.

We wore our masks throughout the speeches, only removing them briefly to drink a toast and to eat the cake. We were ushered through to the adjacent room where a band played for us and we danced into the middle of the night, some wearing masks, others propping them on their heads or holding them like strange trophies.

When the guests left, we stayed. Maria not only offered us a room for the night, but the whole palazzo for several days.

'I'll look after your animals,' she said, fishing in my bag for our apartment keys. 'You two lovebirddogs enjoy yourselves. Spero che trascorriate una luna di miele da sogno.'

Dad kept on sending postcards and I kept on tearing them up. I told Juliana all about it, about mum, and dad too. One of the postcards I'd torn up the day before, Juliana taped back together. She'd made me breakfast and had placed the postcard next to my plate.

'What are you doing?' I said.

'Making you breakfast. Coffee?'

'You know what I mean,' I said, picking up the postcard and reading it again. It said 'I miss you more than you know.'

One of the cats jumped into my lap. I put the postcard down and petted her. She purred and padded at my thighs until she was comfortable.

'You're the one who burned my things,' I said, as Juliana poured me coffee. 'You're the one who said I don't need the past.'

'This is the present and your dad is trying to make amends.'

She picked up the postcard and pinned it to the wall above the table.

'Can you make amends after trying to kill your daughter?'

'He's trying.'

I drank my coffee and stroked the cat's head.

'I'm here for you,' she said. 'There's nothing to be afraid of.'

I didn't receive another postcard for almost a month and when I did it was back to talk of Edinburgh, about a gallery he visited, his chess club. Still no return address. Juliana put them all on the wall. Days could pass with no postcards, but it was all I could think of. It made me angry, how manipulative it all was. There was still no return address.

'Write to him anyway,' said Juliana.

Instead, I took them all down and packed them away in a box. The latest one I threw away, but I fished it out later, coffee stained and stinking.

I got in touch with Tim. Do you know where he lives? Do you have his address? Have you seen him? Tim had met him several times, giving him my address, telling him to reconcile.

'"How can I make amends?" he'd said. I told him just to get in touch,' Tim said. 'I hope I wasn't wrong.'

He gave me his address and I didn't know what to do. I didn't know what to say. I sat down and I wrote:

'youcowardlysonofabitch
youcowardlysonofabitch
youcowardlysonofabitch
youcowardlysonofabitch'

I wrote another: 'Is this your idea of atonement? Telling me about your drawing classes and your fucking chess club?'

And another: 'I'm well. I'm glad you're well.'

And another: 'I'm married now. I'm happy.'

And another: 'I tried to drown myself. I was saved by a fat bald Italian who called me a stupid bitch and left me on the side of the canal. But now I'm well. I'm glad you're well. Your chess club sounds fun.'

And another: 'Fuck you and fuck your fucking chess club.'

And another and another, until I had my own box of unsent postcards. Finally, I had one I put a stamp on: 'I'm well. It's been good to hear from you.' It sat on my table for a week before I sent it. Juliana and I would look at it over breakfast.

'Today?' she said.

'No,' I said. 'Not today.'

Then the day came. I shuffled it into a pile of other mail, hiding it, pretending it wasn't important as I dropped them all in the post box.

It was the start of months of correspondence, not going much beyond the mundane. I told him about my history tour job, about Juliana and our wedding, about my published photographs and articles, and all the cats and dogs and birds I took in. I told him he would love it here. I imagined him coming. I imagined going to Edinburgh.

He sent me a letter one day. His handwriting on the envelope, that familiar British stamp. I didn't want to open it, but I did. He wasn't one for many words. It simply said, 'I'm sorry for what I did. I blamed you. But it wasn't your fault. I love you and I'm sorry I failed you.'

I let Juliana see it that evening and she held me in her arms as I cried.

I didn't respond directly to the letter. His postcards kept arriving as normal and we shared the mundane as normal, but there was a lighter tone. We teased each other. Made each other laugh. We wrote about him coming here, about me going there. But we never met again. I received a letter from a member of his chess club to say he'd died of a heart attack on 22nd January 1973.

Maria and Gio looked after the animals when Juliana and I went to Edinburgh for his funeral. It was a small service, with a handful of people.

His chess club was there. There were four of them after dad had gone, in their seventies and eighties apart from Aaron, a teenage grandson of one of the members. They knew everything about me; dad had never let up talking about me.

'But he was sad when he talked about you,' said Aaron. 'It was as if you were dead. We all thought you were dead until the postcards.'

Not everyone kept in touch when the circus had disbanded, so we weren't able to notify all the old circus folk. We put a notice in a national paper and picked up some people that way. There was Marv and Horatiu, Angelina and her wife, and old Louise who now looked like a wizened crone. A few of them I didn't know; they'd joined the circus after I'd left. They all said how sorry they were but they couldn't look me in the eye.

We had a wake back at dad's flat. It was quiet and awkward at first and I clung onto Juliana. Once the drink had taken effect the circus folk all came over to me, Marv surprising me with a long hug and telling me over and over what a great man James was. By the end of the evening Marv, Horatiu, Angelina, old Louise and I were all in a corner together, drunk and reminiscing. Juliana drifted round the room, talking with everyone, topping up drinks. Old Louise started singing "We'll

Meet Again" and the room grew quiet, everyone turning to watch her: 'Let's say goodbye with a smile, dear, just for a while, dear, we must part, don't let this parting upset you, I'll not forget you.' Juliana sat with me and I leaned into her, crying silently as we listened to old Louise.

People started to leave after midnight, but the circus folk stayed, talking and singing into the early hours, falling asleep on the floor, on the couch, under the table, just like when I lived with mum and dad. There was a subdued melancholy in the morning, everyone leaving to catch trains or buses, making false promises to keep in touch.

A couple of days after the funeral, Juliana returned to look after the animals and I stayed on to sort out dad's affairs and his possessions. Dad owned the flat and had a small amount of savings. I gave most of the savings to the chess club, some to animal charities and kept the rest to cover travelling. He was frugal and didn't have much; a few books, and two photo albums. I sobbed as I pored over the photographs of mum, of the three of us together.

I spent some time walking the streets of Edinburgh and getting lost down all the old closes. One of dad's chess friends told me dad had spent a lot of time walking along Portobello promenade, so I followed in his footsteps.

I didn't want to sell the flat, so we kept it and we went to Edinburgh on holiday two summers in a row and on our second visit I asked Juliana if she wanted to stay. She took time to think about it, but we'd both been talking about how Venice was changing; more hotels, more tourists, and several of our friends had already left. Juliana felt stuck in her job at the gallery and liked the idea of a new start. We brought Monty with us and Maria took in all our other strays, phoning every week telling me what animal had peed on what piece of priceless furniture. We moved into dad's flat and Juliana made the spare room into an art studio. Our friends came over for holidays, which eased our transition; a constant stream of Venetians sleeping in Juliana's studio. We both worked part-time jobs – Juliana a waitress in a local restaurant and I was a cashier in a local shop before getting a job doing ghost tours. It took Juliana a year until she got a job at the National Gallery, and it was then we felt finally settled.

And here I am still. Juliana and Monty are gone but I am here. Or there I was. I should be there, but not now. I'm in London with the flames and the stench and the rotting corpses. I'm in London and everything has turned to shit.

London, 18 January 2012

I sit having breakfast with Tim, staring at the morning paper.

'Are you ready to tell me?'

'Not yet,' I say as Monsta strokes my hand, soothing me.

I read the headline over and over until the words become meaningless:

91 YEAR OLD WAR HERO ACCUSED OF 1939 MURDER.

Tim picks it up.

'Do you mind if I read it?'

'No.'

I drink my coffee, watching him.

'It says you were a witness. To the murder.'

I nod.

'You were nine years old.'

He reads the rest then folds up the paper and throws it on to the table. I pick it up.

'I don't think you should read it,' he says.

'Why not?'

'I just don't.'

I start to read and he says, 'Please, Goblin, don't read it.'

I look up at him.

'What does it say about me?'

'Nothing.'

'That I'm a batty old lady? An unreliable witness?'

'Delusional.'

'Delusional?'

'The family of the accused, they say you're delusional.'

I laugh.

'You don't need to protect me, Tim.'

'No? Tell me what happened, G. I want to help.'

'I know you do. Just let me read.'

He stares at me for a moment, his face impassive, then gets up and gathers the plates. As he washes the dishes I sit and read, spectre-Monsta by my side.

Linda Cartwright had interviewed Detective Curtis, but he didn't say anything other than that there's strong evidence connecting the war hero to the murder. Linda writes that this strong evidence has to be more than the unreliable accounts of an old man and woman. She asks why Mac and I didn't go to the police in 1939, suggesting we have an agenda, suggesting we have something to hide. She interviewed the war hero's daughter: "My father is a *hero*. He doesn't deserve this. He's old and this has been causing him a lot of stress, and for what? The crazy ramblings of a delusional old woman. This could kill him, it very well could kill him and I'll hold this woman responsible." Linda writes that she met me and I was confused, often losing my train of thought. She said I couldn't keep my story straight. She ends asking what it is I have to hide.

Ben comes in from walking Mahler and Sam.

'Jesus, old lady,' he says, 'Why didn't ye tell me?'

'Morning, Ben. Nice walk?'

'Dinnae change the subject. I thought we were friends.'

'We are,' I say. 'Why wouldn't we be?'

Mahler rushes over, puts his paws on my lap, and licks my face.

'Friends talk to each other,' he says, taking his coat off. 'Tell each other their problems.'

'Ben,' I say, looking up at him. 'It wasn't just you. I didn't tell anyone.'

'That's right,' says Tim, drying his hands, 'she didn't tell me either.'

'Aye, but she should have,' Ben says to Tim before turning back to me. 'Ye could have told me. Ye know that don't ye? Ye can tell me anything.'

He sits opposite me and throws his copy of the paper on the table.

'I know,' I say, not looking at him. 'It was just difficult.'

I stroke Mahler's head.

'Did ye do it?'

'What?'

'Murder. Wis it you?'

I stop stroking Mahler and turn to Ben.

'Jesus, Ben. Don't believe everything you read.'

'Well, what do I know, eh? Ye dinnae tell me anything.'

'I didn't murder anyone.'

'Well, ye should sue.'

'What?'

'That reporter. For casting aspersions.'

'She didn't actually say I murdered anyone.'

'Aye, but she may as well have.'

I stand up.

'Do you want some tea?' I say, walking over to the counter.

'Always changing the subject,' says Ben as I put the kettle on.

Tim rubs my arm and says, 'It's okay.'

'It's not okay,' says Ben, twisting round to face us.

'She'll tell us in her own time,' says Tim.

'Her own time? It's been seventy years—'

'Seventy-two,' I say.

'Seventy-two, then. She'll be dead before she tells us the truth.'

'You're acting like I've been lying to you. I didn't lie.'

'Aye, ye just hid it. That's just as bad.'

'Don't you have any secrets?'

'Not from you.'

I don't know what to say to that. I go back to the table,

sinking into my seat.

'I'm sorry,' I say, looking down at my clasped hands. 'It wasn't personal, Ben. I know I can trust you, that you're there for me. I just don't know how to talk about it.'

'It's okay, old lady. I didnae mean to be angry with ye, I just—'

'I understand, Ben,' I say, looking up. 'I'll tell you,' I say, looking from Ben to Tim. 'I'll tell you both everything from beginning to end and back again.'

Chapter 13

London, 27 January 2012

You're a storyteller, aren't you, Goblin?

Yes.

I want you to tell me the story of this photograph. Of all of these photographs.

He spread them out across the table, but he keeps the focus on the one in front of me.

Let's start with names. Who are they?

London, 6 September 1939

We were in the worksite; me, Devil, Mac, and Stevie on lookout. We crept until we came round the side of the rubble and there was another animal pit, and in the pit were the neighbourhood bullies who'd hurt David and me that time after the cinema. There was Jack, Simon, three others, and David on his knees. I couldn't see him properly at first. The light was going, his face was bloody. When I saw it was him it took me a moment to make sense of it. I had just been thinking of him at home, I had an image of him in my head. He was supposed to be stretched out on his bed, smoking a cigarette, telling me to leave it, telling me he didn't want to hear another bleedin' bible story. But he wasn't there, we weren't there, we were here. My brother was on his knees and Jack had a gun to his head.

They all flicked on torches, focussing the light on David. They moved in, turning the torches on themselves, creating floating skulls. They all had a dead pet hanging round their necks like stoles. Simon kept his torch pointed at David's face. The sun was descending, the clouds clearing as it sank down into the horizon, casting shadows and a strange orange glow across the scene.

I remembered I was gathering evidence, remembered I was going to take photos to prove the fat German bastards were here. I clutched at my camera and turned to Mac.

'We'll take photos,' I whispered, 'of the Nazis. Then we'll make a plan and we'll rescue David and we'll go to the palace and we'll have a feast.'

'They're not Nazis,' he hissed, grabbing at my arm.

I shrugged him off.

'Goblin, it's Jack Alexander, Simon—'

Mac looked sick, he was shaking his head and backing away. 'Goblin—'

I raised the camera and we fell like Alice down the rabbit hole tumbling in the darkness hail thee O lizards in the darkness in the depths. In a moment, in a second, with a click, it was over. I had pressed the camera shutter, Jack had pulled the trigger, David fell. When Devil barked they turned on us, another shot and Devil was hit. I dragged him behind the mound, found the hole from the time we played Frankenstein, Martians and Nazis, and down we went, the disappeared.

London, 27 January 2012

When I came back from Cornwall, I'd said, 'Ma? You seen David?'

I'd witnessed his death, I'd taken a photograph of the exact moment, but I wasn't sure what I'd seen. The light was fading, it had happened so quickly. I blocked it out and buried the camera, the only thing that could make it real. When I came back from Cornwall I still expected him to come walking through the door and say, 'Goblin, who said you could go to the ocean without me, eh? Did you see the kraken? Did you swim in the sea?'

But he didn't walk through the door. He wasn't sailing with

pirates, he hadn't settled in Venice. He went down below, not with the lizards but with the pets, cradled in their paws, resting on their fur, rotting in their mass grave, sharing maggots and worms, holding paws with Charlie's parrot-cat, going down down down, feeding the earth, leaving bones, leaving skulls cracked by a clumsy Goblin-child who blamed the enemy, the Germans, the Nazis, a Goblin-child who made up stories to keep from going down down down with David, with parrot-cat, with Ruby and Devil, with the thousands of pets who don't matter, their paws pulling, holding, scratching, their glacial eyes glinting in the dark. To keep David and the no-matter pets at bay, Goblin-child made up stories, Goblin-adult drank it all away, what does it matter? Dead bodies everywhere. Dead things can't die.

I buried the camera with Devil. I thought I'd never see that film developed, but here it is, evidence.

'Ben,' I'd said. 'Have you ever seen someone die? Someone you love?'

It was final. I'll never see David again, because here it is, the evidence, as simple as that, as plain as day. A decorated war hero's first shot, and he hit the mark.

London, 26 March 2012

WAR HERO ON TRIAL FOR MURDER

The photograph has been leaked. All the major papers have picked it up. It's all over the internet. There's commentaries on whether it should be shown at all, discussions over whether it was doctored. Every news outlet in the country wants a piece of me. I'm the photographer who caught the exact moment David was shot in the head.

What's the truth? I say. What's the truth? David has gone. He went on an adventure to the sea. He escaped, like he said he would. That's what I know. The photo is doctored. It isn't

David, it isn't him, it isn't anyone, it's 'let's pretend'. All these corpses and we obsess over one. Bones and truth and DNA, it's all a game. What kind of person wouldn't bury the past? Who lives there in the stench in the flames in the rotting corpses? It is hoped, it said, someone will claim these bones. Time has collapsed and space has collapsed and they have emerged from the darkness below, Goblin and Devil and Monsta. Someone will come forward. It is hoped. It is thought. It is said. It is hoped, it said, someone will come forward. It was decided the photographs of family members should be published in the hope someone will recognise them. Although, it said, there is much debate about this. Because of the angle from which most of the photographs are taken, it has been suggested the photographer was a child. There are several of what are assumed to be family members. Some of the photographs, it said, could assist in identifying the photographer. Most importantly, there is a photograph depicting the aftermath of the pet massacre, an event which remains largely undocumented. Many of them record events in London during World War II. The developed photographs are particularly valuable. The film, it said, is in remarkably good condition. Bones, doll parts, a shrew head, a camera.

THE END

Acknowledgements

Thanks to:

My husband Paul Wilson (aka Cinnamon Curtis) for his love, support, and the beautiful *Goblin* cover.

Rach and Gav for helping me get to this point. I wish Rach could be here to share this.

Mum and dad for their support and café dwelling.

Manic Street Preachers for saving my life. Stay beautiful.

Book Group, Granny Club and Art Club for their friendship (Kristi, Carolann, Kathryn, Ser, Smu, CherryBee, Cat, Emma, Ollie, Dream, Jo, Megan and Stewart).

My writing group for keeping me sane (Catherine, Peikko, Ali, Frances, Alison, Sil, Mairi, Mark).

My readers, Nacho and CB, for suffering an early draft.

Nacho, Ryan and Dream for Venice adventures.

Deb, my Edinburgh Book Fest buddy.

Peter, for advice and delightful correspondence.

Sue Rew for her friendship and mutual gushing over Dirk Bogarde. She is missed.

Gillian for providing a second home through the Looking Glass when I needed it most.

Book Week Scotland, Jenny and Gillian for the pitch opportunity.

I will be eternally grateful to Jenny Brown and Adrian Searle for believing in *Goblin*.

Helen, Rodge, Ryan and Robbie for helping to make *Goblin* the best it can be.

All at Freight Books for helping to launch *Goblin* into the world.

My translators and good friends, Sil and Anna.

John Hughes for Queer Theory.

Em, for making my soul-destroying office job less soul-destroying with book, film and TV chat.

Julie at the Advice Shop for helping me navigate the nightmare of governmental bureaucracy.

Fellow MA students, and Sam, David and Stuart for their teaching, support and guidance. The MA changed my life.

Terry Gilliam for *Tideland* and Jenni Fagan for *The Panopticon*.

A tip of the hat to Shirley Jackson, Angela Carter and Nietzsche.

All freaks and goblins.

Jabba and Belle for owning us. Our lives would be barren wastelands without you.

Thanks to all who work to eradicate speciesism. Praise the lizards! A salute to Corporal Pig.